Praise for SWEET REVENGE

"Unforgettable . . . This bold mix of an unlikely romance, a gritty setting, and a page-turning thriller will leave readers craving more."   —*Publishers Weekly* (starred review)

"Revenge can be sweet, smart, sexy, and make for a fast-paced, non-stop read when Archer's the storyteller. Creating heroes to die for and empowered women and bringing them together in powerful action/adventures with depth of emotion and sensuality are her forte. To readers' pleasure, she brings an amazing cast of characters, a strong plot, and romance to the first in her Nemesis, Unlimited series."
     —*Romantic Times BOOKreviews*

"*Sweet Revenge* is an intense, fast-paced read. A strong plot, memorable characters, genuine emotions—not to mention plenty of heat. What more can a reader want?"
     —Sherry Thomas, author of *Tempting the Bride*

"*Sweet Revenge* is a sexy, action-packed romance with a to-die-for hero and a true love that will make you swoon."
     —*New York Times* bestselling author Courtney Milan

"A dark, riveting tale from beginning to end. Zoë Archer's books are not to be missed!"
     —*USA Today* bestselling author Alexandra Hawkins

ALSO BY ZOË ARCHER

Sweet Revenge

DANGEROUS
Seduction

ZOË ARCHER

St. Martin's Paperbacks

This is a work of fiction. All of the characters, organizations, and events portrayed in this novel are either products of the author's imagination or are used fictitiously.

DANGEROUS SEDUCTION

Copyright © 2013 by Zoë Archer.

For information address St. Martin's Press, 175 Fifth Avenue, New York, NY 10010.

ISBN: 978-1-250-01560-0

Printed in the United States of America

St. Martin's Paperbacks edition / December 2013

St. Martin's Paperbacks are published by St. Martin's Press, 175 Fifth Avenue, New York, NY 10010.

10 9 8 7 6 5 4 3 2 1

To Zack, for his boundless strength

ACKNOWLEDGMENTS

Special thanks to the Secret Facebook Feminist Collective for their wisdom, activism, compassion, and commitment to sharing TMI.

CHAPTER 1.

Trewyn, Cornwall
Wheal Prosperity Copper Mine
1886

The granite room shook. Hissing and grinding filled the chamber. The huge machine crouching within it might crush a man into a paste of flesh and a powder of bone if it spun out of control.

Three men stared across the large pump engine at Simon Addison-Shawe, their arms folded across their chests. The men's eyes were hard, mouths fixed in thin, severe lines.

These buggers probably think they look intimidating, Simon mused. He fought to keep from smiling. Years ago, echoing across dusty grassland, he'd heard the rhythmic pounding of Zulu warriors beating on their shields in preparation for an attack. In a dank Whitechapel alley, he'd faced down a dozen underworld toughs with nothing more than a rusty pipe for defense.

Three copper-mine managers were as threatening to Simon as three old, toothless dogs.

But they were dangerous men. Men who couldn't be crossed without consequences, not just for himself, but

hundreds of others. Being deferential didn't come naturally to Simon, yet the success of his mission relied on it.
He had a role to play. The long game, Marco called it.
Almost nothing could be transformed with immediate
action. It took days, weeks, sometimes months to get the
job done—impatience or unwanted emotion could spell
disaster for an operation.

"If you want this job, Sharpe," one of the managers
said, "show us what you can do. This pump engine hasn't
been working right for the past two days. Fix it."

"Yes, sir," Simon answered, tugging on his cap. He
roughened his accent from its usual genteel tones, just as
he'd donned the coarse but clean garments of a working
man. Under the judging eyes of this tribunal, he kept his
gaze directed toward the floor in a semblance of humil-
ity, though the wealth of Simon's estate in Norfolk could
buy and sell the entire village of Trewyn ten times over.
The Addison-Shawes didn't have a title, but their family
name and holdings dated back to the time of the Restora-
tion. From the moment of his birth, he'd been instilled
with the knowledge that he was a gentleman.

And yet to the three managers of the Wheal Prosperity
copper mine, he had to pretend to be Simon Sharpe, itin-
erant machinist, who could fix a water pump but knew
nothing about the etiquette of a Society ball.

He immediately got to work repairing the pump. The
bag of tools at his feet was his own, purchased from a
dockyard machinist in London. Shiny new tools would
only dispel the illusion that Simon was a laboring man.
The wrench he grasped now wore a proud patina of use.
As he adjusted valves and tightened fittings, he recalled
the instruction about water pumps he'd received back in
London prior to setting out on this mission. He'd inter-
viewed men and read volumes of books—all to ensure

that he could confidently maintain the pumps that kept the Wheal Prosperity mine from flooding. Floods were among the worst dangers a copper mine could face.

Cracks webbed across the engine's pressure gauges, and rust crusted its bolts. Most of the machinery at the mine needed replacement, not repair.

He and the managers stood inside the wooden engine house near the mine's shaft. Aside from the chugging of the other machinery, silence hung over the hills outside. It was working hours, which meant that most everyone was currently belowground, clawing copper from the earth. Through the small window in the engine house, Simon spotted outbuildings and chimneys dotting the landscape.

The managers—Gorley, Murton, and Ware—looked on impassively as he worked. It was imperative that Simon did this job correctly. He didn't need the money, but he needed this job. The workers of Wheal Prosperity had never met him, not a one would recognize him or know his real name, but they needed him to get the job, too.

Several weeks earlier, a typewritten letter had found its way to the Nemesis, Unlimited, headquarters in London.

Dear sirs,

I have been informed through sundry sources that when proper justice cannot be obtained, your organization can provide it. Should this letter reach you, I urge you to investigate the Wheal Prosperity mine in Cornwall. Horrible abuses occur here, rendering the miners all but slaves. Any attempts by the miners themselves to remedy the situation have been met with the harshest of retribution. I, myself, am powerless, but perhaps Nemesis Unlimited can achieve success where others have failed. The situation here is quite desperate. I hope for all our sakes

*that this missive reaches you, and that you will
heed this plea for help, and soon.*

The letter was unsigned. They weren't uncommon,
anonymous letters like this. At least three a month arrived
at headquarters. Some were just outraged ramblings about
imaginary or minor offenses. But others, like the one about
the mine, demanded attention.

Now it was Simon's task to figure out what, exactly,
these alleged abuses were, and, if they indeed existed, how
he could stop them. Anger clouded his eyes at the thought
that anyone in England, this so-called bastion of civilization and integrity, could exist in a state of near slavery. Yet
he knew it happened every day, in nearly every city, town,
and village.

Nemesis might not be able to create perfect equality,
but its operatives fought damned hard for it.

As Simon worked, he said, "If I may ask, sirs, what
happened to the man who had this job before?"

Murton—or was it Gorley? Simon couldn't tell these
mustachioed, self-satisfied men apart—answered causti-
cally, "Never you mind that, Sharpe. All that matters is
that we have ourselves a vacancy. So if you want the situation, stop talking and keep working."

Simon ducked his head deferentially, but he caught the
shared wary glances between the managers. *Hello, boys.
That'll need some looking into.* If they gave him the job.

Half the lights inside the engine house weren't working, so Simon labored by the illumination coming through
the window and open door. A shadow suddenly darkened
the section of the pump engine on which he worked, and
he glanced up to see who stood in the doorway.

The light behind the figure blocked any physical details, but the voice that came from it was assuredly female.

"How are we to eat our bread," the woman said, "or make our pies if we haven't any butter? I ask you, gentlemen"—she almost sneered that last word—"*how*?"

"What now, Miss Carr?" Gorley asked wearily.

Simon straightened as the woman stormed into the engine house. As she did, he finally caught a decent glimpse of her.

Strictly speaking, Miss Carr wasn't beautiful. Her face was too angular, with a pointed chin and a thin nose. Her eyebrows were straight and dark. In the indistinct light of the engine house, he couldn't determine the color of her eyes, but they seemed bright and full of fire, ringed with thick black lashes. A wide mouth offset the sharpness of her features. She'd pinned back her dark hair, but a few stray tendrils drifted across her cheeks.

She wore the sturdy dress and thick apron of a balmaiden—one of the women who broke up the copper ore into small pieces—an ensemble far from fashionable, but it revealed her to have a slim figure with a narrow waist and gently rounded bosom. There was little that was soft about her appearance. This young woman worked, and worked hard, to earn her living. She even carried a heavy bucking iron—a flat hammer used for smashing ore into a sortable and transportable size. She gripped it tightly, not like a tool but a weapon.

Miss Carr's shoulders were set straight and her chin tilted upright. Simon had learned, over the course of his thirty-five years, how to read people in an instant. Miss Carr was a woman to be reckoned with. She certainly had more energy and dynamism than any of the machines in the engine house.

Her gaze flicked over to Simon, back to the managers, and then to him again, lingering for the barest moment. Though her expression barely changed, a tiny furrow appeared between her brows, as if trying to puzzle out a mystery.

She cleared her throat.

Simon had honed the ability to make himself invisible—not an easy task for a man over six feet tall and burdened with a face many women had called "pretty as a new-minted coin"—but sometimes it was necessary to become as inconspicuous as possible. Valuable information could be gathered when one appeared to vanish.

He did so now, making himself proverbially disappear, moving around to another side of the engine.

It had the desired effect. Miss Carr turned away from him to face the managers.

"The butter at the company store," she said, her voice accented with the hard *r*s and dropped *t*s of Cornwall. "It's on the verge of going rancid."

"But it hasn't yet spoiled, has it?" Ware asked, condescension seeping from his words.

"In a few days, it won't be fit to eat by man or beast," she fired back. "It needs to be replaced. The store needs to stock fresh butter."

"And as soon as the current supply is bought up by the villagers, it will be," Gorley answered.

"By which point it will have made everyone sick."

Gorley continued pedantically, "It's simply not economical for the company store to replace almost a hundred pounds of butter just on your say-so, Miss Carr."

"But—"

Murton sighed. "This matter is closed to discussion. We have important business to deal with here, and you're taking up our valuable time." He pulled a brass-cased pocket watch from his waistcoat. "The mine closes for the night in fifteen minutes. Go home early." He produced an indulgent smile.

"We haven't—"

"Go on, now." Ware made a shooing motion with his hands.

Throwing them all a scowl, Miss Carr turned on her heel and stalked from the room. But not before sending Simon one last, speculative glance. His own curiosity stirred. He watched her as, once outside, she threw her bucking iron aside and marched with wide strides away from the mine.

Silence followed her departure.

"Termagant," Gorley muttered.

"Virago," added Ware.

"Pain in the arse, more like," said Murton, and the three managers laughed.

"Begging your pardons, sirs," Simon interjected as humbly as he could manage. "She's got some years on her, but a fair hand can make her run smooth."

"Are you talking about the pump engine or Alyce Carr?" Gorley chuckled at his own wit.

"Alyce Carr, sir?"

"The delightful young woman that just shrieked at us," Ware said. "Imagine, a damned bal-maiden who thinks she can run a mine better than the professionals." He shook his head, as though to dislodge the patently impossible idea.

Gorley fixed Simon with a piercing look. "Avoid Alyce, Sharpe. She'll only lead you into trouble."

"That's assuming I get the job, sirs," Simon noted.

All three of the managers' brows rose at his quick response. But Simon wouldn't obtain the position if he pretended to be a dullard. Machinists needed to be clever in order to stay on top of maintaining the equipment, or if there were ever an emergency.

Whatever the mission needed him to be, he'd play the right role. Marco, the wily, government-trained bastard, had the gift of complete transformation. No one could fault Simon for his own disguises. He'd convincingly acted as a stevedore, a wealthy French banker, an East End housebreaker, and half a dozen other personae.

His grades at Harrow had been abysmal—he saw more of the nearby village and the local girls than he did the inside of a classroom. Yet he'd shone when acting in school theatrical productions. Nobody played a better Sir Andrew Aguecheek. Seemed that he was already familiar with the idea of wanting to be someone other than an Addison-Shawe. A skill that served him, and Nemesis, well.

Simon turned the engine over and started it. The pump chugged to life with more strength than it had demonstrated before he'd worked on it. "So, am I in?"

There was a quick, muttered consultation before the managers turned back to him. "You're in," Gorley said.

Grinning, Simon stuck out his hand, and it was reluctantly shaken by the three men. "Thank you, sirs."

"Payment packets are handed out every Friday," Ware said. "You're paid in scrip, which you can spend at the company store. It's got everything you'll need."

Including nearly rancid butter. "I've got an ill father in Sheffield, and usually send him some of my wages. Can't do that with scrip."

"That's how Wheal Prosperity is run, Sharpe," Murton answered, not an ounce of sympathy in his voice. "Either take the offer as it stands, or apply for work somewhere else."

Scratching his head beneath his cap, Simon pretended to debate the idea. If he truly needed a job that paid, he'd have told the managers to take the express train straight up their arses, but it was more important for him to thoroughly fathom the corruption at Wheal Prosperity—and how to end it.

"Hasn't been a lot of work available lately," he muttered. "No one's hiring." He shrugged. "My sister does piecework in Buxton, and she sends our da money, too.

Guess it's better that I should have food in my belly than for both me and my father to have nothing." The words tasted sour as he spoke them.

"That's the spirit, man." Ware slapped Simon on his shoulder.

He hadn't been in the managers' presence above half an hour, but already he fantasized about plowing his fist into each of their faces.

They took a few moments to sign some paperwork, Simon careful to disguise his Harrow-trained penmanship.

Once that was finished, Ware said, "Head dead east from the mine, two miles, and you'll reach the village. Once you get there, someone will point you toward the single men's housing. Here." He fished a small brass coin from his pocket and handed it to Simon. "That'll pay for your meals for the week, until the next payday."

Simon studied the coin. It had a triangular piece cut out from the center, and stamped on it were the words "Wheal Prosperity Mining Company, Five Shillings, Payable in Merchandise, Non Transferable."

"Thank you, sirs." He nearly gagged on the words. These men didn't know it, but they'd just opened their doors to the agent of their destruction—offering a job and roof to dynamite.

"Work starts at seven in the morning," Murton said. "Every minute you're late, you're docked, so best to be on time."

"Yes, sirs." He grabbed his bag of tools, tipped his hat to the men one final time, and left the engine house. A satchel containing his few belongings waited for him outside the door, and he grabbed this, too. His father would have turned purple with mortification if he'd seen his son travel with anything less than three steamer trunks full of Savile Row's finest, but Simon had grown well used to his father's many shades of mortification on his behalf.

He pushed thoughts of Horace Addison-Shawe from his mind, as he'd done so often, and concentrated on what needed to happen next.

First part of the job's taken care of. Now the real work starts.

His years in the army and with Nemesis had shown him the value of gathering intelligence. He needed to know who had written that letter, for one thing. Then there was untangling the complicated web of corruption ensnaring Wheal Prosperity. And if there was any person who knew the lay of the land at this copper mine, that person was Alyce Carr.

He told himself that was the only reason he hurried to catch up with her.

Alyce strode back to the village on a path she knew as well as her own heartbeat. Generations of miners in their heavy boots had worn a track into the green hillsides. They left their legacy both beneath the earth and upon it. Just as she did. But her steps were fast, and she kicked up dust with each angry footfall. If all of the miners had walked with the same amount of fury that she felt, the path would be a trench, six feet deep.

As she walked, the conversation—or rather, *lack* of conversation—with the managers dug into her mind, like shards of metal.

It's simply not economical for the company store to replace almost a hundred pounds of butter just on your say-so, Miss Carr.

"Economical, my arse," she muttered to herself. They always had some excuse, some barely thought-out rationale. Would it make any difference to them if she was a man instead of a woman? Would they listen to her, take her grievances more seriously?

Doesn't matter, does it? Since I'm the only one trying to make a change.

"Miss Carr! Miss Carr!"

Caught up as she was in her own roiling thoughts, she barely heard a man call her name, or the sound of boots hurrying to catch up with her.

Only when he said her name again directly behind her did she stop walking. Had to be a surface captain, ready to chastise her for leaving work early—even though she had the managers' permission. She was just about to say so, when she turned to face the man pursuing her.

It was *him*. That stranger who'd been in the engine house.

"Seeing as how it's my new home," he said, "I was hoping you could show me the way to the village." He didn't sound at all winded, even though it looked like he'd been running to catch up with her. With his thumb, he pushed back the brim of his cap, revealing a thatch of wheat-blond hair.

In the engine house, she'd only had a brief glimpse of him beneath the gaslights—seeing mostly the winter blue of his eyes—but now that they were out in the sun, she could observe him more clearly.

"Got the job, then?" she asked.

"Good thing, too," he answered. "I need the work and that pump engine needs a nursemaid."

He wore a laboring man's clothes, filling them with a leanly muscular body that had seen its share of work. Growing up and living among men who spent hours a day tearing ore from the ground made her no stranger to the sight of a young man in prime condition. But something about *this* man—the confidence with which he carried himself, the stretch of rough wool across his broad shoulders and down his long legs—made her aware of his physicality.

"Men aren't nursemaids," she pointed out.

He gave an affable shrug. "A friend of mine told me that the definition of a man is that he does whatever's necessary. And if that pump engine needs me to change its nappy and rock it to sleep, then I'm the man for the job."

She tried to concentrate on what he was saying, but her thoughts briefly scattered like startled thrushes when she got a good look at his face. Blessed saints, she didn't know men could look like this. All clean lines, high cheekbones, and elegantly carved jawbone. His lips were thin, but the bottom lip was unexpectedly full. Someone long ago in his bloodline must have birthed an aristocrat's bastard, for there was no denying the natural nobility in his features.

It seemed a strange contrast to the clothing he wore and his accent—which she placed somewhere around Sheffield, and not the nice parts of that city, either.

A face was just a face—nobody had power over how they looked. It didn't matter how handsome this man was, he was only that: a man, like any other.

She pointed to the path, worn into the ground. "If you're looking for the village, follow this for another mile and a half. It'll take you right there."

"Since we're headed in the same direction," he said with a smile, "may as well keep each other company."

For all her bold talk, she was a woman, and not entirely immune to a handsome man's smile.

Still, she said indifferently, "As you like."

Setting down one of his bags, he extended a broad hand to her. She hesitated for a moment, not really wanting to touch him, but he glanced down at his hand and saw that machine grease smudged a few of his fingers.

With an apologetic grimace, he wiped his hand on his trousers—drawing her attention to his thigh—and then offered her his hand again.

"Simon Sharpe," he said. "Just got hired as a new machinist."

It would be downright rude not to shake his hand, so she did so. The contact of palm to palm sent a fast shiver of awareness through her. "Alyce Carr," she said, trying for a level voice. "And you'd be wise to take up your bags and find work elsewhere, Simon." Only the managers and bosses referred to the miners and workers by their last names.

She let go of his hand and walked toward the village. He quickly fell in pace beside her.

"Wheal Prosperity's the only mine that's hiring right now," he said. "Don't have much choice in the matter."

"There's always emigration. Or you could try something different—like the music halls."

"I get seasick something terrible, so crossing the ocean's out. And as for the music halls"—his low, husky laugh trailed along the nape of her neck—"they'd only pay me *not* to sing and dance." His gaze was sharp and curious as he looked at her. "*You* work at Wheal Prosperity, but if it's as you're implying, why don't *you* leave?"

The managers rode by on their trap, trailing thick clouds of dust as they returned to the village, and paying her and Simon no attention. Coughing, Alyce tried to wave the dust away. Finally, it settled, the trap already a speck in the distance.

For a moment, she debated whether or not to be honest with him. There was always the possibility that he could be yet another of the owners' snoops, hunting out agitators. But she'd never made a secret of her complaints, and she hadn't yet been fired.

Because they know I can't do a damned thing against

*them, and I'm one of their best bal-maidens. To them,
I'm just a gnat. A very productive gnat.*

"Can't," she answered bluntly. "I assume they gave
you a chit to pay for your food and lodging for the week."

"Five shillings' worth."

She whistled. "A princely sum. And did you read the
words on the bloody thing?" She recited them from memory. The words themselves were stamped upon her very
brain. "'Payable in Merchandise, Non Transferable.'
That's how we're all paid now. With that damned chit."

"And there go anyone's hopes of saving actual money.
Couldn't even buy a train ticket to carry you to someplace new."

"Just so."

A narrow stream dotted with rocks crossed the path
they walked. Every so often, some enterprising person
from the village thought to lay a wooden plank or two
across the stream to make it easier to cross, but the planks
never lasted. People rather liked skipping across the
rocks—a little reminder of childhood play.

Simon nimbly jumped from rock to rock and landed
on the other side of the stream with just a few strides. He
set his bags down and reached out a hand for her. To help
her across.

The gentlemanly gesture flummoxed her. It was so
natural for everyone who lived in the village to cross the
stream that no one ever thought to give anyone assistance. And she still didn't like the idea of touching him.
No, that wasn't quite true. She didn't like the sensations
in her body caused by touching him. This man who was
an utter stranger.

Ignoring his outstretched hand, she picked up her
skirts and leaped from one rock to the next until she
reached the other bank. There wasn't any harm in him

seeing her ankles. Her boots were nearly as stout as his. Nothing provocative about heavy, sturdy leather.

Even so, when she dropped the hem of her skirts, something like disappointment flashed in his eyes.

She continued walking, with him right beside her. "Besides, all I know is working at the mine, and everyone I've ever known is here. My father worked here, as did his father, and his father's father. My brother, too. And all my foremothers were bal-maidens or took care of the babes at home. This is my life." It surprised her, the defiance in her voice—or was it self-defense?

No, she was proud of the work she did, and the people around her. She had no pride, however, regarding the men who ran the mine. Outsiders, the lot of them.

Like this man—Simon. A complete stranger. Granted, an extraordinarily handsome stranger, but a man unknown to her. Well, she could learn a few things, too.

"Where are your people?" she asked. "Parents, siblings . . . wife?"

Her cheeks heated that she should ask so bold a question.

He didn't seem to take offense. "Sister's in Buxton, and my father's in Sheffield. No wife."

No reason at all for her to feel a twist of pleasure at that—none at all.

"You could've stayed in Sheffield," she noted. "Plenty of work there."

"Everyone I knew worked in the knife factories." He shook his head. "The world's a narrow place behind a grinding wheel. Joined the army for a spell—engineering corps. That's how I learned the way of different machines."

"And did you?"

He quirked an eyebrow. "Did I what?"

"Make the world less narrow?" She'd only been as far as Newquay, and then for only a half-holiday. The rest of the globe seemed a terribly fascinating, terribly big place. How lost she'd feel, out in the middle of everything with nothing but her own name to anchor herself.

"Oh, aye. India, South Africa. Fascinating places. Remind you that there's more to life than being English." She must have looked surprised by his answer, because he said, "Seems I've caught keen-witted Miss Carr by surprise."

"Most of the men I've spoken to who were soldiers called those places savage or heathen. Not fascinating."

He slanted her a smile. "All sorts of men in this world. Some don't fit perfectly into the uniforms they've been given."

She was beginning to learn that he didn't. Looking off to the hedgerow on her right, she saw the old elm tree, its branches bent from the winds that swept down into the valley. She'd seen that tree twice a day, every day, for the whole of her life. Yet for the first time in a goodly while, the long walk from the mine to the village held something new and surprising. That something was him, with an aristo's looks, a working man's accent, and a philosopher's outlook. She saw now the military bearing in the way he carried himself, posture upright, as if he hadn't spent decades crouched in a mine but marching boldly across the globe.

"Wheal Prosperity isn't like other mines, either," he noted. "Most pay with actual money, not scrip. I thought that was something they only did in America, in their coal mines and logging camps."

He may as well know the history of the place if he was determined to work there. "Ownership changed about ten years ago. The American and Australian mines drove the price of copper down. More than half the mines in

Cornwall shut down. We all believed we were goners, then thought it a blessing when a new group of adventurers offered to buy the mine out." She shook her head. "None of us knew the cost. Not until it was too late."

Those had been terrible days. Every morning waking up with fear cold in her belly, wondering whether any of them could go on, or if they'd lose everything. She'd been afraid, truly afraid. Poverty had hovered like a thin-faced ghost over the village and the mine, as everyone had anxiously gathered on stoops and in the two taverns, waiting, waiting. Would they have a way to keep the rain off their heads? Would their children go to bed complaining about the emptiness in their bellies?

Alyce had been only fourteen at the time, and her parents had still been alive. She'd heard her father and Henry talking in low voices by the fire.

We've got a little money set by, Henry had said.

But not enough, my lad, her father had answered. *Not enough to support all four of us.*

I have to run away, Alyce had thought. *One less mouth to feed. Maybe I can get work in London at a shop or in a house, and send my wages home.*

The following morning, Alyce's mother had found the pillowcase stuffed with Alyce's meager possessions. Instead of giving her a scolding, however, Alyce's mother had enfolded her in a hug, scented of mineral ore, chimney smoke, and warm, maternal flesh. *We stay together,* her mother had said. And that had been the end of that.

How happy they'd been when they'd learned the mine had been bought out. How the village had celebrated: everyone in the high street, singing, dancing. Toasting their good fortune with glasses of ale.

Now there was rancid butter in the company store, and no one would or could do anything about it.

She pushed the discouraging thoughts from her mind.

She *would* find a way to make things right, but the *how* of it was something she hadn't figured out. Yet.

"Sure this is where you want to work?" she asked Simon again. Dusk had begun to fall in a violet haze, and the lights of the village could just be seen beyond the next rise.

"Like I said, not many places hiring now, and I don't fancy reenlisting."

Alyce only shrugged. She'd done what she could. If Simon found himself trapped here in a cycle of poverty and debt—just like everyone else—that was his business, not hers.

They made the rest of the trip to the village in silence, for which she was grateful. Talking about the old days only reminded her of what everyone had had, and lost. Reminded her of the invisible shackles around her ankles, the same shackles binding every man, woman, and child in Trewyn. The few hours between shifts at the mine belonged to her, and she wouldn't waste them on anger or despair.

After crossing the last hill, they reached the village. Alyce had been born in Trewyn, and had woken up and fallen asleep here every day of her life. Yet, with Simon walking beside her, she tried to see it now with a stranger's eyes.

Houses of granite crowded the high street, with more creeping along the winding alleys leading off the main avenue. Some sported optimistic flower boxes, and a few doorways had cheerful vines of ivy twining around them. At either end of the high street stood the villages' two pubs, quiet now since the men hadn't yet returned from the mines, but a few old men sat outside on benches nursing their ales with a measured, deliberate pace.

No shops presented cheerful, merchandise-filled windows to the street. There used to be, but they'd gone, and had been transformed into more houses. Only one place to buy anything from mutton to muslin in Trewyn.

"You need to make any purchases," she said, "that's where you go." She pointed to the company store looming at the top of the street.

"It's one of the only wooden buildings in the village," he noted.

That he should notice this detail surprised her. "Yet it holds the most gravity—even more than St. Piran's." She nodded toward their plain little church set up on the hill. A rueful smile curled her mouth. "Funny that the store stands at one of the highest points in the village, as if water—or money—should flow *away* from it, the way it might in nature."

"But nature's rules don't apply here."

"Everyone's work and toil flows *up* into the store. Unnatural, that's what it is."

"There's that scientist bloke—Darwin," he murmured. "He said that creatures adapt to their environment, no matter how unnatural it might be, or else they don't survive. Seems like you've done the same here."

"We haven't got any say in it."

He cast her a glance. "You're ignoring your own decision to endure. But that's just what you've done. You made a hard choice, and stuck with it."

She peered around the village. Trewyn wasn't a pretty place—she'd seen illustrations and photographs of nicer villages and towns, laid out in neat grids, with public squares, subscription libraries, and tea shops. It was a village born from need, built by a people who never expected luxury or even softness from life. Not pretty, but practical.

An unexpected throb of affection beat in her chest. *My home.* All she'd ever really known, and, shabby as it was, she'd defend the village until the last of her blood stained the soil.

Alyce cast a quick, surreptitious glance at Simon, wondering what he saw. After all, he'd been many places, in England and abroad, places far grander than Trewyn.

Yet she didn't see disgust, or contempt, or dismay in his eyes. Instead, he seemed to be *studying* all that he saw, his gaze sharply perceptive, taking note of everything. As if looking for strengths and weaknesses. As though readying himself not for a new job in a new town, but preparing for a siege.

Military habit, I suppose.

Even so, it surprised her to see how he'd changed subtly. The faintest trace of danger emanated from him, like a concealed knife. Unseen, but that didn't lessen its potential.

A shiver danced up her spine.

"I feel as if I should offer you some kind of welcoming gift," she said. "A pot of flowers or loaf of bread. Knitted blanket."

The wariness in his eyes faded slightly as he smiled. "An old bachelor like me would just kill the flowers, devour the bread, and turn the blanket threadbare. But thanks for the sentiment." He glanced up and down the high street, as if searching for something.

"What are you looking for?" she asked.

"Trying to figure out which one of these houses is yours. I expect you've got some kind of banner flying out front, like one of those old-time knights. Seems only right for the Champion of Trewyn."

A shocked laugh burst from her, to be painted that way. But then, it did make a kind of sense. She seemed to be the only one in the village who regularly complained to the managers about the conditions at the mine and at the village.

Strange that Simon, who barely knew her, saw her as a guardian or knight. Strange, and flattering.

"Any particular interest in knowing where I live?" She surprised herself with the sauciness of her tone.

A corner of his mouth turned up. "I might be out taking a stroll and get lost. I'll need someone to show me the way back."

She frowned a little. Was he *flirting* with her? "It's impossible to get lost in Trewyn. We've only got one street."

"Maybe the place is more complicated than you know."

Before she could answer, the rumble of hundreds of men's voices and the thud of booted feet drifted into the village. She and Simon had left the mine fifteen minutes ahead of quitting time, but now the rest of the workers had caught up with them. Women's higher tones wove through like flutes. Some laughed, relieved after the end of the long day, but most spoke in low voices, too tired to do much more. Alyce could almost identify every single person, even with her eyes closed. John Gill and his rough chuckle. Danny Pascoe, who still talked with the piping notes of a lad despite his age. Cathy Weeks, whose voice was as deep as Danny's was thin. Henry was somewhere in the crowd, as well, but somewhere toward the back, since she didn't hear him yet.

Alyce moved aside to give the returning workers room as they trudged up the high street, and Simon did the same. She greeted many as they passed, and took a bit of good-natured ribbing from some that she'd left work early. Dozens of curious gazes fixed on Simon, intrigued by the stranger. More than a few bal-maidens let their gazes linger for a bit longer. Alyce gave many of the curious her own silent, speaking glance, letting them know that she'd be by later to give an accounting of the newcomer. But as for making introductions—he'd have to do them on his own. She had enough to manage without becoming the unofficial welcoming committee.

From a narrow alley, three blue-uniformed constables

suddenly appeared, including barrel-chested Tippet, the head of Trewyn's constabulary. A murmur of unease rippled through the crowd. Alyce sensed Simon tensing beside her. Curious. Had he been in trouble with the law before?

Tippet and his colleagues—Oliver, heavy-jawed and small-eyed, and Freeman, nearly handsome in a unfinished kind of way—shouldered their way through the column of returning workers. They tugged two men from the throng, dragging them roughly to the side, as everyone else could only look on.

"Here, now," Tippet said, shaking one of the men by his collar. Alyce recognized him as Joe Hocking, and the other miner was George Bevan, who grimaced as Oliver clenched his shoulder. "Did you think you'd get away with it? Think the masters are stupid, do you?"

"Don't know what you're talking about," Joe said. Though he'd been a miner all his life, the hard work and lack of enough food had taken its toll, prematurely aging him. His whole body was thin and shrunken. In another year or two, he wouldn't be able to go down into the pit anymore.

By contrast, Tippet was almost obscenely robust, filling out the jacket of his uniform with sturdy brawn.

Tippet smirked. "Right. 'Course you don't." His smirk twisted into a sneer. He flung Joe against a wall, and the older man grunted and went ashen. Joe looked like a fragile weed, clinging to the side of the building.

Tippet dug one end of his truncheon into the underside of Joe's jaw, and the miner grimaced.

Fury roiled up inside Alyce. Tippet never wasted an opportunity to rough up the villagers, even someone who presented no physical threat, like Joe.

Men and women gathered in a semicircle, jockeying to get a view. Restless anger rumbled through the crowd, like thunder before a storm. They were closing the ten-odd feet of distance between themselves and the constables.

"Everyone, keep back," Oliver growled.

"Not a step forward," Freeman added. He shoved back one man who tried to edge closer.

She had to take action—help Joe and keep the crowd from turning ugly. She took a step forward, ready to push the truncheon off Joe's neck.

Simon suddenly emerged from the throng. He tripped over the bags he carried, colliding with Tippet. Both men stumbled.

Tippet whirled around, face twisted in anger. She felt the crowd collectively hold its breath—just like her. What would Tippet do?

Then she saw the hard gleam in Simon's eyes as he faced the constable. Tippet wasn't the only threat, here. Simon was just as dangerous.

CHAPTER 2.

Growling, Tippet shoved the end of his truncheon into Simon's shoulder. As if defending himself, Simon quickly stepped to the side, one hand upraised. His other hand pushed against Tippet's outstretched arm, right into the constable's elbow. Tippet's hand gave a small spasm, causing him to let go of the truncheon. Suddenly, the heavy cudgel was in Simon's hand.

"Easy now," Simon murmured. "No harm meant, Constable. Just being clumsy."

"Who the hell are you?" Tippet demanded.

"Simon Sharpe," he answered. "New machinist."

"This doesn't have anything to do with you, Sharpe," Tippet snapped, though a faint tremor of uncertainty sounded beneath his words. "Give me back my baton and go about your own sodding business."

Yet Simon did neither. He turned the truncheon over and over in his hands. "I've held a Zulu kerrie before, but never something like this." He hefted its weight, letting one end slap against his open palm. "Could cause a big man a serious injury with this weapon." With a puzzled frown, he glanced at Joe and George. "They don't look that big to me."

"It's not the size of the man, but the crime he's committed." Tippet jutted his chin at Joe. "The company's got fine ways of running things. Everything's set up so they're dealt with fairly."

"This one made a good arrangement with the bosses," Freeman added. "The lode he's working is a poor one, so he gets thirteen shillings out of twenty shillings' worth of ore he digs."

"And that one"—Tippet jerked his head toward George—"he's working a rich lode, so he only gets one shilling out of twenty shillings' value. Keeps things honest."

A dark mutter moved through the crowd when Tippet said "honest." Alyce's own stomach clenched at the ironic use of the word. The constables seemed to be trying Joe and George right here in the street—justifying why they were dragging the two men off.

"But them two tried to get the better of the masters," the head constable continued. "Hid themselves off in some dark corner of the mine and did an exchange, then divided the gross profits."

"We didn't!" George protested, but his voice trailed off in a hiss when Oliver gripped his shoulder harder.

"Managers don't seem to think so," Oliver said.

"It's all trumped up," Alyce interjected hotly.

Many pairs of eyes, including Simon's, turned to her. Voice inquisitive, he said, "You sound certain of that."

"I am." She took another step forward. "George and Joe have been telling the managers that the lodes they're working aren't safe and should be closed down. This is the bosses' way of shutting them up."

Tippet snorted. "More baseless rabble-rousing from Miss Carr. We've got a witness who saw everything."

"Who?" she demanded. There had been rumors for a while that some of the miners were paid eyes for the managers, but so far, no one had been able to figure out the spies' identities.

"That's not our burden to prove." Tippet glared at Simon. "Unless you want to get hauled off to the clink, too, you'll give me back my baton."

Though his posture and affable expression didn't change, Alyce sensed Simon coiling, readying to fight. Though he had the same muscular build as any other laborer, it seemed as though he could do more than brawl—he could actually fight, maybe even kill, if he had to.

Then, just as subtly, the tension eased from him. He took a step back. The head constable held out his hand for the return of his truncheon.

Just before Tippet's fingers could close around the baton, the weapon dropped from Simon's hand. It clattered onto the ground.

"Clumsy, again," Simon said with a self-deprecating chuckle.

Tippet muttered and groaned slightly as he bent down to retrieve his truncheon. Once he had it back in his hand, he straightened and puffed out his chest. "Trewyn's a decent place. A safe place. I make sure it stays that way. So do everyone a favor and learn to be less clumsy. Or I might not be so lenient next time."

"Yes, sir," Simon answered, though he didn't appear cowed in the slightest.

Tippet hauled Joe up, and Oliver shoved George in front of him, with Freeman bringing up the rear. "The rest of you, head on back to your homes," the head constable said, addressing the gathered crowd. "But know that the company only wants what's best for everyone. When you step out of line, you make things troublesome and dangerous for everybody else."

Folding her arms across her chest, Alyce scowled as the three constables dragged George and Joe away. Oh, Tippet cloaked his actions with pretty rhetoric, pretending that he protected the miners and workers from themselves. But they were only meaningless words. All that mattered was that two innocent men who'd dared to speak out were now being punished.

No one moved until the five figures disappeared around a corner. As soon as they were gone, mutters churned up from the crowd, and most everyone resumed their walks home. Some faces wore expressions of fear, others anger, but most looked resigned. This was their lot, and there wasn't anything to do but accept it.

Simon picked up his tool bag and satchel. His movement was swift and nimble.

Realization hit her. "Nothing *clumsy* about you," she said in a low voice, stepping close so no one but Simon could hear her. "You didn't trip against Tippet and accidentally take his baton. It was all on purpose."

"Maybe I *am* clumsy," he answered casually. Yet his voice was also pitched low, keeping their conversation private despite the people nearby. "Haven't seen me try to dance. It's like a second Waterloo on the dance floor."

"I know what I saw. I was the only one standing close enough to notice—all of that was deliberate." When he gave no response, she pressed, "Why'd you do it? Defend two men you don't know?"

He only shrugged. "It seemed an unbalanced fight. I like balance."

She stared at him, trying to puzzle him out. "Joe and George could've been guilty, and you'd have stood up for them."

"Were they?"

"God, no!" The idea appalled her. "The company's using them as an example. Of what happens when you speak out."

A corner of his mouth turned up. "And yet you're still roaming free."

Her own mouth flattened into a line. "Better watch

any more instances of your *clumsiness,* or else you'll make an enemy of Tippet."

"I'll cry myself to sleep if that happens."

"Alyce! Alyce!"

She turned at the sound of her brother's voice. He edged his way through the crowd until he stood before her and Simon, scowling. Though he glanced briefly between her and Simon, the majority of his ire was for her.

"Heard there was a dustup between the constabulary and George and Joe," he said angrily. "Yet I'm not surprised to find you in the middle of it."

Her cheeks heated. Henry was only three years older than her, but since their parents' death, he often treated her as if she were a reckless girl in danger of tumbling down the mine shaft. Being spoken to like a child in front of Simon didn't make her feel very charitable toward her brother. "Tippet's made false accusations about Joe and George divvying up their ore."

Henry's expression clouded. "That's daft."

"Exactly what I said."

"No reason, though, for you to shove yourself in the middle of someone else's fight."

"I didn't *shove* myself into the middle of anything."

He rolled his eyes. " 'Shove' or 'push' or 'stick your nose where it doesn't belong.' Whatever words you use, the upshot's the same."

"I'm telling you," she said through gritted teeth, "I wasn't involved."

But he wasn't listening to her. As usual. "Haven't I said it again and again? Don't get mixed up with these brawls. Damn it, Alyce, you want me to sound like a chattering parrot?"

"Parrots are prettier."

Henry opened his mouth as if readying to give her a blistering set-down, but Simon spoke first.

"Begging your pardon—Mr. Carr, is it?—but it wasn't your sister who got between the constables and the accused. It was me." He set down his tool bag and offered his hand. "Simon Sharpe. Got hired today as a machinist."

Henry warily shook Simon's hand, and Alyce couldn't help but note the contrast between the two. Both Henry and Simon were young, strong men who worked hard for a living, but Henry stood several inches shorter than Simon—lack of height being an advantage when crawling around in dark tunnels all day—and had dark hair, where Simon was blond. But these were only superficial differences.

"Welcome to Trewyn," Henry said stiffly. "I'm Henry Carr. Alyce's brother."

Wide as Henry's shoulders were from wielding a pick six days a week, they were still bent, bowed from an invisible burden. He kept his chin lowered, his expression cautious.

Simon stood fully upright, chin high, his face and posture free of timidity. "You share the same frown," he noted, and Alyce had to stifle a sudden laugh.

That frown deepened. "Married, Simon?"

"Not that I know of," he answered with a smile. "Never woke up from a binge with a ring on my finger."

Again, she found herself fighting a giggle.

Henry, however, was much less amused. "Then it's the bachelor lodgings for you. Edgar here can show you the way." He tugged on the sleeve of Edgar Hayne, an unmarried man who was passing by. "Edgar, be a lad and escort Simon here to the bachelor housing."

"Sure thing, Henry," he agreed. Turning to Simon, he said brightly, "Come along, then. Supper's in half an hour, and they won't tolerate anybody being late. Got your chit to cover it, I hope."

Simon patted his pocket. "I'm ready to receive the bounty of Trewyn."

Chuckling at that, Edgar started up the high street, but stopped when he saw that Simon wasn't following. Instead, Simon gave another nod to Henry, then turned his attention to Alyce.

"No one's had a more interesting introduction to a place," he said wryly. "Cheers for that."

"I've given you plenty of warnings," she answered. "There's still time."

He lifted his shoulders dismissively. "And I said it before: I don't have any other choice. Besides," he added, his gaze warming as he looked at her, "maybe I'll find something that makes this place worthwhile."

For a woman who heard the rough language of men without so much as a blush, her cheeks now flamed.

"Oi," Henry said darkly.

Simon ducked his head, but it was just a small gesture. "No disrespect intended. The people of Wheal Prosperity seem like good-hearted folk, and I'm glad of it."

"Lively, now," Edgar called from up the street. "Or we go to bed hungry tonight."

Giving them each a little bow, Simon murmured, "Henry, Alyce. Sure we'll be seeing each other soon."

"It's a village of five hundred," Alyce replied, "and four hundred thirty of us work at the mine. Chances are good we'll run into each other."

"Right, then." With a final, wry smile, Simon turned, and hastened after Edgar. He had a fluid way of moving, sleek and direct. Unable to look away, she watched him walk up the high street. Disappointment flickered in her chest when the two men vanished inside the large house reserved for bachelors.

Henry snorted beside her.

"What?" she snapped.

"In the generations of Carrs that have lived in Trewyn and worked Wheal Prosperity, not a one of them drew trouble as you do." They both walked down one of the narrow lanes, heading toward home.

"And look where that got them." She glanced over her shoulder, toward St. Piran's and its churchyard full of worn stone tablets commemorating brief lives. The name Carr had been chipped into many of them. Every Sunday, she'd leave church, and there it was—the reminder of how short a time one walked this rough earth. Hardly more than the beat of a moth's wings, and then it was over. "Maybe if some of them caused a little trouble, we'd all be in a different place."

Lights ahead signaled that they were almost home. Sarah, Henry's wife, made sure to keep a lamp in the window so that their homecoming was always a warm one.

"Think that all you like," Henry said. "But nothing changes our path. Rattling bars only makes things noisy." He stopped in front of the door to their house. Inside, they could hear Sarah bustling—as fast as a heavily pregnant woman could bustle—with the sounds of her getting their supper onto the table and humming to herself.

Henry's usually serious expression turned even more sober. "Stay away from that Simon Sharpe."

"Warning me off him?" Alyce's eyebrows climbed. "We're not wee children anymore, Henry. Both of us are full grown, and we make our *own* decisions."

"He's already gotten mixed up in strife."

"It was an accident," she said, though she knew it hadn't been.

"Still don't trust him. We have plenty of explosives at the mine, Alyce. We don't need any more."

"Good thing I know my way around a stick of dynamite."

Muttering to himself, he opened the front door and stepped inside, greeting his wife. But Alyce didn't follow him in. Instead, she stood out on the stoop, breathing in the cold evening air and looking up at the emerging stars. How many different skies had Simon seen? Had he looked up at different constellations? Had he wished for impossible things, as she did now?

"Alyce?" Sarah called. "Don't let all the warm air out, darling. We're down to our last bits of coal until the next pay packet."

Heading inside, Alyce turned her gaze from the sky and her musings from the blue-eyed stranger. But her mind was never at rest, and she knew he'd be in her thoughts later. A little-heard, almost girlish voice in the back of her mind murmured, *It'd be nice if he thought of me, too.*

With each step away from Alyce, Simon cursed himself. He shouldn't have done anything when the constables had dragged those miners from the line. Just watched, gathered information, and kept quiet. He couldn't afford to attract attention to himself, not when he needed to gather intelligence.

But his impulses had gotten the better of him. The two miners wore the gray skin and thin frames of the prematurely aged. Beaten down by life. Whatever the law had accused them of doing, it didn't warrant being thrown around like sacks of meal. He'd had to stop it somehow. A well-timed stumble, and he'd been able to keep those men—briefly—from more abuse at the hands of the bully of a chief constable. Trouble was, now the law had taken notice of Simon.

Marco always warned Simon about that—despite his time as a soldier, his gentlemanly impulses to defend the weak could get him into trouble when on assignment. Easy for Marco to stick to keeping a low profile. Working in intelligence for the English government for nearly two decades could make a man slippery as an oiled kipper. Silence and subversion came naturally to him.

For now, Simon needed to keep his head down, blend in with the other workers of Wheal Prosperity, and learn what he could.

It didn't help, though, that Alyce Carr muddled his thoughts with her sharp tongue, incisive mind, and the fierce gray-green of her eyes. Getting distracted by a woman while on a mission was a cardinal mistake. He ought to avoid her. Except she seemed to be one of the best sources of information about the mine. She could be the mystery correspondent—though typewriters seemed outside of a bal-maiden's financial means. And the way she spoke didn't quite match the tone of the letter.

At the least, facing off against the constables brought him closer to her. She'd be a powerful ally.

Simon followed Edgar into the building that would serve as his temporary abode for the next few weeks. Of course, no one here knew that his time in Cornwall was temporary, and so he looked around the bachelors' lodgings with the eye of a man settling into his new home.

"Here 'tis," Edgar said with a sweep of his arm. "Our very own manor house."

"Reminds me exactly of the Malwala Palace," Simon noted.

Edgar chuckled. "Aye, I'm sure it does, even if I've never heard of the place."

Two rows of wooden-framed cots ran the length of the long room. Coarse woolen blankets covered the horsehair mattresses. The beds were jostled next to one another in an attempt to cram as many men in one chamber as possible. Bare planks made up the floor, and dirt and smoke streaked the whitewashed walls. A battered kettle sat atop the single coal-burning stove in the middle of the room. Laundry draped from the exposed rafters—underwear and shirts hanging like ghosts.

Fifteen years fell away. The resemblance to an army barracks was uncanny.

Men sat on their cots or leaned against a few battered wooden dressers as they stretched and yawned and made the myriad sounds and gestures of men at the end of a long workday. Some eyed Simon with curiosity, and he caught a few whispers: "That's the bloke who got Tippet riled." "Heard he beat Tippet's face in." "Yeah, well I saw it happen—Tippet nearly blacked his eye."

Simon quelled a smile. Gossip fed small communities as much as meat or bread did.

"There's a free cot fourth on the left," Edgar said. "You can take that one. Privies are out back, and the water pump and bathhouse are at the end of the lane, but most do our washing up at the change house at the mine. Can't come tromping home covered in dust and dirt, even if we're unmarried."

More men came ambling into the lodgings, all of them wearing the haggard pall of weariness. Impossible to say how old many of them were. He'd seen it in London, he'd seen it in the army: an arduous life stole away years, stripping men, women, and children down to the bone, down to the core of themselves, leaving nothing but exhaustion and emaciated hope.

Murmuring greetings and exchanging nods, Simon made his way toward the empty cot. He stopped briefly now and then to introduce himself and tell his "history," and was unsurprised to find that all the men he spoke with had been born in the village. A cloak of defeatism hung over the room. It wasn't always like this. Even in the factories in Birmingham or the grim corners of Whitechapel, the human spirit had a special way of enduring, grabbing at brief pleasure and moments of beauty where it could.

The few hours he'd spent at Wheal Prosperity and

Trewyn proved otherwise. These were beaten people, trapped by circumstances they couldn't control.

He felt it—that need, pushing him, forcing him to balance the scales. It always shoved at him, as if the highborn blood that ran through his veins would eat through him like acid if he swaddled himself in privilege and indifference.

Simon set down his bags beside his cot. He nudged his tool bag under his bed, then began to unpack his minimal possessions into the dresser next to his bed. His working man's clothes were part of an assortment of costumes, different identities his work for Nemesis might require. Fishmonger. Dockside laborer. Banking clerk. Rarely did he take missions outside of London. As he stacked his shirts, his fingers itched at the lack of a weapon. Traveling with his revolver or trusty Martini-Henry raised eyebrows.

Tippet claimed to care about the welfare of the town. Bollocks to that. Maybe the chief constable told himself that lie to reconcile his need for bullying—but that fiction would crumble apart in a moment in order to keep the villagers and miners under his control.

Did the people here ever fight back against Tippet and his bosses? What would happen if they tried? Of if Simon tried?

If it ever came down to it, Simon would find a way to arm himself. Gentleman by birth he might be, but he was also resourceful.

He set two photographs in his dresser, beside his clothes. One of an old man, and another of a young woman, both fair-haired like him, and both wearing neat but plain clothing. His "father" and "sister." He'd purchased the photos from a secondhand-goods shop. In London, Harriet had even penned him a few letters, signing them, "Your sister, Nell," and Marco had forged the postal marks. Those letters he set beside the photographs.

No books—that was a difficult sacrifice. Hopefully, there'd be newspapers at the pub. But Simon Sharpe, former soldier turned machinist, wasn't a lover of literature. Laboring men who read were often viewed with suspicion as potential agitators. Reading led to thinking, and thinking led to dangerous ideas about equality and fairness.

He'd no doubt that one of the mining company's spies would rifle through his belongings just as soon as they could.

The photographs gave nothing of his real self away. He felt nothing when looking at them. Two nameless strangers standing in for those he cared about.

Alyce suddenly popped into his mind. She shone in the darkness of this place. She worked just as hard as any of the men or women here—when they'd shaken hands, not only did he feel her calluses, but the strength in her arm and grip. Yet something within her continued to burn, some inner fire. Her people may have given up, but she hadn't. Damned hard not to admire her fortitude. And it surprised him, but he wanted to know more about the woman beneath the brazen words and bold gazes.

So, had she sent the letter to Nemesis? It seemed hard to think of anyone he'd met so far who would have the grit to do so. He'd nose around mine and village further before asking. It'd be a bloody disaster if he revealed himself as an agent of Nemesis too soon, and to the wrong person.

What if she hadn't written it, and he had to explain to her who he truly was? What Nemesis, Unlimited, was?

Staring down at the picture of his "sister," an imagined conversation with Alyce ran through his head.

It's just what the name promises, he'd say. *Justice by any means.*

Justice for who? she'd demand, which made him smile

to himself. Even when she was a figment of his imagination, she didn't lose her fierceness.

Those who can't get it for themselves. Maybe because of their position in the social hierarchy. Maybe other circumstances. You've seen it yourself. It's a sodding corrupt, inequitable world that sees too many people ground beneath the boot heels of the elite. So that's what Nemesis does. Makes things a little more even, a bit more just. If someone can't stand up for themselves, Nemesis does it for them.

Would she scoff at him? Think him a fool? Or a hero?

He smiled again. If anything, he was a little of both.

And God knew that the people of Trewyn were in dire need.

More men drifted into the lodgings. They were all ages, from men who resembled the craggy granite hills to boys who couldn't yet grow a beard. Simon fingered the stubble along his cheeks. A scrubby veldt was the best he'd ever been able to coax out of his own facial hair. Not especially useful. Mustaches and beards served as a good disguises. But clean shaven, even he couldn't deny that he resembled his gently bred ancestors.

A clock on the wall chimed the half hour. Almost as one, the men in the room stood or straightened from where they'd been lounging and filed out of the chamber through a door at the far end. Simon fell into ranks with them, following as they crossed a narrow corridor to emerge into another long room. The ceilings were higher here, and instead of beds, rows of tables filled the chamber, but otherwise it looked exactly like the dormitory. A long trestle table stood at the end of the room. Tall, battered pots lined the trestle table, steam wafting up from their contents. Men already lined up at the table, waiting for their food.

As Simon entered the room, a man with large sideburns

and an apron tied around his waist held out a hand to stop him.

"You're the new bloke?" At Simon's nod, he said, "I'm Kemp, the landlord."

"Then you'll be wanting this." Simon handed him the scrip.

Kemp didn't smile, but the frown bracketing his mouth lessened. "Queue up before it's all gone."

Someone waved at him from the line. Edgar, with several men standing with him. "Over here."

"Oi," a man snapped, "no cuts!"

"Be kindly to the lad," Edgar answered. "It's his first day."

"I can stand at the back of the queue," Simon offered, but Edgar brushed that idea aside as if it were a gnat.

"We're giving you a proper welcome, and that's final." Edgar stared meaningfully at the objector.

"Today only," the man grumbled.

Simon slipped into line. "You're a gentleman."

The muttered reply contradicted that statement—at least, as far as language went.

Fortunately, the queue moved quickly. Simon grabbed a bowl and cutlery, then made his way down the long table. Adolescent girls in aprons ladled stew from giant pots, moving like automatons, their gazes far away.

Once he'd gotten his food, Simon found Edgar and his companions already seated, and Edgar again waved him over. Simon sat between two of the men, who gave him polite nods and smiles.

"Thanks. I didn't know where I'd be welcome."

"A new face is always welcome," Edgar said.

"We've heard each other's stories so much," another man said, "I can't remember whose memories are whose anymore."

"Don't think anyone would want my memories," Simon noted.

"Can't be any worse than the time Fred got drunk and fell into the cesspit," Edgar said. "He stank for a fortnight."

Everyone but one man—Fred, presumably—laughed. He just poked at his food, muttering.

Simon chuckled. "Haven't fallen into a pit of shit. But I've seen some bloody combat, and that's not something a bloke wants living in another man's head."

"A soldier?" pressed one of the men. "Go on, tell us your stories. Anything's got to be better than hearing Nathaniel talk about the one time he thought he ate rancid mutton but it turned out it wasn't."

"It tasted strange!" Nathaniel objected. "Gave me the winds something terrible, too."

"Please spare us, Simon," Edgar pleaded.

Simon couldn't help but laugh. So, he talked of his military service—careful to omit any details that might reveal his origins. Some old soldiers liked to embroider their stories, make themselves into heroes. But being in the army was like any job—a job where you'd be bored to death for weeks, months, and then suddenly, men you didn't know were trying to kill you.

He tried to downplay the action he'd seen, but the men seated around him stared, letting their mutton stew go cold and untouched.

"You've seen 'em, then?" Edgar asked. "The savage Zulus?"

"They're no more savage than you or I," Simon answered. "Courageous as hell. Never seen a more organized, more disciplined fighting force. Make no mistake, lads, their army's as good as Britain's."

He'd buried the dead soldiers the Zulu had left behind at Isandlwana. The circling vultures, the buzzing of flies over hundreds of bodies, the scavengers both human and animal picking through the field. The stink of the corpses rotting in the sun had clung to the inside of his nose for months.

And he'd faced the Zulus, himself. But all he wanted was to eat his supper, flavorless and tough as it was, not blather on about the past.

The men gathered around him now fell silent as they contemplated the idea that any army—especially one that wasn't European—could be the equal or even better than Britain.

"We've had a few lads go off and join the army or navy," Edgar said after a long pause. "But most everyone who's born in Trewyn stays in Trewyn to work the mine. We used to lose a few people every year, heading off to London or America, but"—he lowered his voice—"ever since they changed over to scrip instead of money, nobody can afford to leave. Got no means to pay our way out."

"Ever thought about unionizing?"

The men's eyes widened, and Nathaniel made a hissing, shushing noise. "Nobody says that word," he muttered. "Not unless they want to get their face beat in."

"A botched effort, then," Simon deduced.

Edgar glanced around the dining hall, making certain that no one was eavesdropping, before speaking. "About a year after the changeover, we tried. Demanded that they go back to paying us with actual money. We even went on"—he lowered his voice to barely a whisper—"strike." He shook his head. "The owners brought in thugs. Things got violent. Some good men died, more were hurt."

"They said they'd bring in scabs if we didn't get back to work," Nathaniel added. "And this was back when the other copper mines were drying up. Everyone stayed."

Alyce's earlier words of caution echoed in his head.

She'd warned him to leave before he got in too deep. Maybe she'd seen it, the strike. Maybe even took part in it. Then saw the brutality when the strike got ugly.

She'd have been fourteen or so, at the time. A young girl caught up in the middle of that madness. God, he hated to think it. Yet, if she'd seen that viciousness, it hadn't crushed her spirit.

The other people of Trewyn, however, bore the scars of that conflict. Even now, years later, Edgar, Nathaniel, and the other few men seated nearby were ashen just speaking about it, their shoulders hunched, eyes darting from side to side. Anticipating retribution for simply speaking about unions and strikes.

Not all strikes turned bloody. They could be used as effective bargaining tools and the means for creating compromise, but clearly, the ownership of Wheal Prosperity weren't interested in compromise. Just profit. Organizing the miners into a union wouldn't solve the problems here. The threat of violence hung over the valley like a black snare, especially with the precedent already set. And the workers had bugger all for leverage—no strike fund to fall back on, no other work to escape to.

Edgar cleared his throat, and it was obvious from his expression that he wanted to change the subject. "You were with Alyce Carr earlier."

Simon had mingled with the most worldly crowds in glittering ballrooms, was no stranger to the sophisticated pleasures of the bedroom, and spent weeks haunting the vice-ridden alleys of East London on assignment. Nothing shocked or embarrassed Simon.

Yet now he felt heat creeping into his cheeks.

It's because I'm Simon Sharpe, he told himself. *He'd blush at the mention of her.*

"She showed me the way from the mine to the village," he muttered.

The men around him chortled and sent one another knowing looks. "That's a rocky hill to climb, lad," Nathaniel said. "Mind, it's a pretty hill, with all sorts of lovely . . . bumps. But rocky, just the same."

Simon took a drink of beer. "No one's willing to, ah, try the climb?"

"Oh, blokes have tried," Edgar noted.

"What stopped them?" he asked with deliberate nonchalance as he loosened his grip.

"*She* did," answered Nathaniel. "Turned 'em all down. Though, if you ask me, she did 'em a favor."

"Mind," Edgar said, pointing his fork at Simon, "a woman can't survive in Trewyn unless she's got some spine to her. But Alyce Carr's got a little *too* much spine. Always speaking out, acting like she's got the same rights as a man. Overly independent, if you ask me."

Simon gave a wry smile. "Thanks for the warning."

It was a rare event when a woman could challenge him, who spoke so plainly and with such confidence. There were exceptions: mostly female Nemesis agents—and he never tangled romantically with his fellow operatives. Well—he'd tried, with Eva, but she'd been smarter than he, and turned him down flat. Years of being a gentleman's son as well as a member of Her Majesty's Army had taught him important lessons about when, and with whom, he could drop the disguise of decorous behavior.

The women he knew from his upbringing were taught at an early age to be ornamental, to make themselves agreeable to future suitors, to fill their time with social calls, parties, and the occasional useless charitable organization. He'd never really known women to be any other way—until he'd left the protective shelter of wealth and privilege.

Yet for all the strong and intelligent women he'd encountered over the years, Alyce wasn't like any of them. Her defiance, her will—whatever it was, it kept her sliding back into his thoughts. Bold as she was, she held a core of mystery, a part she kept close to herself, a fist locked around her truest self. The lure of that mystery was irresistible—beyond just the job.

She was a firebrand, and clever. A dangerous combination.

She was also the best lead he had on how to take down Wheal Prosperity's corruption.

"Eh," Nathanial said with a genial shrug, "it's no loss, lad. I'd rather have my freedom than be tied down to a wife."

"The only woman who'd take you to wed would have to be blind and deaf," Edgar goaded.

"And have no sense of smell," added Fred.

Nathaniel scowled as the others laughed. "Here now, you're saying you'd rather have to hand over your pay packet every week to a woman? Being accountable to her for all your waking hours?" He snorted. "I've already got managers and bosses telling me what to do all day. The rest of my time is for me, and no one else. And if I want to spend the rest of my night at the pub, then, by God, I'll do it, and not have to explain myself to anybody."

Murmured agreements rose up from the other men.

"Women don't just manage the larder," Simon felt obliged to point out. "They've got the keys to another important place."

Edgar chuckled. "Company town, lad. There are ladies here who'll take chit in exchange for time in their beds. Fine, churchgoing women. They just add a little something to their earnings. It's all kept on the quiet, but I can point 'em out to you if the need . . . arises."

More snickering came from the men. Simon couldn't

pretend to be shocked at the commerce of sex, even in a little village like Trewyn. It was a constant, no matter if one found himself in Bombay or Birmingham.

"Generous of you," Simon replied. "I don't think I'll be a regular customer, though. It might be kept on the quiet, but all the same, I don't want word getting out."

"So you're looking to settle down," Nathaniel said.

"God, no," answered Simon immediately, instinctively. "I've settled down behind a barricade with my Martini-Henry and a box of cartridges. I also settled down in India with a row of stitches in my leg and a month of fever."

"A wife would feel like a seaside holiday after that," Edgar said.

"I'm not carrying a bride across my threshold." Even if he didn't work for Nemesis, he couldn't imagine himself with one woman for the rest of his life. Perhaps his reluctance stemmed from his youth, when it had been made clear that one day he'd make a strategic Society marriage.

"Ah," Nathaniel said, waving at the long dining hall, full of the men hunched over their bowls, the air thick with the scent of grease, "but what young lass wouldn't find this a bridal paradise?"

The idea of being anyone's pawn repelled him down to his very bones. For his parents' marriage had been organized by their famiies with all the care and tenderness of a military invasion. They didn't hate each other, his parents, but after his mother had produced the requisite number of heirs, she and his father treated each other like acquaintances who occasionally shared a house.

He'd left home before anyone could make definite plans for him.

"You ass," Fred said to Nathaniel. "Married men don't live with their wives in the bachelors' lodging."

Nathaniel rolled his eyes. "Smart as a vole, you are."

"I don't know," Simon mused. "We could honeymoon

by the water pump at the end of the lane. Then come back to this glorious nuptial palace."

He needed freedom. To go where he wanted, when he wanted, and be responsible only to himself and his duties to Nemesis. He had a few regular paramours in London: rich, sophisticated widows who asked few questions, made no demands. A countess who'd lost her husband after a decade of marriage and felt no inclination to replace him. A wealthy woman who happily existed on her settlement. Her importer husband had died from fever in Sumatra. For Simon and his widows, it was a mutually beneficial arrangement. All a man could ask for.

"I can just see a woman's dainties hanging from the rafters," Edgar snickered.

"Right across from Nathaniel's flannel combination with the holes worn through in the arse," Fred added.

Simon laughed, but he was only half paying attention as the men continued to badger each other. What if he did have someone, a woman who was entirely his, and to whom he belonged completely?

No rise of terror greeted this idea. And damn him, he knew the culprits behind this sudden shift of attitude.

Jack and Eva Dutton.

Nemesis had blackmailed Jack into helping them ruin a corrupt nobleman, partnering him with Eva for the job. She was the daughter of missionaries, a tutor by profession. A skilled operative.

Having learned as much as he could that day about the mine, Simon allowed his thoughts to linger over Jack and Eva.

Jack was no missionary's son. Not by birth, and sure as hell not by deed. A mean and tough bastard, he'd been spawned in Bethnal Green, earning coin as a bare-knuckle brawler, then a bodyguard. Prison had been his next destination after he'd tried to kill that shady nobleman. But even

Dunmoor Prison hadn't been able to hold Jack. He'd broken out to try to wreak his revenge against Lord Rockwell.

"Vengeance at any cost"—that was Nemesis's unofficial motto. And they'd proven it by sinking their claws into Jack. They'd forced him to work with them to bring Rockwell down. Not the precise formula for romance, but somewhere along the way, Eva and Jack—the two most disparate souls that ever walked the earth—fell arse over teakettle in love. Only weeks ago, they'd gotten married in a small London ceremony attended only by Nemesis agents. Simon had served as best man.

Jack and Eva were currently in the process of moving to Manchester, to start a new branch of Nemesis, and establish a school for the poor and unwanted children of the city.

What would it be like, to have what Eva and Jack had? What if it wasn't a loss of freedom, but companionship and a shared sense of purpose? Purpose that went beyond just missions for Nemesis. A true partner, in every sense of the word.

A strange ache set itself up in the center of his chest, as though the wind had crept through a previously unseen fissure in a wall, spreading its chill.

He shook his head. What Jack and Eva possessed was as rare as a water lily in the depths of winter. Singular. Unrepeatable.

He was content with his life as it was, and wouldn't waste time thinking on impossibilities. Still, that cold ache continued to pulse between his ribs. Something had to warm him, but he didn't know what.

"Oi, Simon." Edgar waved his hand in front of Simon's face. "We've been asking you for the past five minutes if you want to go to the pub."

"A drink or two sounds bloody perfect," he said.

CHAPTER 3.

"My one-woman battle for fresh butter was trounced," Alyce said, stepping into the cottage. "They won't give in."

Sarah, Henry's wife, looked up from stirring a pot of nettle soup, steam wafting around her face in curls as delicate as the blond ones tumbling around her face. "Did you tell them that it's on the verge of spoiling?"

"It was like yelling at a wall of macassar oil and arrogance." Alyce hung her apron on a hook by the front door, then bent to untie her boots. She lined them up next to Henry's. Sarah always insisted that they change out of their work boots immediately after setting foot inside the door, or else she'd spend her every waking hour sweeping up the tracked-in grime.

It was no punishment to take off her heavy footwear, and Alyce sighed as she slid her feet into a pair of worn, often-mended slippers. She pulled tin plates down from the cupboard and set them down on the table at the center of the room. "It made no difference. A matter of economics, so said the smug brigade." Bitterness edged her voice.

Sarah eyed the pieces of sausage frying in a cast-iron pan, then turned her gaze to the ceramic jar next to the stove. "Guess we'll have to make do with drippings. It won't be the first time."

Grabbing bowls from the cupboard as well, Alyce forced a smile, though her anger hadn't dissipated. "Drippings or butter, nobody cooks better in Trewyn than you do. Henry's got to fight the other men from his pasties, don't you, Henry?" she called up the stairs.

"There's fisticuffs at every luncheon," he shouted back down.

"A pair of foolish flatterers, the both of you," Sarah chided, but she grinned and continued to stir the soup. Her other hand rested on the bulge of her stomach, where the next generation of Carrs awaited its entrance into the world. Another two months, the doctor had said, provided everything went well with mother and child.

No one—not Henry, or Sarah, not even Alyce—dared voice their fears. More than a few headstones marked tiny graves in the churchyard. Or worse, some graves accommodated two. One of Henry and Alyce's siblings had been stillborn, and two more hadn't survived their first five years.

A perilous thing, to be a pregnant woman or a small child, especially in Trewyn. But it was a testament to human resiliency that more survived than didn't.

As she set the cutlery beside each table setting, Alyce eyed her own flat belly. So it would remain, for she'd bring no new life into this world of hardship. A small twist of sadness threaded in her stomach, that she'd never know what it was to be a mother, but she'd made her choice and refused to regret it.

Henry clomped around upstairs, doing God knew what, but even the lightest tread in this cottage sounded like the rattling of hippopotami. Granted, Alyce had never *seen* a hippopotamus, but she'd looked at pictures, and had an imagination. The creatures wouldn't lightly caper across an African plain.

They were lucky enough to have a two-story cottage. Many families lived in a single room—father, mother, children, and sometimes even grandfolks. Granted, the Carrs' home was simply two tiny rooms stacked one atop another, with a rickety wooden staircase connecting them. The only door in the entire cottage was the front door. Upstairs was for Sarah and Henry, and, eventually, the baby. Downstairs was the kitchen, and where Henry smoked his pipe each night as Sarah did her knitting and Alyce read and reread the few books she owned. It was also Alyce's bedroom, her cot shoved into a corner and hidden behind a curtain of faded calico. A miserly attempt at privacy.

Still, she had it better than most, and she wouldn't begrudge her cot and her corner.

Henry came down the stairs, the wood groaning beneath his feet. He immediately crossed the room and pressed a kiss to his wife's temple. "The best part of my day," he said.

"Because you know supper's almost on the table," she countered.

"Ridiculous lass. I'll go to bed with an empty stomach, so long as you're beside me."

As Sarah and Henry kissed, Alyce looked away, sensing once again that dull ache. Bad enough to feel that she didn't quite belong in her own village, but even at home, she sensed herself out of place, set apart. From the time Henry and Sarah had known each other as children, they'd been mad for each other. Two years of marriage hadn't changed that. But there had been no one like that for Alyce. No one whose face she couldn't wait to see, whose voice made her heart speed up.

Strangely, Simon's face flashed into her mind. He *had* been flirting with her—hadn't he? And wouldn't it be nice if he had?

Sarah announced that the meal was ready, and she and Alyce dished up the soup and sausages as Henry waited. Once all the food had been distributed—Alyce making certain that Sarah received more than herself—everyone bent their heads and said grace, thanking the Lord for the bounty they were about to receive.

A very unreligious thought crept into Alyce's mind—doubtless the Carrs' definition of "bounty" differed from the masters'. Those men lived in a large house a quarter mile from the village, and she'd seen the delivery wagons carrying huge sides of beef, fresh vegetables, and even crates of fine imported liquor all headed out toward the house. Despite Sarah's attempts to stretch their food, there never seemed to be quite enough. What would it be like to go to bed with one's belly aching because it was full, not empty? Things would only get more difficult once the babe was born.

Everyone began to eat. Alyce tried to pace herself, though she could've simply tipped her plate to her mouth and devoured everything at once. But she'd take a bite and carefully set her fork down, making sure to chew slowly, as though she could fool her stomach into thinking it was getting more than it really was.

"Tell me of the outside world." Sarah dipped her spoon into her nettle soup and looked back and forth between Henry and Alyce. "I never thought I'd miss being a bal-maiden, but staying at home and doing piecework leaves a lass cut off from society."

"Things are just as they always were," Henry said.

Sarah rolled her eyes. "And you say that every night. Do I have to torture news out of you?" She dug her finger into his ribs, and he snorted a laugh. Always ticklish, poor Henry. And too cautious of his wife's condition to fight back.

Alyce decided to spare him. "They've hired a new machinist."

Immediately, Sarah stopped tickling Henry. "Promoted someone, you mean?"

"No, a new hire from elsewhere."

Sarah's eyes widened, her face alight with excitement. "An outsider!" She gave Henry a playful swat. "You weren't going to say a word about it. Haven't you any pity for your poor, housebound, pregnant wife?"

Despite her teasing, Henry shrugged. "Not much to say about him. His name's Simon Sharpe, and he'll be maintaining the pump engines."

Alyce stared at her plate and carefully cut herself another piece of meat, chewing it with more deliberateness than usual.

"Where's he from? Is he young or old? Handsome or homely?"

"Bless me, Sarah, how in goodness' sake should I know?" Henry answered gruffly. "He's a man with two legs, two arms, and a face. What else is there to say?"

With an exasperated sigh, Sarah turned to Alyce. "I know bal-maidens don't usually rub elbows with machinists, but did *you* get a look at him?"

Alyce kept her gaze on her soup, watching the nettles swirl on the surface of the broth as though it were the most fascinating thing in the world. "I did. Walked with him back from the mine to the village."

Sarah threw her hands up into the air. "Lord preserve me from these lead-tongued Carrs!"

Best to just get it over with, like tearing off a sticking plaster. Alyce spoke quickly. "He's from Sheffield. Looks to be in his early to middle thirties. He spent time in the army."

"Oh! A military man! How dashing!"

Henry grumbled.

"Which isn't to say that a copper miner isn't dashing, of course," Sarah added hastily. "Soldiers can be downright unmannerly and coarse." She turned to Alyce. "Was he?"

"No." She poked her spoon into her soup. "His manner was . . . nice."

"He wasn't so nice when he nearly came to blows with Constable Tippet," Henry fired back.

Sarah clapped her hands over her mouth. "Never say! He sounds like an unpleasant character to me, going up against the law like a hooligan."

"He wasn't being a hooligan. It was . . . an accident. And would it have been so bad if he'd stood up for Joe and George, which was a sight more than you would've? Always with you it's keep the peace, head down, don't make noise."

"You'd rather rattle the bars and get a beating for your trouble," he retorted. "Da and Granda knew the best way, but you're a mule-stubborn girl who thinks she knows best. I'm upholding the family name, the tradition that's been ours. Peace at Wheal Prosperity."

"Look at the cost, damn it." She waved at the bowls of soup and plates of sausage. "Hardly enough to feed the three of us, and Sarah's eating for the babe, too. And we're the lucky ones. Vera and Charles Denby have five little ones, with another on the way. The youngest looks as frail as thistledown. Another bad winter and that little boy won't survive."

"Hush," Sarah said. "We don't talk of those things."

Alyce dipped her head. "Sorry," she muttered, humbled.

Henry spread his hands. "What would you have me do, Alyce? None of us have leverage against the masters. There's no choice but to make peace with it and hold out hope."

"Hope for what? Butter that doesn't make us sick?"

"Hope that through common sense and talk, we can get the bosses to see what needs to be done. That won't happen if you keep shrieking at them like a hawk protecting her nest."

"I don't *shriek*. And I won't wait and smile and plead for the masters' attention. Those pompous dolts don't listen. Not unless we pry their ears open."

Brother and sister glared at each other across the table in a stalemate. Minutes ticked by.

"You Carrs are stubborn as cats," Sarah exclaimed in frustration. "And it doesn't say much about me that I've married into this madness. Can we please just calmly finish our supper and save the sulking for later?"

Grudgingly, Henry and Alyce returned to their meals, and Sarah sighed in relief.

Another few minutes passed before anyone spoke. Sarah murmured to Alyce, "So, this Simon Sharpe—is he handsome?"

Alyce's face heated as images of Simon's patrician features and dashing grin flitted through her mind. "It's wise to be wary of him. He *is* new to the village, after all."

"Maybe you're wary of him *because* he's handsome," Sarah answered, smiling.

"I didn't say that."

"Your red cheeks did."

Alyce resisted the impulse to press her palms to her face, as if she could hide what Sarah had already seen.

"Accidentally or no," she said, "Simon Sharpe caused trouble today. When Tippet gets riled, things get rough for all of us."

"That's Tippet's problem," Sarah noted, "not Simon's."

"I don't like Sharpe," Henry answered. "He could be a bad influence on you."

Alyce rubbed her hand across her eyes, where a

headache brewed. "I'm four and twenty, Henry. Nobody *influences* me but me. And I just met Simon. I'm not so pudding-brained that a handsome stranger turns me into his puppet."

"If we don't change the subject," Henry growled, "I will run over to Adam Peeler's and herd his pigs right through our house—dirty, dirty pigs with filthy trotters."

Sarah turned ashen. She stared at her scrupulously clean floors, then back at Henry. "The weather's been pleasant lately," she managed.

Satisfied that the subject of Simon Sharpe had been dropped, Henry continued eating. Alyce did her best to avoid Sarah's knowing look, focusing instead on finishing her meal. But that didn't keep thoughts of Simon from circling inside her like magpie moths on a warm summer afternoon. As a little girl, she'd never been able to resist their pull, dancing with the moths until the sun sank below the horizon and she was called home.

It wasn't the first time Simon had walked in a long column of men. He'd done a considerable share of marching during his stint in the army—sometimes beneath blazing blue skies, sometimes through soaking monsoon rains. Muddy roads, dusty tracks, or straight through choking jungle. There'd been camp followers, too: an assortment of women and native people who tended to the sundry needs of the regiment.

Even so, as he headed toward Wheal Prosperity with miners and bal-maidens, his shoulders knotted, his body tensed. Maybe he wasn't marching into battle, but the danger was still real. The mine wasn't a place of safety.

And somewhere in this vast column of humanity was Alyce. She'd skipped in and out of his restless dreams last night.

It was barely past sunrise, the sky pale gray, and a low-lying mist was draped between the craggy hills. Sheep bleated from the tops of the hills. Hedge-dwelling birds sang the morning chorus. The workers murmured as they walked toward the mine, and his sense that danger lurked ahead sharpened. Yet he felt an odd kind of peace.

London's unofficial motto seemed to be, "Noise at every hour." Especially between the hours of six and ten o'clock in the morning, which had to be filled with the rattle of wagon and omnibus wheels, the shouts of vendors, people cursing one another in the street—under penalty of law. Anyone caught being quiet would be immediately subject to fine, and the punishment of tin pots tied to the offender's legs.

But he wasn't in Cornwall on holiday, and the quiet wouldn't last. Mines, their machinery included, ranked as some of the noisiest places on earth. And he was here to do a dangerous job. Peace was not part of his agenda.

"I don't see George or Joe," Simon noted to Edgar beside him.

"Joe didn't come back to the lodgings last night," Edgar said. "And George's wife said he never made it home. Reckon they got put into gaol."

"How long will they stay there?"

Edgar shrugged. "Depends on the will of the masters. It could be we'll see 'em tomorrow. Or maybe we won't see 'em again until Michaelmas."

That was three weeks away. The conditions in the local gaol probably weren't the most salubrious. A few days there could wreak havoc with a man's health. At least the law here didn't flog, the way they did in the army—even though the practice had been theoretically abolished. Out on campaign, imprisoning a soldier for an infraction wasn't possible; the lash or flog served for punishment. He'd seen many a man tied to a post or tree and flogged until the poor blighter had mercifully passed out.

Thank God, Simon had never earned such discipline. He'd come damned close a time or two. Almost got caught sneaking back into the cantonment after a night gadding about the pleasure quarters of Secunderabad. He'd made it back just in time for morning inspection with one hell of a throbbing head.

"That can't please George's wife," Simon murmured. No wonder Alyce had tried so hard to keep the two miners from being taken away. Men in prison earned no chit, and she knew it.

"Nor his kids, neither," said Nathaniel. "But there's nothing to be done." He patted Simon on his shoulder. "Don't you fret, Simon. Do your job, stay quiet—which means no more tripping into constables—and you won't see the inside of the gaol."

"Maybe in gaol I won't have to hear Edgar snoring," Simon answered, earning him guffaws from Edgar, Nathaniel, and the few other men he'd met last night.

Yet he didn't miss the cautious glances thrown his way by many of the other miners nearby, or the wake of space around him. Keeping their distance.

"Haven't been in Trewyn a full day," he said in a low voice to Edgar. "I'm getting a lot of chary looks."

Edgar made a scoffing sound. "Folks around here have a goodly number of reasons to keep to themselves."

Gazing around the long column of workers, Simon noted most of the men walked in groups, chatting and swinging their lunch tins, sleepy and careless in the early morning. But not everyone. Others were sharp-eyed, too attentive. As if they were eavesdropping on conversations. Taking mental notes in case anyone spoke seditiously.

Spies. Not much of a surprise there. The managers had some of the miners in their pockets, serving as their eyes and ears above and below the surface. He'd have to be wary around them, and committed their faces to memory.

One of the spies kept one hand in his coat pocket—tapping his fingers on what looked like a pencil for writing notes. Another man—a chap with a squashed-in face—had been sticking close to Simon for most of the walk toward the mine. But something else must have caught the spy's attention, because he moved off, leaving Simon with a moment's opportunity.

"People can keep to themselves around me or not." Simon spoke loudly enough so that more people nearby could hear him. "But they ought to know that I don't work for the company."

A handful of men looked shocked by this statement, and even Nathaniel and Edgar sputtered their surprise.

"Who I work for," Simon continued, "is the *miners*. I'm at Wheal Prosperity to keep the pumps running and the shafts safe. I may draw a salary, but it's the miners who are my real bosses, not the managers."

As he'd hoped, his words were circulated among the miners in quiet murmurs. The mistrustful glances faded. Some even looked at him with friendly consideration. Hopefully, word would spread that newcomer he may be, Simon was on the miners' side. That would make the next steps of the mission easier to accomplish.

A flash up ahead of a woman's dark, pinned hair and slim neck caught his attention. Was it Alyce? He forced himself to keep from hurrying to catch up with her. She walked with several other women, and they talked quietly among themselves. One of the women said something to make Alyce laugh—a low, throaty laugh like honey over smooth river rocks. He'd never heard her truly laugh before. The sound surprised him. Even more surprising was how the sound traveled through him in electrical pulses.

Her back suddenly stiffened, and she cast a glance over her shoulder. As if drawn by a lodestone, their gazes found each other immediately.

She looked as momentarily stunned as he felt. Her steps faltered. Then she whipped her head around, facing forward.

He kept his own steps even and measured, and feigned interest in whatever it was that Edgar spoke about—an indicator of Simon's discipline if ever there was one.

What the hell is wrong with me? No denying she's important for the mission. I can flirt with her, get the information I need. But I've got to keep my head.

They crossed over the next rise, and came to the main part of the mine. He'd seen it yesterday when applying for the job, but today he was struck by the rough, industrial scars upon the rolling green hills of Cornwall. Granite buildings and chimneys rose up, and the metal bars of the beam winding engine were unburied bones sticking out of the earth. Perched atop the structure were deathless, unblinking eyes: the large wheels of the winder that watched the miners and bal-maidens mercilessly.

All hint of green had been stamped out by wagons, carts, thousands upon thousands of boots treading on the dirt. Nothing grew in the soil. The only source of fecundity lay hundreds of feet beneath the earth. Heaps of rocky debris were piled like ancient graves around the mine site. Simon recalled that this rubbish, separated from the valuable ore, was known as "deads," and so it seemed—lifeless and thrown aside.

Steps leading to different structures had been gouged out of the ground. Men were already emerging from the change house, where they'd donned their rough, dirty work clothes, some still damp from yesterday. A transformation from men to miners. They wore helmets with candles affixed to their fronts with lumps of clay, like creatures from folklore. Nothing magical about the work they were about to perform. As they readied to go down into the shaft, down into the darkness, many took one last look at the sun feebly poking through the morning haze. Hours would pass before they'd see its light again, feel its warmth. Down below, it was infernally hot, dank, cramped. Dangerous.

God—to do that day after day, climb down into the depths of the earth, uncertain whether or not there'd be a collapse or flood, and never see daylight again . . . Respect for these tough men swelled in Simon's chest. Maybe they didn't have the means to fight their corrupt masters, but they had bollocks of steel to earn their living this way.

Simon headed across the hard-packed dirt toward the engine house. He nearly stopped short when Henry Carr passed by, throwing him a suspicious glare. But then Henry's attention turned elsewhere at the sound of men arguing.

"It's been three damn months, Ralph," one man angrily asserted. In contrast to the coarse, dirty clothing worn by the miners—including Ralph—this man sported a relatively clean white coat.

"I'm telling you," Ralph answered, just as heated, "I gave it back."

"Then it's turned invisible, hasn't it? Because I can't bloody find it."

People nearby, miners and laborers, stopped what they were doing to watch the row. Any moment now, and the two men would start swinging at each other.

To Simon's surprise, Henry walked over to the men. Without hesitation, he clapped a hand on each of their shoulders.

"Lads, why the fuss?" he asked calmly.

The men shouted in unison, until Henry said to the man in the white coat, "Owen, let's start with you."

"Ralph borrowed my best pick. 'Just for a few days,' he said, 'until I can buy myself a better one.' Three months it's been, and where's my damned pick? I'll tell you where. The bugger's gone and nicked it."

"I gave it back," Ralph shouted. "Isn't my fault that you've got granite for brains, and can't remember. Besides," he added sulkily, "you've been promoted to underground captain, and haven't got a need for a pick anymore. You just watch us work and strut around like a bloody prince. Like you're not one of us anymore, but one of *them*."

The disease of mistrust and anger between management and workers had spread deeply through Wheal Prosperity.

Owen opened his mouth to fire back a retort, but Henry spoke first. "You've made your family proud by getting that promotion, Owen. It's true, though, that you haven't got much use for a pick anymore."

Ralph looked smug, until Henry said evenly, "Maybe you ought to search your tools once more, Ralph, just to be sure you didn't overlook Owen's pick. Who knows? Perhaps you thought you returned it, but it slipped your mind. We've all got heavy burdens right now. Tough to keep the thoughts straight. Easy to think you took care of something, but actually forgot to do it."

Both men made grudging, grumbling sounds, as men are wont to do when caught in the snares of their own egos and sense of righteousness.

"Who knows?" Henry continued, still clasping the men's shoulders. "Ralph might find that pick, and maybe Owen might let him borrow it for a while longer. Everyone's satisfied."

The men muttered again, but with less animosity.

"An agreement then." Henry smiled amicably. "Go on, lads. It's a long day ahead of us, and we're only making it longer." He let go of their shoulders, giving them each imperceptibly slight pushes to send them in opposite directions.

Masterfully done. Simon nearly congratulated Henry on diffusing the situation, but held back. The man wouldn't want his commendation. For a brief moment, the shadows beneath Henry's eyes deepened, and his face sagged in exhaustion. Clearly, he'd been playing the role of peacemaker for a long time. Like wearing a heavy suit of armor, such responsibility was a burden, dragging him down.

Without acknowledging Simon, Henry walked on to the change house.

Simon glanced over toward the area where the balmaidens and some men waited, holding their hammers and shovels in preparation for breaking up the ore. A warm feeling like the stroke of a hand passed over him, unexpected in the cold morning. He turned around, searching for the source. And found Alyce looking at him. She didn't turn away from him this time, instead tipping up her chin, as if in a dare.

Alyce and Henry Carr—two different sides of the coin. One, a firebrand, trying to rouse the workers of Wheal Prosperity to action. The other, a peacemaker, seeking the path of least resistance in order to ensure calm.

Both stances were admirable, but Simon was himself a rabble-rouser, always had been. He'd never have created Nemesis if he had been satisfied with the status quo. Surely there were times when Henry's cautious approach worked, but not always, and not for Nemesis. Slow, gentle progress didn't fit their modus operandi. They wanted results. The best way to get those results: action.

It gnawed at him again, the idea that Alyce might have been the one who wrote to Nemesis. If she did, she might have access to more information about the owners and managers of the mine. That information could help him find the means of taking the corrupt structure down.

The company would have to be replaced with something else, however. Hundreds of men and women could lose their only source of employment. A conundrum, that was. One he knew he'd be able to reason out. But it'd take time.

So, was Alyce the mysterious correspondent? It had been written on a typewriter. Even if he had a sample of her handwriting, he couldn't make an analysis. And typewriters were costly. Maybe she'd sneaked into the mine's offices late at night and used one of theirs. A damned courageous thing to do—if she'd done it.

One of the other bal-maidens elbowed Alyce. He realized then that he and Alyce had been staring at each other across the yard. They both turned away at the same time.

He walked up the hill, toward the engine house. He'd faced some difficult missions before, but this one was going to be a long, tough voyage

Simon introduced himself to the weary night-shift men monitoring the pumping engine. He'd never expected water to be one of the biggest problems when it came to mining, but so it was. The deeper they dug, the more ground water seeped into the shafts. The lapse of even an hour could be a bloody disaster—making shafts and chambers flood. So men were there at all hours, operating the pumps. The three men seemed more than happy to meet Simon, offering rough, grease-stained hands to shake. Feet dragging, they hauled themselves from the engine house for the long walk home.

Two men entered the engine house. One of the chaps had a full, dark mustache, and introduced himself as Abel Lawrey. The other was Bill Dyer, with a face as cragged as a rough morning. His fellows on the day shift. Three more men attended to the boilers, shoveling coal to keep the engine and its pumping rods in continual motion. Everyone made quick introductions and exchanges of history before getting to work.

He'd been in this building yesterday, but had been focused on getting the job more than scouting the location. A massive pumping engine dominated the building, one of the marvels of this modern era. It towered over Simon and the other men, a titan of brass, pipes, and moving parts. Two hundred years ago, what would men have thought of such a creature? Did it herald the beginning of a new, glorious era for humanity or the end of it? He'd seen the mills and factories of the north, the smokestacks that pointed accusing brick fingers into the air as if to blame the spirit of progress that smothered England in coal smoke.

The world changed so quickly now. There were fortunes to be made, new horizons to explore. And tens of thousands of people to be crushed beneath the machinery of progress.

"Won't do you any good to be woolgathering this early," Abel called to him from the other side of the pumping engine.

"I'll be sure to drink more coffee tomorrow," he answered, and made himself useful.

The labor itself alternated between mindless and complex. Attend to the valves. Bleed the pressure. Tighten what loosened and loosen what seized up. Thank God he'd done his research ahead of time, and that he had a good head for remembering things. He could perform his tasks without hesitation. Soon, his jacket was off, his sleeves rolled up, as he kept a careful eye on the pumping engine.

It didn't matter how often he wiped his hands on the cloth tucked into his back pocket. Grease and dirt were inexorably part of the job.

A old conversation with his father flashed through his mind.

Our family has responsibilities, Horace Addison-Shawe had lectured a seventeen-year-old Simon. Simon hadn't been looking at his father's face, but was studying the patterns of the Turkey carpet on the study's floor. Someone had made that carpet, an unknown craftsman joined to England by the remarkable power of steamships. Simon's thoughts had often spun off into such tangents, about how the world was separate and yet connected by a massive web.

A reputation, his father had continued. *We don't simply stick our arms into the mud because it amuses us.*

Better to be dirty and immersed in life, Simon had retorted, *than stuck up here in this airless tower of privilege and turn into dust.*

His father, as always, had been unrelenting. *Just because you're a second son doesn't absolve you of your obligations to this family or to Society. You will go back to Oxford, and we'll talk no more of apprenticing yourself to some ruddy gunsmith. Coming home every day with oil beneath your fingernails—my God, your mother wouldn't leave her bed.*

She doesn't now, anyway. Why should she? She's bored senseless.

That had earned him a slap across the face.

It hadn't been the first or last time he'd been called before Father. It was a wonder his ears weren't permanently scarred from all the blistering lectures he'd received.

Fortunately, Horace Addison-Shawe was safely tucked away in his club in London, and couldn't see his son now, in a working man's clothes, hands grimy, and sweat filming his back. No ornamental society bride on his arm.

What would Alyce Carr make of the other Simon—not Simon Sharpe, machinist, but Simon Addison-Shawe, who knew all the sacraments of fine Society? House parties, shooting parties, dinner parties with ten courses and enough wine to drown a horse. The Season, with its debutantes in white tulle and men in their bride-hunting uniforms of black wool and starched shirtfronts.

She might not know such a world existed. But if she did, was it something she longed for? Or maybe she sneered at it? Maybe it was a complex mixture of both for her. The devil knew Simon's labyrinthine feelings about his different lives.

As he made an adjustment on a valve, the nerves along the back of his neck tightened. Someone—a man—approached him. It took all his willpower not to give in to ingrained habit and spin around, brandishing his wrench like a weapon. Instead, he continued on with his work until he heard a familiar voice behind him.

"Sharpe, is it?"

"Constable Tippet," he answered, turning around.

"*Chief* Constable Tippet," the man reminded him sharply. He gripped his badge-adorned hat with thick fingers.

Abel and Bill stared from the other side of the pump engine, their own tasks momentarily forgotten.

"Something you need, *Chief* Constable Tippet?" Simon glanced past the lawman. Two other constables stood off to the side. He recognized one from the other night, the one with the blockish, thick jaw and eagerness to hurt someone. The other constable had his hands clasped behind his back. Simon didn't remember him from last night. He wore his uniform like someone forced to attend a fancy dress party, and his gaze continually shifted to the side, as though avoiding looking at an old man dressed like a Casanova—embarrassed for both of them.

"You're a long way from the village," Simon noted. "I thought the mine had its own men for keeping order."

Tippet's face darkened. "I've got permission from the managers to patrol here, if I think it necessary."

"If you think there's something threatening or dangerous."

The constable gave a clipped nod.

"So you're here," Simon went on, "in the pumping engine house." He glanced over at the giant machine. "Just take a look around, Chief Constable. Everything's in working order. Nothing a bit threatening or dangerous."

"It needs to stay that way." Tippet's eyes narrowed as he stared at Simon. "Things have a certain order here at Wheal Prosperity and in Trewyn. For everyone's safety. When things don't function right, if, say, one little cog decides it's got other ideas about how the machine works, then everything falls apart. People get hurt. I don't want anyone getting hurt."

"The cog winds up getting crushed, too," Simon noted.

The constable gave a thin smile. "No wonder they hired you, Sharpe. Got a good understanding of how these things operate."

"Naught to trouble you over here, Chief Constable. A man can get clumsy, but that doesn't make him foolish. You and me, we want the same things."

Simon's glance moved to the other constables.

"That's my deputy, Oliver," Tippet said, "and the other one's Bice."

Bice's attention whipped to the constable, just as his posture snapped upright. The chief constable added, "Reports anything dodgy to me."

Bice's mouth pinched into a line, and once again his gaze danced around the interior of the engine room, keeping from focusing on any one item.

Wonder if they have a typewriter in the constabulary's office. And who uses that typewriter most often.

"You've made a long walk from the village for no reason," Simon finally replied. "As I said, I have no intention of letting anything get out of line. I'm just doing the job they hired me for." He kept his expression pleasant, inoffensive. But this was a part of the job he always enjoyed. Letting the target believe one thing, when Simon had his own ideas.

Tippet's thin smile widened, but it was no more pleasant than it had been before. "Good lad."

Much as he liked stringing along his quarry, Simon silently gave thanks that the constable didn't try to slap him on the shoulder in a gesture of patronizing approval, or else the wrench Simon held would have to be removed by a blacksmith from Tippet's skull.

Instead, Simon said, "Wouldn't want to keep you and Deputy Oliver and Constable Bice from your duties. I figure a man of consequence like you must have many responsibilities."

Tippet puffed out his chest. "That I do. Can't waste any more time here." He set his hat on his head and stalked from the engine room, self-importance wafting from him like an invisible toxin. Oliver followed in his wake.

For a moment, Bice stared directly at Simon, his mouth opening and closing. "You—"

"Bice!" Tippet shouted from outside.

At once, the young man jammed on his cap and trotted out after the constable. He didn't even cast a glance over his shoulder in parting. Simply ran off, too afraid.

Simon returned to his tasks, ignoring the curious stares of Bill and Abel. The machine on which he worked was somewhat old, but it was still a complicated and intricate engine that required careful operating. Yet the dynamics of Wheal Prosperity were far more convoluted, and demanded much more subtle handling. It wasn't just grease and gears, but blood and bone, the people of the mine and the village. Good people like Edgar, and Nathaniel. Alyce and her family. None of them knew it, but it was his job to keep them safe. And he wouldn't—couldn't—fail.

CHAPTER 4.

Energy and rhythm moved through Alyce's shoulder as she swung her hammer. It was a familiar, practiced movement. The metal head crashed down onto the bread-loaf-sized rock at her feet, sending a jolt up her arm and shattering the rock into smaller pieces. Reddish mud spattered, clinging to her boots and her apron.

All around her came the sounds of women softly grunting with effort, rocks breaking, and the scrape of shovels. Almost soothing, in its way—the noises repeating over and over again. Every day but Sunday was spent just like this.

Prisoners break rocks, too, she thought with a grim, inward smile.

Leaning on her hammer gave her a welcome moment of rest, and she breathed deeply as she waited for Deborah Mayne to shovel up the pile of stones and load it into a cart. A girl of twelve, her face grimy and expression set, pushed the cart toward the stamp mill. Was it Vera Devon? Alyce could hardly tell beneath the red dirt streaking her face. It seemed like only a month ago she'd been a little girl, kicking balls made of rags down the lane.

She watched Vera push the cart to the stamp mill. The

machine ground up and down, relentless as life, as it crushed the ore into even smaller pieces.

We all start out big as boulders, and we're hammered at until nothing but dust remains.

Evelyn Fields pushed another cartful of ore chunks toward her. She tipped the cart, and more lumps of rock, freshly pried from the earth, clattered at Alyce's feet.

"Ah, you're a angel," Alyce said. "Here I was worrying I'd have nothing to do for the rest of the morning."

Evelyn snorted. "Just be grateful there's ore in the pit to mine. Once these stop coming, we're all hobbled."

A sad truth, that. And one that the managers had pointed out whenever Alyce had voiced a complaint. *Be grateful you even possess employment, Miss Carr. There are many who would envy your lot, for they have nothing.*

Even so, as Alyce raised her hammer once more, the rocks heaped at her feet turned into the smirking faces of the managers Gorley, Murton, and Ware. Her hammer smashed against the stone with so much force, the rocks turned into tiny pebbles. She grinned to herself. If she could only take her hammer to the walls of the count house, smashing the granite to dust, splintering the desk behind which the managers shielded themselves, and sending the men running in terror for the hills. What a glorious vision: herself as a hammer-wielding angel of destruction.

"Isn't that Chief Constable Tippet, Deputy Oliver, and Constable Bice?" Evelyn asked.

Alyce's hammer stopped in midair, and she frowned as she lowered it. Tippet, Oliver, and Bice formed dark blue silhouettes against the rock-strewn yard. Like the other above-ground workers, she stared as the lawmen deliberately made their way across the mine, with Tippet and Oliver striding ahead and Bice following at a distance like a reluctant hound.

"They don't come out here," Deborah muttered. "Not unless there's trouble." Fear tightened her voice. With good cause. George and Joe hadn't come to the mine today. If Tippet wanted to haul someone else to gaol, or give them a cautionary thrashing, not a soul could stop them.

When the chief constable and two other lawmen entered the pump engine house, Alyce's heart leaped into her throat.

"Who do you reckon they're going to see?" someone asked.

"I'll be blessed if I know," Evelyn said. "Only machinists and the boiler men in there, and none of them have been causing any disturbances."

"That new lad's in there, too," Deborah noted. "I forget his name . . ."

"Simon," Alyce said through numb lips. "Simon Sharpe."

A whole night had passed since Simon had *accidentally* tripped against the chief constable. A night could last a long while, giving Tippet ample time to mull and stew, to nurse a grudge. Tippet wielding a grudge was an ugly thing—he'd nearly lamed a man a week after the poor sod had made a joke about the constable within hearing distance. Tippet had given some thin pretext as to why the man deserved a beating. Something about respect for the law kept the village safe. Not a soul contradicted him. Including the man he'd almost crippled.

"Shame," another bal-maiden said, and tsked. "He's a comely chap."

Evelyn shook her head. "Well, he likely won't be, after Tippet's done with him. And Oliver likes to give a good beating, too."

Cold sickness wrapped itself around Alyce's stomach. Should she do something? Run to the engine house and try to talk the chief constable out of his anger? Talk hardly worked on Tippet. He seemed uninterested in thought and logic—a guard dog fed on a diet of resentment and bullying. Alyce's presence might make him angrier.

And you don't want to risk your own neck, a sly voice whispered in her head.

She barely knew Simon and owed him nothing. Even so, shame burned her cheeks. A fine champion of the people she made, rooted to the ground like an old stump because she feared what Tippet might do to her if she intervened. No woman had been hurt by him, not yet. There could always be a first time.

Tippet and Oliver suddenly marched from the building. Seconds later, Bice followed. All three mounted their horses tethered nearby and rode toward the village.

"That didn't take long," Deborah said.

"Maybe Tippet only boxed his ears," somebody offered.

Her legs demanded that she run to the engine house. Her mind kept her stuck in place.

Then, like a gleam of sunlight, Simon appeared in the doorway of the engine house. He didn't sport a single bruise, nor favor a leg. Unexpected dizziness threatened to drag Alyce to the ground, but she used her hammer for support until her head cleared.

"If it *was* that Sharpe lad Tippet wanted," Evelyn said, "seems like he only wanted a talk. Lucky for Sharpe."

"Lucky for *us.*" Deborah winked. "It'd be a pity if anything happened to his face."

"Or other important parts," another bal-maiden said and snickered. The rest of the women added their laughter. Alyce couldn't force a chuckle, or any noise. Relief robbed her of sound.

Casual as a cat, Simon rolled himself a cigarette, using tobacco and paper he kept in a pocket in his waistcoat. He shook a match from a box and struck it against the wall, then lit the cigarette. For several moments, he leaned against the door frame, leisurely smoking. His gaze swept over the yard, past her, where it lingered for a second, then moved on. Despite his easygoing pose, and the distance separating them, she felt his alertness.

He pushed away from the door and ambled across the yard. Though he walked at an easy pace, he still moved with direction and purpose.

"Pinch your cheeks and bite your lips, lasses," Evelyn said. "He's heading this way."

The older, married bal-maidens just chuckled, but some of the young, single girls tugged off their heavy gloves to smooth their hair and straighten their clothes. Deliberately, Alyce did none of these things. She lifted her hammer and struck the chunks of ore heaped in front of her. Even when Simon came nearer, threading his way through the giggling, smiling bal-maidens, she kept on with her work.

For several minutes, he simply watched her. Every so often, he'd lift the cigarette to his lips and take a drag, then slowly exhale smoke. He held the end between his index finger and thumb, which mysteriously fascinated her. All the chaps in Trewyn wedged their cigarettes between their index and middle fingers, but he made this ordinary action exotic. She tried not to watch him, focusing instead on her task, yet from the corner of her eye she caught small details: the shape of his lips as he drew on the end, the way he let his arm casually drop after each inhalation, how his fingers curled around the cigarette itself to keep it protected from the slight breeze. How smoke drifted up from his mouth in a way that was almost . . . sensuous.

She'd seen dozens, maybe hundreds of men smoking. But only he made it look like a rough seduction.

"You can't smoke on the dressing floor," she said

without looking at him. It felt vitally important to act indifferent to him—a kind of balm after the fear that had
twisted through her earlier.

He immediately knocked off the cigarette's smoldering end and pinched it shut, then tucked it in his pocket.
"Still learning the rules."

"Is that why Constable Tippet came to see you?"

One of his eyebrows rose. "Five other men work in the
engine house. Tippet could've been talking with any of
them."

She swung her hammer again, splitting apart another
hunk of rock. "Abel, Bill, and the others, they know their
place. The rules. Not you. There's something about you
that warrants keeping an eye on."

"I'm harmless as eiderdown," he answered, sticking
his hands in his pockets.

She laughed at that. "Don't forget, I saw *everything* last
night." Lifting her hammer once more, she said, "You're
anything but harmless." She swung again and smashed
apart more hunks of ore.

He eyed the pieces of rock. "I could say the same
about you. My arms ache just watching."

"Can't get paid if I don't keep swinging. Besides," she
added, "I've been spalling nearly seven years now, ever
since I got big and strong enough to wield the hammer.
Before that, I was carting away deads." She nodded toward a group of girls carrying barrows heaped with the
discards and rubbish that remained after the ore had
been cleaned and sorted. "That's not light work, either."

Lifting her arm, she flexed. "This isn't a fine lady's
arm. Not a bit soft."

She almost jumped when he reached out and gently
squeezed her bicep. It was a quick, impersonal touch, but
it made her heart leap like a miner catching his first sight
of daylight.

"It's a powerful arm," he said. "Much better than a limb that's yielding and weak."

Was he having her on? From what he'd said about himself, he'd been around working women for years, so he wouldn't be shocked by a female with muscles. But, outside of mines and factories, women were supposed to be supple, delicate creatures. She'd seen a few fashion journals—though they'd been at least two years out of date. All the ladies in those magazines had smooth, white arms. One could hardly think they had bones, let alone muscles.

Proud as Alyce was of her strength, she knew she wasn't the height of femininity. Dainty women didn't put bread on the table. Men did have their fantasies about what women were supposed to be, and that didn't necessarily mean a woman who could wield a bucking iron.

Yet she thought she saw real admiration in Simon's gaze, and his voice was low and earnest.

He *liked* that she was strong. Just as much as she did. A quick, swift pleasure coursed through her.

The constant thump and clatter of the dressing floor stopped. All of the bal-maidens and the other workers stared at her and Simon with open fascination. Women normally didn't go about flexing their arms and men didn't squeeze their biceps. Especially not a man and a woman who'd met just the day before.

Damn, we'll be the talk all over the village.

"You'd best be getting back to manning the pump engine. We can't have our lads swimming down there."

"That we can't." He started to turn from her, then stopped. "Does Tippet report to anyone?"

"Why? Do you want to lodge a complaint against him?" The very idea made her laugh.

He shrugged. "Just wondering if he's the final word here."

"It's the managers who run the circus," she answered.

"Not the owners?"

She snorted. "They're snug and oblivious in Plymouth. So long as their profits keep coming, they don't give a parson's belch what happens at Wheal Prosperity." Her eyes narrowed. "That's why you came out here, to ask me about Tippet and the fat-bellied owners?"

It was his turn to chuckle. "I'm just a machinist. As the good constable phrased it, I'm only a cog in the engine. If I'm desperate enough to take this job, I wouldn't do a bloody thing to make me lose it."

She had to admit, that made sense. Still, she pressed, "Then why'd you come out here?"

He grinned, and she thought she heard some of the other women sigh. "Maybe I find a nice bit of sunshine in your company."

He tipped his cap at her, and then at the other balmaidens, before strolling back to the engine house. He didn't look back.

Once he'd gone, Alyce felt dozens of eyes on her. She stared them all down, until everyone returned to their hammering, shoveling, and carting. She, too, got back to work, but the arm he'd touched continued to pulse with the echo of sensation, and she turned the words over and over, like pretty, smooth stones.

Much better than yielding and weak. I find a nice bit of sunshine in your company.

Careful, she warned herself. *He's still just a stranger.* A flirtatious stranger, but unknown, just the same. And if the eyes of the law were on him, she needed to keep a protective distance. She couldn't make a difference at the mine if the managers and constabulary watched her every move. Better to keep away from Simon—the bright blue of his eyes and his warm grins and the way he matched her, thought for thought, the way no other man in the village had ever done.

It was the right choice to hold him off. Yet when she swung her hammer again, it felt a little heavier, as if the pull of gravity had grown stronger.

Picks in hand, Simon crouched beside a large strongbox in the managers' office. He inserted the thin metal tools into the lock and began to carefully manipulate them. Shadows blanketed the room, and desks and filing cabinets made dark, blocky shapes in the empty chamber. A clock on the wall chimed twice. Little danger that an enterprising clerk might show up in the middle of the night, catching Simon in the middle of ferreting out the company's secrets.

Simon worked by touch. He couldn't risk a lamp, no matter how much he dimmed it, and he didn't need to see what he was doing. Long ago, Marco had made every Nemesis operative spend weeks practicing opening locks of all varieties—from basic padlocks to top-of-the-line safes—in total darkness.

It's like making love, Marco had said. *You don't need to see what you're doing to do it properly.*

It doesn't hurt, though, Simon had added. *Watching's part of the fun.*

Then watch yourself get carted off to prison because you need a lamp to get that damned lockbox open.

So, they'd practiced breaking into safes, and practiced some more, until everyone could get into the toughest coffer or padlock within minutes. Now Simon hunkered down, carefully manipulating the picks to get inside the lockbox that held the mine's latest financial records. He felt the tumblers sliding into place, the shift of metal against metal. For all the teasing he'd given Marco, there was something deeply satisfying, and oddly sensual about gently, delicately liberating the secrets from a lock. The initial tension, then the seduction, the yielding, until, at last, the lock opened itself to him, inviting him in. Better that the lock released itself than trying to blast his way in like a brute.

He never wanted an unwilling partner.

As he worked on the strongbox, his thoughts drifted to Alyce. Since that day a week ago, she'd stayed clear of him during the long walks to and from the mine, surrounding herself with other bal-maidens, or else marching so quickly ahead that he'd be forced to jog to keep up with her. He couldn't smoke where the women dressed the ore, but she'd made no attempt to keep him company when he'd taken cigarette breaks close to the engine house. And whenever he'd tried to talk with her, she'd given him terse little answers. Nothing like the badinage they'd shared earlier.

She was deliberately avoiding him. Had he said or done something to offend her? Or did she suspect him of being more than just a machinist? Neither option pleased him, but if she *was* wary of him, he had to make sure that she didn't share her doubts with anyone else. Right now, success in this mission meant keeping himself invisible.

There! Another tumbler fitted into place, but he wasn't in yet.

He'd have to keep working on Alyce, too. She knew the most about the mine, and had already proven herself a valuable source of information. She was also a voice for change, and could be a useful ally when his plans were finally set in motion. He'd subtly tried to glean knowledge from Edgar, Nathaniel, and a few of the other people he'd come to know, but self-preservation made them deliberately ignorant. It was Alyce he needed.

For the mission, he reminded himself.

With a quiet snick, the lock to the strongbox opened.

Inside, leather-bound ledgers were stacked one atop the other like conspirators huddling in the shadows. He hunkered down on the floor and began pulling them out, one by one, flipping through their pages. Back when he'd been in the army, he'd often been picked for night patrols, his vision nearly as good in the darkness as it was during the day. So reading the rows of numbers and precise handwriting filling the books didn't offer much difficulty.

The only trouble came from the tedium of reading each ledger. As he finished one, he'd slip it back into the strongbox, then begin on another. What he found didn't give ample comfort.

If a company could be brought down for shortchanging its workers' wages, then all the businesses in England would shut their doors for good. Wheal Prosperity earned far more than it paid its employees. The managers kept a tidy sum for themselves, and the rest went to the owners in Plymouth. Meanwhile, the miners, machinists, and bal-maidens scraped by. Hardly newsworthy or scandalous. Nothing he could use.

He cursed softly as he put the last ledger back into the strongbox. Then cursed again silently as the light from a patrolling constable's lamp flashed through the office's windows. The door to the office rattled when the constable unlocked it, and the floorboards creaked beneath his heavy boots when he stepped inside. The room brightened as the lamp swept from side to side, lingering briefly on the strongbox. But the door to the safe was closed. Nothing was out of place.

Simon held his breath as he folded himself beneath a desk. Thank God the desk had a solid panel in the front, shielding him from the constable. But there was always the chance the patrolman felt particularly ambitious that night, and he might conduct a more thorough search of the office.

The lamplight stopped on the desk Simon hid beneath. Quick scenarios played through his mind. He could pull his knitted jumper up enough to hide part of his face and pretend to be a burglar. None of the constables carried firearms. It'd be the work of a moment to leap out and knock the lawman unconscious, then plant evidence that the "burglar" had been looking for money. Might make things a little sticky in the morning, setting the law on alert for thieves, but he'd rather face that than have the managers know his true purpose or the real threat he posed.

He was just about to tug up the collar of his jumper, his body preparing for a fight, when the light moved on. More heavy steps on the floorboards, and then the constable locked the door to the office behind him.

Five minutes passed. And then another five minutes. Finally, Simon unfolded himself from beneath the desk. A strange mixture of frustration and excitement thrummed through him. He was almost—*almost*—disappointed he didn't get to fight the constable. Back in London, he trained at a gymnasium every day, and as exhausting as manning the pump engines was, it didn't quite compare to the satisfaction and freeing of energy that came from sparring in a ring. He craved the release of tension.

The ledgers hadn't shown him enough financial misdeeds to take down the owners and managers of the mine, either. He'd have to find another tactic.

And he knew exactly what—more precisely, *who*—could help him.

Alyce waited outside as men emerged from the change house. Some were still wiping rags across their faces, scrubbing away the traces of red copper mud, and leaving their cheeks chafed and ruddy. Others were tucking in their clean but worn shirts as they walked out. Everything smelled of damp and minerals and sweat. For all that the miners tried to clean themselves after a day down in the pit, they only had a long basin for washing—or so Henry told her. She'd never actually been in the change house. Probably the miners would just get missish and shriek if she caught a glimpse of them in only their drawers.

The idea of big Hal Martin holding a tiny rag up to his chest and squealing like a terrified girl made her smile. Hal weighed at least sixteen stone and towered over most of the men in Trewyn. She'd no idea how anyone could get so big on the bare scraps of food the miners were able to afford.

She exchanged greetings with some of the men as they left the change house. Wives and daughters who worked as bal-maidens joined Alyce in her wait. The long walk home was always better with company. Evelyn Fields waited for her husband, Ted.

"Waiting for your machinist?" Evelyn asked.

Heat crept into Alyce's face. "Machinists don't need to use the change house."

Evelyn shrugged. "Maybe he got himself all slick with grease from the machines and wanted to make himself look pretty for you."

"It's Henry I'm waiting on," she answered. Her brother wasn't an ideal companion; they almost always found something to quarrel about, but she'd rather make the trip back to the village with him than run the risk of meeting up with Simon. "Besides, that machinist"—she didn't want to refer to him by name—"doesn't come around the dressing floor to prattle on anymore, so he doesn't give a tinker's damn if he looks pretty for me."

The disappointment in her voice was a surprise. She hadn't realized how much she liked talking with him until their conversations had stopped. It was her doing, too. For a few days, he'd made up excuses to come and chat with her—the other machinists were arguing and trying his patience, he wanted a woman's opinion about a birthday gift for his sister—but she hadn't taken the bait. Eventually, he'd gotten the hint, and didn't come around anymore or try to catch up with her walking to and from the mine.

The right choice, she reminded herself. Looking out for herself had to be her top concern. He could be a lodestone for trouble.

But it surprised her how, after knowing him for such a short time, she missed him. His wit. The tiny dent in his cheek when he smiled. It was like she'd been given a little sip of sweet, cool water and discovered she was thirsty.

She'd heard through gossip that Tippet hadn't bothered Simon since that one day. No one else had anything to say about Simon, except that Jenny Grigg and Nan Bassett had both set their caps for him, and both baked him meat pasties to have for his luncheon yesterday and today.

Maybe Alyce had been too quick in spurning him. Maybe she ought to have Sarah teach her how to bake a meat pasty.

The thought made her snort. A fine day it would be when she'd go begging for a man's favor, luring him with food like she was trying to trap a badger.

Ted Fields came out of the change house, and, smiling, took his wife's hand. Together they joined the procession heading back to Trewyn.

No husband or sweetheart would emerge from the change house for Alyce.

Instead, her brother marched out, tugging on his coat and looking cross. Before Alyce could say a word, he was already scolding her. "Charlie Pool said he saw you going into the managers' offices this morning."

Annoyance prickled up her spine. "Did he tell you I

had an itch on my nose and needed to scratch it, too? Seems like everything I do in the village or at the mine is everyone else's sodding business."

"Itches I don't care about. Let your nose fall off for scratching it. But riling the bosses makes life tough for all of us."

"The butter at the company store's gone rancid," she fired back. "I warned them that it would, and it did. Nobody will be able to work if they're all sick from bad butter. You'd think the managers would have sense enough to understand that."

"Maybe so," he conceded, "but storming into their offices and shouting at them won't get much done."

"I wasn't *shouting*. I was being resolute." For all the good it had done her. She'd been forcibly escorted out of the office by Constable Freeman and told that she'd be docked pay if she wasted any more her time harassing the managers and not processing ore.

Henry gave a long-suffering sigh. "There's a better way to get things done, Allie."

A retort formed on her lips, but before she spoke, someone behind her and Henry spoke. "Not interrupting any family business, I hope."

Recognizing the voice at once, she swung around. Simon stood right behind her and Henry, with a faintly apologetic smile. It caught her off guard, how seeing him again, and so close, made her heart beat a little faster. *It's just because he surprised me.* Either she and Henry had been arguing loudly, or Simon had moved with particular quiet, for one moment, he hadn't been there, and the next, there he was, bright as refined and polished ore.

"Nothing worth hearing," Henry said with a sharp look at Alyce.

She glared back at her brother before turning to Simon. What should she say when he tried to talk to her? Should she brush him off again? Should she try being warmer to him?

But after a polite nod in her direction, Simon's attention fixed on Henry. "They tell me you're the lad to talk to about rugby," he said.

"I'm captain for the mine's club," Henry answered with the pride a man uses when he isn't trying to sound too boastful, but wants the other man to know how impressive he is, just the same. "And set up the matches against other mines." He narrowed his eyes. "Interested in joining up?"

"If the club's got room for me."

"What position do you play? Don't tell me—second-five."

Alyce scowled at the implied insult—that Simon was just a pretty face who didn't do much for the team—but Simon only smiled affably.

"Winger, actually."

This caught Henry's attention, and Alyce's, as well. Wingers were known for speed, and they scored the most in a match. "Where'd you play?"

"I wasn't always dodging bullets in the army. Lots of time between pitched battles with the enemy."

"How was your record?"

"Scored seven tries in a game," Simon noted, also using the same tone of humble boastfulness.

Henry whistled, impressed. "I play flanker, myself. Have a record of five tries in a match."

"So," Simon pressed, "can you use me?"

Real regret sounded in Henry's voice. "We've already got Rob Turner as our winger, but he's rubbish. And our season runs from Whitsunday to Lammas, so we're done until next year."

Simon looked disappointed. "Shame."

"We host trials at Easter." Henry knocked a fist into Simon's shoulder. "You should give it a go."

With a smile, Simon said, "I just might."

Alyce glanced back and forth between her brother and Simon. Neither of them seemed to pay her any mind, and the dislike Henry had carried for Simon had been brushed off like so much dirt from a jersey.

"You've got some stories to tell, I'd wager," Henry said.

"And you," Simon answered.

Henry waved Simon forward. "Come on, then. It's a long walk back to the village."

Stunned, Alyce followed as Henry and Simon chatted like the oldest of chums on the trek homeward, recounting tales of different rugby matches they'd played over the years. She knew all of Henry's stories—she'd watched every match from the sidelines and heard them told again and again until she could recite each maneuver and play from memory. She'd heard there were men who made it their life's work and passion to study one particular time in history—ancient kings of England, say, or Egypt and its monument-building rulers.

Either accidentally or on purpose, Simon had found Henry's beloved history: the rugby matches of Wheal Prosperity from the past fifteen years. And Simon actually listened as if these stories of rivalries between copper-mine rugby clubs were the most fascinating subject in the world. Alyce liked a good match herself, and they certainly livened up a summer Sunday, but for the love of all that was sacred, did she have to hear *again* how Henry scored the winning try against East Wheal Bolton in the last seconds of the game?

She was much more interested in hearing about the matches Simon had played in. But Simon kept asking Henry question after question about local matches, and her brother was eager as a puppy to talk about them—and his own heroic role in each game.

And not once did Simon glance back at her with a smile, a wink, or even a look acknowledging that she was there. She'd half a mind to stomp off on her own, but she just couldn't seem to make herself move on ahead.

It didn't hurt that walking behind her brother and Simon gave her a nice view of Simon's arse. Good and tight, it was, with a high round shape. Was it as firm as it looked?

She pressed her lips tight to keep from laughing, imagining herself pinching Simon Sharpe's bum as if she were some randy old codger groping serving girls in a pub. But it was an interesting idea . . .

Finally, they reached the village, and the long column of workers broke apart as they each headed off toward their homes. As she, Henry, and Simon reached the entrance to the lane that led to their house, she fully expected Henry to wish Simon a good night and part ways.

Instead, Henry said, "Listen, Simon, I want to hear everything you've got to say about creating gaps in the other club's defense. Sounds like you have some good strategies."

"A few, yes," Simon answered.

Henry tilted his head toward the lane wending toward their house. "Come to my home for supper tonight."

Alyce's mouth dropped open. *This* from the same brother who warned her to keep her distance from Simon? Now Henry invited him into the privacy of their house for a meal?

Treachery, thy name is rugby.

"You sure you can spare enough for another head at the table?" Simon asked.

Henry smiled affably. "My Sarah can stretch a meal so far, you'd think it was made of India rubber. But her cooking tastes better."

"If that's the case," Simon said, taking off his cap, "I'd be most honored."

"Half past six, and no later." With that, Henry ambled down the lane. "Don't dawdle, Alyce."

"In a minute," she called after him. She stared at Simon, who finally turned and looked directly at her. He gave her an irresistible grin, mischievous as one of the fairy folk they spoke of in old stories.

Protectively, she crossed her arms over her chest. "You never mentioned that you were a winger."

"It didn't come up. And blokes generally don't start most conversations with ladies by reciting the number of tries they've scored in a match. Not interesting chaps, anyway," he added. "But Henry cares, and it got me what I was after."

She raised an eyebrow. "So you had a hidden motive."

"Of course I did," he said easily. "I wanted to see you again, and now I'm going to have supper with you. Sounds like I got even more than I'd hoped for."

His blunt confession—and what it meant—left her briefly speechless. She could only gape at him. No man had ever pursued her so directly or with such determination. Moths fluttered through her belly.

He put his cap back on and gave it a tug. "See you at half six." Whistling, he strode up the high street, toward the bachelor lodgings. She stood staring at the place where he'd been, as if he'd left behind his words. Words that hovered in the air like glowing lanterns.

CHAPTER 5.

A chair and spare plate had to be borrowed from the Penroses, their neighbors, and Sarah added extra barley to the stew in order to make it feed four rather than three. Much as Alyce disliked cleaning, and little as the snug house needed it, she still swept the place out and spent ten minutes making and remaking her bed, even though it was hidden behind the screen.

Glancing at herself in Sarah's hand mirror, Alyce decided against trying to dress her hair in some attempt at elegance. And neither she nor her sister-in-law owned any cosmetics. Alyce set the mirror aside with a shrug. She'd make the house appear as tidy as she could, but there was no changing her appearance, and she was fine with how she looked. Her face was her face. She was a bal-maiden, with the rosy cheeks to show for it, and a fancy hairstyle would be silly—and desperate. "Silly" and "desperate" were two words she made sure didn't describe her.

Still, with just a few minutes until half past six, she fussed around the house and hovered over the stove, causing Sarah a bit of annoyance.

"I think you let a butterfly in with you, Henry," Sarah said to her husband as she cooked.

"Just swat her with a rolled-up newspaper," he answered.

"You don't *swat* butterflies, lummox," Alyce snapped. "And I'm only trying to be helpful."

"Be helpful and *sit still*."

At her sister-in-law's gentle but firm command, Alyce sat down and folded her hands in her lap. Her toes tapped briskly against the floor, until Sarah's warning look forced her to be calm. As calm as she could be, given the circumstances.

You're being thickheaded. It's only one supper.

But he wants to see me, *even after I'd been so cold to him.*

At least he'd stuck with it, with her, when most other men had just crumbled away. That counted for a lot.

A knock sounded at the door. Alyce nearly leaped out of her skin. Checking the clock, she saw it was exactly half past six. She forced herself to stay seated as Henry opened the door and welcomed their guest. Only when Simon stepped inside did she finally get up and give him a nod. Her heart seized when she saw the posy Simon carried—oxeye daisies, meadow buttercups, wood cranesbill. The season for wildflowers was in its wane, and the blossoms themselves looked a little tired, but they still brought welcome bright color into the drab house.

Henry frowned at the bouquet of flowers, and Alyce could guess that he thought it too forward of Simon to bring them to her. But Simon held the posy out to Sarah.

"Mrs. Carr," he murmured. "My thanks for making room for me at your table."

Sarah's cheeks flamed as she stammered her thanks and took the bouquet. She glanced around in confusion until Alyce stepped forward with an earthenware jug. In went the flowers, with some water, which Sarah set in the middle of the kitchen table. She kept lightly touching the petals as if unsure they wouldn't fly away.

"No wooing my wife," Henry warned sternly, but his smile undercut his threat.

When Henry turned away to help dish up supper, Simon gave Alyce a quick wink. Her own cheeks probably turned as red as Sarah's. And she had to admit, it was a smart strategy on his part. No one could find fault with a man who brought charming gifts to a hugely pregnant married woman, especially right in front of her husband. Sly, he was, and that made him dangerous.

Once the meal had been set out on the table, everyone sat, though with each week that Sarah's pregnancy progressed, it took some careful negotiations to get her down into her chair. Henry helped ease her down and made sure that the pillow placed at her back was in the right spot. Henry sat next to Sarah, with Alyce facing her brother, and Simon seated to her left. The table wasn't large. If she leaned just a little, she'd brush shoulders with him.

Once Sarah had been situated, Henry asked Simon, "Care to lead us in saying grace?"

Confusion and panic crossed Simon's face for the barest second, then he said, "It'd be my honor."

They all bent their heads and folded their hands, and waited.

Simon cleared his throat. "Lord, we're grateful for the riches beneath the earth, for the means to bring your hidden treasure above into the sunlight, but most of all for the ability to provide for those we care about most—our friends and families. Amen."

"Amen," she, Henry, and Sarah echoed.

It had been a brief and simple speech, but Alyce had felt it echo deep within her. She wondered if Simon knew how his voice had deepened when he spoke about providing for those he cared about—or was aware of the faintest note of longing in his words. Did he miss his own family? And he never mentioned any friends, but perhaps he had old army chums. It seemed like a lonely existence: wandering around England, looking for work.

Then again, she'd never left Trewyn. Getting out of here sometimes sounded like paradise.

Almost as soon as they began to eat, Henry launched an avalanche of questions about rugby at Simon.

"For pity's sake, Hen," Alyce said, "let the poor man get a mouthful of stew before you bury him alive."

"Sorry, Simon," Henry muttered.

"No apology needed," Simon answered, "but I've got to say, Mrs. Carr, that this is the best thing I've eaten in months. No, years."

"Not surprised, given what I've heard about the food at the bachelor lodgings," Sarah said, but she smiled at the compliment. "And he's a passionate man about rugby, our Henry." Sarah laid her hand over Henry's and looked at him with fond forbearance. "He doesn't get to talk about it at home."

"Well, if you'd let women play," Alyce said, "the way I'd suggested, you wouldn't have to head down to the pub to get an earful about it."

"No one's going to let a woman out on the pitch," he answered. "Either she'd be crushed to bits, or else she'd score a thousand tries because nobody'd want to tackle her."

"Me and the other bal-maidens swing bucking irons all day. We're not that fragile. I bet I could tackle Davy Bale without a lick of trouble. Remember how I used to make you cry for Ma when I'd leap out and knock you to the floor?"

"Don't remember that at all," her brother said, shooting a look at Simon. "Besides, not every woman's a mad she-devil like you, Allie."

"But I made you a better player, didn't I? Think how fast you got, dodging me."

He whispered loudly to Simon: "Don't tell anyone my special training weapon was my savage little sister."

Simon nodded solemnly. "Your secret goes with me to the quiet of the grave."

"What do you think, Mr. Sharpe?" asked Sarah. "Do you think women should be allowed to play sport with the men?"

Alyce turned her full attention to him as he answered.

"Cricket maybe," he said after thinking for a few moments. "But I'd have to agree with Henry. Don't think most men would feel entirely easy getting into a scrum with women."

"What if the *women* are comfortable with it?" Alyce challenged. She tore at a loaf of bread. "Shouldn't that be their decision to make?"

"Absolutely. And I know some women who are damned, I mean, very strong and courageous." He gave a little secret smile at that, and she wondered who he was referring to. His sister? Some past sweetheart? "They'd be bang-up additions to a rugby club—but even if a woman wasn't that strong, it's a truth that most men can't let themselves hurt a female. No matter how willing she is to get hurt."

"Rather a good thing, I'd think," Sarah murmured.

But Alyce wasn't mollified. "I still think it should be the girls' choice."

Simon took a contemplative bite of stew. "What if you formed a women's rugby club?"

"You mean, women playing against women?" Henry asked.

"It could work just like the clubs for men from the different mines, but with all female teams. You'd have your matches after the men's on Sundays."

"And then everyone would go to the pub after," Alyce said brightly.

"Maybe they'd trade off hosting each other at home," Simon suggested. "Slip a little whiskey into the tea."

Henry sat back and folded his arms across his chest. "Blast me, that actually sounds like a good idea."

"It really does," Alyce added. How was it that she hadn't thought of it before? She'd been so busy trying to shoulder her way into the ranks with the men, she hadn't thought of any other option. And maybe this way, she could convince more women to play, since they wouldn't be afraid of being pummeled into the ground by hulking forwards.

Simon laughed. "You don't need to act so surprised. I work with complicated machines all day—other complex issues, too."

"And you were in Her Majesty's Army," Alyce noted. "Organizing groups of people to batter into each other ought to be a walk on the seaside."

"A very noisy, rough walk on the seaside," he added. "But if the women are willing, why should anybody stand in their way? As you said, Alyce, the choice is theirs to make."

A slight lull fell on the conversation as everyone attended to their meals, but in that quiet, Alyce felt something inside her grow warm and supple. It was all she could do not to stare at him and sigh like the silly girl she'd never been.

Family dinners at the Addison-Shawe home had been chilly affairs: long silences punctuated by the click of silverware against Meissen china and the occasional terrifying interrogation from Simon's father. His mother had barely spoken. His siblings had answered questions with as much brevity as possible. And for his own irreverence— flinging peas at his sister, making his brother snicker at a whispered, filthy limerick—Simon had been sent from the table without being allowed to finish his meal. Many times. He'd never gone hungry, though. After his father had retired to the study for brandy and newspapers, Simon would sneak down to the larder and charm the cook's assistant into fixing him a plate. He'd take his real dinner down in the kitchen, warmed not only by the huge iron range, but the servants' gossip and comfortable ways.

They'd known they could speak and act openly around him, and he wouldn't go tattling.

You're not like the other ones, the head housemaid had said. *Got mischief in your heart, you do.*

And roast chicken in my belly, he'd answered. The cook always gave him leftovers from the servants' meal— meat pies and roasts and other simple fare, instead of *ris de veau grillés* or *poulet sauté au fenouil.*

But you shouldn't make your father so cross, the butler, Tindle, had said. *You eat more of your dinners down here with us than you do upstairs.*

Simon remembered looking around the kitchen, with its bustle and noise and jokes and chaos. *I like it better here,* he'd said.

And he liked it better here in the snug kitchen of the Carrs, as brother and sister exchanged loving barbs, and Sarah took it all with affectionate patience. He'd been eating in the bachelor lodgings all week, and it had been much like his time in the army. Insults, stories, or the quiet of tired, hungry men shoveling food into their mouths as fast as possible. Sometimes the different members of Nemesis would take a meal together at their headquarters— business being the main topic of conversation, and business meant nefarious deeds against nasty men. Not exactly cozy, comfortable environs.

But here, with the Carrs, warmth blanketed him. For

as much as Henry and Alyce badgered each other, real fondness and concern shone in their eyes when they looked at each other. And Sarah formed a buffer—against the siblings, against the world outside, keeping the space of their shabby little house as safe as possible. Heroic, in her own way. Especially carrying a child, both she and her husband occasionally placing a protective hand against her round belly.

In those moments of intimacy, both Simon and Alyce studied their plates intently. They shared glances, the looks of people on the outside.

He'd never believed a wife and family would be his. He still didn't. And he didn't want them, either. But watching the way Henry and Sarah looked after each other and their unborn child, sitting at this small table with clever, pretty Alyce, that strange emptiness in him filled slightly. A tiny, glowing warmth, small and flickering as a tinder lit in the wind.

Careful. Getting too involved puts the mission in jeopardy. He wouldn't be able to think with a level head.

Yet he fought against himself uselessly. This place, these people—Alyce—already shaped him. Stole the distance he needed to get the job done. But he was a veteran of more than one campaign. He'd find a way to make everything work out.

Whatever he planned, it'd have to involve the Carrs—especially Alyce. They were key to figuring out Wheal Prosperity, where even a simple family supper turned into a debate between the siblings.

"While other mines have been shutting down, ours has been making a good profit," Alyce contended. "I don't see why we can't push for an increase in wages."

Henry shook his head. "*Push*—no. The managers are mule-headed bastards. Push them and they just push back. It's got to be worked at slowly, subtly."

"Too slow and there won't be enough to feed the baby when she comes."

"When *he* comes, and I'll make my suggestions to the managers—in my own time."

Having seen the ledgers, Simon knew how vast the disparity was between the mine's earnings and the miners' portions of that profit. Even Henry, who sought peace between the two groups, would be brought to a rage if he understood. But Simon couldn't very well tell them that he'd broken into the managers' office, picked the lock of the strongbox, and reviewed all the numbers.

"Someone has to give them a shove," Alyce fired back. "If you don't, then I will."

"Naturally. Steam-shovel Alyce just storms ahead, and forget about if it lands you in gaol or you lose your position."

Sarah gave Simon an apologetic smile. "Henry should've warned you. It turns into a regular battle royal here every night."

"Only because Henry insists on moving as fast as a drunk tortoise when it comes to change," Alyce said.

"It's because my sister has a good heart but the subtlety of a charging bull."

"Sounds like you want the same things," Simon noted. "Only there's a basic difference in tactics."

Alyce rose. When he scooted his chair aside to make room, their arms grazed. She began to clear their empty plates, and he immediately got to his feet to help. She tried to wave him off, but he wouldn't be dissuaded. Their fingers brushed as they passed dishes back and forth. With the table cleared, she set a kettle on the range and took down three mugs from their hooks on the wall.

"Damn," she muttered. "I forgot to borrow an extra one from next door."

She dashed out before he could tell her that he'd forgo tea.

Simon eased back into his chair, but, despite the fact that the fire in the stove still blazed, it felt as though the heat and light had gone out of the room.

"She'd throttle me if I tried to apologize for her," Henry said.

"Nothing to apologize for," Simon answered at once.

"She's always been headstrong, but when our da died in the mine six years ago, and then our ma took sick and died soon after for want of a good doctor, Alyce became a woman on a mission."

A smile curved Simon's mouth, even as his heart contracted from the loss of the elder Carrs. Their stories weren't uncommon, but that didn't make them less painful. Sometimes he wondered if he'd have an easier time with his work for Nemesis if he cared less—but if he cared less, he wouldn't risk his life over and over again. "I understand having a mission."

He always had goals, objectives. A never-ending fight. But, unlike Alyce, he never fought for himself. Just others. Even when he'd been in the army, struggling for survival, he'd mostly worried about keeping his fellow soldiers safe.

Thinking on it now made him frown. Why hadn't he taken up any battle on his own behalf? Always it was for someone else. As if . . . as if he didn't merit the fight. Easier to take up another's struggle than his own.

Odd, that. When it came to his own conflicts—with his family, his role as a gentleman—he'd turned away. Found somebody else's war to wage.

A troubling thought to have, especially in this place, now.

"Here we are." Alyce came back inside, brandishing an earthenware mug. "It's only got one chip it in, which means it goes to our guest. Keep the handle on the right side so you don't cut your lip."

She bustled about, getting the tea ready over Sarah's objections. "I can take care of that," Sarah complained.

"And stagger around with that giant belly of yours, knocking everything to the ground? No, thank you." Yet Alyce's words were teasing and affectionate, and her sister-in-law only smiled.

The kettle whistled, and Alyce added milk to each cup before pouring in the tea. No sugar. Soon four full mugs were set on the table, along with a seed cake, unwrapped from a soft muslin cloth. Simon held his cup close to his face, breathing fragrant steam deeply. It was better than what they served in the bachelor lodgings, but hardly more than twigs compared to the special blend that his father drank—a mixture of Assam and Formosa oolong—and always with the milk added last. Simon sipped this gratefully. It tasted damned better than any custom blend served in a Sèvres.

Leaning back in his chair, he asked Alyce, "Is yours a one-woman crusade to change things at the mine? Anyone else willing to stick their necks out?"

"Not as far as I do," she said with a rueful smile.

"Then why do it?"

"Someone's got to. Why shouldn't it be me?" She set her mug down on the table and spread her hands upon its rough wooden surface. "Seems to me that everyone's deserving of self-respect, no matter if they're a lord or a lackey."

"I don't know," Sarah said, hesitant. "If people keep to their places, we can just be content."

"Think of all the good that's happened in the world because people weren't content," Alyce countered. "The abolitionists, for one. And Dr. Blackwell."

"Who's that?" asked Henry.

"A woman doctor who campaigned for education and health care for women," Simon answered.

For a moment, he and Alyce stared at each other. It seemed neither expected the other to know who Elizabeth Blackwell was—but they both did.

"It all seems so risky," Sarah fretted, but Simon barely heard her. His attention stayed on Alyce, just as hers remained fixed on him.

"Things worth having come at a price," Alyce said, though she never took her gaze from Simon.

His heart took up a steady, thick beat in his chest.

They wanted the same things, he and Alyce Carr. Only he went about his goals in a more indirect manner. She came barreling in, guns blazing, immovable in her demands. Barefaced and bold.

He had to use subtlety and strategy in order to gain justice. He didn't have the luxury of a frontal attack. It was all subterfuge. Disguises.

Now here he sat, having finished a simple meal in a tiny kitchen, in a clean but ramshackle little house that consisted of only two rooms—one downstairs and one upstairs. Alyce's bed lay behind a curtain, but it was the only thing hidden here. Everything, and everyone, was exactly who they presented themselves to be. Complete honesty. The only pretender was him.

His clandestine investigation had taken him as far as it could. An idea for action was formulating, and he needed their help to accomplish it. And he didn't want to pretend anymore—not with her.

The mission would benefit, but the nascent trust between him and Alyce—that could be broken. But that was the cost of being in Nemesis. Jobs always came first. His own personal wants and needs would continually be pushed aside.

It was a price he accepted—embraced, maybe.

And now, it was time to drop the disguise.

Some subtle change came over Simon's face, as if he were readying himself to jump across a chasm. Unease immediately crept up Alyce's neck. She forced herself to remain still instead of jump up and run away.

"There's something you all need to know." His voice was pitched low, as if he didn't want anyone outside of the kitchen hearing him. "I didn't come to Wheal Prosperity to get a job as a machinist. I came to stop the corruption—in the company, and in the local law. I'm here to help."

No one moved. Nobody spoke. It was as if all sound and movement had been frozen.

Cold spread its fingers through Alyce. She spoke through numb lips. "You're not Simon Sharpe from Sheffield."

He gave a tiny smile. "My name *is* Simon. Can't give you my actual last name, but I'm mostly from London."

Cotton wool filled her head. She shook it, trying to rattle loose what she was sure had to be a mistake in her hearing. But no, she could hear it now. Simon's rough Sheffield accent was gone. He spoke with the round, elegant accent of the elite. Even the mine managers would sound like coarse countrymen compared to Simon.

Sickness curled in her stomach. Everything beneath her feet became quicksand. *Dear God, who* is *he?*

Henry shoved to his feet. "Get the hell out of my house."

Simon looked grim but unsurprised. He didn't get out of his chair. "I've come to the mine to help, Henry. That's what we do. There are injustices in England, and we try to correct them."

"We?" Alyce demanded.

"Nemesis, Unlimited."

Slowly, Henry sank back into his seat, eyes wide. Even Alyce stared in wonder.

"Been lying to us," Henry said after a moment. "About who you are. All that talk of rugby—"

Simon didn't look apologetic. "I did play in the army."

"And Nemesis," her brother pressed. "*That*'s real?"

"It is."

"There'd been rumors, tales," Henry murmured. "We never dared believe . . ."

Alyce had heard stories, gossip that had started surfacing a few years ago. Letters to folks with kin in London, and those letters became stories. Fables. A shadowy group of people in London who made it their business to get justice for people who couldn't get it for themselves. The stories had been cloaked in exaggeration and half-truths, deeds Alyce had never really believed—kidnapped and enslaved children freed, corrupt judges disgraced. Not so long ago, she'd heard that Nemesis had uncovered evidence that a nobleman had committed treason, and the lord himself was killed in mysterious, ugly circumstances.

It had all seemed too good to be true. The world favored the rich, the powerful. People like Nemesis didn't exist in real life.

Except here was Simon, claiming that they *did* exist. And that he'd come to help.

The help she'd wanted for so long.

"You're a goddamn liar," she growled.

"Alyce!" Sarah exclaimed, shocked.

But Simon didn't look offended. And when he spoke, he sounded cool, almost distant. "You'll have to trust me. I am who I say I am."

"Trust you!" She pushed back from the table. "Up until a few minutes ago, you claimed to be somebody else. You even *talked* differently."

"Nobody'd believe a machinist with an Harrovian accent."

"Where's Harrovia?"

"That's what they call students who go to Harrow."

Oh, Lord. That fancy public school for the sons of the elite. God, he was one of *them*. "How do we know you aren't some spy the owners sent to squirrel into our ranks, learn our secrets and turn us in?"

"You don't." He also got to his feet, and even in that little action, she could see a change in the way he moved, polished, confident. The plain clothes he wore now seemed like a disguise. She could easily picture him in some natty, expensive suit, custom-made by one of those shops in London. "All you have is my word."

"I have no idea what your word is worth."

"Maybe not, but you have to believe me when I say that I'll need your help if I'm going to make a difference here. You want off scrip and to get paid decent wages, then you side with me. And you're key, Alyce. You've always been key to my mission."

A sudden, horrible thought burst inside her mind, and she backed slowly away until the wall stopped her. "All that flattery, the flirting—'the pleasure of your company'— that was for your mission. It wasn't me you were interested in. I was just a tool, no different from a pick or a bucking iron."

The fact that he didn't immediately deny it caused a cold, hard lump to form in her belly. And when he glanced aside quickly, avoiding her gaze, the lump grew, heavy as ore.

Henry advanced on Simon, face dark as thunder. "The hell? Flirting with my sister? Playing with her?" He grabbed a handful of Simon's shirt—but Alyce had the feeling Simon *let* Henry grab him. "I'll bloody kill you."

"Alyce is the linchpin of the mine and village. If anyone knows anything important, it's her. I had to get close to her." Simon turned his gaze to her. Regret flickered there. "But you're a damned excellent woman, Alyce. It wasn't a hardship."

"Ah, that makes everything better," she said through a clenched jaw.

" 'Justice by any means necessary.' " He pried Henry's fingers from his shirt and stepped around her brother. "It's how Nemesis operates. Why our operations succeed. Whatever has to be done to see injustice corrected, we do it." He strode to Alyce, and she forced herself to stand her ground, when all she wanted to do was bolt. "If your feelings were bruised . . . I'm sorry."

She gave a low, hard laugh at this apology.

"There's more at stake here than your injured feelings," he continued. "You and I, we can get rid of the corrupt managers and owners, but the only way we can do that is if we trust each other."

"You've done nothing but lie ever since you got here," she fired back. "A *gentleman* posing as a laborer. Playing sweetheart when you just wanted information. I don't have any reason to trust you."

For a long moment, he was silent. His lips pressed together, and lines bracketed his mouth. "No, you don't," he finally said. "But I'll give you a reason."

He strode to the door and opened it. Before he left, however, he faced Sarah. "Thank you again for your hospitality, Mrs. Carr. It truly was one of the best meals I've eaten in a long time." Looking at Alyce and Henry, he added, "Don't tell anyone about me. Not yet."

"Why shouldn't we," she demanded, "when you've played us all false?"

"It's not the right time. And I've had my motives for everything I've done. Think whatever you like, but believe that."

Without another word, he turned and walked out into the darkness. His footsteps faded into the night.

"Where are you going?" Henry demanded when Alyce grabbed her shawl from its peg.

She paused on the threshold. "To see just how trustworthy this Simon Whoever-He-Is really is." Then she, too, plunged into the shadows.

Alyce kept a goodly distance between her and Simon, ducking around corners in case he looked over his shoulder—which he didn't.

The hour was early enough that people still walked up and down the high street. Mostly men. Families were all at home, either finishing their suppers or settling in for the evening. A few wild children knocked along the lane until their mothers shouted at them to come inside. Simon walked with directness and purpose, nodding now and then at the men he passed.

None of them knew. Nobody understood who he truly was. The smooth elegance of his stride was gone, and when she heard him wish Tommy Grewe a good evening, his genteel accent had disappeared. He was back to being Simon Sharpe, slipping into the role so easily even she would've denied that he was actually wellborn, despite the proof she'd just been given.

Part of her wanted to stand in the middle of the street, pointing a finger and calling him out as a liar in front of the village. But she kept silent—were his lies true? Who was he?—as she trailed after him like a wraith.

He didn't go straight into the pub, as she expected, and he passed the bachelor lodgings. She waited to see if he'd go to the managers' house, high on the hill, to give a full accounting of what he'd learned. He didn't do that, either.

Instead, he continued up the high street. The company store perched at the top like a vulture. Lights blazed in the windows and figures passed back and forth as evening shoppers made their final purchases of the day. The store stayed open until nine, making certain that the people of Trewyn could be swindled until well into the night. The church tolled that the hour was quarter to nine, leaving fifteen minutes left for business.

Yet Simon didn't go into the company store, either. He turned down a nearby lane, vanishing off the main road.

Alyce slowed her steps. Should she follow? That lane wound along a low wall, past a few cottages, and then led to a yard behind the store, where deliveries were made. There wouldn't be many places for her to hide, but she couldn't let Simon slip away. So, carefully, she trailed him, creeping along the shadows.

Rounding a corner, she saw his lean shape silhouetted against a wall, and she shrank back. Every few minutes, she'd peek out, but he was still there, barely distinguishable from the darkness. She could just make out that his arms were crossed over his chest, his posture that of a man who seemed to be waiting.

The church bell tolled nine times. Noise from the high street quieted. Even the sounds from the pub dimmed. Village ordinance mandated that the pub be closed by nine-thirty Monday through Thursday. Though the mine was open on Saturdays, pay packets were distributed on Fridays—which made for a profitable night at the pub. On Fridays and Sundays, it stayed open until eleven. Many men came to work on Saturday and Monday with red eyes and gray skin.

For all that Henry annoyed her, he never pissed away his pay at the pub, and if he did go get a drink after supper, he was gone only for an hour, and he'd return almost as sober as when he left.

Too many people lay buried in the church yard because of drink—either the men themselves or their neglected families. Another part of life linked to the mine that had to change. If conditions weren't as bad, if the pay were better so families could save, then maybe numbing ale wouldn't be so needed.

Which was why she couldn't let some outsider like Simon trample his way into the village and make everything into an even bigger mess than it already was. Though— she had to admit—he hadn't trampled anything, sneaking in as he did without disturbing even a fleck of soot.

But she ached, anyway. He'd admitted to using her, and the knowledge of it felt like rusted picks in her chest. Here she'd fancied herself as strong and thick-skinned as an ox, yet a few clever, shrewd words from a handsome man, and she was nothing more than a bleating, defenseless lamb.

It doesn't matter. You don't know him. You never did. And he never knew you.

It *did* matter, and that confused and hurt her all over again.

The clock struck the quarter hour. She peered around the corner to check on Simon.

He was gone.

Careful to muffle her steps, she hurried up the narrow lane, then came to a stop when she emerged in the yard behind the store. The lights were all out, and she couldn't hear anyone moving around inside. Hartley Evans, the store manager, always closed up quickly at the end of the day. He might be in the company's pockets, but what was the use of earning a little extra if he couldn't go home and enjoy the fruits of his crooked labors?

But where was Simon? There was no sign of him.

Her need to know more kept her rooted in place, tense and silently waiting. And she almost would have missed it, the movement was so subtle, so utterly noiseless, but her ma had always said she had the senses of a cat. It had been impossible to claim that Father Christmas had visited when Alyce had seen and heard her parents trying to silently put Christmas oranges on the kitchen table.

Now she caught the shift in the shadows, a tiny motion by the back loading doors to the store. Something resonated within her, like glimpsing a light in the distance and knowing it was her destination. She knew with that same intuition that the motion by the doors was Simon.

He had to be mad. That was the only explanation. He'd be beaten, or killed. And she could be in danger, too, simply by being there. She hoped that what she saw wasn't true—but it was.

He was breaking into the company store.

CHAPTER 6.

Alyce watched, baffled, as he slipped inside the store, shutting the loading doors behind him noiselessly. For a moment she hung back before quickly crossing the yard, then hunkered down below one of the windows. Slowly, she peered over the sill.

All the lamps inside had been extinguished. It was dark as a tapped-out chamber in a mine in there, but she'd been in the store enough times to know its layout. Lidded barrels holding flour, oats, and sugar stood in a row. Tall cabinets and glass-topped long counters lined two walls, holding all sorts of dry goods and household supplies— anything someone in Trewyn could ever want, to make sure all profits went right back into the owners' hands. A locked till sat upon one of the counters, but anyone who tried to rob the store would find it empty. Hartley Evans brought the contents to the managers every night, along with his accounting ledger.

Besides, should someone ever break into the till and find it full, it'd look terribly suspicious if they suddenly had a big influx of scrip. Another way that the owners and managers kept the workers well trapped.

She scanned the darkened shop, looking for the tiniest

hint of movement. No sign of Simon. Then the shadows shifted. There—by the heavy doors that led to the cold storage. A bent, humpbacked figure appeared. It had to be Simon. Strange how she knew exactly what he looked like, but she didn't truly know him at all. He shut the cold storage doors behind him and moved carefully toward the back of the store.

Alyce scurried away, back across the yard, to hide behind a wall. She poked her head out in time to see Simon closing and locking the loading doors. No one would know he'd been in and out of the store. But what had he been doing there?

On his back, he carried a large pack. Strong as he was, he bowed beneath its weight. He moved quickly, though, as he eased away from the store. And though he was still a stranger to the village, he moved purposefully toward another destination, as if he had his route already mapped.

The night was further along, the silence of the village and the valley deeper. She checked her every step, making sure not to knock any loose pebbles or snap a twig beneath her boots. Despite the heavy burden he carried, Simon glided down more lanes, until he left the main part of the village. He kept to the cover of a low stone wall and followed it as it climbed a hill.

Alyce nearly stumbled when she finally realized his destination. At the top of this hill stood the managers' house. It made an impressive sight—two stories, built in a modern style with pointed eaves, several chimneys, and large, plentiful windows. Trimmed hedges and flower beds surrounded the house. It even boasted a stable and carriage house. The managers' home was the finest-looking building she'd ever seen. Whenever she caught a glimpse of it, envy and anger sunk cold talons into her heart. The pastor preached that it was wrong to have those feelings toward someone, but she couldn't help it.

No one in the village would ever live like that. Not even Tippet.

Illness clogged her throat when she thought about how fine the owners' houses must be, miles away in Plymouth. The luxuries they surely enjoyed. Nobody in their homes had to sleep behind a screen in the kitchen—except perhaps a servant, but she'd wager even the servants had actual rooms of their own.

The managers had a few servants. A cook, three maids, a coachman. Comfort that Alyce had never known. Nor would she.

But why was Simon heading toward the managers' house? A new sickness choked her. Was he going to report her? Or spill all the secrets he'd learned since he'd come to the mine?

Anything he told the managers wouldn't be new information. And she could always turn the tables, letting the managers know that he'd stolen from the company store. So she continued to follow him, both making their way closer and closer to the big house.

A few lights glowed from behind heavy curtains—one on the ground floor, and a few more on the next story, and two in the servants' attic rooms. Simon hunkered behind an elm, so Alyce followed suit, hiding herself beside a large granite boulder that had long ago tumbled down from a higher peak. They waited a long while, her thighs aching from crouching, and the tips of her fingers stinging with cold.

Hours seemed to pass. It was only the pain in her legs and hands that kept her alert. Finally, one by one, the lights in the house went out.

Simon tarried nearly half an hour more before moving. She tailed him, fighting a groan as she had to use her stiffened limbs again. But he didn't seem affected by the cold, the wait, or the burden he carried. Instead, he slipped around the back of the house, sleek as a dream.

She skulked in his wake, then drew up short when she came to the rear of the house. A cobbled yard stood between the house and the stables, and off to the side was a gravel path that looked as if it led to a slate-tiled terrace surrounded by potted plants. A wrought-iron table and chairs stood in the courtyard, ready for one of the managers to enjoy a meal or cigar in the outdoors. When the weather was mild, it had to be awfully pleasant to sit out there, fresh air all around and a cup of tea or drink of fine whisky within easy reach.

Simon was nowhere to be found. He could be in the stables—but the undisturbed horses only pawed and snorted as they slept. Had he taken refuge in one of the gardens? Maybe he'd concealed himself behind one of the large potted plants on the terrace. She hesitated, uncertain what to do.

"Come to join me for a bit of breaking and entering?" whispered a deep, familiar voice in her ear.

She spun around, and there was Simon, his hands on the straps of his pack, and looking not at all surprised to see her.

Simon knew better, but the shocked look on Alyce's face almost made him chuckle. But her pride—and the mission—wouldn't permit it.

"How long have you known?" she demanded in an undertone.

"Since I left your home." At her continued shock, he said, "This is my *work,* Alyce. If I couldn't tell that I was being followed, and by a tyro"—she sputtered in outrage at that—"then I'd have to become a machinist for real." She'd actually done a fair job of tailing, which was the greater surprise, but he'd been at this game for too long to not know when someone followed him.

"Or," she hissed, "go back to the aristo world you come from."

His mouth tightened. "Nobody can help the circumstances of their birth. It's what comes after that defines them." He took a step closer, and noted that she didn't back away. Good. He didn't want her shrinking from him. "Now, are we going to stand here all night, praying that someone catches us, or are you going to help me get inside?"

She eyed the managers' house suspiciously. "You could be leading me into a trap."

"Then stay out here. Or go home. But make a choice." He slipped past her, ignoring her almost noiseless gasp of chagrin. Now he needed focus, and whatever she decided to do, he couldn't let her distract him. But she was damned distracting . . .

The servants' entrance was at the bottom of steps leading to a partially subterranean story. The transom above the door and a few narrow windows would let in light during the day, though with the house being so modern, he'd no doubt there were gas lamps to light the servants' work. Right now, it was dark and quiet inside, thanks to him cooling his heels for the past hours. Whenever he had to wait out servants, he knew it would take a long while.

He eased down the stairs, then settled himself in front of the door with his lock picks.

"Someone could be awake in there." Alyce crouched close beside him, and he caught the scent of cool night air and her skin.

"Everyone's asleep, even the maids." He slid the picks into the lock.

"You sure of that?"

"I've been watching the house for the past three nights. They keep to the same schedule. Servants are the first up and last to bed," he added, making minute adjustments to his tools.

"So you've got a lot of experience with servants." Her whisper was sharp with bitterness.

He should've expected her anger over his necessary duplicity. Even anticipated her resentment because he was a gentleman's son. It was all part of the job. Dozens of times he'd ruthlessly made use of someone to ensure a job's success.

And if that person became angry or bitter—it didn't matter. The only important thing was justice.

He'd even treaded lightly with Alyce.

Yet her hurt had somehow migrated from her into him, and he felt a strange pain to see the betrayal in her eyes, hear it in her voice. It shouldn't bother him—this mission was about more than her, it concerned an entire village and all the workers at Wheal Prosperity.

It shouldn't bother him—but did.

"I've had to go in disguise as a servant, too," he said, which was true. Granted, he wouldn't have known as much about the lives and habits of domestic workers if he hadn't grown up with them, but that wasn't any of her business. "A tutor. Coachman, footman. Nobody knows how much footmen get pinched and prodded by ladies—and some gentlemen. I'd always find new bruises under my livery."

She fell silent, and he glanced over to find her staring at him as if he'd crawled out from the ocean. "Tutors, coachmen, footmen." She shook her head. "It's a wonder we can breathe the same air. And *that*." Her gaze slid to the picks he was manipulating. "Do they teach housebreaking at Harrow?"

"Studies supplementary to the curriculum."

A little flare of triumph lit in him when she fought a smile. Then they both quieted as he continued to pick the lock. Finally, it opened with a gratifying click.

He slipped inside, Alyce at his back. It wasn't easy to move with his usual stealth with the heavy weight he carried, but he'd managed under tougher conditions. The door opened into a corridor that stretched into pitch-darkness.

"Put your hand on my shoulder," he whispered. "I'll lead us."

"Lead us *where*?" But she did as he asked.

Good as his eyesight was, he had to find his way by touch, his hand running along the chair rail lining the hallway.

She took a deep sniff. "God, that *smell*. Is that . . . ?"

"Rancid butter." Though he was aware of the sleeping household all around, and the danger of the situation, he smiled in the darkness. "Hope I can wash that stink out of my clothes, or no one will sit next to me in church."

Her hand disappeared from his shoulder. "Are you really going to—"

He fumbled for, and found, her hand, and put it back onto his shoulder. "Enough talk. From now until we're half a mile from this house, we work silently. Give my shoulder a squeeze if you understand."

The feel of her strong fingers tightening around him caused a sudden pulse of heat to flare. A woman with strong hands and a strong will . . . The possibilities . . .

He shook his head at himself and his thoughts. *This isn't how you get a mission done.* He'd prided himself on his spotless record for Nemesis. Not once had he let his cock cloud his judgment. He never involved himself with any women in an operation—unless circumstance demanded it. There were all sorts of secrets and information to be learned in a willing woman's bed. He'd learned many, many secrets swathed in fine linens and expensive perfume.

But that wasn't the plan here. Alyce was no bored

magnate's wife. The only reason he'd have to take her to bed was because he wanted her.

Goddamn it, get your sodding brains out of your trousers.

As he edged deeper down the hallway, toward the kitchen, he kept his senses on alert for any sounds or signs of movement in the house. But his thoughts remained focused on the slim, strong hand on his shoulder. The problem was that he *liked* Alyce. Simple lust could be shrugged off, or taken care of with a cold bath or time alone with his hand. But actually enjoying a woman's company, admiring her—that made things a hell of a lot more complicated.

They reached the kitchen, where light from the windows fell in cool squares across tiled surfaces, gleaming cooking pots, a china cupboard, and a large, modern range. A stone sink stood beneath the windows with spigots for hot and cold running water. Alyce slowly straightened up from her crouch. Her eyes narrowing, she turned in a slow circle.

She didn't speak, but she didn't have to. This was probably the first time she'd been in a kitchen this expensive and modern. By comparison, the kitchen at her cottage looked medieval, humble. That Sarah Carr could cook such delicious food, and with such limited means, testified to her skill and resourcefulness. And soon, Sarah and Henry would have a child to feed from that modest kitchen. They'd probably have another, and another. Simon had seen the large, tumultuous families of Trewyn. Babies came faster than the parents could support them. But support them they did—under the meanest conditions. Everyone was always hungry. Even Simon felt the continual gnaw. There was never enough.

Yet this kitchen, bright and clean and new, fed only

three men who mostly sat behind desks all day. The kitchen also provided meals for the servants who waited on the managers, but their fare would be simpler, cheaper.

Fury crossed Alyce's face and her hands trembled. She looked as though she wanted to tear the shining copper pots down from the wall and throw open the cabinet to shatter the china cups and plates. Here was visible proof of the cavernous gap between the workers and the managers, proof at its most elemental: food.

He took a warning step toward her, but he didn't need to bother. She drew in a shaky breath, calming herself. The work of Nemesis was always emotional, but the trick was to keep those feelings buried so the mind could be clear.

She spread her hands, asking silently, *Now what?*

A heavy door stood at one end of the kitchen. He opened it, and cool air rushed out, lightly scented with beef and dairy. The larder. It smelled of cold prosperity.

Alyce slipped in beside him, and again he heard her suck in her breath at the massive amount of food stored here. Haunches of meat hung from the rafters, with one flank large enough to feed a family of seven. Despite the darkness of the larder, he could see the sheer greed in her eyes. She probably wanted to steal one of the joints of beef—there'd been a minuscule amount of meat in Sarah's stew. Alyce's hand hovered close to the piece of beef. But she pulled away.

She knows. A theft like that wouldn't go unreported. Every cottage and home would be ransacked by the constabulary, the thief arrested and sent to a county gaol.

Proof again of her intelligence. She thought beyond immediate desires, to the larger scheme.

He set the pack of rancid butter on the stone floor. Opening it assaulted his nose, and she reared back, covering her nose and mouth. He began stacking the wrapped blocks of butter on the marble counter. She started to help, both of them moving quickly and silently to empty the pack of its contents.

Once it was empty, he lifted a large glass cloche. Beneath were more blocks of butter, pale and creamy in the soft light. He bent close and inhaled deeply. The milky scent brought him straight back into childhood and slices of bread thickly spread with sweet butter served with his tea in the nursery.

He glanced pointedly between the fresh butter and his pack. Her eyes widened with understanding, then she grinned wickedly. Her smile arrowed straight through him.

She ducked out into the kitchen, then returned a moment later with a roll of paraffin paper. Again, he nodded his approval. Together, she and Simon wrapped each block of fresh butter and carefully set them in his pack. When all the butter had been loaded, hands soon glistened, so he wiped them off on a nearby square of toweling. A groan caught in his throat when he glanced up to see Alyce leaning against the counter, eyes closed, licking her fingers. Her expression was nothing short of ecstasy.

It felt like a deliberate punishment, taunting him with what he couldn't—shouldn't—have.

He wanted it to be *his* tongue running up and down her glossy fingers, sucking them into his mouth, tasting butter and her flesh. And if he didn't care as much about the mission as he did, he would've done exactly that— walked up to her and licked her slowly, watching her face the whole while. Maybe she would've slapped him. Maybe she would've wanted more than her fingers in his mouth.

He'd never know. There was no overlooking that they were deep in the house of the enemy, their situation precarious. He could forget himself with her. Easily.

Quietly, he cleared his throat. She glanced up at him, the tip of her index finger still between her lips. Her gaze was carnal but cruel as she lowered her hand.

As he shouldered his pack, she unwrapped all the blocks of rancid butter, choking a little on the smell, then covered as much as she could with the cloche. He and Alyce left the larder, and she stuffed the paper far back into the stove's cold firebox. In the morning, the cook would unknowingly destroy the evidence when loading up and setting fire to wood to heat the stove. He smiled again at Alyce's ingenuity.

Quickly, they made their way out of the kitchen and out of the house. He made certain to lock the door behind him.

And then they were hurrying away from the house, down the hill, neither of them daring to speak until the house was just a dark, looming shape on the knoll. They stopped for breath beside a hedgerow.

"And now?" she whispered. Her eyes gleamed. Not with fear or anger. With excitement. She was *enjoying* this.

Goddamn it.

"Now, we finish a little game the Americans call the 'switch.' "

The hour was late, but Alyce knew there would still be a constable or two on patrol. So she and Simon made their way quietly, stealthily to the company store. He quickly picked the lock to the store's back doors. Her mind reeled as she watched him deftly break in. In a single night, he'd changed so many times, her head spun like a mill wheel. From machinist, to gentleman, to Nemesis operative. And now to this—expert burglar.

Who *was* he? The mystery of him kept unfolding, like a map being opened one small corner at a time. She thought she'd known his whole geography, but then another piece of the map was revealed, leaving her disoriented. Lost.

Anger still singed her. The whole time he'd been lying. Lying to her.

He had his reasons. Are you going to be a sulky child, or are you going to help?

The back loading doors to the store opened, and together, they crept inside. Darkness smothered the inside of the shop, but she knew the place the way she knew recurring bad dreams. She followed him to the larder, a small room that wasn't half as cold as the insulated chamber inside the managers' house. It gave off a faint stink. The meat on its hooks and racks here was tinged gray, not red, and bottles were filled with cloudy liquid that was supposed to be milk—unlike the opaque, brightly white bottles of milk at the house. She noticed a gap on the wooden counter where the butter had been.

Without speaking, she and Simon unloaded the blocks of wrapped, fresh butter. They worked quickly together. Every so often, he shot her a glance, ripe with awareness.

"What?" she whispered, torn between annoyance and interest.

He shook his head. "It'll have to wait."

She would've thought that breaking and entering—twice in one night—would've bothered her. Every Sunday saw her at church, dutifully listening to sermons and believing herself, in essence, a good person. Yet she'd be a liar if she said there hadn't been something almost . . . *fun* . . . about burglarizing the managers' home, and again here in the company store. Technically, she wasn't actually *stealing* from the store, since they were putting merchandise back, but these weren't Bible- or law-abiding deeds.

For a good purpose, she reminded herself. She wasn't about to start a life of crime after tonight.

With the butter all unpacked, Simon hefted his empty satchel.

"We're going to have to tell them," she said under her breath.

He frowned. "That we've stolen from them?"

"Not the managers. The women of the village. They've gone without fresh butter for over a week. They need to know it's here."

His expression turned doubtful. "The new machinist showing up at their doors in the middle of the night—I'd be turned in to the constabulary before I got a word out."

She smiled at him. "That's why I'm coming with you."

It wasn't the fastest process, and they couldn't visit every household in Trewyn, but they made slow, steady progress, all the while steering clear of the patrolman.

Alyce and Simon approached another home, careful to keep to the shadows. Amazing how she'd learned the skill so quickly in the course of a night. But now she felt almost as comfortable in the darkness as she did with a bucking iron in her hands.

Stories about Nemesis had trickled into the village. Some of the younger lads had fled without a single penny to London, walking or hopping trains to get there. And once they did, they slept on the street and sought work as navvies digging trenches, or whatever jobs they could scrape together. And some of those lads wrote home, telling of their adventures, and passing along rumors of Nemesis. In a few of those letters, Nemesis was described as a benevolent, charitable organization, not unlike the Salvation Army. But other letters told very different tales: Nemesis was a gang of dangerous vigilantes, patrolling the London streets with cudgels and brass knuckles, waiting for any chance to start a brawl.

Now she knew—Nemesis was something else entirely. They stole, lied, ruthlessly used cunning and guile. All to get what they wanted: justice. Glancing at Simon, who moved with rangy muscularity, she didn't doubt the operatives of Nemesis could go toe-to-toe, if the situation demanded it. Would tonight find them in one of those situations?

She scratched on the door. None of the homes were big, and they were all rickety as a bundle of reeds. A knock on the door at this hour and in such small dwellings would sound like a battering ram. People moved around inside, whispering, muttering, pulling on dressing gowns or shawls.

As they waited, Alyce studied Simon. He kept watch on the street, his gaze never at rest, his long body primed and ready. Though she couldn't be sure, *this* seemed like the true Simon: a man of strength and energy, fiercely intelligent, ruthless. Then he winked at her—damn him for being so sodding handsome—and against her will, she felt her insides heat. His charm seemed the most dangerous thing about him. At least she could protect herself against his lies, his physical capability. But her defenses against his allure kept sifting away, bit by bit, as if breaking ore down to tiny granules.

At last, the door opened, and both Lester and Joan Willis appeared in the doorway. Joan clutched a shawl around her thin shoulders, and Lester's hairy calves and feet appeared beneath the hem of his nightshirt. Farther back in the dimly lit cottage, several children of different ages strained to see who their late-night visitors were. While the wife wore a look of worry, Lester appeared suspicious, hostile, particularly when he stared at Simon.

Simon only gave the man a small nod, the look on his own face giving away nothing.

"Something wrong at the mine?" Joan demanded, her voice thin. "Flood? Collapse?"

"It's all right, Joan," Alyce whispered. "But you need to get to the company store tomorrow and buy butter."

Both husband and wife looked baffled. "The butter's all spoiled," Joan said.

"Not anymore, it isn't," Simon noted. His accent had gone back to being the machinist from Sheffield—making Alyce's head spin again. How many different selves did he have? How could he keep track of them all? She'd be certain to make a mistake.

Was it a quality to be admired, the way he could shift like clouds across the moon? She needed to be especially careful around him.

"The managers and that thieving bastard Hartley finally listened," Lester said. "Got rid of the bad stuff."

Alyce shook her head. "Not exactly. But let's say they *provided* the fresh butter."

Joan and Lester's eyes widened. "How—?"

Simon cut them off. "Better if you don't know too much about it."

Lester winked, tapping the side of his nose with his finger. "Right you are, lad."

They had a lot more homes to visit, and the hours were growing smaller, heading closer to dawn. "Have a good sleep," Alyce said, "and make sure you get to the store tomorrow."

With that, she and Simon left the Willis home, and continued their task. It took hours. Sometimes the people were hostile, but most beamed their appreciation. Drippings were a poor substitute for butter, and she'd heard from more than a few women at the mine about their children growing haggard, desperately missing that important bit of fat in their diets.

All the while as they worked, Simon's gaze kept returning to her, lingering longer. Turning . . . hungrier. But he said nothing. Made no move to touch her.

"We're skipping Dyer, Gundry, and Poole," Simon murmured as they continued their progress.

"Because they're snitches." Alyce shouldn't have been impressed that he'd been able to figure that out, when some of the miners themselves didn't even know. But not much seemed to slip past Simon's cutting awareness. "A shame, though, since Gundry and Poole have wives and children."

"Can't take the risk that they'll go squeal."

She nodded. It was unfortunate, but the men had made their choice to spy on their fellow miners in exchange for some extra chit. The consequence was theirs to shoulder.

As she and Simon skirted the edges of the village, heading back toward her home, the morning birds were already beginning to sing from the privets. She sighed. "Not everyone is going to get to the butter in time. It'll be sold out."

"Then it'll ensure there's no excuse not to reorder."

She slanted him a look. "Thought this out, haven't you?"

One corner of his mouth lifted. "Jobs are like chess matches—no, they're like wars. Every battle's got to be planned. You can't go running into the field, shooting your Martini-Henry at anything that moves. Either you'll waste bullets or wind up hurting an ally. This way, we know we're getting results."

"We did get results, didn't we?" The thought made her grin. In just one night, she and Simon had been able to accomplish something that nearly two weeks of complaints and accusations hadn't. An odd feeling rose in her chest, a lightness that made the graying sky and familiar hills almost beautiful. It took her several moments to understand the feeling—happiness, maybe. Satisfaction. A problem had been solved, and she and Simon had been the ones to solve it. So often, she found herself running up against a granite wall, gaining only a headache and frustration in the process. But not tonight.

"And we worked well together," he added, almost thoughtful.

"Sounds like you weren't certain I could help you." She tried not to be put out when he didn't immediately deny it.

"I always knew you could help me, somehow. That's why I kept close to you when I first got here. But we were both unknown quantities," he said. "When I left your house earlier tonight, you didn't think you could trust me."

Never one for mitigating her words, she answered, "No, I didn't."

The unspoken question hung in the chilly air. Did she now?

They finally reached the lane that led to her home. Morning approached, with ashen light lining the hilltops to the east. In less than an hour, people would rise from their beds and ready themselves for another long day at the bottom of a pit or smashing stones with picks and hammers. She ought to feel tired, having gotten no sleep, and the evening full of danger that had made her heart pound. But instead, she felt that lightness again, that sensation she could accomplish anything, right any wrong.

A little burglary and all of a sudden I'm Robin Bleeding Hood.

Stopping at the entrance to the lane, she turned to Simon. To make certain that they couldn't be overheard by an early riser or a passing patrolman, she stepped close to him. There was no denying the caution in his gaze. Or the heat coming from his body. She still hadn't said whether she trusted him or not, and her answer was important. For more than just the mission.

"What next?" she asked. The implication being, *Yes, in this, I trust you.*

His expression eased slightly. "Got a plan in mind. It won't come readily, though. I'll need the backing and cooperation of the miners."

"That'll take some doing."

"You're a stubborn lot," he said with a wry smile. "I'll give you that."

She did her best to keep her chuckle quiet. "Cornishmen and Cornishwomen can be downright mule-headed."

"And that's a compliment?" He shortened the distance between them, until only a few inches separated their bodies.

The heat of him soaked into her, or was it the intensity of his gaze? Though the sun hadn't yet risen, she could've sworn his eyes gleamed bright as aquamarines. Her pulse, which had been kept at a rapid clip all night, suddenly beat even faster. Throughout the evening's adventure, she'd been aware of him, the leashed strength of his lean body, how he moved with such precision and confidence. Like no other man she'd met. Up until now, she'd told herself she hadn't noticed, not really. But she had.

"Oh, aye," she said, abruptly breathless.

He inhaled sharply. "I've held myself back all night—for sake of the job." His voice was a low rumble. "Tonight's maneuvers are over. Leaves me free to finally do this."

He brought his hands up, but slowly. Giving her a chance to move away or push him back. Yet she didn't. She let his large hands cup the back of her head. Her own hands stayed at her sides, testing him.

Either he tipped her head up, or she tilted it back. She couldn't quite tell. But then he lowered his head, and his mouth found hers.

His lips were soft, nimble. They brushed back and forth across her own lips, learning the feel of her and letting her learn him. Then he seemed to want more than this gentle exploration, the kiss deepening, both of their mouths opening to feel each other's warmth and slickness. His flavor was rich, dizzying. It wasn't an uncertain kiss. Yet she could feel how he held himself at bay. Was it for her sake, or his?

She wasn't a delicate puff of milkweed. His kiss roused needs in her, needs that, for her own protection, had been kept buried beneath piles of granite. But as dawn edged closer, and the night's events still swirled around her, and she was here, with *this* man, she couldn't shut the gates around her desire. She wanted to break free.

She touched her tongue to his. His control seemed to snap.

Groaning, he moved one of his hands to the small of her back and pulled her closer. His mouth grew more demanding. She met his need, fed off it. Her fingers dug into the hard round shapes of his shoulders, the flesh barely yielding beneath her grip. Her breasts pressed into the rigid wall of his chest.

He was just a little rough as he kissed her, held her, and it felt so incredibly *right*. The other kisses she'd shared had been nothing more than boys' tentative fumblings. Maybe a little bit of pleasure, but nothing like this. Simon was a man. He kissed like one. And her whole body stirred to life, a burst of electricity cascading through her. She wanted more.

Damn, he is *dangerous.*

He broke the kiss with a muttered oath. Took a step back. And then another. He raked his hand through his hair. His chest rose and fell on fast breaths. But he didn't turn his back on her.

For a moment, they stared at each other. Her hands slowly drifted back down to her sides, and she blinked, as if waking. Sure enough, her head felt thick and cloudy, as if she'd been dreaming moments before. But no, she'd been wide awake. The sensation humming through her body told her so.

"We're not . . ." His words were raspy, and he cleared

his throat. "Getting involved with someone who's integral to a mission isn't wise."

"Those the official rules of Nemesis?"

"No official rules. But we all know an assignment takes precedence." Still, his voice was gravelly, and his breathing had barely slowed. "This next step can't happen without your help. It's got to be planned and executed carefully."

"It isn't planned or careful, kissing me witless."

He exhaled roughly. "You make me lose my head, Alyce. Can't let that happen."

Maybe she shouldn't feel flattered. Maybe he flung out compliments like that all the time. Yet his words had been plain, open in their admission of desire, and that filled her with a new heat and weightlessness.

He was right. There was work to be done, work that she'd wanted carried out all of her adult life. She wasn't going to ruin that because of vivid blue eyes, sharp wit, or kisses hot enough to melt ore. Besides, she still didn't know him. Not truly. It would be easy to be reckless around him, and she needed to protect herself. Protect her family and her village. She couldn't do that if she was mooning after Simon, hoping for another kiss. Or something more.

"Deal," she said. "No more of this." She waved at the space between them, that still seemed to shimmer with the heat they'd created.

"No more." It sounded like real regret in his voice.

It felt ridiculous to shake on it. Instead, she pulled her shawl tighter around her shoulders. "I'd best be getting back. The whole village will be rubbing sleep from their eyes soon."

"No sleep for us, but a full day's work ahead."

She couldn't stop her smile. "I don't regret the sleeplessness. Not a jot. Can't think when I've had a better night."

He raised a skeptical brow. "Following me, breaking into the masters' house to steal butter, then spreading the news through the village? That's your best night?"

She shrugged. "Life is very, very quiet in Trewyn." But then she grew serious. "I'm not daft, Simon. I made a difference tonight. *We* did. Nothing's better than that." She couldn't help adding, "The kiss was a nice little side benefit, too." A benefit she wouldn't experience again, but for good reasons.

He gave another frustrated groan, then started toward the bachelors' lodging. He'd only taken a few steps before he stopped. "Kissed you *witless,* did I?"

Her lips curled into a smile. "Like an asylum inmate. Now, go. Flattery's for weak men and it's nearly dawn."

He tipped his head and continued walking. She had to fight the urge to watch him go, reminding herself of all the reasons why now, of all times, she needed distance from him. Instead, she hurried down the lane to her house, and slipped inside.

Not a moment too soon. She had just enough time to change back into her work clothes before Sarah came trundling down the stairs, one hand on the rail, the other pressed to the small of her back.

"Up already?" Sarah asked, moving toward the stove to ready breakfast. "Where's the peevish girl I usually have to shake out of bed?"

"Restless night," Alyce replied.

"Aye," Sarah said with a shake of her head. "Mr. Sharpe's revelations threw us all. But I suppose I shouldn't call him Mr. Sharpe. What was his real name again?"

"He didn't say." He was still a stranger, even though moments earlier she'd had her lips pressed against his. "Just call him Simon, for now. To keep him safe."

Sarah narrowed her eyes. "What happened to the Alyce who called him a liar and shot fire from her eyes?"

"He might've won my trust. A little," she added hastily. Then she yawned hugely into the back of her hand. Weariness suddenly made her arms and legs feel like lead. "Extra strong tea for me this morning, dear. Oh, and get to the company store early this morning. As soon as the doors open. Make sure you buy butter."

Upstairs, Henry's heavy footfalls and coughing announced that he was awake. At some point, she'd have to tell her brother what she'd learned about Simon. He was a stranger, but an ally.

Now Sarah's eyes went wide. "Alyce Carr, what did you do?"

Despite her tiredness, Alyce smiled. "Something real and useful. For a change."

CHAPTER 7.

The news about the butter already hummed like riled bees by the time the workers made the long morning trudge to the mine. Simon wasn't surprised. With a small village like Trewyn, nothing moved faster than gossip. Especially if it involved two of the most hated institutions—the company store and the managers themselves.

"I heard that Hartley Evans hired thieves from Truro," Edgar said to the nearby men and women. "Paid them to break into the managers' place and get the fresh butter so he could finally clear his wares."

"Maybe he stole into the managers' house, himself," Nathaniel suggested.

"Nah," said another man. "Hartley's a damned muttonhead. He can rig the prices at the store like some mathematical genius, but when it comes to breaking and entering, he'd be a sodding buffoon."

"He opened the store early, too," a woman named Evelyn added. "Women were pounding on his door, wanting in. The butter was sold out in a quarter of an hour."

Several people rubbed their hands and licked their lips. "Been too long since we've had good butter," someone said gleefully. "My kids miss it something terrible. But we'll have butter with our bread tonight!"

Simon and the rest of the workers walked beneath a leaden sky, and though the dark clouds did little to dispel his exhaustion, he couldn't help the bright gleam of satisfaction within. He didn't risk a glance at Alyce, walking beside him. It'd be too easy to share a conspiratorial smile with her. It would be too easy just to smile at her for no reason at all. Or look at her because he simply wanted to.

It'd been a mistake to kiss her last night . . . or was it this morning? A mistake to get involved with someone so crucial during a mission. But the twist of it was—he didn't feel sorry at all. He wanted to kiss her again. Soon. Feel the heat of her, taste that spicy-sweet flavor of her mouth, know the strength of her will and her body.

Last night, she'd been with him through every step, every twist. Worked almost as well as any seasoned Nemesis operative—but she wasn't. She had no training, the way he and the others had. Alyce was a bal-maiden in a Cornish mining town, but her adaptability, her willingness to take risks, her clever and sharp mind—not to mention her sharp tongue—revealed someone extraordinary. But the mission always had to come first, and nothing—and no one—should affect that. He shouldn't want more of her. Yet he did, especially after last night.

Keep focused, damn it. It's for her *that you're doing this.*

"I heard the managers sent Hartley packing," a woman chimed in, bringing Simon's thoughts back from dangerous places. "Had Tippet stand in his doorway and give him thirty minutes to get his gear together, then ran him out of the village."

Edgar spat on the ground. "Good riddance. That bastard never lost a chance to cheat us."

"They'll just find another toady to mind the store," Nathaniel said darkly.

"Change might be coming." This, from Henry, who'd been silent up until that point. "Couldn't that be so, Simon?"

Simon gave a noncommittal shrug. "Lots of things could happen. Things we can't know or control." It was a little too early to play his hand.

"Maybe we've got more power than we know," Alyce said, also breaking her silence.

He did glance at her then, slightly cautioning. She might've done a bang-up job last night, but she wasn't a Nemesis agent, who knew how to keep secrets and led two lives as easily as most people led only one. A lone misplaced word, and everything could fall apart like a house made of wet paperboard.

Her mouth tightened, but she gave a little nod of understanding. A tough-willed woman like her wouldn't take easily to being told what to do. In this case, though, she seemed to understand that his experience was their key to toppling the managers and owners.

But stealing the butter had served its purpose: getting decent food into the mouths of the workers, and gaining Alyce's trust. A success on both fronts.

All the miners and workers continued on their long walk to the mine, talking of nothing except the butter and Harley's scheming. Simon kept silent, and, thankfully, so did Alyce. She'd shown herself to be trustworthy, yet she was still green.

Finally, everyone reached the mining compound and its industrial sprawl—machinery and buildings spreading like thick scabs over wounds in the earth. The smell of damp minerals hung in the air. As the men and women broke apart into groups—the bal-maidens picking up their hammers and tying on their heavy aprons, and the miners off to the change house before heading down into the pit—Alyce drew close to Simon.

He ignored the quickening of his heartbeat as she neared him. He couldn't ignore the shadowed circles beneath her eyes, though, or the squeeze of concern in his chest that she'd be working all day without any sleep.

"Don't push yourself too hard today," he said, low and gruff. "Swinging that bucking iron—you could hurt yourself."

She gave him an indulgent smile. "Today's not the first day I've worked on the dressing floor wanting sleep. I know how to keep from smashing my foot."

His nod was terse. Alyce was a grown woman, capable of taking care of herself. He'd worked with colleagues—even female operatives like Eva and Harriet—in dangerous situations, always trusting them to see to their own safety. He didn't abandon them when they were in need, but Nemesis functioned because of that mutual sense of skill and capability. Yet a strange feeling had been uncurling within him over the course of the night and morning: protectiveness.

It didn't serve Alyce and it didn't serve him or the mission to shadow her, second-guess her.

"A mine can't be won through butter," she pointed out. "There's got to be more that we can do."

"Already considered," he answered.

She raised a brow. "Are we going to play I'm Thinking of Something, or will you tell me straight-out?"

"This isn't a parlor game. Everything I do has its reasons. That goes for not revealing my plans, as well."

Crossing her arms over her chest, she said, "Convenient for you, leaving us poor peasants to just do as you command without question."

"Easy," he said in a low voice. He didn't look around, but he could feel the curious looks he and Alyce were attracting. He hoped the people nearby thought he and Alyce were only having a sweethearts' tiff. "Not now. Not here."

"When, then?"

"When I think it's safe," he answered. "I've done this more than you. You have to trust me when it comes to doling out information."

Her frustration was a palpable thing, but she finally nodded. "Be careful," she muttered.

A quick, painful contraction gripped his heart. "You, too."

Without another word, she turned and headed toward the dressing floor, joining her fellow bal-maidens.

He wanted to chase after her to say his silence really was for her protection. But he had to get to the engine house. The workday had begun.

That night, he had even more work to do. There'd be no rest for him. Not for a long while. And Alyce herself both energized him and left him with a foggy head.

In London, he belonged to a gentlemen's club and visited there often to hear the latest news and scandal. Several times, he'd found missions just by catching snatches of whispered conversations—brothels that catered to men who had a taste for children, political machinations that devastated whole communities. The club itself was over a century old, with dark wood paneling, deep leather chairs, the air scented with expensive tobacco and brandy. All conversation was kept to a polite, discreet murmur, and the servants moved as silently as liveried ghosts.

As he entered the engine house, with its clanging machines and smell of grease, he longed for a cup of his club's strong coffee. It was going to be a long, long day and another long night.

* * *

There were few horses in Trewyn. Too expensive, and nowhere to keep the animals. Most of the horses were kept by the constabulary, making the beasts even more risky to steal. It was ten miles to St. Ursula, the nearest town with a telegraph office, and Simon had to trek each one on foot.

He'd managed to catch a few hours of sleep before slipping out of the bachelor lodgings unobserved. Nothing to complain about. He'd gone three days marching through the Transvaal with only a few scraps of sleep stitched together here and there, with the fear of attacking Zulus always gnawing at the back of his mind. Soldiers had been known to snap like twigs under the terror and deprivation. Not him. He'd pushed himself until they'd reached the safety of the outpost. And then he'd slept for seven hours, and reported for sunrise muster.

The Cornish countryside in the depths of night offered fewer risks—he didn't worry that a rustling bush held warriors lying in wait. The only animals he encountered were sheep and goats, not black mambas, crocodiles, or huge, vicious hippos.

He kept his pace brisk as he passed darkened villages, other mines, farmhouses. Away from London, the sky dazzled with its lavish display of stars. Everything around him was still, shuttered. The decent people of central Cornwall were all abed.

Including Alyce. They hadn't spoken much since that morning. That had been his doing. He didn't need her for this next step. Better, in truth, that this journey was made on his own.

But, hell, he found that he *missed* her.

It didn't make any sense—he'd traveled farther on his own without problem. His mind always buzzed with ideas, from recent Nemesis objectives to pretty widows he'd met at dinner parties to the latest news from the far-flung reaches of the British Empire. A long walk in the night wasn't dull, either. He knew all the constellations, and could amuse himself for hours reciting or making up their legends. He was a man fully comfortable with being alone.

Not tonight.

Absently, he dug the heel of his palm into the center of his chest, as if soothing an ache.

He kept clear of open roads on the off chance he might meet some other late-night traveler, so he crossed open fields and dug his way through hedgerows. Lightly, he leaped over low stone walls, and climbed stiles. Finally, he saw the dark outline of St. Ursula ahead. No lights shone in any windows—but that wasn't a surprise. Even though this town was bigger than Trewyn, boasting not only a telegraph office but an actual minuscule train station, it was still a modest little Cornish settlement. No one would be awake at two in the morning.

Still, he kept to the shadows along the high street. St. Ursula wasn't a mining town, and it wore its prosperity in the form of well-paved avenues, a few shops with large, merchandise-stocked windows, three different pubs, and an inn. Nothing luxurious. Only serviceable. If he hadn't just come from Trewyn, he might've thought St. Ursula to be a slightly shabby place—but he knew better.

He finally reached his destination, and quickly picked the lock to get inside. There was a counter, and behind the counter, a large piece of equipment sat upon a table. He headed straight for it and fired the device to life. The telegraph machine looked about ten years old, far from the recent advancements made by Edison, but it would suit his purposes.

Working by the watery moonlight coming through the window, he tapped out a message. Coded, of course. But the recipients would know exactly how to read it. Just as in three days he'd receive an encoded response at the St. Ursula telegraph office.

Once he completed his task, he set everything in the telegraph office back to rights. No sense in arousing suspicion in another town.

The whole business had taken less than half an hour, but he had hours ahead of him to return to Trewyn. Hopefully, he'd be back with enough time to catch a little more sleep before the workday began. But without Alyce's presence beside him, the journey was cold, dull, and lonesome.

A knock sounded on the door just after Alyce had finished clearing the supper dishes. A quick, single rap upon the wood. She exchanged curious glances with Henry and Sarah. None of their neighbors called at this hour, and on the rare times that they did, their knocks didn't sound so . . . cautious.

She opened the door. Simon stood on the threshold, his expression serious. Her stomach knotted.

For the past three days, they'd been circling each other warily, their conversations brief but fraught with things unsaid. He kept his plans to himself. For good reason—or so he'd have her believe. Still, it gnawed at her that she couldn't be told what, exactly, he planned.

She couldn't forget their kiss, either. She'd toss and turn in bed, body and mind restless. Had the heat and desire between them been a result of the excitement of that night? Did it mean more? At least twice she had had to stop herself from marching up to the bachelor lodgings in just her nightgown and shawl, and pound on the door, demanding answers. Any answers.

These thoughts flew through her head, and she realized she'd been staring at Simon wordlessly for a good second or two. She probably looked daft.

Stepping back from the door, she tipped her head, signaling him to come inside. He did, ducking as he entered to keep from hitting the low jamb. The cold night clung to his clothing. He smelled of cool wool and man. She caught herself inhaling deeply.

She shut the door behind him. For good measure, she locked it. Only the managers and the store locked their doors. It seemed ridiculous for any of the workers to lock their doors—no one had anything worth stealing—but some enterprising builder generations ago had fitted locks into all the houses, and tonight was the first time she could remember making use of it. But the look on Simon's sternly handsome face was enough to tell her the precaution was needed.

He stood in the middle of the small room, not anxious, exactly, but filled with a restless energy that seemed to press against the walls and fill the little kitchen with his presence.

"Tea?" a nervous Sarah asked.

"That's kind of you, Mrs. Carr, but I have to decline. Business brings me here, not social calls."

"What kind of business?" Henry demanded, rising from his chair with his pipe in hand.

As Alyce leaned against the front door, Simon glanced back at her. Their gazes caught and held for a moment, before he looked away.

"This business." He produced a folded piece of paper from his pocket, then held it out to Alyce.

She took the paper, her fingers briefly brushing against his. Unfolding it, she saw it was a telegram. She herself had never received one, but Will Penrose had gotten a telegram a few years ago when his cousin had been killed in a boiler explosion working on a naval steamship. The news had been sad, but most in the village had been amazed that the accident had occurred on a Wednesday, and it had taken only a day for news to reach Will. No waiting for the post.

Not that Alyce got letters, either. Everyone she knew lived within shouting distance.

But now she focused on the telegram she held.

She rubbed her eyes and frowned down at the paper. She stared and stared, minutes going by. "The dame school we went to wasn't as fine as Harrow, but I can read, and I can't make a crumb of sense of this. All I can see is that it came from London." She held the telegram out to him.

He took it and slipped it back into his pocket. "It's encrypted. Marco came up with the code. Nemesis uses it for all our communications."

Who Marco was, she had no idea, and she didn't especially care at the moment. "Then why show it to me?"

"Because you need to know the plan's in motion."

"Ah, so now I'm allowed in on the scheme." It was difficult to keep the tartness from her voice, but, damn it, she didn't like being on the outside of things, especially if they concerned the mine or the running of the village.

He gave her a dry look that said he wouldn't rise to the bait, and a brief wave of annoyance washed over her. He was the professional here, not her. When it came to matters of justice, he was the expert—galling as it was to admit, even to herself.

"And because I'm going to need you for the next step," he added.

"I'm in," she said at once.

Everyone in the room looked at her, but only Simon's glance lingered. Then he retreated behind cool expertise. "You'll be taking a risk. A big one."

"I'm still in."

"Alyce—" Henry said warningly.

"You want your child born into poverty and corruption?" she replied.

Henry looked startled. Both he and Sarah placed their hands protectively on her swollen belly.

Doubt always clung to him, with a wife and coming baby to protect. He'd avoid risk—but Alyce had a freedom, and burden, Henry didn't. She had no husband, no children. But the village and workers . . . they were her responsibility. She couldn't back down.

"What do you need from me?" she asked Simon.

He tore his glance away from the picture Henry and Sarah presented. "The names of the most trustworthy miners. And a place where we can all meet without worrying about Tippet or any of the company's cronies finding us."

She didn't know what he planned, but the fact that he entrusted her with what had to be a crucial part of his mission filled her with satisfaction. And pleasure. All the workers at the mine knew how hard she labored for them, but only Simon treated her as if she were as capable as any man. He had faith in her.

"I can do that," she said.

Lanterns threw swinging patches of light upon the cavern walls, revealing in wild arcs stone walls streaked with red. The cave echoed with the sounds of two dozen men in heavy boots. Their voices didn't carry as far. Most of the men kept their talk to a minimum, walking in tense silence, wending deeper into the cave. Though Alyce knew these men almost as well as her own family—including Henry, who made up part of the crowd—they kept throwing her wary glances. Maybe the looks were for Simon, striding beside her. Either way, no one was at ease.

"This place is safe?" Simon whispered.

"Most everybody in the village knows about Carndale Cavern," she whispered back. "Used to be a slate quarry, but it shut down over twenty years ago. Now it's a place for being alone when you're walking out with someone. Once you get married, though, you stop coming to Carndale."

A corner of his mouth inched up. "Might get embarrassing if we run into some buck and his sweetheart getting familiar with each other."

"Even lusty lads and lasses are snug and asleep in their own beds at this hour."

"What about you?"

She lifted one brow. "I'm not in bed." She glanced down at her feet, then back up, her eyes wide. "Maybe I'm sleepwalking."

"I mean, did you ever come here?"

Now it was her turn to smile. There was a slight gruffness in his voice, belying the casual way he tried to ask his question.

"A time or two," she answered and, despite the tenseness of the situation, she almost laughed at the brief look of ill temper that crossed his face. The lantern light made him look angular, severe. "But it was always too cold down here," she added. And, in truth, it was. A damp chill clung to the stone walls like an unpleasant memory.

"You needed to find the right lad to warm you."

Oh, he was a cheeky one—*that,* she knew for certain.

"In any event," she pressed on, "the cavern's completely hidden from the village. No one knows we're here."

The stone floor sloped abruptly, but she knew to expect it, and nimbly climbed down despite Simon's offer of help. He, too, jumped down to the next flat expanse, agile as a fox. The men continued to walk ahead, casting long shadows, the gleam of their lanterns curving up the cavern walls. Everything beyond the lanterns was covered in darkness. The miners paid it little attention—all of them used to being belowground, in the dark.

Women and children weren't allowed into the mine or below the surface. Alyce resisted the impulse to wrap her arms around herself, despite the eeriness of the place. The few times she'd been here, she'd been too young and foolish to give the cave much thought, but now old legends of dark fairy kingdoms beneath the hills came flooding back to her.

She glanced at Simon through her lashes. Though he was blond, not dark, she could easily see him sitting atop a fairy kingdom throne, with that charmer's smile, those sharp cheekbones and vivid eyes. The kind of creature who beguiled mortal girls, luring them away from the hearth fires of home, never to be heard from again.

Of all the times to spin silly fantasies. She kept walking.

His hand on her elbow stopped her. "These men," he said quietly, flicking a gaze toward the men marching ahead. "They're to be trusted? None of them will run to the managers?"

"You asked me to pick the most trustworthy of the miners," she answered, "and I did. None of them are loyal to the owners or managers. They want what we want. But that doesn't mean getting them on our side is going to be a May Day fair."

"Never expected it to be. But," he added with a gleaming smile, "I can be persuasive."

She sniffed. "Don't overestimate your charm."

"I got you to say 'we' and 'us,' instead of 'you' and 'I.' That's worth something."

She hadn't even realized that she'd been doing that, damn him. But somewhere over these past weeks, especially after they'd made the theft and switch of the butter, she *had* started thinking of their cause as a united one. That they worked together as a unit rather than two individuals who happened to be walking down the same road.

The kiss they'd shared hadn't helped to keep her mind clear, either.

"I can't win them over on my own," he added. "They don't know me, not truly. There's only one way I can get the miners on board with my plan. Only one person they genuinely trust." He gazed meaningfully at her.

She started. "You mean Henry."

"No, I mean you. They know you want what's best for them, what's best for everyone. Maybe you don't see it, but I do. When the workers look at you, it's with respect. With faith. And for good reason. Because you give a bloody damn, and not many do." He drew in a deep breath, as though calming himself, quieting his voice. "They'll follow you, Alyce."

The revelation shook her. Here she'd been thinking that her rabble-rousing had been only tolerated, but now that she gave it closer consideration, she realized that there'd been hundreds of tiny instances when men and women at the mine had approached her, asking for advice. Should they press for a promotion? One of the bosses had been leaning hard on them—what should they do? All this time, she thought those questions had been typical, the kind idly kicked around like footballs. But people didn't approach Evelyn with the same questions. They didn't ask Edgar for advice.

God—had she been a leader, and never truly known it?

So strange, this odd mix of feelings: surprise, pride. Even . . . modesty. It was a hell of a duty.

He seemed to sense her wavering feelings. "Just yesterday, there was an argument among the bal-maidens about divvying and weighing the dressed ore."

"How'd you hear about that?"

"Nothing's a secret at Wheal Prosperity. I heard that they came to you to help figure out how to portion everything properly, so no one got cheated. And you did. But things like that seem to happen every week, if not every day. *You're* the one the workers respect, the one they trust. Where you lead, they'll follow."

God—the responsibility. It could crush her, if she wasn't strong enough. But she had to shoulder the burden. Hell, she'd been carrying it all this time, and remained standing.

Finally, she nodded. "I'll try to convince them. *If,*" she added, "I agree with your plan. You've got to convince me, first."

His smile returned. "Never thought otherwise. Now, we'd better catch up, before they start getting restless." As she and Simon continued walking, he asked, "Where are they heading, anyway?"

The snaking tunnel opened up, and she spread wide her arms. "Here."

The cavern arched overhead, streaked with more minerals, lit by nearly a dozen lanterns. A large underground lake filled most of the cave, shining dark as ink. Where the lantern light touched its surface, the rocky lake bed revealed itself, shallow in some places, then disappearing into the recesses of the cave like gateways to other worlds. A few empty bottles littered the ground and the bottom of the lake—testament to the lads and lasses who'd come here to escape the tight bounds of the village and their families. More than a few babes had been born after visits to Carndale.

Thank God no one had ever tempted Alyce enough to take that risk. Most of her female friends were married by now, with passels of children. Much as she looked forward to the coming of her future niece or nephew, she couldn't see herself as anyone's mother. But she'd be a good auntie. If the baby survived its first perilous months.

Pushing those dark thoughts aside, she faced the men who gathered at the edge of the underground lake. They looked warily at her and Simon.

"Why'd you bring us here?" one of the men demanded, breaking the silence. His voice echoed sharply off the stone walls, and he clapped his mouth shut.

"We're not here for a bit of slap and tickle," Edgar said, more quietly.

"No offense," Simon replied, "but you lads aren't my sort." He stared at each one in turn. "I've asked Alyce to gather you here because she tells me you're the most trustworthy men at the mine. That you aren't the managers' toadies."

"Like hell we are!" Christopher Tremaine said, then also quieted when his voice, too, echoed. "But who the devil are you?"

Alyce realized that not all of the men knew Simon—most were married and worked in the pit, and had little occasion to cross paths with him. "This is Simon," she said. "He's the new machinist. But more than that, he's here to help."

"With what?" a man asked.

Simon spoke before she could. "With the fact that, in order to talk about your jobs, you've got to hide in a cave."

The men muttered in response.

"Wheal Prosperity's changed," Alyce said. "Everyone knows it. Scraping by just to earn chit. The profits going into the owners' and managers' pockets, and none into ours. We can't even say a word of protest without fearing that the constable thugs are going to beat us senseless or drag us to gaol."

"None of this is news, lass," Christopher said. "Same as the fact that we can't do a bloody thing about it."

"But you can," Simon answered. "With my help."

"You're just a machinist," a miner retorted. "An outsider, at that."

Simon drew himself up, and it amazed her, the way he gathered power and confidence around him like a king's robe, all by the determined gleam in his eyes and standing a little taller. She'd sensed his potency when they'd been on the heist, like an electrical current all around him. Now she felt it stronger than before, and it made her pulse jolt.

He said with quiet authority, "I'm from Nemesis."

The men's muttering abruptly stopped. Complete silence fell. They stared at him, afraid, awed. Only Henry looked unsurprised by the announcement.

"*The* Nemesis?" Dan Bowden asked.

Another man chimed in. "The folks that shut down all the opium dens in East London?"

"Who freed a hundred children from a brothel?" someone asked. "And slaughtered the madam and a dozen bully boys?"

"We didn't shut down *all* the opium dens," Simon answered. "It was three unlicensed dens, and they were robbing and murdering their clients. Also, there were a dozen children in the brothel, and no one was killed when Nemesis freed them. But we did get the madam and her bully boys brought before the magistrate and imprisoned."

More silence as this information soaked in. Alyce herself was stunned. She'd heard about some of Nemesis's exploits, but clearly not all of them. What she heard now knocked her breathless. The more she learned about Nemesis—about Simon—the more she felt a strange distance. He was just a man, and yet, he'd done so much, accomplished things few others could.

"You were in the army, too," Edgar added. "In India and South Africa."

Travis Dyer, a man given to skepticism, snorted. "Next thing, you're going to tell us you were at Rorke's Drift."

"Spent most of the fighting at the mealie-bag walls. It reached the point where the Zulu were climbing over their own dead to get to us. I can show you the scar from the spear I took in my shoulder."

Alyce fought from gasping aloud. Small and isolated as Trewyn was, even she and the villagers knew of the two-day battle. Instead of a sermon, one Sunday the vicar had read from the newspaper to the congregation, telling them of the heroism of the men at Rorke's Drift. She remembered being aware of nothing but the sound of the vicar's voice, her mind trying to imagine the incredible scenes. The soldiers had faced impossible odds against their Zulu foes—nearly a hundred and fifty British against several thousand warriors—and emerged with only a few casualties, while the enemy had retreated, with massive losses on their side. Only a day earlier, over a thousand British troops had been slaughtered by Zulu warriors.

And Simon had been there. Taken part in that desperate battle. Survived.

If the men gathered in the cavern hadn't been impressed with Simon when he'd revealed his connection to Nemesis, now they were completely overwhelmed. Even Henry looked stunned. She could hardly blame him or the others.

Simon's a man, like any other. A remarkable man, but made of the same flesh and bone as any of us.

He'd kissed her hungrily, as a man, not a legend. Extraordinary he might be, but he desired her, too.

"Over the next few days and weeks," he continued, "I need you to follow my instructions. It's the only way to get things right at the mine, and make life better for you and your families."

As she expected, suspicious Travis spoke up. "You claim you're from Nemesis, and maybe you did see action in Africa, but why should we do what you say? Maybe we'll be one of Nemesis's failures."

"We don't fail," Simon answered flatly.

"Ever?"

Before Simon could answer, Alyce stepped forward. "I know you're worried, Travis. Didn't trust the blighter, either, when I first found out about him. Who was this bloke, this outsider? Yes, he might be from Nemesis, but what did that matter here, at Wheal Prosperity? If he could fool me into thinking he was just a machinist from Sheffield, what else was he hiding? How slippery a character was he?"

The gathered men mumbled, their suspicion and uneasiness riled.

"Not being very helpful," Simon muttered to her.

But she pressed on. "How many of you enjoyed fresh, sweet butter on your bread these past few days?"

Men nodded.

"Because of him," she continued, tipping her head toward Simon. "Wasn't a big gesture. It didn't change the pay system from chit to real money, but it did something else instead. It proved he's truly here to help. He knows what needs to be done in order to get our mine and village back. Besides," she added with a small smile, "it takes a slippery character to get results and bring about change. That's what he's offering us—change. And I don't know about you lads, but I'm ready for change. It starts with Simon. With us."

More quiet from the men. "They'll want to talk about it," Henry said.

Instead of arguing, Simon nodded. "Ten minutes. The longer we're out here, the more likely we are to get caught."

Henry, Edgar, and the other men gathered in a circle, their voices pitched low. Hands waved in the air, and the lanterns revealed the hard expressions of men who had to make a difficult, meaningful decision.

Alyce set her lantern down, then she and Simon edged

into the shadows. Giving the men privacy. Though she couldn't see Simon's face well, she felt him looking at her.

"If they don't agree to let me help," he murmured, "we know it's because of me. Your speech was . . . incredible."

Warmth spread through her. "I meant every word." She faced him. "You want all of my trust? You don't have it. Not all of it. However, there's one thing I do believe—you'll do everything you can to help us."

She felt him smiling in the darkness. "Suspicion is healthy. Keeps us alive."

"I plan on living a good, long life."

"That's my plan for you, too."

She started to speak, but quieted when she heard footsteps approaching. It was Henry.

"We've reached a consensus," he said.

"And?" Alyce demanded, her heart pounding.

Henry glanced back and forth between Simon and Alyce. "We're going to work with Simon. We'll do what he asks us."

Alyce exhaled, and Simon stepped closer to the ring of men.

"I've got a plan," he said. "And it starts now."

CHAPTER 8.

Simon didn't ask if the men were certain, or congratulate them on making the right choice. Hesitation now—on his part or theirs—could send the operation into a downward spiral. And the longer they remained in the cavern, the greater the possibility that someone might discover them. He pulled a piece of paper from an inside pocket in his jacket and held it out to Henry.

"I'll need each of you to sign this at the bottom," he said.

Henry took the paper and studied it. "There's nothing on it."

"But there will be. And what's going to be on that paper is going to help you win the mine." From another pocket, he fished out a pen and bottle of ink. "You can all write your names, can't you?"

Travis sniffed. "'Course we can, but we don't sign anything without knowing exactly what we're putting our names to."

Simon glanced at Alyce, looking for support. But she folded her arms across her chest. "Not an unreasonable request," she said coolly.

He bit down on his frustration and reluctant admiration. Of course she wouldn't blindly agree to whatever he proposed. It was part of what made her so maddening—and so beguiling.

"This paper," he explained, "will be part of the incorporation documents that will ensure the ownership and management of Wheal Prosperity will belong to *you*. To all of you, not the men managing the mine now, nor the owners in Plymouth."

The miners broke into excited, confused murmurs. Edgar said, "Wheal Prosperity? Belonging to *us*?"

"All policy, all decisions on the distribution of profits, everything that has to do with the running of the mine—all of it will be in your hands. Not *theirs,* but *yours*."

Alyce stared at him with cautious wonder. "How's that going to happen? None of us have the money to buy them out, and they sure as the devil won't just hand us ownership of the mine."

"Nemesis earned its reputation by making the impossible possible." At her continued look of skepticism, he said, "I've already been in touch with my colleagues in London, and we've got a plan in motion. But in order to make it come to pass, I'll need your signatures."

Everyone, including Alyce, remained where they were. No one took the offered pen.

His patience frayed. "Once, some Nemesis agents and I holed up in a Whitechapel rattrap to plan an assault against a gang leader—but we stayed too long, and his mob found us. Had to fight our way out. It's time for us to clear out of here, or you'll have much more to worry about than a piece of paper. It'd take all night for me to explain the plan. But our top people have got all the pieces in place. I'll be the one sticking my neck out in order to make everything work. You only need to sign." He stared at each man, and Alyce, in turn. "Want my help? Then trust me, and I *will* make things better for you and your families."

Another stretch of tense silence. Then Henry took the pen. He smoothed the piece of paper over a flat-topped rock on the ground, and signed his name. As he did, men queued up behind him, and, in turn, put their signatures to the paper. Once every man had signed, the pen and paper were given back to Simon.

He turned to Alyce, who had been looking back and forth between the men signing the document and Simon. Her expression was guarded—but hopeful, the desire for change plain in her face.

"You, too." He held the document and pen out to her.

She started. "Me?"

"Think of Dr. Blackwell. And women own businesses, too. Lady Olivia Xavier in London, for one. Greywell's Brewery belonged to her. Exceptions are rare, but that doesn't mean *you* can't be one, too."

Still, for a moment, she didn't move, as if too stunned. A few of the men called out their support, even her brother giving her an encouraging smile. Simon made sure to keep his own expression as neutral as possible, knowing that she wouldn't like being cajoled like a reluctant child. He simply continued to offer her the paper and pen, letting the decision be hers alone.

She took one step closer. Then another. With a look of wonderment, she took the pen and document. Crouching down next to the flat-topped rock, she signed her name, her hand moving slowly over the paper—either because she wasn't familiar with writing, or because she wanted to savor the moment. He suspected the latter. She was being given the same rights and privileges as a man, and treasured them. And he could help make that happen for her. His heart contracted, a sweet pain threading through his chest.

Damn it, this is supposed to be a job. Nothing else.

But he couldn't stop the satisfaction flowing through him as Alyce put her name on the document that would, hopefully, make her one of the owners of Wheal Prosperity.

When she finished, she brought the paper and pen back to him, her chin tipped up and pride in her gaze.

"You're the best of the lot," he whispered to her. "The one most suited to the job."

She allowed herself a small smile. "Don't want anyone to feel left out, poor lads."

An unexpected laugh burst from him, and even more warmth filled his body as she shared in the laugh. A small, private moment for Simon and Alyce alone. He hadn't heard her laugh very often. It was low and rough, like raw silk, a laugh of real pleasure rather than calculated flattery or something engineered to sound charming. Unselfconscious. Genuine.

Like her.

He slipped the paper into his jacket, careful to keep it unwrinkled. Marco would need it as smooth and unblemished as possible—though with his skills, Marco could take a wadded-up, muddy playbill and make it look as pristine as the queen's own Bible. Amazing what they taught agents of the crown. Simon was almost glad he didn't know the extent of Marco's abilities. He'd probably never turn his back on Marco again if he did.

"And now?" asked Henry.

"Now, you go about your lives, just as you have been. Change is coming, change that's going to make things rocky for a time. But I know," he added before anyone could voice concern, "that you're all strong and courageous enough to face whatever happens."

Only he heard Alyce's soft snort of amusement. She seemed to know exactly what he was doing—plying the workers with careful flattery. Still, the men needed to know what lay on the horizon, and none of them could afford uncertainty.

"Time to head home, lads." Simon waved toward the entrance of the cavern. "We'll leave singly every five to ten minutes, lanterns off, to make sure no one sees us."

He'd commanded troops before, and the men of Trewyn responded to his order like obedient soldiers. Gradually, they filtered out of the cavern, until only Simon, Alyce, and Henry remained.

"I'll see her home," Simon said.

"Hold, now," Henry objected. "I don't think that's proper."

"We broke into the managers' home and stole butter together. Not entirely proper, either, but she's safe with me."

Scowling, Alyce planted her hands on her hips. "And the *she* in question hasn't got a say in it."

He turned to her, making himself the model of courteous decorum. He could still rely on his old training as a gentleman's son. "Alyce, after your brother leaves, may I walk you home?"

Despite the dim lanterns, he could've sworn that she blushed. And though her scowl faded, she seemed careful to keep her expression aloof. "Very well."

"But—" Henry began.

Her sharp look cut him off. "I'm four and twenty, Henry. Go home."

The mulish look that crossed her brother's face was so familiar, so like her, that Simon almost laughed. Wisely, he didn't. Instead, his heart starting to pound hard within his chest, he watched as Henry picked his way back toward the entrance of the cavern. Within minutes, Simon and Alyce were alone.

It was an eerie place, the cavern, made more so now that the others had gone and taken most of the light with them. But there was a strange comfort in its oddness, its space within space, tucked into the Cornish hills. A sense of time removed from the rest of the spinning, exposed world, with he and Alyce in its hidden heart.

They now stood at the edge of the underground lake, its surface a black mirror.

"You helped," he said, "but you didn't make it easy on me."

"Why should I?" she answered. "If you can't win them over, how can I be sure you'll succeed with anything else?"

He smiled a little, and walked along the rim of the lake, as if daring any creature that lived beneath its surface to make a grab for his ankles. That had always been his way. As a boy, if he ever heard of a place reported to be haunted or inhabited by fairy folk, he ran right for it, not away.

"There's a Nemesis operative I think you'd get along with very well," he said. "Either that, or you'd butt heads so often, you'd both be lying unconscious on the floor."

"He must be a cunning, brave lad." She strolled beside him, and he saw that she'd picked up one of the smooth pebbles that lay along the edge of the lake.

"Oh, she is. Went toe-to-toe with an escaped convict and never blinked, never backed down."

"*She?*" No mistaking the edge of ice in Alyce's voice. "I mean . . . there are women in Nemesis?"

"Three, at last count. Eva, as I said, Harriet, and Riza."

"Forward-thinking for a group of vigilantes."

"We're more than vigilantes, and you know it."

She shrugged. "It makes sense. If anyone sees more than their share of injustice in this world, it's women."

"That's the damned truth of it." He kicked a rock into the water, and the wet noise it made echoed through the cave. He waited for something to slink up from the depths, but of course, nothing did.

"And this Eva," Alyce continued. "How long have you

and she worked together?" Again, a slight tightness in her voice, as if wanting but not wanting to know the answer.

"Three years or so. She's up in Manchester now, running a school and doing more of Nemesis's work up there with her husband."

"Husband?" She sounded shocked. "He lets her keep on with her dangerous work?"

Simon chuckled. "Jack doesn't just *let* her, he *helps* her. He was the escaped convict she faced off against."

"So they've both got reasons to fight for justice," she murmured. "And they do it together." She shook her head. "I never would've thought such a thing possible."

"Why not? It was you and I who handled that butter heist."

Moving away from him, she ran her hand along the wall of the cavern. The sight of her slim fingers trailing along the multicolored rock roused a dark need in him. He knew the strength of her hands, yet they had a surprising sleekness, an elegance that seemed to defy the tough life Alyce led.

"I don't know how Nemesis works," she said. "Maybe you meet in some hidden lair beneath the streets of London, guarded by passwords and clockwork devices— like they have in those adventure books that sometimes make their way to the village."

The idea that Nemesis would have enough money to fund such elaborate, fantastical mechanisms nearly made him laugh aloud. "We're just a group of men and women who meet above a chemist's shop in Clerkenwell. Nothing like you'd find in an adventure book."

She turned back to him, her lips curled intriguingly. Heat flooded him as he remembered suddenly the feel of her lips against his, and the passion she'd unleashed. The whole of this evening, he'd worked to keep his focus on the mission, not her, but she'd made it a difficult task, with the sharpness of her mind, her strength of will, and that alluring curve of her waist. His palms suddenly itched to touch her there, feel her softness and living, fiery strength.

"There you go," she said with a smile, "smashing my pretty illusions."

"I never mistook you for someone with illusions."

To his dismay, her smile faded a bit. "Aye, there's not much air for fantasies and dreams at Wheal Prosperity. They suffocate quickly in the dust."

"But we're going to change all that," he reminded her.

"We'll *try*, at least."

He shortened the distance between them, and she pressed back until she leaned against the cavern wall. He planted his hands on either side of her head. "When a mission succeeds," he said fiercely, "it's because we believe it will. No room for fatalism, or hoping. If we want something to happen, we *make* it happen."

"And no complications? No obstacles?"

"There are always complications and obstacles. But we're clever people."

"Silver-tongued, too."

He felt her gaze on his mouth, just as his own fell to her lips. Despite the coldness of the cave and its resonant damp, he caught her scent of soap and skin, clean and real. He'd seen her face in daylight and in darkness, and didn't need a lamp to know the shapes of her cheekbones, or the sharp point of her chin, or the storm of her eyes. In every way, she was striking. Time in the village, these past weeks, hadn't dulled that impression. In truth, the more he was around her, the more she intrigued him. He felt almost . . . enthralled.

"I'm going to Plymouth," he said.

She blinked at the sudden change of subject. "That's where the owners of the mine live."

"Exactly why I'm going there. With this." He patted the paper inside his jacket. "I'll be posing as a solicitor. As I said, Nemesis already has parts of this plan in motion. Now it's my turn—*our* turn—to make the rest of it happen." He tilted his head as he considered her. "How good are you at feigning illness?"

She frowned. "No idea. I'm never ill, and if there's work to be done, I do it. But I don't understand what pretending to be sick has to do with the owners in Plymouth."

"You're going to have to learn the art of malingering, and soon." He smiled. "Because when I go to Plymouth, you're coming with me."

Between his nearness and the events of the night, it took Alyce several moments to understand Simon's words. And when she did, they still didn't make sense.

"Me? Going with you to Plymouth?" She frowned. "You've been inhaling too much engine grease."

"I can't get that smell out of my head," he conceded. "But my thoughts are running as smoothly as one of the pump engines. In order for the next part of the plan to work, I'll need you with me in Plymouth."

She ducked beneath his arms and paced away. "To do what?"

"Remember how I said I was going to be posing as a solicitor? In order for the solicitor to get the current owners of Wheal Prosperity to trust me, I'm going to have to bring my wife with me."

Ice coursed through her. He'd wooed her. *Kissed* her. "You never said anything about your wife."

"Because I don't have one." He stepped closer, his gaze warm. "But I know a woman who'll make a perfect solicitor's bride. One who's got the brains and confidence to handle this ploy. I can't lie to you, Alyce. It's going to be a difficult job. A confidence game. Neither of us will be able to drop our disguises, not for a minute, and if we make the slightest misstep, say the wrong thing, then the whole plan's up in flames."

She swallowed hard. "Will it be dangerous?"

"The owners might consider themselves civilized men, but if a man's wealth is threatened, the veneer of civilization peels off like a snake shedding its skin. There's a poison adder beneath, and it'll strike without warning." He planted his hands on his hips. "I'll do my best to protect you, yet sometimes I won't be able to. But I need you for this, Alyce. I need *you*."

Wrapping her arms around herself, she considered his proposition. She'd always wanted to deal a serious blow to the owners of the mine, always knew that to do so meant putting herself at risk. Every time she went up against the managers, it was a gamble. Still, what Simon proposed went far beyond anything she'd ever considered. Disguises. Confidence schemes. Traveling all the way to Plymouth—a city she'd never visited—pretending to be, of all things, a solicitor's wife. All she'd ever been in her life was a miner's daughter, a bal-maiden. Simon could slip in and out of identities like an actor in a traveling troupe. He'd even been careful to keep his Sheffield accent when talking to the men earlier, to keep them from being too suspicious and wary.

But what did she know of confidence schemes? She'd only been Alyce.

"You could get one of those other Nemesis women to play the part of your wife," she said. "They've probably got cartloads more experience than me. Especially when we're talking about disguises and fancy schemes. I'll wager they've had training that included more than swinging a bucking iron." This was so much more than simply marching into the managers' office and voicing complaints. Far more than stealing butter under cover of darkness.

For the first time, doubts choked her, thick as coal dust.

"Alyce." Simon's voice broke through her thoughts, and she looked up sharply, seeing the clean planes of his face in the lamplight, the certainty in his gaze. "It has to be you."

Trewyn was *her* village, *her* community. No one wanted it to thrive more than she did. She had to make sure that the people and the workers were being represented by one of their own. Someone who cared about them. A woman from Nemesis might care, but not as much. How could she? This was Alyce's home. The women and men were her neighbors, her family. She wouldn't trust the fate of Henry's child to a stranger.

Don't forget your pride, a wry voice whispered in her mind. *You're too stubborn and proud to trust this to anyone except yourself. And Simon.*

She released her tight grip on her arms, and let them fall to her sides. "When do we leave?"

The corners of his mouth twitched, as if he were fighting a grin, but then he lost the fight, and he beamed at her. Suddenly, the air in the cavern became scarce.

"Tomorrow night," he said. "We'll have to sneak out after everyone's gone to bed. This isn't anonymous London, where you can come and go without anyone noticing."

"And that's why you want me to pretend to be sick."

He nodded. "Tomorrow, at work, you'll make everyone think you're coming down with a nasty case of the ague. Henry will make the excuse to the managers the next day, so you can miss a few days of work."

She wouldn't get paid for those lost days, but she'd be willing to trade scrip for tossing out the corrupt owners. "And you?"

"Edgar and Nathaniel will cover for me. I'll be rushing off to my father's deathbed."

"Without permission from the managers? You might not have a job to come back to."

"At that point," he answered, "it won't matter."

She took a step toward him. "It's a lot of faith you're putting in me."

His gaze, bright blue even in the cavern's dimness, was level. "Because I know you can do it. The miners bring the rocks and ore up from the ground, but you're the one who breaks those rocks apart and makes them valuable. Without you, they're just worthless lumps of minerals."

"That's my job," she muttered. "No different from any other bal-maiden."

"No—you've got something no other bal-maiden has. Not just physical strength, but strength here." He tapped the center of his chest. "I'd wager there's nothing you can't do, not if you want it badly enough."

Her back suddenly itched, as if wings were about to sprout there and send her soaring toward the stars.

Freedom spiraled through her. Anything she desired, anything she wanted, she could have. It was all possible.

Her gaze moved across the contours of his face. So sharply carved, those shapes, the hollows of his cheeks. His deep-set eyes. Lips that verged on too thin, but she knew from experience their feel, their softness, and their strength.

Anything, she reminded herself. *I can have anything.*

He seemed to sense her intention, even as she held herself perfectly still. The black of his pupils nearly swallowed the ring of blue around them. His breathing roughened. She took another step closer, until their bodies pressed tightly together. Simon wrapped one arm around her waist, and walked them backward to the cavern wall. She brought her hands up to grip his shoulders. He turned them, so her back leaned against the stone, and his other hand cradled the back of her head, protecting her from the rock. Heat blossomed out from everywhere he touched. She felt the broadness of his hands, their strength, the tight-knit muscles of his body against her. Coldness from the rock spread across her back. But his heat chased the cold away. She felt only him.

They inhaled together, sharing breath. And then she rose up onto her toes and kissed him. They had kissed once before. This was a new discovery—the discovery of knowing him and the anticipation of what he might feel like again. The give and demand of his mouth on hers. His taste of tobacco and coffee, and his own flavor. His need as powerful as her own. And his confidence. Here was a man who knew how to kiss a woman, and shamelessly used his skill to weaken her knees and send pulses of hunger through her.

She wasn't sophisticated, like him. Could count on one hand the number of men she'd kissed—with him among that number. But she didn't care. Cultured seductress or not, she understood the wants of her body. And feeling the thickness of his erection pressed against her belly, she understood his wants. Basic, animal.

Yet more. Even as she urged herself closer to him— her breasts growing heavy, small groans escaping from the back of his throat—she felt another pull, almost as strong as desire. He was the only one. The one man who didn't back down when she challenged him. The one man whose gaze heated when she spoke her mind.

His hand came up, tracing up the curve of her waist, then cupped her breast. She gasped, and he growled. *God.* It felt so right, so delicious. It didn't matter at that moment that he was a gentleman by birth, an agent of Nemesis, or she was a unworldly Cornish girl. Their bodies had selves beyond blood and place.

She cupped his hips with her own, but muttered her frustration at her skirts and flannel petticoats tangling around their legs, keeping her and Simon apart. He rocked into her. Bolts of hot sensation shot through her, as if someone had poured molten copper into her veins.

She growled her disappointment when his hand left her breast. But when she felt him gathering up her skirts, cool air rushing up around her legs, and then the sensation of his hand upon her stocking-covered leg, she gasped in pleasure. His large hand skimmed up her leg, over the coarse wool, tracing patterns of heat. He reached her garter, slid his fingers beneath the elastic strap to touch her bare thigh—all the while making low, animal sounds that fueled her need even more.

At the touch of his fingers to her uncovered skin, she gave a soft moan. No one but herself had ever touched her there. It was strange to have him stroking her thigh. Strange, a little frightening. But wonderful.

Suddenly, she was cold. Cold everywhere.

Her eyes blinked open, and she saw Simon standing almost a yard away. He was gasping for breath, and kept raking his hands through his hair as if needing to do something with them. Something other than cupping her breast or caressing her thigh. His expression, normally so calm, so assured, looked wild. There was no missing the long, thick shape of his erection, either—the sight both aroused and alarmed her.

"Don't stop," she managed to gasp. She reached for him, but he edged away.

"I don't always have sterling manners," he rumbled, "but I don't fuck virgins in caverns."

She started at his coarse language. "But I want you to."

He swung away. "Hell, I shouldn't touch you at all."

More coolness flooded her, then anger began to take its place. "You don't want me."

"Of course I bloody want you," he snarled. "But I

can't have you. If my brain's in my cock, I can't make sure the mission succeeds."

"I'd wager you've got enough brains for your head *and* your . . . cock." Much as she knew the rough ways and language of men, she was indeed a woman, and a virgin. She couldn't pretend to be comfortable saying words like . . . like *cock*.

"I won't imperil the mission, and I sure as hell won't put you in any danger." He turned to her. "I'm—"

"No saying 'sorry,' " she snapped. "We both wanted—want—this. We're both responsible. Nobody's at fault. And it won't happen again." Still, frustration and thwarted desire left her tight, aching, and tense.

He gave her a clipped nod, looking about as unsatisfied as she felt. He strode to his lantern and picked it up. "I'll walk you home."

"I know the way." She hurried through the caverns, hearing his footsteps echoing behind her. He called her name, but she wouldn't slow or stop.

Until she reached the entrance to the cave, and froze.

Constable Tippet stood just outside the cavern. The lantern he held cast long, leering shadows over his face. He smirked at her.

"Alyce—" Simon reached her, then also came to an abrupt stop when he saw the chief constable. A bit farther off in the shadows lurked Freeman, waiting, it seemed, for the signal to pounce.

"Lover's tiff?" Tippet smirked. "Damned shame."

"You know how irrational women can be," Simon answered, wrapping his arm around her shoulders. "Just because I said I didn't like the way she makes mutton stew—"

"It's my mother's recipe," she snapped. "If it was good enough for me and my family, it's good enough for you." Her heart pounded in her throat. Had Tippet and Freeman come by the caverns only a few minutes earlier, they would've seen all the miners or, worse, heard their plans.

Tippet chuckled. "Ought to learn better timing, Sharpe. Don't complain about a lass's cooking when you've got her horizontal. Once you get what you want, *then* feel free to criticize."

She fought a wince as Simon's fingers tightened on her shoulder.

"I'll remember that for next time," he answered.

Another chortle from Tippet. "If there *is* a next time. Better make with an apology, and quick, or you'll have to find another lass to bring to Carndale."

Alyce's own fist ached with the need to punch the chief constable right in his lecherous, smug face.

"I might," Simon replied breezily. His tone just as off-hand, he asked, "Carndale part of your usual patrol, Chief Constable?"

Tippet shrugged. "Not usually, but sometimes I come up here and give the randy kiddies a scare. Keeps 'em honest and pure. We don't want any bastard babes in the village."

Probably just wants to watch the lustful goings-on, the filthy son-of-a-bitch.

"Given my lass's dudgeon," Simon said wryly, "there's no chance of that tonight. So we'll wish you a good evening, Chief Constable. And Constable Freeman," he added.

"Evening," Tippet replied. "Better luck next time." With another lewd chuckle, he and Freeman ambled down the hill.

Neither Simon nor Alyce spoke until they were certain the lawmen had gone. Only then did she exhale. Simon cursed softly. They shared a relieved but wary glance, each knowing how close they'd come to disaster.

Or how close they'd come to making love, with Tippet catching them in the act. Only Simon's rejection had kept that from happening. Anger surged in her again.

"I'm going home," she said, her voice clipped. "Alone."

"It's a moonless night—"

"I was born in Trewyn and I'll probably die here," she answered, a biting edge in her voice. "There's not a rock or tree I don't know. Even in the dark."

"I won't—"

"Again," she said, cutting him off, "it's not your choice to make. But don't worry," she added tartly, "I'm still going to be your wife."

With that, she sped down the hill, letting the night's darkness smooth over the rough edges of her confusion.

Standing at the large oak tree at the outskirts of the village, carrying his rucksack, Simon half anticipated she wouldn't meet him that night. Yesterday evening, they'd parted . . . well, he had no idea what to think of the way they'd parted. Angry. Frustrated. Aroused. He'd had to take the longest possible route back to the bachelor lodgings, practically running up and down the hills to burn his need for her out of his body. And when he'd collapsed into bed, his hands still felt the soft weight of her breast and the satin of her thigh. His cock had continued to ache.

But privacy was in short supply where the men slept, so he'd had to try to sleep without getting a measure of self-provided relief. Not an easy night. But those had been few ever since he'd met Alyce.

He checked his pocket watch—the dented, cheap one he used when on assignment, not the Vacherin Constantin his brother had given him after he'd retired from military service. Nearly nine o'clock. If she didn't arrive soon, they'd never reach St. Ursula in time to catch the late-night train. And the longer he waited here, the greater the chance someone might spot him. He'd already given his excuse to the managers that he'd be rushing off to see his dying father. They didn't like it, but he'd marched from their offices before they could issue any threats.

Still, it'd look suspicious if he was found lingering at the edge of the village, when he was supposedly halfway to Sheffield.

He hadn't seen Alyce all day. God, had he turned everything into a damned mess by kissing her again? Or made it worse by not making love to her, as she'd wanted?

As we both wanted.

He gritted his teeth and fought the urge to pace. Pacing would only make him more visible if anyone happened to be out. So he held himself still, though he seethed with the desire to move, to act. To find Alyce, wherever she was, and kiss her breathless, feel her melt against him— though he suspected she had too much spine to melt. It would be a luscious battle the whole time, each of them fighting, pushing, and giving. Exactly the way he liked it.

Enough, idiot. The mission was ongoing. He couldn't let his thoughts wander, not for a moment, even if the path his thoughts took was awash in erotic images.

A twig snapped close by. He crouched low, blending into the tree's shadows. A woman's slim silhouette appeared from the darkness, her steps cautious. He stood.

"Here," he whispered.

Alyce emerged out of the night, wearing a woolen cloak, and carrying a small bag made from carpet pieces. Her eyes were wide in the darkness, but her steps didn't falter as she approached him.

"It's taken care of," she whispered back. "I made a good show of it at work today, coughing as if I were pounding on death's door. No one came within five feet of me. Made my throat raw, though." She did, in fact, sound a bit more raspy than usual. "Henry's covering for me for the next few days, telling everyone that I'm too contagious to go to the mine."

He nodded, pleased at how coolly and efficiently she and her brother were handling the machinations of the scheme. "Time to go. It's ten miles to St. Ursula."

Without another word, they headed off toward the other town. They trekked wordlessly beneath the star-strewn sky, crossing fields and farms and sleeping little villages. Tension silently radiated out of Alyce. She kept throwing glances over her shoulder, as if checking to make sure they weren't being followed.

"My sneaking around at night has increased three times over since I met you," she muttered when he helped her over a stone wall.

"Better than just lying in bed, waiting for the next workday to come."

He couldn't tell if her silence was one of agreement, but she didn't contradict him, either. Of the whole population of Trewyn, no one else would've agreed to help him with this mad scheme. Alyce was either reckless or courageous. Or both.

Lights finally glimmered ahead. Almost all the businesses in St. Ursula had closed their shutters for the night, but the tiny railway station was open, a few lamps burning on the platform and one in the biscuit box of a ticketing office. Three men stood on the platform—two farmers and a clerk of some kind—but they were too weary to give Simon and Alyce much notice as they approached.

Ten minutes to midnight. They'd just made it.

"Stick your hands inside your cloak," he said under his breath.

"Why?"

"Because you're not wearing gloves, and I forgot to give you a ring before we reached town." He took her bag from her, and she did as he asked, tucking her hands into her cloak.

He neared the ticketing office. It was only a wooden box

with a counter and a window, and a small stove shoved into one corner. The clerk propped his head on his fist, dozing lightly. Simon rapped on the glass. Snapping to partial wakefulness, the clerk regarded Simon and Alyce through bleary eyes. "What's that?"

"Two tickets to Exeter for me and my wife," Simon answered. He slid coins across the counter.

He felt Alyce tense beside him, but fortunately, she didn't speak.

With dull, mechanical movements, the clerk took Simon's money, then handed him two slips of paper. "Ain't no dining car on the train at this hour."

"We'll manage," Alyce said. As she and Simon stepped away from the ticketing office, she whispered, "There are two meat pies and a flagon of cider in my bag. Sarah was afraid we might starve," she added on a whisper.

"A prime woman, that sister-in-law of yours."

Genuine pleasure lit Alyce's face. "She is at that. Don't know how a dunderhead like Henry managed to trick her into marrying him."

"Must be that famed Carr charm."

"You can't see it, but beneath my cloak, I'm making a very rude hand gesture."

His laugh startled the drowsing men on the platform.

"Why—" she began.

He knew what she was going to ask. "Wait until we're on the train. It's late, so we should be able to find a carriage that's mostly empty. Then I'll tell you whatever you want to know."

She arched a brow. "That's a foolishly generous offer. I've got a lot of questions."

"Looking forward to answering them." He meant it, too. Even with his fellow Nemesis operatives, there was a certain code of secrecy among them. They all led dual existences, kept parts of themselves hidden. A strategy they'd all silently adopted as a way to keep from being completely absorbed by their work. It'd be all too easy to fall down the pit of assignments, never emerging, never knowing life beyond one job to the next. But they had to shelter themselves to some extent, or risk vanishing altogether.

Yet something inside him felt a strange . . . safety . . . with Alyce. Maybe because she was a temporary part of his life. Once he'd completed the mission, they'd part company forever, she to continue on at Wheal Prosperity, and he to the next Nemesis objective. There was a freedom in that.

But he also sensed a different kind of security with her. Her mind was sharp, constantly questioning. Nothing was assumed or taken for granted. With her, he felt . . . real. Body and mind and purpose united into a single self. He could show her both the gentleman and the vigilante. She didn't turn away, but demanded more of him.

And it stirred within him, the feeling that this job was more than a job—helping someone else, righting the wrongs against them. Every assignment held meaning, but this one . . . he needed it to succeed not just for the workers of Wheal Prosperity, but for Alyce herself.

Even . . . for himself.

The approaching train's whistle punctured the night. Alyce started as the hissing, steaming machine chugged to a stop. A few passengers staggered out, and the men on the platform hurried to board.

She eyed the train with trepidation. Alyce never looked at anything with trepidation. She probably hadn't been on a train before. Or, if she had, not that often. Whereas he crisscrossed the country several times a month. Nothing could be more quotidian.

He placed his hand low on her back, not so much for guidance but reassurance. "This way, Mrs. Sharpe," he murmured, and escorted her onto the train. They found a carriage with one man asleep in the corner, and settled into their own seats at the far end. Simon placed their bags on the brass overhead rack. Then he took the seat opposite hers. The lamps in the carriage turned her face pale. She lost even more color as the train lurched into motion.

The seating in the carriage had been designed so that a decent distance separated the knees of the passengers who faced one another. But he leaned forward, narrowing the space between him and Alyce.

"Give me your hands."

The fact that she did so without questioning him indicated how rattled she was. She slid her hands into his—they were chilled, shaking slightly. He frowned. Even when it was bitterly cold outside, she never shivered.

Jesus—she was frightened. She was taking a huge risk, far greater than anything she'd ever done. Damned courageous woman.

She looked down, startled, when he slid a plain gold band onto her left ring finger. Something contracted in his chest as he placed the ring on her. It wasn't the first time he'd gone in disguise as a married man—he'd done so half a dozen times with Eva and occasionally Riza. It shouldn't unsettle him the way it did now. But he'd never put the ring on either of his colleagues' fingers. And now, here he was, sliding a wedding band onto Alyce's hand, in a shabby second-class train carriage.

It felt . . . wrong. As if it, as if *she,* deserved better.

"This makes me your wife, now," she murmured, then added, "Temporarily."

"Temporarily," he agreed.

"Then I claim a wife's privilege." She leaned closer, her gaze flicking down to his mouth.

His body tightened in readiness, though his mind rebelled. They'd agreed not to pursue their attraction—and this was a public train carriage. If anyone spotted them kissing, he and Alyce would be thrown off for indecency.

But all those doubting thoughts dulled as he contemplated the tempting curves of her lips.

"Claim away," he said.

"Dear husband," she breathed, leaning even nearer. "You said we were going to Plymouth, so why the *hell* are we going to Exeter?"

CHAPTER 9.

Alyce carefully watched his face for the slightest hint of surprise, but he seemed perfectly at ease, damn him. Her heart was racing as fast as this awful train; she'd never gone beyond the borders of Trewyn without her family. And he'd casually slipped the bloody *wedding band* on her finger—as if being fictitiously married were something he did every day—looking as calm as a summer sky.

He glanced over at the sleeping man. When he spoke, his voice was just loud enough for her to hear him above the rattling train. "It's for the mission. We're meeting some Nemesis operatives there to help us get ready before moving on to Plymouth." He raised one elegant eyebrow. "Thought I had nefarious designs on your person? After last night?"

Her face heated as she remembered practically *begging* him to make love to her, and his refusal. "I was thrown, was all."

"I can't step off the train in Plymouth claiming to be a solicitor but dressed like a machinist. Marco and Harriet are bringing us clothing, among other things."

She looked at the cuff of what was her very best dress, worn to church, weddings, and funerals—including when

she'd buried her parents. Good as Sarah's needlework
was, anyone could see that the seams of Alyce's dress
had been mended more than once, and the merino had
grown thin and shiny in places. No one in Trewyn had
fine, new clothing. Everything had been handed down for
so many years, it was impossible to know how long a
garment had been in the family.

How shabby she and the other villagers had to look to
Simon. Like . . . like peasants.

Not once, though, had he ever looked at her or any of
them as if they were beneath him.

But she wouldn't let herself feel ashamed. Most of the
world labored for the smallest bit of bread or the possibility of one shiny, new ribbon. There was no embarrassment in working hard and having little.

"Tell me about Marco and Harriet," she said.

"How dare you say that about my parents!" he said
loudly.

"I—"

"They're not in the least bit common!"

A grumble rose up from the sleeping man. Alyce
peered around her seat. The man had awakened and now
stared balefully at her and Simon. Clearly, the passenger
wanted them to quiet down so he could go back to sleep.

She turned back to Simon. "As common as sheep in
Wales," she yelled. "And the way your mother fusses about
everything! 'Oh, dear, are you sure that's the proper way to
boil a pudding? It doesn't seem right to me.' 'Is that really
what you're going to wear?' 'Why is there always a chill
at your house?'"

"Maybe if you were more respectful—"

"Maybe if you weren't such a milksop—"

Muttering angrily, the other passenger got to his feet.
He sent Alyce and Simon one last spiteful glower before
slamming out of the train carriage.

Now that they were finally alone, Simon stretched his legs out, settling in for the trip. Despite the space between them, his legs were so long that his ankles brushed against the hem of her dress. An odd pride refused to let her shift her position and break the intimate contact.

"You play the part of harridan well," he murmured.

"It's easy when I've got such excellent motivation."

"That *was* nicely done," he said. "You transitioned to your role without a hitch. As good as any Nemesis operative."

Brief pleasure surged in her. She could do this. She was more than a woman with a hammer. Her intelligence could be a weapon, too.

"You were going to tell me more about Nemesis before we had to wake our sleeping friend," she said.

"Marco's been with Nemesis since the beginning. Four years, it's been. Back then, it was he, I, and Lazarus. Three strangers who happened to meet in a pub the night they executed William Vale." He looked at her as if expecting her to know who that was, but she only shrugged. "The news of it wasn't sensational enough to make it out to Cornwall, but it was a man's life, just the same. Vale was a low-paid clerk who'd been thrown out of his tenement by a son-of-a-bitch greedy landlord. The landlord kept raising the rent, and Vale couldn't afford it. Not an uncommon situation in London, but Vale had a wife and young son, and no place to go. And it was winter. The woman and child died, and Vale wanted restitution. Not money, but something to make up for the loss of his wife and child."

"He didn't get it," Alyce guessed.

"The police and courts wouldn't hear his complaints, so he took justice into his own hands. Tried to kill the landlord, but failed. They sentenced him to swing, of course."

She winced at the casual note in his voice, but beneath that seeming coolness, his words were edged like blades, and his eyes were hard blue shards of glass.

"The night they hanged him, I found myself in a seedy little dockside pub, drinking and getting angrier by the minute. Since I'd left the army, I'd been . . ." He glanced out the window, but there was only blackness outside, the glass reflecting pale ghosts of her and Simon.

"Lost," she filled in.

He nodded without looking at her. "There wasn't anything to come back to but parties, gentlemen's clubs, and drink. Perhaps marriage to some suitable, well-connected but meek girl and sire a line of children. Maybe go into law or medicine—but I felt too old to start over that way."

She swallowed hard, thinking of the elegant girls that had probably been paraded before him. She'd heard the gentry conducted their courtships like horse fairs, trotting out the latest fillies in hopes of landing a rich bidder. It sounded awful—for everyone.

"And," she added, "you'd been halfway around the world, fighting for your life every day. I'd think the life at home would be dull as blazes."

"Dull," he agreed. "Purposeless, too. Whenever I looked beyond the tidy gardens and marble-faced houses of my class, I saw that there were people living lives of degradation, poverty, hopelessness. Not just the poor, but all the people who'd fallen through the cracks. Shopkeepers and clerks working fourteen hours a day. Women going blind doing piecework. Girls standing alone on street corners, selling . . . selling whatever they could sell. Here I'd been to what were thought to be the most *uncivilized* places on earth, and yet I never saw as much suffering as I did in the great capital of London. Sickened me."

He caught himself, and smiled ruefully. "Get me alone

on a train in the middle of the night and I turn into a nattering magpie. You don't need to know all that dull stuff."

In truth, it was all she could do to keep from hanging on his every word, her mouth agape. This was the most he'd ever spoken of himself, and she found herself fascinated, learning things about him—not just where he'd been and what he'd done, but the hidden riches within him, like undiscovered ore, gleaming in the darkness. She couldn't imagine many men of privilege thinking about those without such advantages, or caring about them.

Yet she had a feeling if she begged him to reveal more of himself to her, he'd close up like a strongbox—and she didn't have the skills to pick the lock.

"How far to Exeter?" she asked instead.

"Forty miles."

"Not much else to do besides talk. And if I'm going to be working with the lunatics of Nemesis, I need to know more about them. You said you and some other lads met in a tavern . . ." she prompted.

" 'Lunatics'—an apt term. We didn't know each other at the time, Marco, Lazarus, and I, but drink and anger loosened our tongues. It seemed a gross miscarriage of justice that the man who'd been wronged was the one punished. The law and society had failed, so we decided we'd take matters into our own hands."

"Did any of you know the executed man?"

"Only from what the papers had told us."

She frowned. "Then why risk yourselves on his behalf?"

"Because no one else gave a damn." His hand curled into a fist that pressed tightly against the armrest. "If it wasn't us, then nobody would care."

The heat of his words startled her, as much as the feelings behind them. It was impossible to miss how much he truly *cared*. He was a gentleman. Born into the ranks of the elite. The world belonged to him and men like him. Everything was weighted in his favor. Yet that wasn't enough for Simon.

"You didn't . . . murder the landlord, did you?"

He scowled. "We never kill in cold blood."

"Not an entirely comforting answer," she said, shivering.

"Some things can't be avoided."

Logically, she knew he'd been a soldier. And one who'd fought at Rorke's Drift, where the Zulu casualties had been enormous. Simon had killed before—that was part of his job as a soldier—but to kill in peacetime, *here,* in England . . . He seemed ringed by a new shadow of danger. Not to her, but to the world at large. He had the appearance and manners—when he chose to use those manners—of a highborn gentleman. That was only one facet of a much more complex truth.

"Then tell me what you *did* do to get revenge on the landlord," she said.

He drew a breath, as if calming himself. "Marco's a government intelligence man," he went on. "Knows everything and everyone. He got us in touch with Harriet. Nobody can work a financial ledger or the numbers of a banking account like Harriet. She helped us set up a ruse. Got the landlord to invest in a sham scheme."

"And it fell apart."

For the first time in a while, he smiled, but it was a cold smile. "The bastard lost everything. His money. Possessions. Ownership of the tenement. Found himself out on the street just like William Vane. Last any of us had heard, he was begging outside Charing Cross Station and sleeping in a rented pile of straw in Whitechapel. But he could be dead by now."

He shrugged, unconcerned about the fate of the greedy man. Alyce discovered she didn't care about the landlord's fate, either, but she felt a dark satisfaction knowing he'd been punished, and that Simon and his colleagues had been the ones to make the punishment happen.

"We found a new landlord for the tenement, too," Simon added. "One who charged a fair rent. And that was Nemesis's very first mission. We didn't know it at the time, or have a name for ourselves, but we'd started something and didn't want to stop. Dealing out vengeance. Righting wrongs at any cost."

He straightened at the sound of the train carriage door opening. A weary ticket collector appeared and held out his hand.

Simon presented their tickets. The collector eyed Alyce for a moment, and, though she wanted to glare back in defiance, she made herself look at her lap like a shy wife.

"Bit late for a woman to be out," the collector noted.

She wanted to snap that it was none of his business, but Simon spoke first.

"We've eloped." Simon took her hands in his, running his thumb over her fingers, especially the band on her left hand. She glanced up to see him looking at her with warm fondness, mixed with barely suppressed desire. Heat blossomed across her face. The look seemed so genuine, exactly how an eloping groom might look at his new bride.

It's all pretend. He might want me, but that's all it is. Lust and opportunity.

The ticket collector gave a soft snort as he punched their tickets. "Enjoy these weeks, lad, for they won't last."

"It'll be different with us," Alyce heard herself retort.

"Whatever the missus says." Then the collector ambled off toward the other end of the carriage. He grunted as he pulled open the door connecting cars, and suddenly there was a loud whooshing sound and the clack of the wheels. Then the door slid shut, and the carriage fell silent again.

Simon smiled at her. "I'm glad you have so much faith in our *marriage*."

She sniffed. "Who's that old buzzard to tell us about our happiness. Maybe we'll be the happiest damned couple in England."

"For the next few days, in any case."

Right. It was all make-believe, as real as the prince and princess with tinsel crowns and a paperboard castle. She wouldn't let herself feel deflated. She could play this game, too. Like any Nemesis operative.

Even so, she kept her hands clasped in Simon's, telling herself it was because she had no gloves and his hands were so warm.

"And that's how Nemesis came to be," she said.

"Harriet's the one who came up with our name," he explained. "Nemesis—the goddess of retribution against evil deeds. It was she, too, who urged Lazarus, Marco, and me to spread the word on the street about us. Whispers here and there. Before we knew it, we had people searching us out, begging for help because no one else would. We don't take every case—it's just not possible. Haven't got the manpower or financial resources. But since then, we've added a few more members. Eva. Desmond. Riza. Jack."

"So you're not all highborn."

He laughed, and she admired the strong column of his neck. "God, no. Jack's a convict from Bethnel Green. Harriet's a clerk. Eva's parents were missionaries. Lazarus was an enlisted man for three decades. Desmond and Riza's parents taught piano and singing. Marco's father is some industrialist. Went to Cambridge, though. And he's the craftiest bastard you'll ever meet."

"What do your families think of all this? Of Nemesis."

He looked appalled. "They know nothing about it. We all keep it a secret. My father thinks I amuse myself at an office a few days a week, moving papers around and acting important but bored."

"You think he'd be embarrassed."

" 'Embarrassed' wouldn't cover it. More likely 'mortified' or 'humiliated.' He was ashamed when I decided to enlist instead of buying a commission. I can only imagine his enraged paroxysms if he ever learned about Nemesis."

She stared at him. He'd *enlisted*. Like a commoner. "But . . . if it's so important to you, I don't see how it's possible to keep something like that hidden."

"We're not exactly models of filial and paternal attachment, my father and I. I wasn't the heir, not even the spare. He left me to my own devices—and I took advantage of that. When we do occasionally meet, we're acquaintances who share a last name, nothing more."

Did he hear the chill in his voice, the disappointment? She'd never spent much time considering the lives of the highborn—why torment herself with something she couldn't ever have?—but never did she think that they could be so cold toward one another, that there wasn't . . . *love*. They had wealth and privilege in abundance, but it just hid a hollowness. A glittering shell covering nothing.

Then he laughed again and shook his head. "Clever lass. Got me to blather on about myself, when I said I wouldn't."

She offered him her own sly smile. "Maybe I'm better suited to this skulduggery than either of us figured."

"That wouldn't surprise me," he said warmly, making it sound like a compliment. "Not in the slightest."

Alyce didn't realize she'd fallen asleep until she felt someone gently shaking her. Blinking, she looked up into Simon's face—not a bad way to wake up, even if her mind felt swaddled in fog.

"Time to rise, my bride," he murmured. "We've arrived."

The train had, in fact, stopped, and she squinted out the window to see a large platform and train station beyond the glass. A sign hung from one of the girders, proclaiming EXETER.

She rubbed her eyes and struggled to her feet. Simon cupped her elbow, smoothly guiding her to stand. He took their bags down from the rack, then offered her his arm. There was hardly anyone around, and yet he continued to play the role of attentive husband. She told herself that it was just an act, and she oughtn't like it too much. Even so, a little ember glowed in her chest as they got off the train and emerged onto the platform of the Exeter train station.

It wasn't much more populated than the station at St. Ursula. A large clock suspended from the metal beams overhead showed the time to be just after three in the morning. The newsagent's kiosk was closed, as were the other shops in the station. A few men milled around, including some porters and a constable—which made her nervous for some reason.

"We've got nothing to fear," Simon said in a soothing, low voice, his breath brushing her cheek. "Just a happy eloping couple."

The constable actually gave them a smile and nod as he passed. Alyce exhaled.

"Just the same," Simon continued, leading her through the station, "let's not dawdle."

They progressed through the building until they wound up on the street. She would have wagered that no carriages for hire would be around at this hour, but the moment she and Simon stepped out onto the pavement, a little two-wheeled cab rolled up, drawn by a single horse with a driver perched at the back.

"Take you someplace, sir?" the cabman asked.

"Hotel Imperial," Simon answered. He helped Alyce into the cab, his hand steady on her waist, then placed their minimal luggage on the floor of the carriage before settling himself in and shutting the door. As soon as he'd taken his seat, the driver snapped the reins, and they were off.

"Don't know how you managed to find a hired carriage at this time of night," she murmured.

"Eva thinks I'm blessed by the god Cabicus. I just have to step into the street, and suddenly, hansoms and hackneys appear."

She didn't doubt it. An air of possibility clung to him— that if he wanted something, he simply willed it into being.

But she didn't say anything, conscious not only of his thigh pressed against hers, but of the strange city they drove through. It was late, the streets almost empty, but the gas lamps were still on, revealing the storefronts and fenced parks. Exeter may as well have been on the other side of the world. It was so much bigger than any other place she'd been to, with orderly paved streets, shops after shops, signs announcing important businesses. The buildings had imposing stone fronts, some with elegant arches, balconies with wrought-iron railings.

She couldn't stop herself from gasping aloud when they passed the most magnificent building she'd ever seen. She nearly fell out of the cab as she strained to take it all in.

"Exeter Cathedral," Simon explained. "Driver," he called up, "slow down for a moment."

She braced her hands on the edge of the cab window and stared. There were fancy words to describe the different parts of the cathedral, words she didn't know, and didn't care to know. But the elaborate flowerlike central window, the rows and rows of holy figures standing imposingly above the door, the soaring towers—all of it left her awestruck.

"How old is it?" she asked.

"I think the final building, this one here, was built around 1400. Not much of an Exeter historian, so I don't know more than that."

"They made all this without modern tools." She shook her head. "The things faith can move us to do."

"Madness or inspiration," he said quietly. "There isn't much difference between the two." He rapped on the side of the carriage, calling up to the cabman. "Drive on."

"Thank you," she murmured as they drove away.

His brows rose. "For what?"

"Stopping the cab so I could get a better look when we're short for time."

He smiled softly. "I'd make a poor guide if we came to Exeter without viewing the cathedral."

Her lips curled. "No doubt you think I'm a terrible rustic, gawking at everything."

"Never put words in my mouth or thoughts in my head," he said with surprising heat. "I don't believe that at all. You've lived your whole life in a small village. Why would I expect you to be unimpressed by an old and beautiful cathedral? Intellectual curiosity—that's the most important thing. You know who's bored or jaded? Narrow-minded dullards. Don't need that kind of person around. I'd be worried if you *didn't* care."

He fell silent, and she wondered if she'd struck a sore spot. Remembering how he'd described his upbringing, she thought he was probably encouraged to act just that way—uninterested, cynical, world-weary. Yet Simon was anything but those things. And he had probably been rebuked for it.

The cab rolled on for a few more minutes through the streets of Exeter, occasionally passing men and women pushing carts, a lone man out by himself, or dustmen already making their rounds. The buildings grew finer and finer, and Alyce more and more uneasy, until the cab pulled up in front of a three-story building with a grand red and gold awning, and brass banisters on either side of its carpeted front steps.

"Hotel Imperial," the driver called out.

Simon hopped out of the cab, paid the driver, and handed Alyce down to the curb. After grabbing their bags, he offered her his arm. She took it and together they went up the steps. Through the glass doors, she saw the lobby of the hotel, its floor thickly carpeted, plush armchairs near a white stone fireplace, even tall plants in big Chinese vases. No wonder they called this place the Hotel Imperial. It looked like an emperor's shiny palace.

The gaslights had been turned down to burn low, and when Simon tried the door, they discovered it was locked. He pressed a little button by the door. Within seconds, a man in a sleek suit appeared.

The man's ready smile faltered when he looked at Simon's and Alyce's clothing. He paused in the act of unlocking the door.

"Can I help you, sir?" the man asked through the glass.

Despite his workman's clothing, Simon stood tall and spoke with his gentleman's voice, polished and clipped. "The Blaines are expecting us."

The manner of the man behind the door instantly changed. He quickly unlocked the door and waved them in. "Of course, of course! Can I get you and your wife anything? Some tea for the lady? Something a little stronger for you, sir?"

"Just the Blaines' room number," Simon answered.

"Number 302," was the reply. "If you like, you can

ascend in our elevator." The man gestured proudly toward what looked like one of the cages used to send miners down into the pit, except this metal box was sparklingly clean and covered in brass scrollwork.

"We'll take the stairs," Alyce said.

"As you wish, madam. If you just give me your bags, I can show you up."

"That's not necessary." Simon pressed a coin into the protesting man's hand, and the protests quickly faded.

"Have a pleasant evening," he said after pocketing the money. Then he backed out of the lobby and ducked behind a swinging door, smiling all the while.

Alyce glanced at Simon. "I'm starting to see the benefits of being a part of Nemesis."

"It's not all smart hotels and obsequious servants," he said, climbing the stairs.

She followed, eyeing the pretty framed pictures on the wallpaper-covered walls, the vases of fresh flowers on tables at each landing.

"Most of the time," he continued, "we're stuck in rented, smelly carriages for surveillance, crouched in alleyways, and hunkered in dark, rat-infested hovels."

"You need to work on your recruiting skills."

He stopped and faced her. Standing on a step higher than her, he looked even taller, more imposing. His expression was grim. "This is a one-time mission for you, Alyce."

"I know that," she said quickly, fighting to keep her cheeks from turning red. Hard not to feel like a chastised child when he spoke to her like that, damn him.

He took several steps down, so that their eyes were level. "Nemesis keeps its numbers small for a reason. The work is dangerous, and only meant for people willing to devote their lives to it. You're here for one purpose, and when that's done, we all go back to where we came from. You go back to an improved life."

"That's all I want," she fired back. She glared at him. "What are we quarreling about?"

He grinned suddenly. "Hell if I know. Lack of sleep, I'd wager." He tipped his head toward the ascending stairs. "We've got people waiting for us."

As Alyce followed him up the steps, her heart began to pound, as if she were about to meet his family for the first time.

In a way, I am.

They finally reached the third story, and Simon stopped in front of the door marked 302. Instead of knocking, however, he scratched his fingers against the door in a pattern. One long scratch, then two short, then another long.

Footsteps muted by carpet sounded on the other side of the door. And then more scratches, this time from inside. Three short, one long. Simon answered with another pattern.

The door unlocked and was pulled open. Standing on the other side was a man with olive skin, black hair, and a neatly trimmed goatee. Aside from Simon, Alyce had never seen anyone with such perceptive eyes, as if he could pick a lock simply by looking at it. He held himself light on his feet, and if it weren't for his expensive-looking dark suit, she would've sworn he was an athlete. His shoulders were broad, his limbs long and powerful.

Standing just behind him was a woman of middle years, striking in her appearance. Her skin was darker than the other man's, a light brown that suggested she had mixed blood, and the sleekness of her hairstyle didn't quite hide the slight kink in her hair. Her eyes were pale, however, and in the lamplight, sharp as cut agate. She had an air of biting intelligence and capability.

Neither of them were people Alyce would ever want to cross.

Nemesis.

* * *

Though Alyce's first instinct was to move back when the olive-skinned man stepped aside to let her and Simon into the room, she walked inside. Both members of Nemesis watched her like falcons as she moved farther into the room.

"Any trouble getting here?" the man asked Simon.

"None. A damned easier train ride than when we dealt with Dalton."

Alyce glanced around the hotel room, as cautious of the luxury as if it could bite her. The chamber in which they now stood appeared to be some kind of sitting room or parlor, with a fine mahogany desk, upholstered chairs and a sofa, and its own fireplace. A door joined the parlor to a bedchamber, and from what she could see of it, it contained a large brass bed and painted wooden cabinet. If she'd been able to take the two rooms of her house in Trewyn and lay them side to side, they'd be dwarfed by this hotel suite.

But the hotel rooms interested her far less than the people in them. She was having her first look at other Nemesis operatives. What she'd heard wasn't just words and stories. It was as solid and genuine as her own flesh. Besides Simon, there were these two others, at the least. He had mentioned many more names on the train.

Nemesis is real, and for now, I'm part of it. Part of them.

They shared Simon's intense perceptiveness—the kind of people who had seen and done much. Never had she felt as unworldly as she did just looking at them across the hotel room. Their gazes were wary as they studied her, and she felt like one of the tunnels in the mine, as if she were being chipped apart to see what she was made of.

No hope for it but to brazen it out.

"Alyce Carr," she said, stepping forward with her hand outstretched.

The olive-skinned man took her hand first and shook it. Unsurprisingly, he had a strong grip. "Marco," he answered.

"Just Marco?"

"Last names can be cumbersome." He released her hand.

She nodded, understanding. Simon had withheld his, as well. She was the outsider on this mission, the unknown element. They would likely give her just as much information as she needed to get by, and no more. For the sake of the mission—and probably her own safety.

The woman came forward next, and shook her hand. Another strong, confident grip. Alyce noticed there was no wedding band on her left hand. They were an unconventional group. But she didn't expect otherwise. "I'm Harriet," the woman said. She boldly looked Alyce up and down, staring at her body in a way that made heat fill Alyce's cheeks—either from embarrassment or anger or both. Not even the freshest man in her village looked at her like that.

"They've got French postcards for that kind of thing," Alyce snapped, pulling away.

"She's getting an idea of your measurements," Simon said. It was the first time he'd spoken since they'd entered the hotel room. "I'd given her as good an idea as I could, but she's the one who'll be making the adjustments."

"You didn't make too poor an assessment," Harriet responded. "The alterations should be minimal." She walked to a trunk Alyce now saw propped in the corner and opened it. Dresses of every color and fabric were neatly folded inside—all of them far finer than anything Alyce had ever worn. And the mission meant she'd have to wear some of them. The thought shouldn't excite her as much as it did.

Wait.

She spun to face Simon. "You told her my *measurements*?" God, he would've had to study her body. Or, hell, when they'd kissed, he'd gotten a good feel.

The intimacy of it robbed her of breath. Partly, she felt acute mortification. Harriet and Marco could probably guess how Simon had gotten such knowledge of her. But she didn't regret Simon touching her.

Simon shrugged, but she could see a flash of something, a memory, perhaps, of when they'd kissed, in his gaze. "I did the best I could without the benefit of a measuring tape."

"I also brought some suits for you," Harriet continued. "But those I took from your flat. No alterations necessary." She even produced two hatboxes. Lifting the lids, she revealed a daytime hat of fine dark brown wool. The other box held an object that struck a bolt of fear into Alyce's heart: a black silk top hat. That could mean only one thing—at some point soon, they'd be attending a formal gathering.

Bold front, she reminded herself. She'd be crushed beneath Nemesis's elegant, ruthless boots if she showed any fear or hesitation.

"There's not much time," she said brusquely, slipping off her woolen cloak. "Time to get to work." Her fingers went to the buttons at her throat. Marco made a choked sound, but Simon rushed forward, gathering up her cloak as if to cover her with it.

"We'll take this into the bedroom," Harriet said. She ushered her to the adjoining room.

Alyce's cheeks heated again. "Right," she muttered.

Harriet returned to the parlor for a moment, leaving Alyce alone in the bedroom. The Nemesis operatives talked quickly and softly among themselves—too quietly for Alyce to understand what they were saying. But it seemed a practiced kind of talk, the kind perfected over years of knowing and working with one another. The way in which she and the other workers at the mine spoke—people she'd known her whole life—in a sort of shorthand that would confuse outsiders.

She had never felt as much of an outsider as she did at that moment. Moving as silently as she could, she peered through the bedroom doorway to see the three members of Nemesis conferring in a close circle. Clearly, they knew each other well. Trusted each other. Even though Simon's expression was taut, he looked entirely confident there, among his comrades, no longer pretending to be a machinist. Oh, he'd been open and candid with her—at least, she thought so—but Harriet and Marco were his people. She'd only ever be a stranger.

Then Simon looked over at her. Their gazes locked. All sense of being on the outside burned away. She wasn't one of Nemesis's trained agents. Her knowledge of Simon went back weeks, not years. But the way he spoke to Marco and Harriet held a kind of distance. They were colleagues. Not entirely friends. They held back from one another.

She'd bet a month's wages he'd told almost no one what he'd revealed to her on the train. That it was intimate knowledge for her and him alone. And it was still there—the heat between them. They could try and push it aside as much as they liked, tell themselves they wouldn't act on it for the sake of the mission, but just because you didn't mine a bountiful vein didn't mean it stopped existing. The promise of its riches might be buried, yet it remained.

Harriet suddenly stopped talking. She glanced back and forth between Alyce and Simon, expression unreadable, but Alyce had a good idea what the other woman thought.

Let her think what she likes. I've got a purpose on this

mission. I'm the only one here with a personal stake in it. Alyce's stake couldn't be more personal. Whatever altruistic goals Nemesis had in changing Wheal Prosperity, they couldn't match her own motivations.

"Don't we have work to do?" she asked, summoning her most lofty tone.

Harriet lifted a brow. "Chaps," she said, excusing herself from Simon and Marco.

The other woman entered the bedroom and shut the door softly behind her. It was the first time Alyce had ever been alone with a Nemesis agent who wasn't Simon. Harriet waved toward a small door. "There's a sink and water closet if you need to refresh yourself, and I've got a pot of tea and some sandwiches." She nodded at a little table that held a tray with a completely unchipped tea set, plus a plate of crustless sandwiches, the bread so white Alyce could've written on it.

An odd, contrary impulse demanded that she refuse all these offerings—pride, maybe. That she wasn't just a simple country lass to be coddled her way through a mission. But Harriet spoke without a speck of pity or even warmth. As one might talk to a fellow worker. That comforted Alyce much more than soft words and sympathy.

She nodded and went into the bathroom. It held a large iron tub, a flushing commode, and a sink with running water. After making use of the facilities and washing up, she studied her face in the mirror mounted above the sink. For a woman far from home, awake in the middle of the night, surrounded by strangers, and about to embark on the most dangerous activity of her life, she had to say that she didn't appear too poorly. Her eyes were clear, her skin not too ashen. Harriet might have a natural poise, and Marco the suave elegance of a panther—and Simon was always sharply, aristocratically handsome—

but she had nothing to be ashamed of. The color in her cheeks came from honest work.

She glanced down at herself. Compared to Harriet's smart traveling costume, Alyce's dress looked faded and shabby. Yet she was a bal-maiden. She'd never smashed apart a lump of copper ore to discover a bolt of expensive sateen inside. And the only fashion journals that reached Trewyn were years old, tattered to the point of being unreadable—and the clothes within them as obtainable as fashions from Mars. What use would she have of a . . . what did they call them . . . a promenade costume?

"Miss Carr?" Harriet asked from outside. "We've got several gowns to alter, and not a lot of time, so we need to get started."

At that word—"gowns"—Alyce's stomach leaped. In a day, maybe even in a few hours, she'd be meeting the owners of Wheal Prosperity. She would know them, but they'd have no idea who she was—or what they were up against. This would be her one chance to *not* be a bal-maiden, and despite her fear and the looming danger, she was determined to enjoy every damned minute of it.

CHAPTER 10.

"You're sure we can trust her?" Marco asked for the fourth time.

"She's green," Simon answered, "but I trust her as much I trust you." Hands in his pockets, he stopped his pacing and stared at the bedroom door, straining to hear the sounds of the women inside moving about.

Bent over the sheets of paper, his pen moving slowly but methodically, Marco shook his head. "Always thought you were a damned idealist."

"It's my fatal curse and eternal blessing. How're the documents coming?"

"They'd be progressing faster if you'd shut your gob and let me work."

"You're the one who keeps asking about Alyce."

"And you're the one who keeps staring at that door as if you could burn it down with your eyes."

Simon clenched his jaw. Herein lay the problem with observant colleagues. "Keep forging. That's what you do, isn't it? Fabricate things?"

As Marco got back to work, Simon paced over to the window and looked out through the curtains. The room faced the street, so he could distract himself with the comings and goings of people on the avenue. Trouble was, it was early as hell, and the distractions were minimal. The Hotel Imperial was located in a relatively genteel part of town. No late-night mischief on the street to keep his mind from wandering into the bedroom—where Alyce and Harriet were sequestered, fitting Alyce with an appropriate wardrobe.

He wouldn't think about Alyce stripping out of her petticoats, down to her combination. The lamplight on her bare limbs. The exposed curve of her neck and slopes of her shoulders.

No, he wouldn't think about any of that. He'd enough to stew over—such as whether or not this gambit was going succeed, or whether he and Alyce would be caught in the middle of it, and everything would go up in flames. There was always a risk to himself, but it was she and the miners that worried him. Far easier for him to walk—or slip—away from a disaster. But Alyce, her family, Edgar, all the men and women he'd come to know over the past few weeks—they'd be the ones to suffer if it all went south.

"Jesus, I can hear you thinking," Marco muttered. "It's like a rusty gearbox."

"As opposed to the smooth, glassy waters of your brain," Simon fired back over his shoulder. "Not even a ripple to disturb the surface."

After setting his pen down carefully, Marco linked his fingers behind his head and studied Simon. "Four years we've been doing this together, and I've never seen you like this."

Simon turned around and folded his arms across his chest. "Like what?"

"Like you're about to kick the walls of the hotel down. This mission's a tough one, no denying that, but you're strung taut. The wrong word, the smallest look and"—he snapped his fingers—"you'll explode like mercury fulminate."

"Of course I'm tense, you ass. Hundreds of people's jobs are at risk. Their lives, too, if things go disastrously."

"And it's got nothing at all to do with . . ." Marco flicked his gaze toward the bedroom door.

Simon stalked the perimeter of the room. Right cozy, it was, and the closest he'd come in weeks to the normal way he lived in London. But he didn't feel at ease or have any sense of respite. Just more tension, all contained within the floral walls of the hotel room's parlor.

"You don't have to worry about me," he growled. "I'll keep my focus. I'll get the job done. She won't affect my judgment."

Marco snorted softly.

"The hell?" Simon demanded.

"Didn't you give Eva a similar warning about Dalton? And she said the same thing in response."

"That mission was a success. Rockley wasn't just ruined, he was killed."

Marco smirked. "There was also that very interesting side effect that Eva and Dalton got married."

Simon forced out a laugh. "Christ, Marco, there's no need to worry on that score. I'm as likely to marry as you are."

A dark look crossed Marco's face. "Spies don't make for good husbands."

"Neither do scapegrace younger sons with secret tendencies toward vigilantism." Even if he hadn't been a part of Nemesis, Simon would have relegated himself to permanent bachelorhood. A wife meant a life of predictability—employment, meals, conversation covering well-trod ground. Wives wanted children, and children needed stability—even the wild ones like him. Stability, predictability. Those things were poison in his blood.

Ironic, then, that the one aspect of marriage he knew he could honor was fidelity. Once given, he never went back on a promise. It might be expected that men of his class kept mistresses, but the thought of making a vow and then deliberately breaking it made his stomach roil. What was he, if he didn't honor his word? As feckless and useless as any other younger son. In that, he'd prove his father wrong.

It didn't matter. Simon wasn't marrying, so vows of fidelity never had to be sworn.

But he wondered about men like him and Marco. Deliberately alone. Not short on female company, but neither of them possessed what Jack had with Eva. A partner. In every sense of the word.

That was the singularity, not the norm. He was an adult man who'd seen a good deal of the world. It was a cold place, filled with cruelty, loneliness, yearning. No reason why his life would be any different. The best he could expect was completing missions for Nemesis, and dying either quickly from a sharpshooter's bullet in his brain, or of old age in a clean, warm bed—alone.

Despite all the battles he'd waged—in India, Rorke's Drift, jobs for Nemesis—he'd never truly taken up his own cause, fought for himself. As though he didn't deserve it. His only real purpose was to help others. But he, himself, held little value.

Yet a voice whispered seductively within him. *The story might have a different ending. You've never met a woman like Alyce before. When she looks at you . . . you're not a hero or a scapegrace. But a man. A man worth fighting for.*

The bedroom door opened and Simon whirled around. Disappointment was a ball of lead in his chest when he saw it was only Harriet.

"How many gowns is she going to need?" Harriet asked.

"Three. Two suitable for traveling and visiting, and one for dinner."

From somewhere in the bedroom, Alyce cursed softly. "You didn't say anything about dinner."

Simon smiled to himself. "It's the last meal of the day. Roast meat is usually served."

Harriet grunted as Alyce shouldered past her and stalked into the parlor. Alyce didn't seem to notice that she was wearing only a corset, a corset cover, and petticoats, leaving her arms, neck, and upper chest all bare and shockingly creamy. But Simon noticed.

He shot a quick glance over at Marco. Sophisticated as Marco was, even he stared at a partially dressed Alyce, his pen hovering over the paperwork.

"I know what dinner is," she snapped. "I didn't know it was part of the scheme."

"We'll have to dine with the owners at one of their homes to make sure that everything goes according to plan," Simon explained. He had an urge to tear the crocheted throw off the back of the sofa and cover her with it, or perhaps punch Marco for daring to look at her. He also wanted to stare at her for hours. Not once would he have suspected that she had a tiny, caramel-colored beauty spot just above her collarbone, as if her Maker had very helpfully indicated an excellent place to kiss her. "This isn't going to be a problem, is it?"

"Unless rich folk eat with their toes, I can manage a fancy meal," she answered. "No need to worry I'll embarrass you."

"That's never a worry."

"What about her accent?" Marco asked. "It's pure Cornish village."

"Not only dresses can be altered," she replied.

Everyone started, for the rough edges of her natural

accent had softened, the *r*s becoming gentler, the *t*s more firmly pronounced.

She smirked at the shocked expressions on their faces. Continuing in the same, more refined tone, she said, "I've heard the managers speak hundreds of times. Quite easy to copy, really. And I've done it a few times. Give the other miners and bal-maidens a good laugh when I ape the managers. 'We shan't take any more of your impertinence, Miss Carr. You are a discredit to your sex.'" She placed her hands on her hips, clearly—justifiably—proud of herself. The movement highlighted the bareness of her arms.

Simon had felt the strength of those arms before, but never seen them uncovered. Though her skin was smooth and milky, little curves of muscles adorned her biceps and triceps, and more muscle shifted beneath the skin of her shoulders. This was not a weak woman.

He respected the mental and physical strength of the women in Nemesis, but their potency never stirred him the way Alyce's did. She would—and had—matched him. Word for word. Step for step. Pushing him back when he pushed. A clash like that, between two people who never backed down . . .

Heat settled in his groin.

Stop it, he snarled at himself. *Doesn't matter how much I want to run my mouth over her shoulders. Or hear that note of challenge in her voice.* As far as he was concerned, he was an astronomer and she a distant star.

Harriet surveyed Alyce's arms critically. Alyce jerked back when Harriet gave her bicep a squeeze.

"Good thing I brought long gloves," Harriet said, and clicked her tongue. "We're going to have to cover these."

Alyce's eyes widened when she finally realized she was wearing only her underclothes and standing in a room with two men who were assuredly not related to her. She spun on her heels and hurried back into the bedroom. Harriet followed, closing the door behind them.

"Intriguing woman," Marco murmured, "your Miss Carr."

"Shut up and keep forging," Simon answered.

He watched the icy sun crest the Exeter skyline, glazing the façades and rooftops with pale light, but hardly breaking through the wash of clouds and haze that hung over the city. Streetlights were turned down. Shopkeepers appeared at their front doors, stamping their feet in the chill as they unlocked the entrances to their businesses. Young maids of all work in coarse woolen cloaks hurried down the street so they could light the fires and have tea ready for their masters and mistresses. Men and women pushed carts stacked with rags, or bottles, or fish, or cheese. A thin boy with a broom stood at the street corner, ready to sweep or hold horses, in the hope of a coin or two.

Morning in any city in England.

Even here, in this university town, he didn't doubt Nemesis was needed. Girls were trapped in brothels. Laborers weren't paid for their work. Wives felt the brutality of their husbands' anger and fists. But Nemesis couldn't protect everyone, couldn't bring to justice all who'd done wrong.

He braced his hands on the window and stared out at the street. "There are too few of us. And it never stops."

Marco's pen continued to scratch across paper. "There's an Italian saying: *Chi non fa, non falla.*" His mother's language ran smoothly from his tongue. "'Those who do nothing, make no mistakes.'"

Turning around and leaning against the sill, Simon asked, "You go to sleep every night, content that you've done all you can?"

"I'm never content." Marco didn't look up from his

work. "None of us are. If we were, we'd be morons. Or government employees."

"You *are* a government employee."

"My name doesn't appear on any payroll. I'll never receive commendation, official or unofficial. And spies have terrible pension plans."

"So you're a moron," Simon said, grinning.

"Oh, quite." Setting his pen down with finality, Marco stretched his neck and cracked his knuckles. "A talented one, however."

Simon approached the desk. He let out a low whistle when he saw Marco's creation. "That should be framed and displayed at the Royal Academy."

Holding up the document, Marco sighed. "It quite breaks my heart to part with it."

"But for a good cause."

The door to the bedroom opened, and Harriet came out. "Did I hear that our masterpiece is ready?"

"You did indeed," Simon confirmed. "And what of your own handiwork?"

"That's finished, as well. Alyce?"

The woman who emerged from the bedroom was entirely Alyce. Same sharp features, same clear, direct gaze, same straight-backed posture. But her hair had been dressed in a sophisticated chignon rather than a plain bun. Small pearls adorned her earlobes—the first time Simon had ever seen her wear jewelry aside from the faux wedding ring. Her old wool dress had been replaced by a slim, stylish traveling gown of dark green moiré trimmed with gray velvet, and a flare-waisted bodice snug around her curves. She rustled as she stepped into the parlor, the result of her petticoat and bustle.

He'd never seen her in a bustle before. Fashionable as she looked, he missed being able to see the sway of her hips and her natural shape.

"Well, *I* think it's lovely," she said, smoothing her hand along her skirts.

He realized he must have looked a little disappointed because she wore a bustle. "It is. You are."

"You've made your own—what's the word for it?—metamorphosis." Her gaze traveled up and down him, her expression midway between appreciation and caution.

While Marco had been busy with his forgery and Harriet had altered a wardrobe for Alyce, Simon had donned one of his own suits. The gray wool with a burgundy silk waistcoat wasn't an especially lavish ensemble—he was supposed to be a solicitor, after all—but compared to his coarse machinist's clothing, he knew he looked a damned sight more modish. These clothes had been custom-made, and the gentleman in him secretly reveled in the excellent fit. He didn't miss his heavy work boots, either, liking how the lamplight gleamed on the fine leather of his short ankle boots.

He'd also put a bit of macassar oil into his hair and combed it back, as well as given himself a fresh shave using a basin and ewer.

"Is this your natural state?" she asked.

"I have no natural state."

"Nobody's more unnatural than Simon," said Marco.

"And nobody's more fond of his own voice than Marco," Simon replied. "Which is a shame, because he brays so, like an Italian donkey."

"Asino," Marco corrected.

Harriet gave a very unladylike snort, which she didn't appear to regret at all.

But Alyce wouldn't be distracted by their badinage. "The truth, now," she said, unsmiling. "Is this how you usually dress?"

"Depends on the hour of the day, where I am, the occasion. I wouldn't wear this after six o'clock in the evening, and never to the races. Or the country." He took a step closer. "But I also wear a navvy's tattered jumper or the filthy apron of a man who works in the stockyards. Whatever the mission dictates." He shook his head. "They're only clothes. None of it matters, compared to the person wearing them."

She glanced down at her dress, her hands hanging at her sides as if ready to pluck the gown from her body. "This feels strange. I feel like I'm being crushed."

"That's the corset," Harriet said.

But Alyce shook her head. "No, it's as if I'm not myself."

"It's a costume," Marco said. "We wear them all the time, just as Simon said."

"You'll be playing a role," Simon added. "But it's still you underneath all this. Some moiré and velvet doesn't change that."

This made her smile. "Of course you know the special names for these fancy fabrics."

He shrugged. "I speak English and aristocrat. Only one of those languages makes actual sense."

"Ladies and gentleman," Marco broke in impatiently, "if we're done playing *Myra's Journal of Dress and Fashion,* I have to catch a train back to London in the next thirty minutes." He stood and pointed to the document on the table. "I've used the signed paper Simon gave me to create the corporation for the miners."

"Is that legal?" Alyce asked.

"It'll hold up in a court of law," was Marco's elliptical answer. "You see that you've signed to become a member and representative of the corporation."

She bent closer, studying the paper. "So I did. Didn't know it at the time."

"Simon can be . . . opaque . . . at times," Harriet said wryly.

"Transparency is for people with nothing to hide," he said. "And we all have something to hide."

Marco cleared his throat, clearly annoyed. "The tour's almost over and the boat's returning to shore, so everyone, *basta*." He produced a leather portfolio and pulled out more documents. "These are the papers that the mine's current owners will sign."

"Transferring ownership from them to the miners' corporation," Simon added.

Alyce frowned. "There's no reason why they'd do that."

He smiled, feeling the electric anticipation of a good hunt. "We'll give them a reason."

Marco dashed off soon after, and Harriet helped pack up the trunk containing their clothing for the next few days.

"Mind," she said, pointing at Simon, "in Plymouth, you'll have to get one of the hotel's maids to help Alyce dress. She can't get in and out of these things on her own."

Alyce pressed a hand into her waist, glowering. "No woman would cheerfully lace herself so tightly. I swear this corset's crushing my innards into mash."

Simon could only offer a sympathetic grimace. "Never worn one myself." But he'd removed his fair share, and they seemed like elegantly designed torture implements. Women always gasped in relief whenever he'd peeled their corsets off. He'd never understood why anyone would willingly subject themselves to that kind of pain. But then, most women didn't have a choice.

"If men had to wear corsets," Alyce said darkly, "they wouldn't exist."

"Truer words were ne'er spoken," agreed Harriet. They both glared at Simon as if he personally had decreed that women must be subject to steel cages wrapped around their torsos.

"Our train leaves shortly," he said.

While they packed, they discussed the plan for when they arrived in Plymouth. The scheme was complex and as winding as the tunnels of Wheal Prosperity—and fraught with just as much darkness and peril. Fortunately, he and the rest of Nemesis knew their way around in the dark. Only Alyce remained the untested element.

Once the final details were outlined, they were able to finish packing and clear out of the hotel room with a minimum of trouble. Simon donned his hat and overcoat, and Alyce wore a smart little ribbon-trimmed hat as well as a dolman coat. In the mirror, they looked the very picture of upper-middle-class respectability. Reflections of people neither of them were—which pleased him.

A porter brought their trunk down, and the concierge hailed Simon, Alyce, and Harriet a hackney for the ride back to the train station. All the while, Simon kept a careful gaze on Alyce. She held herself with straight shoulders and, despite her complaints about the corset, showed no visible discomfort. She even easily navigated the tricky business of sitting in the cab while wearing a bustle—though she confessed Harriet had shown her the proper way to sit when a strange metal cage was strapped to one's backside.

"Fashion's a bizarre creature," Simon murmured, half to himself. "Especially when it comes to women's bodies. One day, they wake up, and *boom,* they've sprouted enormous buttocks."

"Or we suddenly decide to move our waists a few inches higher or lower," Harriet added. "or make them wider or smaller. Simply on a whim."

"Fashion doesn't come to Trewyn," Alyce said. "No suddenly giant arses or waists beneath our armpits. Just as long as we show up and leave work clean, and wear our best on Sundays, who can be bothered?"

"I'd say that you're lucky," Harriet noted dryly. "But

it's never a sign of luck when Nemesis shows up." She shrugged. "Women are clay, shaped and molded as others want us to be."

"What if," Simon said, "one day, women rose up and declared, 'No more. We won't wear these ridiculous garments anymore.'"

Harriet looked thoughtful. "No more corsets."

"Trousers instead of skirts." Alyce sounded excited by the idea.

Simon grinned. "Now *that's* an intriguing notion." He tried to picture Alyce in a pair of trousers. He'd be able to better see the shape and strength of her legs as she moved. No limitations as to where she could go. And . . . he had to admit . . . it would offer a fine view of her arse.

He decided he was in favor of it. He was becoming as revolutionary as a member of the Rational Dress Society.

Harriet snorted. She must've seen the lascivious turn in Simon's gaze. "Trust a man to take something that's supposed to liberate women and turn it into something lewd."

"How else would we know he's a man?" Alyce asked.

"Give me a chance," he said in a low voice. "You won't be in any doubt about my masculinity."

Though Alyce reddened, she didn't look away. One of the many reasons he was growing more and more obsessed with her. She never yielded. They continued to gaze at each other across the narrow space of the cab's interior.

Harriet loudly cleared her throat, breaking the thick atmosphere. "I'd rather not have this hackney burst into flames before we reach the train station."

For his own self-preservation, Simon looked away from Alyce first.

Harriet continued. "Marco was bloody disappointed he couldn't handle this part of the mission. You know how he loves a good confidence scheme, the scoundrel.

But he's just taken on a new case—something involving a widow being cheated out of her inheritance—so it's up to you two, now."

"Eva and Jack?" he asked.

"Already waiting for you in Plymouth."

Alyce's brows rose. "You Nemesis folk do keep yourselves busy."

"Wish we didn't have to," he answered, and he fought again that sense of a mountain slowly, inexorably bearing down on them, he and Nemesis armed only with tiny shovels.

"But you're trying," Alyce said, "which is a damned sight more than most people do."

He only shrugged. There had been people helped by Nemesis who'd thrown around terms like "hero" and "savior." All of those words he pushed away like a plate of bad oysters.

"One other thing," Harriet added, and the caution in her voice made him sit up straighter. "The last couple of weeks, there's been a young investigator from Scotland Yard sniffing around Nemesis. Asking questions in some of the disreputable parts of the city about a secret group of, I think the words he used were, 'Those that think themselves above the law.' "

Simon rolled his eyes. God, the very last thing Nemesis needed was a Yard man determined to make his name through some investigation concerning them. "I wager he wears a cheap checked suit and has an amply waxed mustache."

"His suit's black, and he's trying so very hard to grow a mustache, but alas," Harriet said with a pitying look at Simon's own bare upper lip, "not all men are capable of such a masculine feat."

Alyce glanced back and forth between Simon and Harriet. "You should be more worried about this investigator.

What if he digs up the truth? It'd be a quick trip but lengthy stay in prison for the lot of you."

"He'll be managed," Harriet said with easy conviction.

Though Alyce looked skeptical, she let the subject pass. In truth, Harriet's news tied a small knot of apprehension in Simon's belly. No one in Nemesis could afford exposure. And if they became public, the lives of those they'd helped would likely be torn open, too. Then there were those people Nemesis would be unable to help in the future because they group had been unmasked.

It was something to gnaw over. Something that would have to be handled.

But not just yet. The hackney pulled up in front of the train station, now a hive of activity, and it was time to move on to the next stage in this mission.

On the platform, Harriet gave him a nod and shook Alyce's hand. "No need for me to wish you luck," Harriet said.

"With your excellent tailoring," Alyce answered, already using her more refined accent, "it'd be impossible for us to fail."

"For a woman, a smart dress is as impervious as armor."

"To a point," Simon warned. "Don't mistake this"—he gestured to her dark green traveling ensemble—"for steel and chain mail. Confidence we need, not complacency."

"Look at me, Simon," Alyce said. "Maybe I'm dressed like a lady, but I don't take a single pebble for granted. Could hold ore, could be worthless deads. But I have to make sure."

He had to agree with her on that. Standing on the platform, waiting for the train to carry them to the next and more risky stage of their plan, Alyce radiated determination. She seemed to glow with it, so much so that many men passing by gave her a second look. Simon's glare sent the men hurrying away.

"Take my arm," he instructed her.

"Why?" Yet even as she asked, she slipped her hand into the crook of his elbow. A sense of *rightness* flowed through him.

"Because from now on, we're an inseparable team."

Piece by piece, Alyce felt herself changing. She now rode on a train as if it were the most natural thing in the world. The clothes she wore were proper for a sophisticated city woman. She'd been inside an elegant hotel and eaten delicate, toylike sandwiches.

But these were just superficial alterations. Something within her was being reshaped, transformed. She'd entered a world of forged documents and false identities, and the shock of it, the newness and strangeness, all that began to drift away.

As she watched the countryside speed by in a dizzying blur, she said to Simon, "I feel like that other Alice, the one who stepped through a mirror to find herself in a topsy-turvy world of living chess pieces. And I'm one of the pawns."

"A rook," he answered. "Not a pawn. Pawns just go where they're told."

"Isn't that what's happening now? 'Wear this, Alyce.' 'Travel here.' 'Say these words.'"

At this hour of the morning, the carriage held many more passengers. Men, women with children. The car buzzed with the chatter of daily life, almost comforting in its dullness.

She and Simon sat side by side, leaning close and speaking in low voices. They both wore soft smiles, as if they really were a newly wedded couple. But it was all part of the disguise, part of the game. It was hard to remember that, though, when she glanced up into the blue, blue, blue of his eyes, or felt the warmth of him as his shoulder pressed against hers.

"Rooks have more power than pawns. They're valuable in the endgame. Most of the checkmates are made by rooks."

"Now you're just throwing words at me to keep my head spinning."

He took her hand in his, and she was disappointed that they were now both gloved. But her gloves were of thin kidskin. His heat soaked through the leather, into her flesh.

His gaze held hers. "Whatever you believe, know this: I don't need a pawn, and I don't need a puppet. I need *you,* Alyce."

Curse them both—it would be too easy to think he talked of another need. Not just of his body, but something deeper.

All of this was in service of the mine, though. For the villagers and the workers and her family.

"I'll play my part," she answered. "And do a damned fine job of it."

He grinned at her, a sight that was beginning to feel like a pickaxe to her heart. "Stop stating the obvious."

She spoke in an even rougher Cornish accent than normal. "Oh, but I can't help it, sir. Just a simple country lass, I am."

This made him laugh, and the words formed clearly in her mind. *I'm in trouble. Grave trouble.* Because she was liking them too much, craving them too often, his smiles and laughs, and now wasn't the time, sod it, to start dreaming of what couldn't be.

"Well, my simple country lass," he said, using the same thick accent, "things are about to get awful complicated."

They spent the rest of the trip in silence, but he continued to hold her hand. She didn't object. Everything moved so quickly—she was speeding toward what would be the biggest challenge of her life—and he was warm and solid. She couldn't let him be her strength. Yet it surely helped knowing that he was beside her.

After the metal grandeur of the Exeter train station, the plain wooden depot at Plymouth came as a disappointment. The machinery at Wheal Prosperity was more impressive. As Simon paid the porter and hailed a cab, Alyce laughed at herself and her newfound airs. And all of this was an illusion, anyway, not truly part of her life. In a few days, it would be as if Plymouth's railways didn't exist.

A few days. A lifetime between now and then, and what lay in between . . . she couldn't see. For all of her twenty-four years, the shadow of the mine had fallen across her life. She'd stayed in school as long as possible, but then it'd become necessary to work, and from then until not very long ago, her patterns never altered. Wake, eat, walk to the mine, work, walk home, eat, read before exhaustion set in, sleep. Repeat. Only Sundays saw a disruption in that routine. And her forays to the managers' office, demanding change.

God, it felt so good to break from those chains of habit. Good—and not a little frightening. But she could master that fear.

Simon helped her into the cab. "The Admiral and Anchor," he called up to the driver. "We can't risk meeting Jack and Eva at a hotel," he explained to Alyce.

"If anyone saw us together . . ."

"Disaster. Yes."

As soon as the hackney left the area near the train station, she smelled the heavy, briny sea. And when the cab turned a corner, and the narrow street suddenly revealed a broad vista, she fought a gasp. The bay spread out below

them, the color of iron, and dotted with ships of every
size. White flecks of seabirds wheeled and cried overhead. Plymouth Sound reminded her that the world was
much larger than she'd ever imagined. Ships crossed the
sea, going to faraway places, bringing back exotic
cargo—things *and* people. Impossible not to feel a little
small, when the whole of the ocean stretched endlessly
toward the horizon, and brave ships skimmed back and
forth from that distant line.

"Have you seen the sea before?"

"Newquay, once. But I was just a little'un. Don't remember much except Henry putting sand down the back
of my dress and my ma pulling me away from the water.
I couldn't swim."

"That didn't stop you from trying."

"And getting a lungful of salt water when I finally
jumped in. We went home after that. Not much of a seaside holiday."

"I'd say we could make up for it now, but—"

"This isn't a holiday," she finished.

"Another time, maybe."

"Another time." Which they both knew would never
happen. So she let herself take in as much of the view as
she could, hoping her mind could work like one of those
photographic cameras, and capture the image for her to
return to again and again later. If she did have a photo-
graph of that moment, she'd write on the back, *Simon
and the Sea, 1886.*

Two things that she'd never fully know.

The view disappeared as the cab turned down another
street. Here, just as in Exeter, people of all stripes walked
the avenues, including men in naval uniforms and some
very grand-looking folks, indeed. Alyce tried to remember every image, all the faces young and old, clothing fine
and shabby, the handsome streets and smell of the

ocean—souvenirs for her mind, to take back with her to Trewyn and retell. The villagers were always starved for stories of life beyond their small town's boundaries, and she hoped to sate their appetites with stories when she returned.

She pushed thoughts of the future and going home aside. Everything was about now, and these next few days. Simon had warned against complacency, and that included thoughts of Trewyn.

The cab pulled up outside a stately looking place that she recognized as a tavern by the painted shingle swaying on a brass post.

As Simon climbed down from the hackney, he said to the driver, "Take the trunk on to the Cormorant Hotel. Say it belongs to Mr. Shale, and they'll know what to do with it."

The cabman pocketed Simon's offered coins, and tipped his hat. "Yes, sir!"

Simon helped her down from the hackney, and it seemed so strange, being put into and taken out of vehicles, as if she couldn't manage the task perfectly well on her own two legs. She'd pushed wagons loaded with ore up hillsides, for heaven's sake. This was a different world, however, where women didn't have the same strength and were handled like soap bubbles. She might not pop at the slightest breeze, but in this foreign land, she'd have to follow local custom. And it didn't upset her to feel Simon's hand on her elbow, his hand taking hers as he guided her down to the pavement.

After the cab had rolled off, Simon pushed open the door to the tavern. Sunlight poured in through a bank of windows onto a polished dark wooden floor. The bar itself gleamed, including a well-polished brass footrail. Malty ale and lemon furniture polish scented the air. Tables were arranged neatly around the room, and there were high-backed settles lining the walls. If this tavern was a tall-masted ship with sparkling white sails billowing, the pubs at Trewyn were leaky rowboats.

Though the hour was still before noon, a few men were already at tables and lined up at the bar. They looked at Alyce with harmless curiosity as Simon, his hand on her back, guided her up to the bar. In her respectable traveling dress, and the well-mannered way Simon touched and gazed at her, nobody would mistake her for a woman of loose character. Still, her presence in the tavern was odd enough to attract a bit of attention.

"How may I serve you, sir?" the barman asked politely.

"The Dunhams are expecting us," Simon answered.

"Right this way," was the prompt answer. The barman stepped out from behind his counter and led them down a hallway lined with framed pictures of naval ships. He knocked lightly on a door. "Your company's arrived, Mr. Dunham."

"Fine," came the response—a voice so deep and raspy it sounded as if it emerged from the lowest part of Wheal Prosperity's deepest mine shaft.

The barman didn't open the door. He accepted the coin Simon gave him—where did all these coins come from? Surely he didn't have them in Trewyn—and disappeared back toward the front of the tavern.

"It's me and company," Simon said through the door. The way he spoke, it seemed as if he were warning someone with a large, vicious animal that he was approaching, and they'd better keep their hand on the animal's collar.

Slowly, he opened the door, then ushered Alyce through it quickly. They stood in a small private room, also with dark wood on the floor and walls, a single window, a round table encircled by a few chairs, and a fireplace.

A woman stood to one side of the room, fair-haired

and neatly dressed in a jacket, shirtwaist, and skirt. She carried with her an air of complete control and an intelligence so sharp it could cut steel. The woman stepped forward briskly, and spoke with the same no-nonsense tone. "You must be Alyce. I'm Eva."

Which Alyce could have guessed.

"This is my husband, Jack." Eva gestured toward the other side of the room, and Alyce fought a yelp. She'd known large, powerfully built men before—miners earned their strength honestly—but not once in her life had she ever seen a man like Jack.

He was . . . *huge*. Thick with muscle and radiating so much raw strength, it was a wonder the entire building didn't simply collapse from the force of it. Though he wore a respectable suit, a wildness clung to him, something almost feral.

The name registered in her memory. A realization struck her. This was the man who had escaped from prison.

His dark gaze saw the moment she seemed to understand who he was. A small smile curled in the corner of his mouth, and it wasn't at all comforting.

Simon explained, "Jack and Eva are going to help us in the next stage of our scheme."

Good God, these two dangerous people were their *allies*? And if this powerful man and this sharp woman were their partners, how treacherous was the risk they faced?

She summoned all of her nerve, all of her calm, and straightened her back. "Let's get started."

CHAPTER 11.

Alyce knew she shouldn't judge anyone by their appearance, or even their history. She should be the last person to do so.

Still, when Jack spoke, she expected him mostly to grunt or point or speak in a dialect so low, she'd need a translator to understand him.

That's not what happened at all.

The four of them—herself, Simon, Eva, and Jack—sat at the table in the private room. An aproned server came in with plates of eggs and sausages, and a tray bearing steaming cups of tea. Nerves plucked at her, but she discovered that the sandwiches and tea in Exeter had barely fueled her furnace, and so she, Simon, and the couple fell to their breakfasts with the seriousness of churchgoers. The tea went a long way to revive her after a night with barely any sleep, so she was fully awake when Jack explained his latest activities.

"Been going down to the owners' offices every day, posing as a government man." He did talk with a hard accent— she guessed it came from the kind of place where people fought daily to stay alive—but she understood every word, as well as the equally hard intelligence of the man speaking. "I've been putting the lean on 'em, saying that they owe hundreds of pounds in taxes, and I won't stop breathing down their necks till I get the money."

"You've got them shuddering in their sock garters, I'd wager." Simon smiled over the rim of his tea cup.

"And they believe you're really from the government?" Alyce asked. Though Jack wore a decent suit amazingly tailored for his giant frame, some fine wool couldn't hide the fact that he wasn't a bureaucrat—not that she had much experience with bureaucrats. "You don't strike me as the sort of lad who normally sits behind a desk."

Instead of taking offense, he winked. "More comfortable behind a punching bag than a desk." She believed it. In his massive hands, the knife and fork looked better suited to a doll.

"But Jack's remarkably adept at intimidation," Eva said, glancing at her husband fondly. "And with one of Marco's forged documents proving Jack's from a taxation bureau, it's astonishing what can be accomplished."

Alyce had definitely found herself on the other side of the mirror. Only in the world of Nemesis would a wife take pride in her husband's skill at extortion. She glanced over at Simon, seeking an anchor. He leaned back in his chair, sunlight from the lone window bright along the clean planes of his face and picking out intriguing shadows, like the one below his bottom lip that revealed its slight fullness. Where Jack was a heavy hammer, Simon was an elegant blade.

She wondered if he found this conversation as strange as she did, but he looked perfectly comfortable, cradling his cup of tea in one long-fingered hand as though it were an ordinary morning and they were talking about if the weather would hold.

This mirror world was his, too. *She* was the stranger here.

In that book, the other Alice tried to follow rules that seemed to be made up as they went along, being told by everyone and everything that she was the outsider. The only one who'd been kind to her, who accepted that other Alice, was the White Knight. He wanted her to be a queen, and made sure that happened. The sole figure in that opposite world who'd made Alice feel welcome and believed in her.

Simon wasn't half as foolish or full of ideas for useless inventions as that White Knight, but he'd been Alyce's supporter all along. He'd had his concerns about her at the beginning—she couldn't blame him for that—but once she'd proven herself, he'd stood firm in his belief. He trusted her, and seemed to like her for precisely who she was.

None of the men back home had felt the same. They'd tried to court her, and she'd fielded a handful of proposals. But it was a kindness to everyone that she'd always said no. She couldn't be a sweet girl, like Sarah. She couldn't be biddable.

Simon didn't want her sweet. Or biddable. He cared for *her*. She could see it in the way he looked at her, feel it in his touch.

Oh, the sly bastard. How could she go back to her ordinary life once he left?

Jack wiped his mouth with a napkin, then stood. "Those bastards aren't going to just hand the mine over on their own. Better be getting down there."

"How much time do you need?" Simon asked, still stretched out in his chair.

"Fifteen minutes should do it. Been working them all week."

Alyce couldn't believe that anyone could hold out against Jack for so long, but she wouldn't underestimate the mine owners' greed—even when faced with someone as terrifying as the escaped convict.

"Ready to do battle against me?" Simon grinned.

"Put us in the ring together, I'd snap you like a tinder."

"Won't be as easy as that."

"No, you were always a tough little bugger." Only in comparison to someone as big as Jack could Simon be considered little. Alyce also had to wonder about when they'd locked horns before. And if Simon survived that . . . dear God, what *could* break him?

"Always put up a good fight against you," Simon said.

"That you did." Jack clapped on his hat, and his wife got to her feet. She walked him to the door of the private room, her hand on his sleeve.

"Break some spines, love," she murmured.

"I'll bring 'em to you like a bouquet." He lowered his head and she rose up on her toes for a kiss.

Alyce ought to look away, but she couldn't. So much heat and tenderness in a single, brief kiss, it felt like a fist closing around her heart. They couldn't be more different, this couple, and yet only a sightless man could miss how much they cared for each other. And they'd met because of a Nemesis mission.

She glanced again at Simon. He studied his tea cup intently, as if forcibly not watching Jack and Eva.

Finally, the couple broke apart, and with a final tip of his hat, Jack left. Eva leaned against the door as she closed it. Her expression was tight. "Months now, he's been one of us," she said to no one in particular. "But my stomach knots every time he goes out on an assignment."

"Don't you trust him?" asked Alyce.

"With my life," Eva answered without hesitation. "But . . . I love him. I'll never not worry."

So easily Eva said those words, when Alyce hadn't uttered them once in her life. Would she ever? And if she did, would they be freeing, or would they feel like a mining shaft caving in, robbing her of air, crushing her?

Useless, these questions, when she knew with certainty that those words would never pass her lips. It was safer, more secure, to keep complete in herself. No chance of having her spirit trampled. No deferral to any man. And if she became an old spinster, then she'd feed the village's stray dogs and knit blankets for other women's babies. Not too bad a life.

She'd once thought that a fine way to lead the rest of her days. Simon had gone and ruined all that.

Eva took her seat again, though she only poked at her breakfast now. She and Simon talked of things Alyce didn't understand, things happening in London and involving people she didn't know, and as their genteel voices blended together, comfortable but not intimate, Alyce's gaze kept drifting and staying on Simon as he rolled himself a cigarette between his long, nimble fingers.

She couldn't have him. It was as plain a fact as if it had been printed on the front page of a newspaper and circulated at train stations all over England. And the thought was acid in her chest, as much as knowing that there'd come a time when he'd be off on another mission, and she'd become part of his past. But he'd never be part of her past. He'd always be with her, in his absence, like the twisting empty tunnels at the mine. Once they'd been completely tapped, they'd just be abandoned. They never went away.

Yet that meant getting through the next few days. Beating odds that seemed impossibly high.

She had to distract herself from the doubt and future sorrow that wanted to pull her down. "How long have you been in Plymouth?"

"I've only come down this morning. Someone had to run the school while Jack's been here all week. If everything goes well, I'll be on the evening train back to Manchester."

Alyce frowned. "You're not going to the owners' offices or to dinner tonight?"

"It'd ruin the illusion of Jack as a government tough if his lovely wife accompanied him everywhere," Simon noted. He lit his cigarette with a Lucifer, then blew streams of smoke toward the ceiling.

She remembered him smoking in front of her at the mine. But he held the cigarette differently now—gracefully at the top of his index and middle finger. Even that had been part of his role. But that didn't make watching him smoke now any less beguiling. Now he had a gentleman's languor, despite the fact that he had to be running through the work he was about to do.

Her mind snagged on the words "lovely wife." True, Eva was a handsome woman, and married to the most intimidating man Alyce had ever seen, but did Simon fancy her?

"If you aren't needed to be with Jack," Alyce pressed, "then you don't need to be in Plymouth at all."

"Simon's going to be down at the owners' offices for a while," Eva answered, "and Jack will be there, too."

"Leaving me on my own and in need of a minder," Alyce said wryly.

"You're not a child." Simon immediately lost his gentleman's sleepy calm, leaning forward in his seat, his voice firm. "Yet Plymouth's a big place, and you haven't spent much time at all away from the village. I won't be able to concentrate on the objective if I'm worried about you."

A hand fisted around her heart. He *worried* about her? "I've got enough brains to keep myself alive in Plymouth for a day or two."

"I don't just want you alive. I want you safe." He crushed out his cigarette into a ceramic ashtray advertising beer, his fingers sharp and twisting in their motion.

She felt as if someone had taken a riveter and bolted

her into her chair, right through her chest. It was a forcibly given confession, as if he hadn't wanted to admit any of it. And that made it all the more shocking.

We're trying to halt something that can't stop. Like a cart whose brakes had shattered. The best they could do was hold on and hope they didn't crash or were flung to their deaths.

"Think of me as your personal tour guide to Plymouth," Eva said, breaking the silence. "We can visit Smeaton's Tower, or the Royal Citadel, or," she added, when Alyce showed no interest in these sites, "I can give you loads of gossip about Simon."

Alyce sat up straighter in her chair, as Simon sent Eva a glower. "You've got my attention."

The other woman smiled wickedly. "Nothing better than some entertaining tattle while the menfolk do the heavy lifting."

"Eva . . ." Simon said warningly.

The blond woman glanced toward a clock on the mantel. "Look at the time! Oughtn't you be going, Simon?"

He shoved away from the table, scowling. "It's useless for me to tell you to be discreet, isn't it?"

Eva grinned. "Don't worry, dear. I'll confine all of my gossip to your personal life. No missions will be jeopardized by my revelations."

"What an eased burden." Simon donned his hat and coat, and, taking the leather portfolio with him, headed for the door.

Alyce found herself on her feet and beside him before she was aware she'd moved. She gripped Simon's arms, feeling the solid, lean muscle beneath all that expensive wool, and stared up at him. His expression was tense, but his gaze searched hers, as if trying to figure out a riddle.

She'd answer the riddle for him. Just as Eva had done with her husband, Alyce rose up on her toes and kissed

Simon. It didn't matter that the other woman was in the room. It didn't matter what kind of conclusion Eva would draw from the kiss. All that mattered was that Simon was about to step into the lion's den, and she couldn't let him leave without feeling her mouth against his.

It didn't last long, the kiss, but she felt a shudder pass through both her and Simon—one swift sensation of longing. He tasted of tobacco and tea. A man's taste.

She pulled back just enough to feel his breath across her face and see his pupils wide in his brilliant eyes. "Lie to those bastards," she breathed. "Make them pay."

His smile was as dark as mid-winter. "It'll be my greatest pleasure. For . . . the workers."

"For the workers," she repeated, and then she let him go.

He gave her a final glance before stepping out into the hallway. She listened to his footsteps receding, and then shut the door once again. Turning around, she saw Eva staring at her as if considering a strange plant that had popped up in her garden, and couldn't decide whether or not to pull her up by the roots, or tend her.

"No," Eva said.

"No, what?" Alyce drifted over to her chair, but couldn't find the calm to sit. Instead, she wandered to the window. It offered a glimpse of sky between the buildings.

"It doesn't get easier when they go off on an assignment," Eva replied. She picked up her tea cup, sipped at it, then grimaced and set it down. It must've gone cold. "I thought you ought to know that now. The fear never goes away."

Simon rode alone in a hansom, heading toward the offices of Wheal Prosperity's owners. He drummed his fingers on the window frame—a contrast from the usual calm that enveloped him before a scheme. The cab rolled past a woman with Alyce's hair color. And he could've sworn he saw her standing outside a mercer's shop. But that was impossible.

She was back at the tavern. And so were his thoughts. His lips held the feel of hers, her warmth and taste. He'd kissed many women in his life. But it was hers that resonated, long after the kiss itself was over. It felt as though her spirit burned in him, guiding him like a lantern in the darkness of the mine. For her, he couldn't fail.

And despite her objections to having Eva act as guardian, he didn't regret his decision to have the other Nemesis operative accompany her today. He didn't doubt Alyce could take care of herself, whether she was in Plymouth or Peking, but it sure as hell freed his mind to think of other things, knowing that Eva was with her. No harm could befall her.

He alit from the cab when it stopped outside a handsome brick-fronted building. A discreet brass plaque on the front announced GREATER CORNWALL MINING ENDEAVOR, LTD. He ascended the stairs, and with each step he slipped farther into the persona of a solicitor, giving his posture an extra stiffness, as if rigidly monitoring the world's behavior and finding it slightly below standards. But for the right price, he'd make everything all right.

Inside, the offices exuded decorous wealth, with thick imported rugs on the floor and paintings of idealized mines on the paneled walls. None of the mines looked at all like Wheal Prosperity. The equipment wasn't rusty. The clean, well-dressed miners all grinned as they readied themselves to be lowered over a hundred feet beneath the surface.

The office foyer was furnished with a few upholstered chairs pushed against the walls, ready to receive the arses of supplicants. The air was full of ink, foolscap, and hair oil, and the sound of typewriter keys clacking. Simon maintained his own offices in London where he pretended to be a younger son dabbling halfheartedly in industry—though it wasn't much of an act, since he truly was only dabbling, his real work being Nemesis. The scent of both offices was identical. Except here, he truly cared what happened within these mahogany-paneled walls.

Moments after he stepped inside, a smooth-faced clerk approached him. "May I assist you, Mr. . . . ?"

"Shale. Simon Shale, solicitor." He handed his coat and hat to the clerk, who stared at the items with a puzzled frown. "Where is he?"

"Sir?"

Simon strode down one corridor, passing offices and more clerks. "The government tax man."

"Oh, Mr. Darby." The clerk shuddered. "He's in with Misters Harrold and Tufton, but I really don't think they'd want to be interrupted."

"They will." Men's raised voices sounded from the other side of a door. The name OLIVER HARROLD was painted in gold on the door. One of the voices belonged to Jack, whose deep timbre made the other two men sound thin and nasal.

As the clerk sputtered his objections, Simon opened the office door without hesitation and stepped inside. A middle-aged man with thinning hair but a full beard sat behind a huge desk, his face as red as his waistcoat. Oliver Harrold, presumably. Another man of middle years stood beside the desk, his arms folded across his girth. Simon's research identified him as Victor Tufton. There was a third partner in the ownership of the mine, one John Stokeham, but either Stokeham was out of town or hiding, because the only other occupant in the room was Jack.

Jack whirled and pointed a finger at Simon. "You, again."

The first time Simon had met Jack, he'd been intimidated by his size and near animal ferocity. When it came to sheer strength, there was no doubt Jack could easily beat Simon into the next world. And even though he knew exactly who Jack was, and the role he played, Simon's first instinct was to throw down his portfolio, put up his fists, and growl his defiance.

Training, however, kept Simon's arms at his sides, his expression calm.

"Yes, me, Mr. Darby. Always a pleasure to encounter you again." He produced a calling card from a pocket in his waistcoat and handed it to the clerk. "Simon Shale, solicitor."

The clerk, sending terrified glances at Jack, edged around the room. He handed the card to Tufton, who barely spared it a look.

"I don't know who you are, Mr. Shale," Tufton said. "But these are private offices and this is a private meeting. Linford," he said, turning to the clerk, "show our unwelcome visitor out."

Simon spoke before the beleaguered clerk could move. "Begging your pardon, sir, but I think you'd rather have me here than Mr. Darby. In fact, I *know* you'd rather have me here." He turned to Jack. "You've harassed these good men long enough, Darby. Oughtn't you crawl back into your ditch next to the taxation office? Maybe there's a sewer that needs a new tariff."

Tufton, Harrold, and the clerk all gasped at Simon's flippant remarks. They stared at him as if he'd gone raving mad right in the middle of their offices.

A convincing shade of red filled Jack's face. "It's official government business I'm here on. And no shoddy London solicitor's going to run me off."

"My God, you're a tedious fellow," Simon drawled. "Had you the slightest splinter of intelligence in that massive, bulky head of yours, you'd know that you aren't going to get a single ha'penny from these gentlemen. Especially now that I'm on the case."

Jack stepped closer and Simon kept his own expression blasé, as if nearly seventeen stone of solid muscle weren't looming over him. "I'm not going anyplace until these blokes pay what they owe."

"But we don't owe *anything*!" Harrold exclaimed. "That's what I have been trying to tell you all week! We make certain that we stay up-to-date on all our taxes." He whitened when Jack's gaze turned on him.

"Then you haven't been keeping current with the new laws on mining properties," Jack snarled.

"Mr. Darby," Simon murmured, "you've threatened these poor good men enough for this day. No money's changing hands, not today. As well you know, a new solicitor is afforded proper time to acquaint himself with levies—and the government wouldn't step on that regulation, would it? This *is* Britain, after all, not some corrupt, philistine nation such as France or the United States. So go brawl with drunken sailors, and we'll see you again bright and early tomorrow."

"I—"

"Go on, now, Darby. You've been a good soldier for the taxation office, but a wise soldier knows when to retreat. Think of all the clever things you're going to say to me tomorrow."

Jack blinked, as if genuinely confused by Simon's mixture of insult and flattery. "I'm coming back," he growled.

"Of course you are. All the best diseases do. Good day, Mr. Darby."

A brief silence, then Linford the clerk squeaked, "Shall I see you out, Mr. Darby?"

"Don't bother, milksop. I know every corner of these offices. And they'll belong to the government if you don't pay up." With that, Jack stalked from the room.

A long, slow exhale came from Harrold and Tufton. Then Harrold looked at Simon. "Thank you very much for your assistance, Mr. Shale. But who in blazes *are* you?"

"You ought to go back to the hotel and get some rest," Eva said as they sat in the back room of the tavern. "Doubtless you need it, and there's nothing for you to do while Simon's busy at the owners' office." She stood. "Come, I'll escort you there."

"So you'll sit at my bedside like a nursemaid and watch me sleep?" Alyce would have none of that. "I was too busy scuttling from the train station to the hotel and back again to see anything of Exeter. I won't miss my chance to explore Plymouth."

She didn't think she'd be able to sleep, anyway. Her body felt tight, as if she were strung up on a loom, but instead of being woven into something whole, threads of her kept unraveling. There might not be anything left of her by the time she returned to Trewyn.

"What would you like to see first?"

"The sea," she answered at once.

But when she and Eva stepped out onto the street, and Eva moved to hail a hackney, Alyce stopped her. "I want to walk."

"The Barbican is at least a mile from here."

"I walk four miles to and from work every day. One will feel like a holiday. Unless," she added, "it's too far for you."

Eva bristled. "The best path is to the left."

Together, Alyce and the woman she'd met only an hour earlier began to walk down toward the seafront. The day was at its height, and the streets bustled with activity. Carriages, cabs, and wagons trundled along the avenues. Voices and hawkers' cries were thick in the air. Alyce had never seen so many people in one place before. Easy to feel like one of those bits of seaweed floating along the current, as if she might just wash away in the sea of people and noise.

But she thought of Henry, and Sarah, of her fellow bal-maidens and the rhythms they made as they swung their bucking irons, and the red mud-covered faces of the miners. She thought of Simon and the faith he had in her. The ground grew steady beneath her feet.

"Simon wrote that you work at the mine," Eva said as they moved into a business district full of sober-coated men.

If Eva, with her polished manners and accent, thought Alyce would be ashamed of her work, the fancy lady was in for a disappointment. "As a bal-maiden. I smash pieces of ore with a big hammer. Makes me deucedly strong."

Yet there was no disgust in Eva's gaze. "Jack and I run a school and a boxing studio in Manchester. I do the schooling, he teaches the boxing, but he makes certain I get in front of the heavy bag three times a week." To Alyce's shock, Eva curled her arm, revealing a tight, rounded bicep. "I'm coming along, but it's going to be a while before I can beat you at tug-o-war."

"Or wrestling," Alyce added. She studied the woman walking beside her. "I may like you."

"But you aren't certain." Eva nodded. "That's a good policy: caution. I'd urge you the same when it comes to Simon."

Whatever thawing Alyce might have felt toward the other woman instantly froze. "You heard what I said to him—I'm a grown woman. Any choices I make are my own."

"I'd be the last person to tell another woman how to

think or act." She glanced both ways before crossing a busy street. The smell of seawater and the cries of seabirds grew thicker. "But Jack and I . . . we're a rare exception. Nemesis agents don't involve themselves with people who are part of a job. Safer for everyone."

"I've been hearing a lot lately about my safety. But I work at a mine. Doesn't get more dangerous than that. If I can handle that, managing Simon won't trip me up." The desire between her and Simon was already explosive— but more dangerous were the feelings that tangled through her whenever she thought of him, looked at him. How her heart swelled when he was near, and how it shriveled when he was at a distance.

She and Eva turned down another street, and suddenly a wharf opened up before them. Ferries chugged through the water, and sailboats bobbed in their wake. A few green cliffs rose up on the other side of the harbor, with houses perched atop them, staring out at the water like sentinels. Eva turned right, leading them along a paved waterfront. Gaily painted shops and stone-fronted buildings lined the street, and Alyce even spotted a tea shop full of women wearing ridiculous and beautiful hats.

"He's a gentleman, you know," Eva said as they strolled.

"He's told me. Some rich man's younger son. A rich man who doesn't approve of him."

"If his father ever found out about Nemesis, he'd be disowned. Cut off without a penny." Eva spoke flatly, as if reciting rugby scores. "He wouldn't be welcome at home or at any family gathering. Couldn't appear with them at any public function. In essence, he'd be dead to them, and disgraced, metaphorically dead sons aren't eagerly embraced by the rest of Society."

Despite the sun breaking through the clouds, a chill danced along Alyce's arms and down her back. He'd never talked of his life in Society with fondness—in fact, he seemed to hate it—but to lose all contact with his family, to become a pariah . . . it would be a high price to pay. She couldn't imagine the desperate loneliness if she lost Henry and Sarah.

Still, she said, "He's aware of the risk."

"Of course he is," Eva answered readily. She stopped walking and considered a seagull perched atop a mast, sure-footed even as its resting place heaved beneath it. "All of us are. What we do for Nemesis means too much for us to stop. Even Simon, who has the most to lose."

Anger filmed Alyce's gaze. "I'm not going to show up at his father's doorstep."

"No, you won't. And if you tried, well . . ." Eva smiled a cold little smile that looked like a knife coming out of its sheath. "You'd discover just how ruthless Nemesis can be. Particularly when it comes to protecting one of our own."

"He came to Wheal Prosperity to help. If you think I'd ever hurt him, I'll show you my own boxing skills and knock you right into the harbor."

Eva's smile warmed. "That's all I needed to know."

Crossing her arms across her chest, Alyce demanded, "All this has been a test?"

The other woman didn't seem offended. "My idea, not Simon's. I saw the way he looked at you. How you look back." She nodded toward a group of clouds casting shadows on the harbor. "Desire passes. Provided one takes precautions, lust can be sated without repercussions."

Alyce's face heated. Candid as conversation with other bal-maidens could be, Alyce had never talked of such frank matters with a stranger.

"If you and Simon merely wanted to jump into bed together," Eva continued, "I wouldn't be saying any of this. The two of you could have your enjoyment of each other and that would be the end of it. But I see it goes beyond that." She glanced at Alyce. "Far beyond. Everything I'm telling you . . . it's merely a matter of safeguards, for both you *and* Simon."

Alyce had the strange urge to peel back her gloves and see if her skin had turned to glass. How else could Eva had seen through her so easily? Yes, she'd kissed Simon at the tavern, but one kiss didn't reveal everything. Did it? Or maybe Eva was really that astute, perceiving things that Alyce herself wasn't ready to admit.

"So," Alyce said dryly, "this test. I'm on tenterhooks to know if I passed."

"He made a good choice by picking you for the mission."

Alyce was wry. "That's the best news I've heard in years. Your approval means everything to me."

Eva grinned. "I might like you." Resuming their stroll, she continued. "To keep us all safe, we don't socialize with each other outside of our objectives for Nemesis. Our lives are all divided. My parents don't know. Marco's sisters are completely unaware. Harriet's employers are ignorant. It's a tightrope we walk every day."

"And you all take these risks because . . . ?"

The blond woman's expression darkened. "If we don't, who will? Who'll make sure that the cook who's horribly burned her hands has a way to feed and house herself? Who will make men of power pay when they abuse that power? Who'll keep children out of brothels or factories that pay them less than a penny for fourteen hours of work?"

The passion and quiet anger in Eva's voice was a contrast to the cool, composed way in which she ambled along the waterfront, past the pretty shops and their oblivious patrons. But Alyce saw how the other woman's eyes flashed, the conviction that sank deeper than bone. Admiration reluctantly climbed through Alyce, like a stray cat being lured out from a hedgerow with an offer of meat.

"And who'd care that the workers at one little copper mine were being exploited by the owners and managers?" Alyce added. "Nobody in Trewyn can pay you, you know. There's no reward for everything Nemesis is doing."

Eva seemed an expert in cold little smiles, for she gave another one. "Don't worry. Simon will find a way so that everyone's costs are recouped."

Though she gazed out at a pretty little harbor full of masted ships and sprinkled with sunlight, Alyce's mind saw only Simon in his solicitor's coat and hat, preparing to swindle the mine's owners, ready to face whatever danger confronted him.

Some worry must have shown on her face, for Eva said, "Other than Marco, no one knows the confidence game better than Simon. He'll be fine."

"I know he will," Alyce replied with much more sureness than she felt.

"Tea, no sugar or cream," Simon said to the mystified clerk.

"Uh . . ." Linford glanced at Tufton and Harrold.

"Fetch it for him, Linford," Harrold directed. "If only as a thanks for getting that appalling thug out of our office."

As the clerk bustled out, Simon draped himself in a chair in front of Harrold's desk. Tufton continued to stand, his arms still folded across his chest. Both men looked innocuous enough, like any other man between forty-five and sixty with a comfortable income and the belief they had a blameless conscience. Simon saw past the disguise, to the rot and corruption beneath. Everything in this office, from the imported rugs to the crystal decanters of whisky to the gold stitching on Tufton's waistcoat—all paid for by the sweat and toil of the people of Wheal Prosperity. By men like Henry and Edgar, risking their lives daily on worn-down equipment, and women like Alyce, smashing rocks of ore for hours so that she and her family could slowly starve on minimal rations.

But these men in their tasteful office didn't care. They got precisely what they needed, and saw no reason why they ought to make any changes to a corrupt system.

It was all Simon could do to keep from punching the two of them square in their prosperous faces.

Instead, he smiled blandly at them, crossing one foot over his knee in a posture of utter ease.

"Again, Mr. Shale," Harrold said, "who *are* you?"

Simon took the clerk's offered cup of tea and sipped at it. Excellent tea. Doubtless imported from Suchow, at great expense.

"I'm the man who's going to make Mr. Darby go away," he answered.

"How do you propose to do that?" Tufton demanded.

"Quite simply, really." A familiar but always welcome thrill shot through him, more potent than any tea. "The ownership of Wheal Prosperity is transferred to me, in exchange for three days of the mine's profit and, say, a thousand pounds."

Both Tufton and Harrold sputtered indignantly. "Outrageous!" Tufton exclaimed.

"And how much is Darby bilking you for?"

Sullenly, Harrold said, "Twenty-five hundred pounds."

Simon set his tea cup on the edge of the desk, much to Harrold's displeasure, and spread his hands. "A minimal outlay in comparison. Further, the group to which you'll be transferring ownership isn't subject to the taxes Darby's trying to enforce. The transfer will effectively serve as a barricade to that blockhead."

His bulk must have made standing wearying, because Tufton sank into a large leather tufted chair, but his expression didn't ease. Calm enveloped Simon. This might take some time—these men were shrewd business owners—but Simon would bring them around.

"We've been ruddy careful to keep all this taxation claptrap out of the public's ear," Tufton said. "I've never laid eyes on you until today. So how do you know about our situation?"

Simon made a show of clenching his jaw. "Darby. My income doesn't come solely from my work as a solicitor. I have shares in other businesses and industries. But Darby's been the damn fox in my henhouse. Always finding taxation loopholes to exploit. Wringing me dry."

"Bastard pockets some of his revenue, I'd wager," Harrold muttered.

"He wouldn't have a job with the government if he wasn't crooked." Simon had to remember to repeat that to Marco later. And Marco would agree with him. "I've been tracking the son of a bitch, and heard about your endeavor's misfortune. So, I'm here to help."

Tufton narrowed his already small eyes. "Why?"

"Because I want to kick Darby in the teeth. Because we can help each other."

"You're just a solicitor, Shale," Harrold said, scornful. "You can't help us."

"That's where you're mistaken. I have a few business endeavors in Assam and Karnataka that are exempt from British taxes. Perfect little opportunities for you to hide your income."

"Why would you want our money in those endeavors?" asked Tufton. "That would just lessen your share of the profits."

Simon smiled. "Your capital would make the investments more robust for everyone, including myself. And you, my good gentlemen, would have a lovely chunk of untaxable income. It offers nothing but profit."

Tufton and Harrold glanced at each other. Simon read the pure avarice in each man's gaze and the pleasure at the thought of getting something for nothing. This had been one of Marco's lessons in the realm of confidence schemes: get the mark's own greed to work against him. Nearly every person liked the idea of having it better than someone else, of cheating the system. It fed their sense of a world centered entirely around their own needs, their belief that they were better, more deserving than others.

Clearly, Harrold and Tufton were no exception.

"Once Darby's off your back," Simon continued, "I'll transfer ownership of the mine back to you, and that bugger won't bother you anymore."

Harrold steepled his fingers in a way he likely thought made him look clever. "What's to say he won't come back and start his harassment all over again?"

"It's wondrous what the fear of one's in-laws can accomplish," Simon answered. "What you have here is a London problem, not a Plymouth problem."

"I don't see the bloody difference," grumbled Harrold.

"It's more than a distance of miles, gentlemen, it's mentality. London's my home. I have connections that neither of you possess."

"If that's the case," Tufton said, "you could've taken care of Darby sooner."

"Timing is everything." He uncrossed his legs and leaned forward, bracing his forearms on his knees and clasping his hands together. "*Now* is the ideal moment to get rid of Darby, and if you agree to transfer ownership of Wheal Prosperity to the corporation I've created, he'll be nothing more than a smear beneath the wheel of your barouche."

"Are you certain you can succeed, Shale?" Harrold demanded.

Tufton added, "You keep mentioning this other corporation." He matched Simon's posture—an amateur gesture for someone in the confidence game. "What is it?"

"I have the incorporation documents here." Simon hefted his portfolio. "My own wife has signed the papers—using her maiden name, of course. All you good gentlemen need to do is sign over ownership of the mine to her. She has a brother who's an assistant to the President of the Board of Trade. Edward doesn't think that highly of me," he added, annoyed. "But once he gets word that Darby is harming the business his sister owns, and his own name is getting dragged into it, he'll be motivated to make Darby go away. By the time the government realizes that Alyce is my wife"—unexpected heat pulsed through him at the words—"Wheal Prosperity will belong to you again."

Harrold and Tufton traded doubting looks. It was time for Simon to play his last card in this hand.

"Can't blame you for not trusting me. After all, you've only met me within this past hour. Your caution does you credit."

Naturally, both owners puffed at the praise.

"My wife and I are in Plymouth together," Simon continued. "There's no better way to get a sense of who we are than having us over for dinner. Tonight."

"Damn impertinent of you to invite you and your wife over for dinner," Harrold blustered.

"Your sense of restraint's justifiable. I'm only honoring that. Consider, you'll have ample opportunity to answer the question, Is this blighter to be trusted?"

"And your wife," added Harrold.

It was a reasonable thing to say, but Simon still wanted to leap over the desk and ram his elbow into the other man's throat for even *speaking* of Alyce or questioning her integrity.

Simon continued, "Her, too. We'll be partners in many ways. The mine, my Indian endeavors. Dinner's a perfect opportunity for everyone to get to know one another. A single misstep on our part, if we say or do anything to arouse your suspicion, then the deal is off. Simple as that. Who knows? We could forge a friendship that could be profitable for *all* of us. It's the wisest course of action on your part."

Tufton nodded. "Yes, it *would* be prudent of us to subject you to a bit of close scrutiny."

His expression remained placid, but inside, Simon reveled. There was something so damn satisfying about setting a trap and having his prey waltz right into it, all the while believing the trap was the prey's idea.

Simon got to his feet. "Marvelous. Shall we say dinner at eight? At Mr. Harrold's?"

Blinking, Harrold said, "That would be . . . yes, I suppose . . . Linford will give you my direction on the way out."

"I look forward to it. Gentlemen." Simon bowed and strolled out the door, his every step light with confidence, but he knew that the most unpredictable part of the scheme was yet to come. And it all depended on Alyce.

CHAPTER 12.

Alyce strolled beside Eva as they moved east from the rows of shops, following a road that brought them around to look out at the open sea. A green park sloped down from limestone cliffs, and a striped lighthouse in the park kept its glass eye turned out toward the water. More boats and ships danced along the surface of the sea in their own ageless rhythm.

Landlocked. That was her. All her life. And here was just a tiny sliver of the sea, and ships skimming along the waves. But—aside from Simon—she'd never seen anything so exotic. This was merely someone else's world, as routine to them as the miners plunging every day over a hundred feet underground. Maybe a sailor would gape at the man-engine, the complicated device that lowered the miners far down into the earth.

Simon had been on many ships. Had journeyed across oceans to faraway places. She pictured him on the deck of a ship, his hair wind-tossed, his eyes as blue as the sea around him. It filled her with lightness, that image. It seemed right that he'd have the freedom of the ocean.

In her vision of him aboard the ship, a shadow appeared beside him, flickering like an uncovered lamp.

Her. Could she take her place next to him, flying across the sea?

It'd never happen. Her shadow guttered and went out, and Simon was alone again in her dream. She stayed on the shore, watching him sail off, the horizon eagerly reaching for him, taking him away.

As they walked, she and Eva ate lemon ices from paper cups, using little flat wooden spoons. Her first lemon ice, and despite the brisk weather, the treat tasted like summer holidays she'd never have.

They'd been silent for some time, she and Eva. There seemed no need to fill the air with chatter—Simon wasn't on a ship, but in the offices of the mine owners.

"I can't help wondering if the ruse is going as we planned," she confessed. "Think he'll convince the owners to sign over ownership of the mine?"

"A more persuasive and charming lad you couldn't find anywhere," Eva said.

"But the bloody owners have hearts of rock and brains like tills at a shop, thinking only of pounds and pence." Alyce looked around at the other people strolling by. Probably none of them were talking about confidence schemes and greedy mine owners.

"Simon has a way about him," Eva said. "He'll get it done."

Alyce didn't want to say it aloud, but she agreed. That devil had sneaked his way inside her mind, in the fibers that knit together to make her body. Had it only been a few weeks ago that she'd first met him, on the road from the mine to the village? It felt like the whole span of a life.

She thirsted for more of him. *All* of him. "Why'd he enlist instead of buy a commission?"

Eva was silent for a few moments, considering. "He didn't want to be treated any differently than other men.

So he told me. Started as a rank private. By the time he was at Rorke's Drift, he'd worked his way up to sergeant, and that's where he stopped."

"So he was never a commanding officer."

Eva spooned some flavored ice into her mouth. "I imagine he kept order when it was all going to hell, but no, he wasn't in command."

A sailboat clanged its bell as it skimmed past, the sound oddly cheerful in contrast to what Alyce had just learned.

"His father must've been furious," she murmured.

"That's what Simon told me. Wouldn't take his letters for nearly a year. Of course," Eva added, "the next year, buying commissions was abolished. All that wrath for nothing."

Another chill pierced Alyce as she imagined a younger Simon writing letter after letter to his father and having them all refused. A complete rejection. "Did he know that they'd get rid of the buying of commissions?"

"There'd been rumblings, but naturally Simon wouldn't wait. The cheeky bastard had to make his statement."

Which seemed so much like him that Alyce nearly laughed. It did seem to be something he'd do, just to prove a point, just to show the world that he did whatever he liked, and centuries of privilege wouldn't stop him. And of course he wanted to be with the enlisted men. This was the same Simon who now worked for Nemesis, shoving his shoulder against the giant stone wheel of injustice. Not because it benefited him, but because it was right. And if he got to break a few rules—perhaps even a law or a nose—along the way, so much the better.

Digging her spoon into what was now turning to lemony slush, she said, "Does he . . . in London, is there . . ." She winced inside at her faltering words. "Does he have a woman?"

"It won't be much of a comfort to you if I said that he didn't."

"Does he have a woman or not?"

"He doesn't."

Knots released themselves from Alyce's shoulders and stomach. Then they returned when Eva stopped walking and faced her. The wind tugged at the ribbons of the other woman's hat, but her expression was grave. And when she spoke, there was a curious note of compassion in her voice.

"Having a dual existence plays hell with romantic relationships. They can't last under the strain."

"They might," Alyce countered. "With the right people."

Eva gave her another cool smile. Had she always been this aloof, or had her work with Nemesis made her this way? Either way, it felt bloody strange to talk about romance with a woman as chill as New Year's morning.

"You seem decent," Eva said. "Simon trusts you—a minor miracle in itself. He looks at you like a thirsty man desperate for wine. Never seen him gaze at a woman the same way. I see the way you look back, just as thirsty."

At this point, there was no sense in denying it. Alyce didn't like to lie, either. But she didn't speak.

"To win his heart, it'd take someone very extraordinary," the other woman continued. "I'd wager he thinks he hasn't a heart to win. But he does. With its own needs, its own cravings."

"And those are?"

"Passion, strength of character. But being in Nemesis comes with a curse."

Alyce gave Eva a skeptical glance. "You don't strike me as the sort to believe in things like curses. That's for us peasant folk."

"It's not a curse of fairy gold or crossing a ring of toadstools. But we Nemesis sort—we're fated to be alone.

I'd been, until Jack." The way she said her husband's name nearly made Alyce blush.

Yet something niggled at Alyce. "But you and Simon . . . you've never . . ."

Eva tossed her lemon ice in the rubbish. "Nobody ever suggests that Scotland Yard detectives become lovers."

"Maybe they *do* become lovers, but they don't trumpet it in the papers."

The other woman raised her eyebrows as if conceding the point. "He tried, once."

Alyce had the sudden urge to throw Eva into the rubbish bin.

"I said no," Eva said. "And it didn't wound my sensibilities overmuch when he seemed relieved that I'd rejected him. In truth, I think he made the suggestion out of a sense of obligation. Not any real attraction."

"What a consolation."

"I do like you, Alyce. You seem like an intelligent woman who doesn't yield to anyone. Rather reminds me of myself," she added with a small smile. The smile faded quickly, however. "But I'm telling you again: nothing can come of this thing you have with Simon."

Alyce crossed her arms over her chest. "Bloody cheek! You've got Jack. Whatever happens with me and Simon, it doesn't have a lick to do with you."

"No," Eva allowed, "but he's my friend. If you're both not careful, there's going to be a lot of pain for the two of you."

Alyce wanted to throw her hands in the air, but stopped herself in time. Fine ladies didn't make such gestures in public. Instead, she said hotly, "It doesn't matter. Nothing but the mine matters. Everything else is just deads."

"Deads?"

"The rubbish left over after dressing the ore. Worthless, useless rock. At the end of every day, we cart it away. That's what's going to happen with me and Simon. We'll cart away everything that's got no value. The next day, it'll be like it never happened."

Eva eyed Alyce skeptically, but Alyce only glared back in defiance. What did these Nemesis people know of her? It took a lot of ruddy nerve to make those kinds of assumptions. And if anything Eva said felt like needles shoved slowly into Alyce's chest, she ignored the pain. This mission would come to an end, one way or the other, with the one certainty being Simon leaving. It was the only thing that could be relied upon.

After a few moments, Eva shrugged. "I know the futility of other people trying to argue with me, so consider the subject dropped." She glanced at the little timepiece pinned to her bodice. "Simon ought to be finished by now. Shall we reconnoiter?"

They took a cab up the hill, with the day bright and lively all around them. Yet Alyce's thoughts kept gnawing on Eva's well-intentioned warning.

Her advice had come far too late.

Weariness and excitement danced through Simon's nerves as he rode the elevator up to his hotel room. He fumbled with the brass key, his vision swimming. When was the last time he'd slept? Difficult to remember. On other missions, he'd gone days snatching sleep here and there, falling back on his soldiering habits. But at the moment, he couldn't honestly remember when he'd last shut his eyes. Too busy setting everything in motion. Too busy looking after Alyce. She was still new to this world of plots and schemes, for all her bravado.

Unlocking the door, he pushed it open. A cold stab of panic hit him when he saw that while their trunk was in the room, Alyce wasn't.

He exhaled deliberately. She was with Eva, one of

Nemesis's most capable agents. Nothing would happen to her.

Throwing his hat and coat onto the table, he also loosened his necktie. It didn't help him breathe easier.

What the hell was happening to him? Dozens of jobs, all of them utilizing different people to obtain an objective, and not once in all of those missions had he been so gripped with concern about any of those people. He wouldn't callously use a woman and throw her aside in service to Nemesis's goals—but this acid that burned in him when he thought of Alyce being hurt, this *fear,* that was new.

From the trunk, he pulled out a revolver. The Webley felt good in his hand, solid and trustworthy. He preferred his Martini-Henry rifle, but that proved more conspicuous when traveling. And not convenient when fighting in close quarters.

He doubted that anything that might happen in Plymouth would require a gun—but it was better to be prepared for any eventuality than be caught shorthanded. After checking to make sure that it was clean, loaded, and in working order, he placed the weapon in the little side table beside the chaise. That's where he'd be sleeping—or attempting to sleep—tonight.

He removed his jacket and draped it over the back of the chair. The room here at the Cormorant resembled the one back in Exeter, in the way all hotel rooms of good character but not wild expense resembled one another. It had its own bathroom with a hipbath, commode, and sink. The room lacked a parlor, however. Instead, the chaise longue was arrayed near the fire. The room itself was dominated by a large brass bed heaped with lacy pillows.

They'd be sharing this room tonight, he and Alyce. His mouth went dry. A whole night of lying on that chaise, listening to her as she shifted beneath the bedclothes, knowing she wore only a nightgown. Granted, he'd seen the nightgown that Harriet had packed, and a more modest garment of high-necked flannel couldn't be found. Yet even that would be enough to keep him awake all night.

He glanced at the clock. It was after two in the afternoon. They'd parted before noon. Where *was* she?

To distract himself, he threw himself down onto the chaise and studied the incorporation and transfer papers Marco had drawn up in Exeter. Harriet had mentioned he had a new client—a cheated widow. They didn't collaborate on all the same missions at the same time, otherwise it'd take far too long to get through their caseload. Still, Simon wondered what the details of the widow's case might be. And then there was that Scotland Yard detective making a nuisance of himself.

Simon rubbed his forehead. Always so much to consider. He liked it that way. Better to run from one objective to the next than turn into one of those staid, sedentary men who never seemed to leave the huge leather chairs at the club, ossifying behind their newspapers.

Footsteps sounded in the corridor, then stopped outside his door. He was on his feet in an instant, but didn't reach for the gun. He knew that tread. The lock clicked and the door opened, revealing a tired but tense Alyce.

He wanted to cross the room in two strides and wrap his arms around her. Instead, he asked, "Where's Eva?"

"She dropped me off a few blocks from here, just in case anyone was watching the hotel and might possibly connect her to Jack, and Jack to us." Alyce shut the door behind her and glanced everywhere in the room. Everywhere but at him.

Unease trailed its fingers down his spine. Women had a tendency to reveal things to one another, even women of short acquaintance. It might take two men years before they learned each other's first names, but women seemed eager to share intimacies with total strangers. One of those mysteries of womanhood he'd never quite understood.

What had Eva and Alyce talked about? Eva had promised to gossip about him. God, he hoped she didn't mention that awful peccadillo of his from a year ago—Simon had honestly believed the woman to be a widow, and so she'd represented herself, but her husband was, in fact, quite alive and watching from a secret chamber.

Pressure built behind his eyes. He had the oddest need to tell Alyce that none of it meant anything; it never could. All the women who'd breezed through his life had been diversions—just as he was a diversion to them. Yet he said nothing to Alyce, just watched her as she took a few exploratory steps in to the room.

"The meeting went well," he said, filling the silence. "Jack played his part like a born thespian. Or confidence artist. Same thing. And the owners seemed intrigued by the offer of the temporary transfer."

"What's next?" As she removed her hat and coat, she glanced over at him in his shirtsleeves. Her gaze lingered for a moment, straying on his shoulders and arms, before she looked away.

"Dinner tonight at eight o'clock. I'm to bring my charming wife"—there was that shiver of brightness again whenever he referred to her that way—"and they'll determine whether we're trustworthy enough to handle this deal."

At the word "trustworthy," she gave a short laugh. Then, more soberly, she said, "I've never been to a dinner party before."

"They're dull as hell, but ours tonight will have a little extra zest to it."

"The zest of lying through our teeth."

"Deceit always makes for a more scintillating time."

She stared fixedly at a framed picture of Plymouth Sound, as if she didn't want to meet his gaze. "Will you . . ." Her words came out slowly, each one a struggle. "There's got to be rules to how these dinner parties go, but I don't know them."

She still wouldn't look at him. It cost her so much to admit her lack of knowledge. Something within his chest expanded, trying to fill him completely.

He tugged on the bellpull. In a few minutes, a man wearing the hotel's uniform appeared at their door, smiling brightly. "How may I help you, Mr. Shale?"

"I'll need a tray set for a semiformal dinner. All the glasses, plates, and cutlery."

"Of course," the porter said at once. Thank God the staff was well trained in the art of not asking questions.

"Half an hour after that, I want baths drawn for me and my wife. And a maid to help my wife undress." It was a wonder he didn't stumble over those last two words.

"Yes, Mr. Shale."

Simon handed the young man a shilling, and the porter hastened off.

"I haven't had any schooling for over ten years," Alyce said wryly, when Simon turned back to her.

"You're going to make an excellent student," he answered.

His instincts proved correct. She quickly learned the etiquette required of a dinner, not merely the usage and timing of the plates and silverware, but the ritualized process surrounding something that ought to be basic—the eating of a meal. But if Society could complicate something, it gladly did so.

He and Alyce sat at the table in their room, the dishes arrayed before her as they reviewed the protocol.

"I'm only to say yes or no to a servant," she noted. "Not even thank them? Seems . . . rude."

"It's more rude to say 'thank you.' They're just doing their jobs. Saying thanks implies that they've gone beyond their established duties."

She nodded, but her look was pure skepticism. "All I have to worry about at home is whether I can get the last piece of bread before Henry does. If Sarah doesn't want it," she added quickly.

Some women might resent their pregnant sister-in-law, but Alyce seemed happy—eager—to tend to Sarah. Kindness came naturally to Alyce, but not the saccharine, false munificence of Society ladies who only cared that other people *thought* they were charitable. Alyce's generosity was real. And he savored it.

"A dinner party is the proverbial tip of the iceberg." He leaned back in his chair, linking his fingers behind his head. "Whole libraries could be filled with books on etiquette and proper, moral behavior."

"What a waste of paper."

"But excellent fodder for writing lewd things in the margins."

She stared at him, appalled. "You *wrote* in your books?"

There it was again, the proof that they led disparate lives. The cost of a book meant nothing to him when he was growing up. It didn't mean much now. He had a bookseller in the Strand who often set aside for him items of particular interest—travel narratives, studies of geography, Monsieur Verne's latest novel—and he'd buy them by the stack.

"Boys like me grow up believing the world is ours to scribble on," he said.

"Then they grow up, but they still think they can scrawl all over everything." She gazed at him, contemplative. "Not all of them, though."

He resisted the impulse to shift in his seat. With each glance from her, he felt more and more the weaving of an invisible thread, joining them. He ought to cut that thread, but the idea created a physical pain that ached through him.

"The men tonight," he said instead, "even their wives, they're going to say things that will shock you. Anger you. But above all else, *they can't know this.* The smallest hint from you that you disagree with their beliefs and we'll be out on our arses."

"I'll sit on my hands so I don't punch anyone."

He leaned forward. "Listen to me, Alyce. Class division is the god these people worship. They hate and adore the people above them, and don't acknowledge the humanity of the people below them. If you cast stones at their idol, we'll be crucified."

The earnestness in his voice appeared to shock her. After a moment, she nodded tightly. "It'll hurt like hell, but I'll keep quiet. Or even"—she shuddered—"agree with them."

He exhaled. "There's my lass."

They stared at each other, caught. He'd spoken like a miner, as if she really *were* his lass, and neither of those things was true. They never could be.

A knock sounded on the door. Simon lurched to his feet and opened it, to find the porter standing in front of aproned maids with buckets of steaming water—it was far easier and faster to heat the water on the stove downstairs than try to draw bucket after bucket from the bathroom sink. A burly man in uniform carried a hipbath, as well.

"You ordered baths in half an hour, Mr. Shale," the porter explained brightly. "And thirty minutes have elapsed."

Simon waved the hotel staff into the room. Some of

the maids filled the tub in the bathroom, while the others emptied their buckets into the hipbath now set before the fire. Simon tipped every servant as they filed out, but one maid lingered, glancing shyly at Alyce.

Understanding at once, Alyce stood and strode into the bathroom. The maid followed, shutting the door behind them. Simon waited, drumming his fingers on the mantel, fighting his thundering pulse as he imagined Alyce being undressed. Bodice unhooking from skirts, skirts sliding to the ground, petticoats, bustle, and corset cover being removed. Corset next. Then wearing only a chemise, pantalets, and stockings. Then those were gone, too, and he could actually hear Alyce sink into her bath. She gave a long, luxurious sigh.

The maid emerged, her arms full of Alyce's clothing. She tucked everything back into the trunk, blushing all the while at the intimacy between supposed husband and wife. Simon made certain to keep his hands in his pockets. He didn't want to terrify the poor maid with his aching erection.

"Just give a pull on the bell when you want the missus dressed for tonight, sir," the maid whispered.

"Your gratuity is on the dresser," he managed to growl.

The girl pocketed the coin, bobbed a curtsy, then quickly left. Simon locked the door behind her.

From within the bathroom, he heard the soft, intimate sounds of Alyce in her bath. He bit back a groan. With any luck, the water in his own bath had turned cold.

When she emerged from the bathroom later, her hair was damp and loose about her shoulders, and she was wrapped in a long flannel robe. She stared deliberately at her feet—her bare, pink feet that he, too, found fascinating—until Simon said, "I'm bathed and dressed. No need for modesty."

Simon had slipped on a pair of trousers and a shirt,
but that was as far as he'd gotten. They still had hours to
go until dinner, and he'd be damned if he'd spend all that
time fully clothed. The bath had still been warm by the
time he'd gotten into it, and now a lethargy weighted his
eyes and limbs. He was sprawled on the chaise, with a
book in his lap, but the moment Alyce had come out of
the bathroom, he completely forgot what he'd been
reading.

"It's your own sense of modesty I'm thinking of," she
answered, glancing up. Pink stained her cheeks, despite
her bravado. "Working at Wheal Prosperity, watching
the men come in and out of the wash house, there's not
much I haven't seen."

"I haven't seen any miners come racing out with their
goods uncovered and dangling."

Did she know that her gaze shot straight to his groin
the moment the words left his mouth? He suddenly remembered the book in his lap, and gave thanks for it.

"You remember that lake in the cavern? The boys
bathe there in summer." She sat gingerly on the edge of
the bed. Lace-patterned light drifted across her face as
the afternoon sun wove through the curtains.

He grinned. "Naughty girl. You spied on them."

"Of course I did."

Goddamn it, but he liked her. "Did they get the chance
to return the favor?" He half dreaded her response, thinking of those slavering country boys getting a look at what
he was dying to see.

"Girls couldn't use the quarry."

He exhaled.

"Doesn't mean I didn't sneak out at night and have a
bathe with some of my girlfriends, though."

And there went his breath again, and the throb of his
cock. The image was almost too much: Alyce, sleek and

nude, cavorting in ink-dark water in the lamplight. Doing as she pleased because she'd bend to no one's will but her own.

Desmond had once taught him some special techniques for calming his thoughts, and he used them now. It was either that or lunge for her like an animal. He emptied his mind, filling himself with a bright nothingness, thinking of absolutely naught.

"Simon? You're not ill, are you?"

He blinked back to awareness. "Only tired."

She covered her mouth as she let out a huge, lusty yawn. "I'm starting to see two of you."

Glancing at the clock, he said, "We still have a few hours until we have to be at Harrold's for dinner. Better get some sleep."

"Doubt I could get a wink. I'm too wound up." But she yawned again.

"Soldiers know that if they don't get rest before a battle, they could make a fatal mistake on the battlefield."

"That's not much of a lullaby, Sergeant."

The idea that Alyce knew about his past didn't send immediate needles of panic through him. He was glad, actually. It felt so bloody liberating to be around someone without any wall or distance. As if, for the first time, he was more whole than he'd ever been.

"Just lie down and shut your eyes," he said. "If you sleep, good. If not, lie there and entertain yourself with thoughts of how utterly we're going to ruin those bastards."

Naturally, that idea made her smile. Still wearing her flannel robe, she pulled back the covers and nestled beneath them. The sight of Alyce in a big, welcoming bed was one of the greatest tests of his life.

Or so he thought, until she held the covers open. "Come on, soldier. You need your rest, too."

His body turned to rock, and he gripped the back of the chaise until his knuckles whitened. "Over here is fine for me."

"It can't be as comfortable."

At that moment, it felt like a bed of nails. He said through gritted teeth, "I get into that bed, the last thing we'd do is sleep."

Her eyelids lowered. "So we won't sleep."

God, he was so tempted. So bloody tempted.

"No," he said.

"But—"

"Don't fight me on this, damn it. One of us has to make the right decision."

Her look was pure mutiny. He half expected her to jump out of bed, haul him up by his shirt, and throw him into bed. Almost wished she would. Instead, she turned away from him.

"I'm trying to be rational," he said gently to her back. "I want you. So much. But we just . . . can't be."

A long silence. "You're right," she finally said, still with her back to him. "But I hate it."

"I do, too."

Neither of them spoke. Her body relaxed, and within minutes her breath grew steady and deep.

He let out his own breath. It was easier, actually, with her asleep. He'd never bestow his attentions on a sleeping woman. That was for scoundrels and artless seducers. No, if he was going to make love to Alyce, he'd want her fully awake, ready and eager for his touch.

I need to take my own advice and rest. But that was impossible with his cock pressing like a branding iron against the front of his trousers. No help for it, then.

Noiselessly, he rose up from the chaise and slipped into the bathroom. He almost laughed at himself as he tore open the buttons of his trousers. When was the last time he'd had to hide himself away for a secret wank? Years and years. But this was what he needed.

He fought back a hiss as he took his cock in his hand. Since he'd arrived at Wheal Prosperity, he hadn't had any kind of sexual release. Weeks of tension and need had built within him. With Alyce as the sole focus of all that hunger. Now she slept in the other room, after filling his head with images of her undressing, taking a bath, going for late-night nude swims. God, she'd be so incredible naked. So tight with muscle, so long and curved in all the right places. Would she have dusky or light nipples? Of a certain, the curls between her legs would be dark and silky.

His hand froze when the door creaked open.

In the washroom mirror, his gaze met Alyce's. She gripped the door frame with one hand, and the other pressed against her belly. Her eyes traveled from his face to his hand, still wrapped around his cock. It pulsed beneath her scrutiny.

"Don't," she said when he started to release his hold on himself.

Goddamn it. He grew even harder.

"Then get out of here," he growled, "and let me finish."

She stepped into the washroom. "We're supposed to be married. But the minute we show up at that dinner tonight, they'll know we've never really touched each other. Not very convincing."

He cursed. "Sit on the edge of the tub and watch, then."

"No." She closed the distance separating them, pressing herself to his side. Her breast brushed his arm, the hard point of her nipple a delicious rasp against him. "I'm going to take care of you."

He closed his eyes, praying that he didn't spill right there and then. "You've done this before?" His voice was pure gravel.

"Some fumbling at the cavern. Nothing like this." Her own voice was husky. "Show me what to do."

Shuddering, he let go of himself. Then took her hand in his and wrapped it around his shaft. They both moaned.

"God," she breathed. "I never knew. The *feel*."

"Hard." That was the only word that came to mind. He'd never been so hard in his life.

"Soft, too. The softest thing I've ever touched. And hot." She tore her gaze from her hand around his cock and looked up at him. "I make you feel this way?"

"You make me feel everything."

She gazed back down to her hand encircling his shaft. "What do I do?"

He could barely get the words out. "Stroke it. Move your hand . . . up and down. Tight. Don't be afraid to be rough."

"I'll hurt you."

"You won't."

Her hand began to move, pumping him. Tentative at first, and then with more strength. He'd never felt anything half so delicious. It was all the more exquisite because it was *her* touching him, stroking him. The woman he'd wanted for so long. And she was so strong, so wondrously strong. In every way.

He shut his eyes. If he looked down, if he saw her hand around his cock, it would be over in seconds.

She took some time to circle her fingers around the head, finding the exact spot that scoured him with pleasure. "Yes." He hissed. "Just like . . . just like that."

"Simon," she said breathlessly. From beneath her gown, her breasts quivered against him, and she deliberately rubbed them along his arm. "Feels so good, so wicked."

"Ah, God. *Alyce*. I'm—"

He arched, groaning. The climax shredded him. It

tore from his body, from somewhere deep inside himself, and he reached one arm back to grab the towel bar behind him for support. His body was molten, his throat raw. The world dimmed around the edges. All he knew was his release, and Alyce.

Slowly, her fingers uncurled, releasing him. The small washroom filled with the sounds of their panting. He finally opened his eyes and saw her studying her hand, fascinated. He quickly grabbed a washcloth and cleaned her up, then himself.

They stared at each other. A febrile blush darkened her cheeks, and her pupils were fathomless.

Christ. He'd just had the most intense sexual experience of his life. All from Alyce's hand. From *her.*

"That was . . ." She shook her head, as if unable to find the right words. He understood completely. Words were too small, too defined, for what had just happened.

"I can make you feel more," he rumbled. "Much more. We'll get through this damned dinner and then the rest of the night is ours."

She pressed a hand to her belly. "I won't be able to concentrate, knowing that."

"Don't concentrate on anything now. Just rest." He led her to the bed, then collapsed onto the chaise as exhaustion overwhelmed him.

She got into bed. "Simon . . . thank you."

He managed to choke out a laugh. That she should thank *him* was ridiculous. And wonderful.

Within minutes, Alyce's eyes closed, and her breathing slowed. She was truly asleep.

Yet even after everything, despite his weariness, Simon couldn't sleep. His mind whirled. And his goddamn sodding heart raced.

He stretched out as best as his tall frame would allow on the confines of the chaise. Taking his own advice from

earlier, he envisioned the owners and managers of Wheal
Prosperity shaking their fists at the heavens as their corrupt system was torn away, decimating their fortunes.
They'd rage and scream, but there would be nothing to
stop their ruin. And Alyce happily licked fresh butter
from her fingers.

Simon fell asleep with a smile on his face.

Hours later, arrayed in his formal black-and-white evening clothes, he waited down in the hotel lobby. He exchanged pleasant nods with other guests as they walked
in and out, all the while drumming the brim of his top
hat and trying to keep his foot from tapping. Impatience,
excitement, and a soupçon of concern danced through
him. Going into a scheme with confidence was crucial.
But he wanted, *needed,* this ploy to work, and Alyce was
the means to make it happen.

Currently, she was sequestered in their room upstairs
with one of the hotel's maids, helping her dress and complete her toilette for the evening. Simon had dressed
quickly, his back to the women, and then hurried out.

Simon now gave his starched cuffs a tug and took another look at himself in the pier glass over the fireplace.
He adjusted his white tie and double-checked the studs
on his shirtfront. Everything seemed in order. No one in
his social set knew that he hadn't employed a valet since
he'd returned to civilian life. After dodging Zulu war
clubs and Indian bandits' bullets, relying on someone
else to help him put his clothing on seemed remarkably
ridiculous.

Three chintz-covered chairs were drawn close to the
fire, but he couldn't sit. Too much energy surged through
him. And one of the chairs was occupied by a large orange tabby that regarded him with the disinterest in
which cats seemed to specialize. Simon had no doubt,

however, that the moment he took one of the other chairs, the cat would immediately leap into his lap and cover him with orange fur.

He turned when his peripheral vision caught sight of movement on the stairs. Without thought, his feet took him to the foot of the staircase, and he could only stand there, gaping, as Alyce slowly descended. The maid trailed behind her, but he hardly saw the other woman. His eyes were full of Alyce.

This must have been how Bellerophon felt when he slammed to earth—Simon quite literally couldn't breathe.

Alyce wore an evening gown of silver satin, its flounces, low neckline, and minuscule sleeves adorned with jet beads. Pale silver-trimmed lace tapered down the bodice to end in a sharp point at her waist. The skirt had been artfully draped to recall Grecian statues, and with each step she took, the gown moved with her, gleaming like a pearl, begging for touch.

The fabric only served to highlight expanses of creamy skin—her neck, her upper chest, the slim band of bare flash between her sleeves, and her long ivory kid-skin gloves. Thank God she wore a wrap of dark gray velvet, covering the majority of her décolletage. But he dreaded the reveal that would inevitably come when she'd remove her wrap, because he knew, he *knew* that it would be his first real glimpse of her breasts—the tops of them, anyway—and it'd be bloody difficult to keep up his patter at Harrold's when all he'd want to do was stare at the treasure he'd discovered.

He did catch a glimpse of a jet-bead collar encircling her neck, and matching earrings swung from her ear-lobes, tempting a man to catch her earlobe between his teeth and suck, ever so gently, until she moaned. And the thought of her wearing nothing but the beaded collar sent all of his blood below his waist.

Her hair was pinned up in a more elaborate style, dark whorls and curls held in place with silver silk flowers and jet combs. The hotel's maid had a talent.

All of this was a far cry from Alyce's simple, home-spun clothing in the village, the heavy apron she wore when working, her tightly pinned bun. Even her smart traveling ensemble was a pale flicker compared to the blazing elegance of this gown.

But none of it mattered—not even the glimpses of bare skin—when compared to the expression on her face. He might've expected some shyness or uncertainty. These weren't the clothes of a bal-maiden. Some women in the same circumstance might tug uncomfortably at their garments, or keep their heads down, modest and blushing.

Not Alyce. Her chin was held high, her eyes gleamed brightly, and the color in her cheeks came not from mod-esty or even paint.

No—she was a flame of shining confidence. She looked magnificent, and she knew it. As men in the lobby slowed to stare at her, she took in their gazes as if she were a queen, and their regard were her due.

It wasn't snobbery in her posture or the slight curve of her lips. She didn't put on airs. But he could see her revel in her power, and it was a deluge, drowning him in desire.

She came down the steps, her hand trailing on the ban-ister. Their gazes met. A long, breathless moment. Then she pulled her eyes away, running them deliberately, thor-oughly over him. Taking in the sight of him in his evening dress. He wasn't a fool. He understood that he wore such garments well. But never did that give him more satisfac-tion than at that moment, when her eyes darkened, her grip tightened on the banister, and her nostrils flared subtly.

"Thank you, Maisie," she said over her shoulder, every inch a lady. "You may go."

The maid bobbed a curtsy and hurried away before Simon could add his own words of gratitude.

"I know we're not supposed to thank the servants," Alyce said. "But this"—she waved down at herself—"is extraordinary."

"You can thank a maid or valet, and in this case, she deserves the praise." He couldn't believe such banal words even left his lips, when all he wanted was to grab her, drag her upstairs, and show her just how extraordinary she truly was.

He closed the distance between them and offered her his arm. "It's time to hunt."

She placed her hand in the crook of his elbow. "Hunt the owners? Or each other?"

His grin was as savage as he felt. "I'm hungry enough for both."

She did him one better by licking her lips. "Good, because I'm *starving*."

CHAPTER 13.

Alyce stared up at the front of Oliver Harrold's three-story terraced home. Though similar houses lined the street, all of them built on the same plan of bow windows, columns flanking the front door, and sharply gabled roofs, only Harrold's was built on the blood and sweat of the people of Trewyn. It could've been the world's most elegant home, a grand palace—but to her, it was as ugly as a wound.

As she and Simon walked up the neat path, she murmured, "What was that weapon they had way back in the Middle Ages? The one that could throw boulders into the walls or dead horses over the ramparts?"

"A trebuchet."

"I'd like one of those right now."

"What we've got is better than a trebuchet. This," he said, nodding toward the house, "will be a smoldering crater when we're done."

"You always know the right thing to say."

They climbed the stairs, her hand on his arm. She didn't think she'd ever get used to the feel of his solidness, his lean strength. And for the rest of her days, she'd remember the feel of his cock in her hand, satiny and hard as iron, and the agonized look of pleasure on his face when she touched him.

She had done that. *She* had made him feel that way. She loved that she could give him pleasure, wanted to give him more. And her own body hummed with unspent desire.

Here she was, standing on the front step of her enemy's house, and she wanted to push Simon against the door and kiss him dizzy. They'd reached the most important stage in their plan. She wouldn't ruin it with wayward, hungry thoughts.

But it certainly helped keep the fear scraping in her belly at bay. Simon believed in her. Everyone in Trewyn and Nemesis counted on her. Tonight, she couldn't fail. It just wasn't a possibility. Except that it was.

"Brave lass." Simon gave her hand on his arm a squeeze, and the smallest of smiles. The fear that threatened to grind her up ebbed with his encouragement. He reached for the heavy brass knocker on the door, but his gloved hand hovered over it.

She drew a deep breath. "Go on."

He knocked. The door opened immediately, a stone-faced man in a starched uniform standing on the other side, looking more self-important than Saint Peter.

"Mr. and Mrs. Simon Shale." Simon handed the butler a little card.

There was no change in the butler's expression as he pocketed the card. He stepped aside, permitting Simon and Alyce to enter. "The company's assembled upstairs in the drawing room, sir."

Simon handed his coat and hat to a young man in another uniform—a footman, Simon had told her earlier—and the same footman took Alyce's wrap before retreating. She tried her best not to gape at her surroundings, though this was truly the most expensive home she'd ever really seen. All she'd witnessed of the managers' house had been the kitchen and larder in the depths of night. Now she was above stairs, with the lamps blazing.

She had a brief impression of a checked tile floor, and a marble-topped table holding painted china vases heaped with menacing flowers. But then Simon offered her his arm again, and they began to go up a curving, carpeted staircase. Voices floated out of a room on the next floor—men's strident tones, the occasional woman's fluttering comment. Alyce's heart thudded painfully with each step closer.

"These ancestral portraits on the walls," Simon murmured. "They probably bought them by the dozen."

She smothered a laugh. The thundering of her heart eased.

They stopped in the doorway of what had to be the drawing room. It looked like the inside of a rotting animal carcass—all red and black. Fabric swaddled every surface, from the tables to the windows to the chairs to the mantel. Everywhere her gaze fell, she found objects of wood and china and brass. Plants and wreaths and pictures. An abundance of *things*. The room itself wasn't small, but she felt herself choking as she took a step inside. What was the point of all this junk? Worse still, was that terrible ceramic elephant paid for with money that could've been used to buy fresh beef at the company store?

Still, she schooled her face to appear calm and serene as she looked around at the people within the room. One tall, skinny man stood by the mantel, and the others hefted themselves out of their chairs when she and Simon entered. Here they were—the owners of Wheal Prosperity. The men who crushed the life out of her family and friends.

It was a disappointment to see how *ordinary* they

were. No pointed horns sprouting from their foreheads. No giant boils on their noses. Nobody greedily rubbed their hands together. Except for their evening clothes, they looked like regular middle-aged men. She felt strangely deflated. For all the wrong these men did, couldn't their appearance match their foul hearts?

A man with spare hair on his head but a thick beard stepped forward. He gave them both a reserved bow. "Shale, welcome. Mrs. Shale, an honor. I'm Oliver Harrold."

Simon bowed in return and Alyce curtsied. "You are gracious in your hospitality." There was nothing but sincerity in Simon's voice.

She couldn't quite tell, what with Harrold's beard, but he seemed to give them a wry smile. "Too kind—especially when we're here to assess *each other's,* ah, hospitality."

"Your home is delightful," Alyce said. "Comfortable and attractive without being overly modern."

"All the efforts of Mrs. Harrold." He gestured to a woman sitting on a burgundy sofa. Mrs. Harrold regarded Alyce through narrowed eyes, and gave her a little nod of recognition, the red stones around her throat glittering.

"Perhaps, after dinner, you might give me some suggestions as to the outfitting of our home," Alyce said. "We're newly married, and I would be so grateful for any advice you might have to offer. I want to make certain of Mr. Shale's every comfort."

The frosty expression on Mrs. Harrold's face warmed slightly. "It's a woman's primary duty to ensure her husband's contentment. Everything else, including her own comfort, is ancillary."

Simon's hand covered Alyce's, where her fingers dug into his arm. Any other man might wince in pain from the pressure, but he kept the same bland smile on his face. She slowly released her death's grip on his arm. They couldn't make a single misstep, not here, in the den of the beasts.

"Shale," Harrold continued, "you'll have the privilege of escorting Mrs. Harrold into dinner. And it will be my singular pleasure to escort Mrs. Shale down to the dining room."

As discussed earlier, both she and Simon made sounds of gratification.

"This rather breaks from tradition," Harrold continued, "but considering the circumstances, I'll introduce you to the rest of the party. Shale, you've already met Victor Tufton, but your wife has not. The charming woman in yellow is Mrs. Tufton."

A heavy man, his face already red, nodded. Where he was large, his wife seemed birdlike, her skin pulled tight over brittle bones. Simon and Alyce again repeated their bows and curtsies.

"And you haven't met our other partner. This is John Stokeham." He waved toward the tall, thin man at the mantel.

Alice had seen the names before on a metal plaque outside the managers' office, and now she looked into their faces, saw them as men and not just names or anonymous enemies.

"His delightful sister," Harrold went on, "is Miss Vera Stokeham."

Miss Stokeham looked about the same age as Alyce, but she had a white, glossy plumpness and the sullen expression reserved for babies who always get what they want. Age was the only thing she and Alyce seemed to have in common.

Once more she and Simon curtsied and bowed.

Damn, but this was odd. All these formal words and these practiced gestures. None of them meant anything.

They were empty, like a miner's drained canteen. And none of them spoke of what this evening was really about: deceit.

The butler appeared in the doorway to the drawing room. "Dinner is served."

"I detect some Cornish in your accent, Mrs. Shale," Harrold said. He sat at the head of the table, and she'd been placed to his right. Far at the other end of the table, Simon sat beside Mrs. Harrold, and something he said to her made the older woman laugh, her hand fluttering around her chest.

Alyce felt herself in exile, even though she knew this was how dinners were always arranged. None of the guests sat with their spouses or, in the case of Miss Stokeham, beside her brother. Simon had told her it was supposed to encourage conversation, but it seemed the best way to make someone feel uncomfortable. How could she chitchat with people she didn't know—and worse, hated?

"We aren't so far from Cornwall," she pointed out. A servant appeared beside her, bearing a silver platter heaped with meat in some kind of brownish-red sauce. Carefully, she placed a few slices of beef on her gilt-edged plate, but only just caught herself from thanking the servant before he moved on to the next guest. Already, there had been two kinds of soup, fish, roast partridge, ham, lamb, and oysters. And there was still more to come.

The amount of food paraded past her made her ill. She poked at the meat with her fork, moving it around her plate so it looked as though she ate.

Too bad that her reticule was so small, or else she'd scrape everything off her dish into it and take it home to Sarah. She could make a few slices of beef last for days.

"Yet your husband is from London," Tufton noted as

he sat on her right. He took a much larger portion of meat, going back and forth from the platter three times.

Was this part of the test? These men didn't talk the way Simon did, with elite London's smooth, glossy notes, but they didn't sound like miners, either.

"My father is from Perranporth," she said. "He also used to manage a mine near Dolcoath. Doubtless his accent and speech patterns made an effect on me."

Tufton and Harrold nodded wisely. From the corner of her eye, she saw Simon relax slightly—the barest easing of his shoulder that only she seemed to notice.

"Fortunate, then, that this latest endeavor of your husband's involves a mine," Harrold said.

"Oh, yes! When we discussed the matter, we thought—"

"We?" Tufton's brows lowered. "Mr. Shale actually talked to you about business?"

Everyone, from the men seated nearest her, to the other women at the table, stared at her, aghast. Only Simon's face was perfectly neutral.

"Of course he didn't!" Alyce giggled. "The very idea! I've no sense for these matters, and he never speaks to me of them."

"As well he should," Stokeham pronounced.

The ladies all nodded in agreement.

"As he said to me," she continued, "'Alyce, it would make me very happy if you'd just sign this document.' Naturally, I didn't ask what the document was, I just signed it. Only later he accidentally revealed that the document had to do with a Cornish mine, and I thought it was so funny, you know, because of Papa and *his* mine."

To her own ears, she sounded as if she had dandelion puffs for brains, but from the way the rest of the company at the table looked at her, she'd clearly said the right thing.

Then Tufton's frown returned. "'Accidentally revealed.' Doesn't sound very discreet or wise."

Simon only laughed. "I'm a newly wedded man, Mr. Tufton. Surely you can excuse an occasional verbal blunder in the presence of one's bride. She does make me lose my head, sometimes." The look he sent her down the length of the table could have scorched the flower arrangements. She didn't have to manufacture her blush.

"Besides," Simon continued, "I needn't worry that Alyce will go gossiping to anyone. She's a model of all that's modest and discerning. After we married, we had to pay calls—"

Harrold groaned. "Don't remind me. It's been twenty-three years since Laura and I married, and I still wake up in a terror that we haven't finished all our wedding visits."

"And poor Mrs. Shale," Simon went on, "she was so afraid of indiscretion that she barely could manage a yes or no." He chuckled. "I'm sure it was a disappointment to the people we visited, but a credit to her."

"To you, as well," added Tufton. "Like children and the lesser ranks, women need to be guided by men of sense. They can't be trusted to see to their own well-being. Men such as us have to save them from themselves."

Alyce suspected it would be a breach of politeness to jump up and hit Tufton over the head with one of the heavy silver platters making their way around the room. Instead, she smiled blankly and moved peas around her plate.

At least she knew Simon didn't believe the blather he was spouting. But he played his part so well—so smug, so bloody *superior*—she had to fight the urge to throw something at *him,* too. She maintained a blank smile plastered to her face.

"I couldn't agree more, Tufton," he said. "Not to be too indelicate with ladies present, but with my own business ventures, I oversee as much of the workers' lives as I can. They may fuss and whine about issues of *fair wages* or *living conditions*, yet as I see it, they ought to be grateful for honest employment."

"It's really the best they can expect," Stokeham added.

"Giving ideas about living above their station is harmful." Harrold drank deeply from his glass of wine, and a servant stepped forward to refill it. Alyce resisted the impulse to catch the servant's eye. *Do you hear the complete rubbish these bastards are saying?*

"It's a kindness we're doing," Tufton said. "The lower ranks need us to make decisions for them, or else they'd degenerate into drunken chaos. Have you seen the way they live? Once, I toured the village of Trewyn and saw nothing but squalid little hovels. Families of seven or eight crammed into two rooms. Not a speck of privacy or modesty."

Miss Stokeham shuddered. "Mr. Tufton, pray let's not speak of it, for I'm sure to be put off my pudding, and I was so looking forward to it."

"My apologies, Miss Stokeham." Simon sent her one of his most charming smiles, and the girl practically melted in her chair. "The fault is mine for introducing such an indecorous topic."

"I believe you mentioned you're recently married," Mrs. Tufton said, turning to Alyce. "Where did you go on your wedding journey?"

Alyce's mind spun. She and Simon hadn't discussed this when they'd been plotting out their strategies for tonight. The best someone from her village could hope for was a few days in Newquay, or Torquay if they were being extravagant—which nobody ever was. But these people expected more than some Cornish seaside town. She pictured the map from the dame school she'd attended so long ago, and all the differently colored blobs that represented different countries. Brazil? No, that was all the way across the ocean and full of dangerous jungle. Egypt? Old sandy tombs seemed a strange thing to visit when celebrating a wedding.

"Greece," she blurted. It had lots of little islands that probably made for good places for young couples to learn about the physical side of marriage.

From the quick flash of approval in Simon's gaze, she'd made the right choice.

"How charming!" Mrs. Harrold cried. "Did you see the Acropolis? I just adored the marketplace at Monastiriaki—except for all the impertinent Greek vendors, of course."

"We were only in Athens for a short while," Simon explained. "We'd intended to go to Delphi, but the roads weren't safe. So we took a steamer to Santorini and then on to Crete."

"Ah, so much wonderful ancient culture!" Mrs. Tufton agreed.

"It was very educational," Alyce added. "I mean, charming."

"Do you remember, my dear," Simon said, "how you absolutely fell in love with a baby donkey on Crete and wanted to take it home with us?"

She answered, "You know I cannot resist an adorable ass."

"What happened to the creature?" asked Miss Stokeham.

Simon sighed. "Alas, we had to leave it behind."

"But there are plenty of asses right here in England," Alyce said.

More dishes were taken away, and she almost shouted in relief when she saw the footed platters heaped with fruit and nuts. This torturous part of the evening was almost over. She ached with the force of keeping herself still and silent. Inside, she shook with rage and called these men all the worst names she could think of. *Bastard. Son of a bitch. Eater of shite.* Mentally, she ripped the white cloth and its bright blue runner off the table, scattering dishes, and pulled the plate and china down from the heavy sideboard to smash on the floor with a noise like vengeance. She could still hear Davy Roberts screaming as they brought him up from the pit, his legs crushed by a crumbling support beam that they'd begged to replace. Her ears continued to ring with the tears of Catherine Linsey's husband and children as she'd been buried, taken too soon because the owners didn't have a doctor regularly come to the village.

How would Harrold sound if his legs were smashed? Would Tufton sob the way John Linsey had as his wife was lowered into the ground, his children clutching at the hem of his coat, begging for their mother?

The table in front of Alyce now was spread with crystal wine glasses that glittered like ice. The jewels dangling from the women's necks and ears gleamed coldly. But the room was overly hot, stifling. At this time of year, she, Henry, and Sarah would already be able to see their breath in their cottage. There was never enough coal.

More conversation followed, as thin and pale as the soup they'd been served. Clearly, they were saving further talk of business for after the ladies' departure. She kept silent as they talked of the lack of "really decent" society in Plymouth, sniffing at the social climbers as if they weren't sewn from the same pattern.

Finally, Mrs. Harrold stood. "I think it's time we left the gentlemen to their masculine interests."

All of the men got to their feet as Alyce and the other

women rose. Stokeham was nearest the door, so he held it open. As she left the dining room, she sent one quick glance toward Simon. God in heaven, but he was a lovely sight in his evening clothes, yet he anchored her when she felt herself tipping over the edge. His own calm, his informal, confident air assured her. This mission meant as much to him as it did to her. Yet somehow he found the means to appear casual, assured. She could do the same for herself.

Her heart lifted, though, when he gave her the tiniest nod. A mere hint of encouragement. He couldn't say or do more in a room full of their prey. But it was all she needed.

Following the other women, she glided out of the dining room, feeling like a hawk soaring high above a vole. Flying so high that the brainless little animal below had no idea that it was being hunted.

The gas chandelier didn't actually dim when Alyce left the dining room, but the chamber seemed gloomier, darker without her. Simon manufactured a smile as brandy and cigars were circulated.

Matters weren't helped by the fact that the walls of the dining room were covered in sickly dark green wallpaper, and the cumbersome mahogany furniture crowded in like mourners after a funeral, eager to grab the deceased's belongings. Everything in Harrold's house seemed purchased for its expense. There wasn't a single piece of bric-a-brac or a painting that possessed an ounce of real feeling.

This family is sober and moral, the silver epergne seemed to declare.

What utter fucking hypocrisy, he thought.

"There's a relief, eh, gents?" Harrold said with a

chuckle. He settled back in his chair, one hand wrapped around a brandy glass, the other holding a cigar. "Ladies can be charming but tedious."

"They can't help themselves," Stokeham declared, then drew on his cigar. Exhaling smoke up toward the ceiling, he added, "Their lives can never be as full or important as ours. An excellent cigar, incidentally."

"From Florida, in the United States," Harrold said pompously. "Costs an appalling amount to get them, but it's worth it."

More proud of the price than the actual quality of the cigar, Simon thought.

"The best things cost the most," Stokeham agreed. "Went down to Wroxley's shop and said to the man, 'See here, I want a Norfolk jacket, and I won't pay any less than two pounds for it!' The man had to scramble, but he made one for me from vicuña wool, and charged me three pounds twenty for it." He sat back, exceptionally pleased with himself.

Simon's own haberdasher in London charged him two pounds for a bespoke coat, and that was a fairly outrageous sum. And Simon made sure not to go around bleating about the cost of it.

God, the evening just kept getting longer.

"But to continue what we were talking about earlier— we need women, don't we?" Tufton swirled the liquor in his glass. "To tend to our needs, to ensure our homes are comfortable havens, to keep the children clean and polite."

"And sequestered," added Harrold. He directed a smirk at Simon. "Savor these early months, Shale. You don't have to worry that the children will come racing down from the nursery, demanding your time."

Early on, Simon had learned that, above all, he wasn't to trouble Father. That meant keeping to the nursery, remaining silent at meals unless an adult spoke to him directly, and generally being a paper cutout of a boy to be taken down from the shelf and briefly admired before he was returned to where he belonged.

He never stayed on the shelf. He'd go missing for hours—usually into the woods or, if they were in London, to the zoo or park—and return home for scolding and a scrubbing so vicious, his lye-scented skin would be red until the next morning.

Thank God his older brothers had done their duty and reproduced, ensuring continuity. Simon wouldn't inflict childhood on anyone—at least, not the way he'd been raised.

"Mrs. Shale is eager to become a mother," he said.

"And that's a credit to her," Tufton replied. "Woman's greatest purpose, beyond the solace of her husband, is motherhood."

"They do have other purposes," Stokeham added with a laugh. The other men joined him in his mirth, and Simon forced himself to chuckle.

"Pleasant as the ladies are," he said, "now that they've repaired to the drawing room, we can discuss business."

"Why, Shale, don't tell me you're a prude," Harrold admonished.

"He can't be." Tufton snorted. "D'you see how he looks at his wife?" He heaved a sigh. "Almost reminds me of when Dorothy and I had just wed. But it doesn't last, Shale."

Harrold made a grunt of agreement.

"I'll take that under advisement," Simon answered. But he'd seen it often enough in his own class: marriages conducted more like commercial agreements, just as his parents' marriage had been. The idea of a lasting passion—if that passion even existed in the first place—seemed as impossible as perpetual fire. Eventually, the fuel would be spent, the flames would extinguish, and all that would remain was cold carbon.

But there was Eva and Jack. They hadn't been married long, but he could recognize it in how they spoke to each other, their incidental touches and glances. Flood and famine and war wouldn't keep them apart.

Jack and Eva were the anomaly, not the standard. He never expected anything for himself like what they shared. Never thought that he could find a woman who'd delight and challenge him for the rest of his life. And he was part of Nemesis. What sensible woman could endure his many identities, the constant danger he willingly faced daily?

When an inner voice whispered *her* name, he feigned deafness.

He was a good confidence man—but he couldn't swindle himself.

Now's the time to secure her *future, not think about your own.*

"Having met my wife," he said, "I hope we've gained some measure of your trust."

"An excellent woman," Harrold declared. "She seems entirely guided by you."

"Oh, she is. There's no fear that she'll take any undue interest in our collaboration."

"It's a good sign when a man is in complete command of his wife," Tufton declared. "If he cannot rule at home, where can he rule?"

"It seems that you rule well at Wheal Prosperity," Simon noted.

Stokeham puffed on his cigar. "Our managers run it, but on terms that *we've* determined. Everyone profits."

Except the workers. "It's an unusual system, isn't it, to pay using chit instead of actual wages?"

"The idea came to us from seeing how American

mines were operated," Harrold said. "They may be barbarians over there, but no one can dispute how rich some of them have become. If we can get twice the revenue from the same amount of workers, why shouldn't we? *They* don't know any difference. As I said, I've seen how they live, and they're barely more than animals. Money doesn't matter to them."

"What would they do with more income?" Tufton demanded. "Drink themselves senseless? Have more squalling brats?" He shook his head. "This system is much better for all concerned."

Simon said, "When I researched the running of Wheal Prosperity, saw its innovative system for paying the workers, I was struck dumb with admiration. Think how many men of industry could be even more wealthy if they only adopted your methodology. In truth," Simon continued, "that was the deciding factor in my decision to approach and include you gentlemen in my overseas enterprises. *These are men of innovation,* I thought. Who better to have as part of my commercial ventures than such entrepreneurial thinkers?" He took a sip of his brandy, the taste cloying on his tongue. Harrold probably paid some exorbitant amount for it, too. Damn, Simon longed for a decent whisky. "Mark me, gentlemen, we will *all* profit from our mutual association."

Silence fell, weighted with smoke and schemes. At last, Harrold said, "Why don't you go on and join the ladies, Shale? My partners and I have some discussing to do."

Simon pushed back from the table and ground out his cigar in a gaudy ashtray. "Again, you show yourself men of singular wisdom. I'd be suspicious of you if you *didn't* discuss the merits of my proposal. I shall see you upstairs."

He bowed, then sauntered from the room as if the fate

of hundreds of people—and Alyce—didn't depend on the next fifteen minutes.

Perched at the edge of a low, overstuffed chair, Alyce discreetly sniffed at the tiny glass of liqueur in her hand. Little glasses had been handed around to all the women once they'd reached the drawing room, poured by more blank-faced servants.

She'd been careful not to drink much wine at dinner— the few times she'd had wine, it had loosened her tongue and her inhibitions. If she'd had more than a glass tonight, she'd wind up standing on the dining room table and either throwing cutlery or setting the owners' ears to blistering. Not the best course of action, considering why she and Simon were here in the first place.

She tried to keep from glancing at the door, hoping to see him stride into the drawing room. What were the men talking about? It had to be about the business arrangement he was proposing. He'd seemed assured that the owners would agree to the scheme—he'd run other confidence ploys before—but that didn't keep her pulse steady.

And what if something happened to him? What if the owners had set up an ambush, and three bruisers came crashing into the dining room as soon as the women left, and were at this very minute pummeling Simon bloody? She'd hear something, wouldn't she? She strained to hear above the women's dull patter for any sounds of fists, grunts, or broken furniture. She'd already seen him fight—briefly—once before. He was fast, brutal, and effective. It could be over in moments.

God, she really was walking the edge of sanity right now. Gentlemen—even ones who stole from their own workers—didn't hire thugs to attack possible business partners. Not in the gentlemen's own homes, at least. The furniture looked costly. They wouldn't want it wrecked.

She drew a steadying breath. She just wanted Simon *here* with her. This place was an adder's nest.

Maybe she ought to have that drink after all. It seemed safe enough, and she carefully sipped at it. It tasted of almonds, coating her mouth with sugar. Altogether not too bad. She sipped a bit more.

"My mother passed that receipt on to me," Mrs. Harrold said proudly from the sofa on the other side of the room.

"I didn't know your mother was Mrs. Beeton," Mrs. Tufton answered with a thin smile. "This tastes just like her instructions for homemade crème de noyaux."

"I assure you, it's entirely a family receipt."

The two women politely glared at each other. "*My* elderberry liqueur has been honored many times at local charity functions."

Alyce sat up straighter. For the past ten minutes, the two married ladies had been talking about their children, speaking with pride about the cleverness of little Arthur or how very good young Ursula's needlework was. Unease had been churning in her stomach as they'd chatted. If she and Simon carried out this ploy, these women and their children would lose their money, the means of keeping themselves fed and a roof over their heads. Could she justify destroying their lives for the sake of her own, and the workers of Wheal Prosperity?

It'd be so much easier if she could just paint these people as nothing more than villains, deserving their fate.

"Are you much involved with charity, Mrs. Tufton?" she asked.

"Of course. All women of good morals are. We all have our little handicrafts that we sell at charity bazaars. My ornamental picture frames are in great demand."

"And my embroidered pillow cushions are snapped up immediately," retorted Mrs. Harrold.

Miss Stokeham yawned loudly behind her hand as she stared into the fire. Clearly, charity functions weren't her favorite topic.

"And what becomes of the funds you raise through these bazaars?" Alyce asked.

Mrs. Harrold frowned at her. "I assumed London ladies held charity bazaars and fund-raising events, as well."

"Oh, we do," Alyce answered quickly. "Only, I was curious to know if the fine women of Plymouth had their own way of doing things. Perhaps I could learn from you and pass the information along to my sisters in generosity."

Both Mrs. Harrold and Mrs. Tufton smiled smugly. "The Plymouth Ladies' Beneficial Society *is* known throughout Cornwall and Devon for its munificence."

"And who are the lucky souls who benefit from your aid?"

Mrs. Harrold blinked. "Well . . . I'm not sure. Someone handles those considerations. They're altogether too taxing for me."

"The deserving poor, most likely," added Mrs. Tufton. "Good, honest middle-class people who may have fallen on difficult times. Not like those wretches who live in filth and degradation. And there are so *many* of them. Just last week, I was doing my Wednesday shopping when some horror of a woman and her scrawny babe had the temerity to approach me and beg for charity."

"What street was it?" Mrs. Harrold asked.

"Cornwall Street."

"I shop there thrice a week!"

Miss Stokeham stirred herself up enough to add, "And I'm there nearly every day. They've got the best shops in town."

"I cannot believe a beggar would approach you on Cornwall Street," Mrs. Harrold said, affronted.

Mrs. Tufton sniffed at the indignity of it. "She said her husband was a sailor who'd died in a shipwreck, and she and her children were starving."

Mrs. Harrold's eyes widened. "The nerve! Did you give her any money?"

The other woman scoffed. "And support her idleness? I told her to find some useful employment and stop being a parasite on society."

"Quite right."

Harmony between Mrs. Harrold and Mrs. Tufton had been restored, thanks to the penniless, hungry sailor's widow. Miss Stokeham yawned again, finding nothing of interest in talking about the poor.

It wouldn't be so difficult to ruin the owners, after all.

The door opened and Simon finally walked into the drawing room. The thorns of tension loosened from her chest. But the other men didn't follow him in.

"Ladies." He bowed. "The gentlemen had some additional matters to discuss, and graciously liberated me so that I might indulge in your company."

What did that mean? Why had the owners forced him to leave the dining room? It couldn't be good.

"Mr. Shale, you do have the sleek manner of a solicitor," Mrs. Harrold said, and giggled.

He pressed a hand to his chest. "Let me assure you, madam, that rumors of my profession's tendency toward servility are greatly exaggerated. I took to the law because I believe in *sincerity*. Every word from my mouth is the truth."

"Is that so, Mrs. Shale?" asked Mrs. Tufton.

"My husband is the *soul* of honesty."

"Naturally, you would say that," Miss Stokeham said, rousing herself from her stupor. "He's your husband."

"Oh, but I'm an excellent judge of character. When I meet someone, I'm seldom wrong about them."

"And how do you find us, Mrs. Shale?" Mrs. Harrold asked. Her smile could freeze the ocean.

"Entirely deserving," Alyce answered. *Of getting your arses thrown in the gutter.*

At a nod from Mrs. Harrold, a servant handed Simon a glass of liqueur. Simon downed it in one drink, then grabbed one of the chairs. "Will you forgive my breach of decorum," he asked the women, "and permit me to sit close to my wife? I find even a few minutes out of her company to be intolerable."

"Newlyweds," Mrs. Tufton said. But Alyce couldn't quite tell if she spoke fondly or with some bitterness.

He set the chair down beside Alyce and draped himself elegantly in it. This close, she could see the tiny, tiny lines of tension around his mouth, but to anyone else, he'd look perfectly at ease.

The women took up a discussion of troublesome servants, leaving Simon and her a small bit of privacy.

"And?" she asked him, wearing a smile like a mask.

He gazed at her with warm fondness. "And . . . we'll have our answer in the next few minutes."

"What if they say no?"

"They have to say yes."

"But they might not."

The other women glanced over at them, and Alyce realized she'd spoken a little too loudly, with too much strain in her voice.

"I keep telling you, darling." Simon patted her hand. "The furniture warehouse promised us they'd have the divan you wanted."

"But it's such a popular style," she said. "They might not have it in stock."

"If it turns out that we can't get that particular divan," he answered, "we'll find a different one. I vow to you, one way or another, we're going to get what we want."

She muttered, "I wish I had your confidence." They sat in an expensively decorated drawing room, but really they were balanced on the blade of a knife.

"Trust me," he said, his smile genuine. "Your husband won't let you down."

CHAPTER 14.

Minutes later, Harrold, Tufton, and Stokeham ambled into the drawing room. Simon remained seated. He smiled affably, as if he didn't feel himself strangled by steel cables. Beside him, he sensed Alyce bracing herself, though she also wore a placid smile.

He wanted to leap to his feet and demand, "Give me your answer, you bastards." Instead, he waited as tea was poured and everyone murmured inconsequential words. A reluctant, sullen Miss Stokeham was persuaded to play piano. She banged out Chopin, challenging everyone to keep smiling.

"Shale," Harrold murmured. He nodded toward one curtained corner of the drawing room. "A moment."

Now Simon would have his answer. He rose and followed Harrold to the corner, making certain to keep his expression genial and bland.

He hadn't lied to Alyce earlier. If this plan didn't work, they'd find another way to get Wheal Prosperity out of the owners' and managers' hands—there was no other choice—but it would take a hell of a lot more work, and they'd already poured so much time and energy into this scheme.

"Tufton, Stokeham, and I discussed it," Harrold said, when they'd sequestered themselves. He took a sip of tea.

Simon waited. This was always the crucial, delicate moment. When the mark decided to take the bait or not. You couldn't pressure them into making a decision, in case you appeared desperate, inciting their suspicion. But he couldn't appear too indifferent, lest his target feel as though the risk weren't worthwhile. So he schooled his features to look attentive, like a man at an agricultural fair.

He avoided glancing at Alyce—too much would show in his face if he looked at her.

"Come round the office at ten tomorrow morning," Harrold said. "Bring your wife, as well, so we can make the transfer."

"Very good," Simon answered. He did not throw his teacup down and shout in victory. But that didn't mean the urge wasn't there.

Harrold grinned, a man well pleased with himself. "Can't wait to see the look on Darby's face when he realizes he's been scuttled."

Jack would enjoy letting his rage out. He might even get the chance to break some furniture.

"It promises to be an interesting morning." Simon set his cup aside on a table and bowed. "The hour is late, and we've imposed too much on your hospitality."

"Not at all. Been a very pleasant change from the usual dinner parties Mrs. Harrold hosts. I actually gave a damn. And your wife is a very charming young woman. You've got my envy, Shale."

As quickly as he could, Simon disengaged himself from Harrold. He strode over to Alyce. Judging by the way she clutched at her wrists and the taut muscles of her neck, her composure was beginning to fray. No blame in that. Even he was about to explode like a burning ammunition magazine.

"We're expected at the gentlemen's office tomorrow morning," he said.

She pressed her lips tightly together—he suspected it was to keep herself from yelling in triumph. "Not too early, I hope," she said.

Heat cut through him at what her words implied. *We're going to be up late tonight.*

"Not so early that a cup of bracing tea can't cure any lingering lethargy." But Simon had plans, many plans, between now and sunrise. If everything went as he envisioned, they'd be so exhausted, they would need to be rolled into the offices on wheelbarrows.

Farewells were exchanged with the guests and their hosts, with Stokeham and Tufton giving his hand an extra-hearty shake. Tomorrow, they believed, he'd be leading them directly toward boundless, underhanded profit.

He and Alyce descended the stairs into the foyer, where a footman appeared with their hat, coat, and wrap. Neither he nor Alyce spoke. The air around them crackled, and they didn't look at each other, nor did she take his arm, as if knowing that once they spoke, looked, touched, there'd be no stopping them.

The footman signaled for a cab. A hackney rolled to a stop, and, his touch as light as possible, Simon helped Alyce inside. "Cormorant Hotel," he growled up at the driver. "There's an extra quid in it if you get us there in ten minutes."

If anyone later reported to the local law that a cabman had been driving with reckless speed through the streets of Plymouth, Simon didn't care. All that mattered was that seven minutes later, he and Alyce were going up the steps to their hotel room, and he felt as if he were climbing a stair that led straight to a long-denied paradise.

* * *

She liked that he fumbled with the key. It took him several tries, his hands faintly shaking, before he unlocked the door and ushered her inside their room. He'd picked locks and slipped easily through danger, calm as the night sky. But now, here, with her, he shook, and that made her even more unsteady.

Still, neither of them said anything as he turned up a lamp. He left the flame low. The room felt small and warm as two cupped hands.

She draped her wrap over the back of a chair, watching him as he paced to the drawn curtains, then back. He shoved his hands into his pockets and finally looked at her. A burning gaze. But he stood in the middle of the room, while she lingered by the table in the corner, and made no move to close the distance between them.

Need and eagerness shuddered through her. But she took a kind of pleasure from them, in this stretching out of tension. Maybe the outcome was inevitable. Maybe it wasn't. Just this once, she'd let herself enjoy uncertainty.

But it truly wasn't uncertain. Not really. Not the way he licked his lips when he looked at her, and her breasts already felt tight and heavy, and the lamplight traced the line of his hard cock pulling at the fabric of his trousers.

"It isn't settled yet." His voice was a rasp. "Not until the documents are signed. Even then, there's more."

"What's ever settled?" She took a swaying step toward him. "What do we ever have, except now?"

Standing inches in front of him, she slowly peeled off her long gloves. It was a process—loosening the fingers, the part that covered her hand, and then pulling deliberately at the tight leather. She couldn't go fast if she wanted to, but why would she want to, when he watched her keenly, as if each movement, each little bit of skin revealed, was the most important thing in the world?

One glove came off, and she dropped it to the ground.

She repeated the process with the other glove. Her arms and hands were bare. She felt herself glow—from the light and the need radiating out from him.

She slid her hands down his starched shirtfront. It rasped against her sensitive palms. But she kept them there, pressed against his chest. Beneath the shirtfront and the shirt itself, he was hot and solid, and his heart was like an engine as it raced under her hands.

"Tonight," he growled. "At Harrold's, you were . . . perfect. A warrior."

"I talked like a featherbrain, not a warrior."

"A brilliant disguise. Only the best can pull it off—hide who they truly are. *You* did. All I could think about was that wicked, clever mind of yours."

"Just my mind?" She'd never smiled like this in her life, as if she were the essence of seduction.

"The wicked, clever rest of you, too. Especially your hands. And your mouth."

She was pierced all over with darts of need. "Tonight, I kept thinking about how polished you were, a handsome, smooth talker. In that drawing room, in the dining room. Those *elegant* places. And I thought about your cock in my hand, hard and thick."

He growled.

"Now we're here," she continued. "Alone."

He didn't need the prompting. He cupped her head with his hands and brought their mouths together. Ravenous, explosive. Their kiss ricocheted through her body. He surged against her, and she met his force, straining to him.

Everything she'd tried not to feel for the past hours, days, weeks, she let herself feel now. What she felt most of all was him, his own power and want. Need for *her*. His tongue slicked into her mouth and she sucked on it, tearing a groan from him.

He kept one hand around the back of her head, but the

other he ran all over her: neck, arms, waist, and up again, to curve against her breast.

"You fancy folk and your fancy clothes," she muttered. "I can't *feel* anything."

After pulling off his own gloves, his hands quickly went to work, undoing the many fastenings and lacings of her gown. She didn't know how he did it—she'd watched the maid at work earlier and it had seemed some kind of agonizing, deliberate ritual—but in moments, her elaborate gown was gone, thrown aside with a rustle of silk. He wasn't finished, however. One by one, her layers disappeared. His fingers flew over the hooks of her corset, and she felt giddy with the rush of air—or that might have been him making her head spin like a top.

And then she was just in her chemise, drawers, and stockings.

"You've practiced getting women out of their clothes," she said with a breathless laugh.

His smile was wickedness itself. "All leading to this moment." He pulled her against him once more, and there, *there* he was, his hands shaping her buttocks, skimming up her sides, caressing her breasts. He rubbed her tight nipples through the sheer muslin of her chemise.

She'd never been this uncovered for anyone—but she wasn't afraid. She wanted more.

Sensation flooded her. She felt all of her body, as if every nerve came alive at the same time. Without the barrier of her clothes, she felt him—the fine wool of his evening suit, his taut, long body, the thickness of his erection pressed into her belly. It was still a shock, to feel that part of him, even if she'd had him in her hand only hours earlier. Proof that he was *real*. A man. With her now.

They kissed with swelling hunger, until, rumbling, he broke the kiss. "It's your turn."

Her mind was fogged while her body was alert. "For what?"

He led her to the chaise, sitting her on the edge. Sitting gave her a perfect view of his straining cock.

He pushed her hands away when she reached for the buttons of his trousers. "Not yet. You first."

She didn't have time to ask him what he meant before he knelt before her. A look of utter concentration crossed his face as he undid her garters. His hands glided over her legs as he removed each stocking, and he made a growl of approval. Up to now, only her own hands had taken off her stockings. Each step was a new intimacy.

"I love your legs. Sleek." One of his fingertips traced a muscle along her inner thigh. "Strong."

She couldn't care that she didn't look like a fine London lady, white and soft. Her muscles meant she worked, and worked hard, and she prized each one. Judging by the stark need in his face, he did, too.

He tugged off her drawers. She peeled off her chemise. And there she sat on the chaise, completely naked. Another threshold crossed—her first time fully nude in front of a man. Everything was so much better because it was Simon here with her for all these new experiences. She wouldn't want anyone else.

His hands pressed on his thighs as he continued to kneel in front of her. He stared at her, his gaze hotter than any refinery. "I just want to look. I want to touch. I want everything."

The intensity in his face and voice almost frightened her—but they *did* send another wave of arousal crashing over her. "We've got all night."

"Isn't enough." He leaned forward, kissing her deeply. "But we're going to start somewhere." The kiss continued. One of his hands stroked up her thigh, higher,

higher, until—she gasped into his mouth as his fingers dipped between her legs.

The only fingers that had touched her there had been her own. He caressed her there, lightly at first, and then delving deeper, with an instinct for how she wanted to be touched. As if he were in her mind, in her body. She arched and writhed. His fingers had to be dripping, and she was shamelessly glad that he could make her feel so much. When his finger rubbed against her bud, a sound unlike any other she'd ever made clawed up from her throat. She'd touched herself there before, but it hadn't been nearly as agonizingly sweet.

"God, Alyce," he groaned. "Sweet Alyce."

"Not sweet." How was she able to speak? "Never have been."

"You're wrong. I'll prove it."

He spread her thighs apart and ducked his head. Her eyes widened. Was he really . . . ? Did people *do* that?

They did. She grabbed the back of the chaise, fighting back a scream, when he put his mouth on her. His hands stayed firm, holding her down, as he licked her with long, potent strokes. He toyed with her, commanded her, worshipped her. His tongue circled her bud, and he sucked it gently between his lips. One of his fingers slowly eased inside her, then began to glide in and out. She'd put her own fingers into herself before, but his were thicker, stretching her.

He still wore his fancy evening clothes. She wore not a single stitch. Though he bent low over her, she could make out the high, sharp planes of his cheekbones, the elegance of his gentleman's face. And she could see the exquisite pleasure on that face, the complete concentration and devotion to his task.

She felt the smooth upholstery beneath her naked body and the wooden back of the chaise she gripped.

She felt his mouth, his finger. Felt what seemed like a lifetime of want and struggle and desire building, building. She never would've thought people gave each other pleasure this way—but, God, did Simon pleasure her.

The climax took her. It was freedom and a cage, tightening over her, releasing her. A pleasured scream tore from deep inside. Her body arched completely up from the chaise. But still he held her, gripping her. He was ruthless with his mouth. He wouldn't let her go. Not until she'd come again. And once more.

Finally, she collapsed back to the chaise. All of her bones had dissolved. She couldn't do much beyond watch him as he unsteadily stood and threw off his clothing. Revealing himself bit by bit.

A new surge of energy filled her as she saw him for the first time. Not just the suggestion of muscle beneath his shirt, but the planes and contours of his chest, his arms and shoulders. The barest gleam of golden hair glimmered on his chest. He was lean and tight, sinewy. Each muscle sharply defined in the lamplight, from the ridges of his stomach to the lines arrowing down from his hips toward his groin. More fine golden hair trailed down the flat of his stomach. Scars formed shadows on his body—one across his ribs, another on his shoulder, a line on his calf. He was a soldier. A warrior. Had fought and survived to stand before her now.

He stepped out of his trousers and drawers, then kicked them aside.

His thighs were hard and just as keenly muscled as the rest of him, his calves strong but not thick. He had long feet, and they looked primal and male as he stood on the Oriental carpet. But her gaze didn't linger on his feet. No, her attention fixed on his cock. She'd seen it—touched and caressed it—earlier today. But she hungered at the sight of him, thick and curved, the head dark, shining, with a little bead of liquid at the slit.

He bent and lifted her up in his arms. She felt dizzy, freed from the force that tied her to the earth. As if she and Simon could fly out the window and soar into the night sky.

After pulling back the covers, he laid her down upon the bed.

"You'll join me now, won't you?" She smiled, stroking her hand along the cool sheets.

His answer was to slide into bed and pull her to him. The length of his body burned hers, the small tremors that shook him echoing within her. When they kissed, and she tasted herself on his lips, desire roared back to life. She wrapped her leg around his. He gripped her tightly. His forehead lowered to hers, their breath mixing hotly.

"Alyce," he rumbled.

"Simon."

He rolled her onto her back, easing her thighs open. He was dark and golden above her, severe and beautiful as a saint, but there was nothing saintly in his eyes. Their gazes locked. She felt the tip of him at her entrance. Yet he held himself still.

"Yes," she said.

His eyes briefly closed, as if giving thanks, then they opened again. Slowly, so slowly, he slid into her. She was stretched, filled. Rosy pain spread, petal by petal.

He watched her face every moment, his own tight. "Hurting you."

"It's good." She wasn't capable of lying, not at this moment, with him inside her and the world changed forever. Yes, it hurt, but the hurt was good, and she held it close. Like a prize.

When he'd sunk himself fully within her, he stilled. Breathed in and out harshly. "Ah, God." His whole body shuddered and sweat gleamed over him. Holding himself back—for her.

"More, Simon." She squeezed her thighs around his hips. She wouldn't be refused.

He drew back, sliding out gently, then pushed forward again. More pain, followed by unexpected pleasure. She melted around him, and the pain lessened.

He felt the change in her. His hips thrust with more strength, more speed. His eyes closed. He growled. She reveled in his pleasure, moving past the hurt and feeling only him, everywhere inside her.

Then he made an agonized sound, and pulled quickly from her body. His own body bowed, his head thrown back, and liquid spilled in hot streams onto her belly. It seemed a blissful torture.

With a groan, he collapsed beside her. One arm he flung over his head. But his other hand found hers, and their fingers laced together.

"Goddamn it," he said, his voice edged with self-blame. "Your first time, and I was a sodding brute."

"You weren't."

"The pain—"

"And the pleasure." She turned her head toward him. "I'd thought, wondered . . . but I never knew. How good it could be." It would never be this good again, not after he left. But she couldn't let herself think of that now. "I've also heard," she added, smiling, "that it gets even better the more you do it."

He grinned. "Very true."

He rose up from the bed, and disappointment pierced her when he let go of her hand. But then he went into the bathroom and returned with a dampened washcloth. Carefully, tenderly, he cleaned her, and showed no embarrassment when he cleaned himself. Thin streaks of blood appeared on the cloth as he wiped himself off.

They stared at each other. But she had no regrets. This had been *her* choosing. No promises had been demanded, and none had been given. She expected nothing but this night.

So she plucked the cloth from his hand and set it aside. Set it all aside. Tonight was hers, and for just these few hours, she could pretend that *he* was hers.

They dozed, wrapped together. She didn't know how much time had passed, but when she woke, the lamps were out and moonlight and shadows bathed the room. He stirred behind her, nuzzling the back of her neck, his hands drifting over her body. He stroked her breasts and she pressed herself into his touch. She thought once she'd had her release, she'd be sated, but with his languid caresses, hunger suddenly swelled.

She felt loose-limbed, soft. When one of his broad hands moved down her stomach, then lower, to caress her folds, her need built even higher. She lifted her arms and hooked them behind his neck, leaving herself stretched and open. As he touched her, she moaned, writhing, wanting. His cock was hard and hot against her back. He pulled her legs apart.

Slowly, he sank into her. Pain again, at first, less than last time, and it dimmed and pleasure grew. He continued to thrust deep, and as he did, his fingers circled and rubbed her sensitive bud. All the while, he whispered into her ear. Soft, coaxing words. Telling her how beautiful she was, how they were made for this, for each other, and he wanted to be inside of her forever. The climax hit her with the force of a thunderclap. His own followed right after, with him pulling out and spilling upon the sheets as he rumbled her name.

They quietly panted together in the aftermath. She ought to be exhausted. Her body echoed with lovely soreness and tiredness. The day had been long and tumultuous, exciting and frightening. But with Simon's sweat-dampened, naked body cupping hers, and her mind spinning, she was awake as if it were noon. Time was slipping away, grain by grain. She wanted whatever she could grab hold of.

Eventually, she asked, "Are they all like that? Rich people?"

He stretched and rolled onto his back, pulling her along, so she lay partially atop him, her hand splayed across the tight span of his chest. She thought he might dismiss her question, tell her it was far too late to talk about these things and to just go to sleep.

But he didn't. "Those men—Harrold, Stokeham, Tufton—they've built their wealth because they don't give a damn about anyone but themselves. I've known dozens, hundreds of businessmen who've grown fortunes without treating other people like animals. Or worse than animals." He exhaled slowly. "But the fact that Nemesis exists is proof enough—there are plenty of bastards in the world who'll crush the spines of anyone beneath them. To make money. To feel better about themselves."

He shrugged. "I've seen acts of incredible kindness and cruel brutality."

"There's got to be a meaning to it, a pattern." She stroked her fingers through the fine hair on his chest, memorizing the feeling.

"Wish that there was. I wish we could predict it. The best we can do is encourage compassion in others, and see the signs of cruelty as early as possible so we can stop it."

"And if you bait and blackmail men like Jack Dutton in the process . . ."

He offered another shrug. "To quote Marco, quoting Machiavelli, *'Il fine giustifica i mezzi.'* The ends justify the means." He turned to her. "You're not having second thoughts?"

"Not after hearing those horrible women blather on about the *undeserving poor*. Whatever the hell that means. It's as if . . . they've blinded themselves on purpose. As if they'd rather be sightless than see what's really around them."

"It's a choice many people make."

"Some of us don't have that choice."

He brushed his lips back and forth across her forehead. "That's why we fight back, however we can."

Alyce settled deeper into his embrace, feeling the length and energy of his body, the soft, thick blankets and crisp sheets enfolding them. A moment out of time. A memory that she'd hoard, belonging only to her and Simon. This wasn't real life. Even if the scheme for the mine worked out, she'd go back to being a bal-maiden. Her pay would be better, and every day wouldn't be such a battle, but she'd remain Alyce Carr of Trewyn, Cornwall, helping her sister-in-law as she raised her nieces and nephews. She'd also take a more active role in the running of the mine, and damn anyone who said she couldn't because she was a woman. Her path was clear.

Simon's was, too. Hearing him speak of his work for Nemesis, the determination in his voice, the quiet anger at the brutality of the world—this was what he was meant to do. He was a ruthless scoundrel of dubious but also unquestionable morals. When he left, as he'd have to, it would hurt like hell. She'd never known anyone like him. She never would again. Even if she left Trewyn, left the mine, and sought her fortune elsewhere, there wouldn't be another man like Simon.

"Why does time have to move?" she murmured. "Why can't we stick a pin in it, the way those scientists pin butterflies?"

He let out an uncharacteristic sigh. "Time has wings, but we can't pluck them off, we can't make it stop flying. There's only one thing we *can* do about it." In a sudden move that robbed her of breath, he flipped her onto her back, pinning her arms above her head. His body stretched over hers, hard and relentless. And his gentleman's face was taut with need. "Enjoy every goddamn minute we're given."

She arched up to meet him for a blistering kiss. Though they'd already loved several times this night, they couldn't get enough of each other. She struggled against his hold, wanting to touch him, but that only made him tighten his grip on her wrists. And curse her if his blatant show of strength didn't make her burn all the hotter.

They wrestled against each other, a rough give-and-take that stole thought. All she knew was this wild dance, hot and slick. His cock curved thickly against her stomach. A sudden image filled her mind, her body, making her wetter.

"Let go," she gasped, breaking from the kiss.

"Not a goddamn chance," he growled.

"Trust me." She smirked. "You'll want to let me go."

He raised a brow. A moment later, he released her wrists.

She slid out of bed and hurried into the bathroom. Grabbing another washcloth, she ran it under the warm water tap.

Emerging from the bathroom, she found him stretched out on the bed, the covers thrown off, splendid in his bold nakedness. He watched her with glittering eyes as she climbed onto the bed and knelt beside him, holding the warm, damp cloth.

"Hold on to the headboard," she directed.

His mouth curved at her demanding tone, but he did as she commanded. He reached back and gripped the curved brass headboard, the movement revealing all the lean, solid shapes of his muscles, making the curves of his biceps round even more impressively.

"Don't move, and don't let go," she continued.

"Her true colors come out," he said, his voice low and unsteady. "Dictatorial, that's what you are."

"If that word means bossy, then, yes. Now quiet and let me work."

But he wasn't quiet at all when she began gently rubbing his cock with the washcloth. He groaned and growled as she ran the soft cloth up and down his shaft, caressing him, cleaning him. Circling around the base and then up, to swirl around the tip. She went slowly, so slowly, and with every stroke, he writhed and twisted and cursed.

He started to reach for her, and she gave him a stern look. "Don't let go, I said."

His eyes narrowed with a look that said he'd obey *for now*.

She slid down him, then continued stroking him with the cloth. But it was growing cool, and the last thing she wanted was to subject him to the effects of cold water. So she set the cloth aside. His eyes flashed as she pushed his thighs open and knelt between them. Her heart throbbed in fear and excitement—she'd never done anything like this. But what he'd done to her earlier on the chaise had given her ideas.

This was their night. And she'd deny herself nothing.

So she gripped the base of his cock, and lowered her head. All the while, their gazes held.

Her tongue swirled around the head. So silken and tight, and that tiny kiss of salt beading at the very tip. An inhuman sound clambered up from his chest. Growing bolder, she took the head fully into her mouth. Sucked on it. The headboard rattled as he tugged hard and let out a series of curses or maybe prayers. She couldn't tell the difference.

She lowered down further, taking more of him into her mouth. Her eyes glided shut. She couldn't fit all of him in her mouth, so she wrapped her hand around his shaft. Then moved. Sucking, licking, up and down. Imitating the strokes she'd used with her hand, and the way he'd been inside of her. But deliberate thought evaporated as she lost herself in the pleasure of giving him pleasure, his delicious taste and feel, and how he shook and shuddered beneath her touch.

And still, she wanted more. She pulled him from her mouth. He made only the lowest sound of protest before she straddled him, placing the head of his cock right at her opening. She held herself there for as long as she could stand it. They didn't speak, only stared at each other, both of them gasping, and if she looked anything like he did, they were both ready to level the whole of Plymouth with their need.

It was a trust, too. If he'd wanted to, he could've let go of the headboard. But he held, restraining himself, holding himself down as if she'd captured him. This man who wanted freedom above all else was giving it up, for her.

Her heart strained against the cage of her ribs. And she saw his own heart, reflected in the brightness of his eyes. It was almost too much. She wanted to duck her head to hide from it. But she never refused a challenge or turned away from something difficult. So she lowered herself onto him.

They both hissed as he filled her. His thickness, his fullness—they were everywhere, and she welcomed them, taking him into herself. She paused once he was seated fully inside. Just to feel him. To know this moment.

Her hands braced on the planes of his chest, she began to ride him. Leisurely at first, as she discovered angles and movements. Then faster. She learned that to tilt her hips just *so* rubbed her bud against him, and if she leaned in just *this* way, the head of his cock brushed against a sensitive point inside her, sending shudders of pleasure through all parts of her body. She moaned with every new discovery.

"Yes, Alyce, *yes*," he panted. "So . . . beautiful . . . learning your . . . power."

He was carved like oak, burnished with sweat, strained tight as he gripped the headboard, the cords of his neck standing out. The look of a man who never loved his suffering more.

Control broke. She gripped his shoulders and rode him hard, flesh to flesh, until the orgasm broke her apart. She splintered into fragments of light and sensation. Losing awareness of everything but pleasure.

She crumpled against him, her face to his damp chest.

"I'm letting go," he rumbled, his voice as taut.

In an instant, she was lifted from the bed. Simon carried her over to the chaise as if she weighed no more than a scrap of lace. But for all the decimating potency of her climax, she didn't feel delicate like lace. She felt powerful, durable. Forged strong in the heat of what their bodies had done.

He stood her so she faced the chaise, then guided her hands to grip its back. The position made her thrust her behind out, a bold invitation. She *felt* bold.

"Now *you* don't let go," he commanded.

"Or else?" she couldn't help retorting.

Her answer came as a sharp smack against her buttocks. She jumped. Hot sensation filled her. God, she hadn't been spanked since . . . never. She always ran faster than the teacher with the switch, and they never believed in hitting at home.

She waited for a sense of anger or embarrassment. None came. Only more pleasure.

"Or else that," he said, voice edged with need.

Now she couldn't decide whether or not to be disobedient. That spank had been wicked, glorious. But she also wanted him again, for him to take her as he wished. So she held fast to the back of the chaise.

He gripped her hips with bruising force. The tip of his cock notched at her entrance. And then he thrust in, one sure, thick stroke that was all of him.

"Wanted this," he rasped. "For so long. To lean you against a wall at the engine house or in the village, and take you, make you mine."

She didn't think it was possible for a woman bent over a chaise having sex from behind to blush, but she did. "You've got me now."

And he seemed ready to make full use of the chance. His hips moved, his cock within her, and it wasn't gentle or sweet. It was raw and real, as animal as she felt. She pushed back into him, making eager sounds. Sounds without words, which meant "yes" and "more" and "harder."

She chanced a glance over her shoulder, wanting to see him. His body in motion was a beautiful thing, especially when that motion was loving her roughly. His eyes were clamped shut, his mouth open. He'd never been more glorious. And *she* was the one who put that look of ecstasy on his face.

Growling, he pulled out. Release shot from him, spattering onto her buttocks, her back. It felt incredible, but just once, she wished he could climax inside her. A wish that couldn't come true. Not without the possibility of consequences.

For a long while, they remained as they were: her bent over the chaise, him continuing to hold her hips. But then he moved, and he found one of the discarded cloths, using that to clean them both.

Slowly, stumbling like drunks, they got back into bed.

The moment they lay down, he wrapped her in his arms, their bodies weaving together. He tipped her chin up and kissed her, once, sweetly.

"Simon," she breathed, and in that one word, in his name, was all her hope and fear and need and dread and pleasure. Things she'd never shared with anyone else. Only him. Two little sounds in his name, but they held everything she couldn't admit, not even to herself.

Too soon, it'd all be taken away.

"I know, love," he said. "I know."

Love, she thought as she drifted off to sleep. *Yes. Love.*

CHAPTER 15.

The carriage ride to the owners' offices revealed that nothing in the world had changed. Men and women walked to and from work, the sky was a watery gray, the smells of damp pavement rose up, and a nautical bell tolled distantly. A dog barked, a man shouted in complaint against a thoughtless driver. Just another day.

How could everything look and act exactly the same, but everything for Simon had shifted as completely as the poles reversing? It didn't help that the woman who'd come to be his North Star rode across from him in the cab, scattering his thoughts whenever they tried to gather.

He went over the steps in his mind—presenting the documents to Harrold, Stokeham, and Tufton, the exchange of property, signing more documents, Jack's appearance, Simon's response—it was just the same as reviewing a battle plan, thinking of all possible steps, every contingency.

No sooner did his thoughts alight on these details than he'd remember the night before. *Alyce beneath me, above me, all around me. Her taste. Her smell. The feel of her.* And her boldness that set his blood to flame.

The need to fight rose up in him. For her. And . . . for *himself.* She'd given him that.

There she sat across from him in the cab, wearing another of Harriet's expertly tailored traveling ensembles. Alyce's hands knotted in her lap, and she couldn't seem to keep her gaze still. It slid out the window to blankly watch the passing streets, then skittered around the interior of the hired carriage, to finally land on him. She attempted a smile.

And, *damn it,* there went those knives into his heart again. Her bravery never stopped.

He wanted to say something to her. Anything. To reassure her. To let her know that last night had been the culmination of every dream, every desire. Yet they both knew that dreams never lasted in the light of day. So they both kept silent, rocking slightly with the movement of the carriage, until it drew to a stop outside the offices.

She took his arm as they went up the front steps. Before he could place his hand on the doorknob, Linton the clerk had already flung the door open.

"Welcome, Mr. Shale." Linton glanced at Alyce, waiting for an introduction, but Simon hadn't the interest or patience to go through the standard rituals.

He gave the clerk his coat and hat. "Where are the others?"

"In Mr. Tufton's office. I'll show you the way."

Alyce didn't speak as they made their way through the workplace, though her gaze touched quickly on the rich furnishings. No doubt tallying what everything cost and comparing it to what that money could've bought the workers of Wheal Prosperity. Yet she looked cool and mildly uninterested, as a woman of her class might when presented with the mundane activity of earning a living.

The young clerks at their little desks all watched her pass. She wore a bronze and blue traveling ensemble with a little feathered hat, and carried a fur and satin muff against the autumn chill. In this masculine fortress, she had to seem a welcome respite. A visitor from the realm of the inconsequential. Little did any of these clerks know that Alyce was a living weapon disguised in moiré silk.

Inside Tufton's office, Harrold and Stokeham also waited. They rose from their chairs, smiling, and offered handshakes and bows at Alyce and Simon's entrance. Linton was sent to fetch tea.

"Thank you again for your hospitality last night." Simon waited until he'd seated Alyce in front of Tufton's desk before taking his own seat.

"I've never had a more enlightening evening," Alyce added.

Harrold laughed indulgently. "Happy we can be so enriching. A shame, though, that you live so far away in London. We could make such evenings a regular occurrence."

"What a pity," Simon said. He hefted his portfolio. "Shall we get to the matter at hand?"

At Tufton's nod, Simon arranged the paperwork on the desk. "First, here are the documents pertaining to my overseas properties. These are stocks. They'll serve as collateral against the return of the mine. When the mine's back in your hands, you'll pay for the stocks—and everyone's satisfied."

"How soon will we see a profit?" Stokeham demanded.

"The profits are small but steady from these investments," Simon said. "The real benefit, however, is that the money isn't taxed, nor can the British government touch it. Profit in protection."

The men chuckled, and Harrold accepted the stocks.

Simon pushed other documents forward. "As you see on this sheet, it has Alyce's maiden name indicating she's the representative of the Cornish Mining Collective. This ensures the venture has her brother's protection. It just needs your signatures transferring ownership."

"Cornish Mining Collective?" Harrold said with a frown. "Is it a genuine corporation?"

"I created it," Simon explained, "and I'll dissolve it. Most important is that my wife's signature is on it."

The men eagerly put their pens to the paper, and, with a flourish, Harrold handed the pen to Alyce. Only Simon saw how her hand trembled slightly when she signed the document.

And then it was done. The transfer had been made. Wheal Prosperity no longer belonged to these bastards.

Alyce set the pen down, then sat back in her chair with a barely audible sigh. He had to commend her—she didn't look at him or give any sign that this bit of paper shuffling was anything more than a slightly mystifying nuisance. The sign of a green confidence player was revealing too much through nonverbal cues. A shared look. A quick smile.

But she played her part exactly as she was supposed to. Goddamn, but she never stopped fascinating him with the many people she could be, and yet still remain herself.

"Well, gentlemen—"

The door banged open. Everyone, even Simon, jumped. Jack loomed in the doorway.

"I've come back again, like I said I would," he growled. "Every day until you pay what you owe." His gaze caught on Simon. "What the hell are you doing back here?"

Simon rose from his chair. "Ensuring your ugly face doesn't, in fact, return."

Jack stalked forward. "Listen—"

"Ah, no, my gargantuan friend, I believe it's time for *you* to listen." Simon held up the sheaves of paperwork.

"All of this ensures that you haven't got a leg to stand on. Wheal Prosperity doesn't belong to these men anymore. It belongs to my wife."

Harrold, Tufton, and Stokeham looked on with wide eyes and gaping mouths, like an audience at the latest melodrama.

Jack sneered. "Then I go ahead and tax her, don't I?"

"You can't. First, because the ownership is a now a collective that falls outside of your department's purview. It's exempt from your thieving taxes. And second, because you might want to take a look at my wife's signature."

"The hell would I want to do that for?" Still, Jack snatched the paper from Simon's hand and peered at it. He did a convincing job of turning pale, then going red.

"You're not entirely a simpleton," Simon went on, "so I'm sure you recognize her name. Carr. As in Edward Carr. As in the assistant to the President of the Board of Trade. A man you most certainly wouldn't want to cross, and whose name you wouldn't want to damage."

Jack shook with rage. "This is just paper. I could tear it up, and no one would know any difference."

"But I have a duplicate set of documents, also signed. Destroy these. It won't matter." Simon plucked the documents from Jack's massive hands, and set the papers aside. "The bell has rung, Darby. The match is lost. Get out of here before you make an even bigger fool of yourself than you've done already."

Jack spun around, glaring at everyone, including Alyce. She had the good sense to recoil from the blazing intensity of his anger—either excellent acting on her part or a genuine response of fear. Simon couldn't blame her. Even when pretending, an enraged Jack Dutton was terrifying. The owners themselves seemed to try to crawl into the flocked wallpaper.

Only Simon faced him calmly. He had to fight to keep from smiling. This was always part of the confidence scheme he enjoyed—a relic from his schoolboy theatrics.

Jack stalked to Simon, looming over him by a good half a head. "I could also beat you bloody in front of your wife and all these fine gentlemen. No damn papers can stop that."

Simon had never seen Jack fight during his boxing and brawling days, but he had seen him fight a time or two during their last mission, and he'd been a force unto himself. Simon and Jack had also never become friends—mostly because of Eva, but they'd still butted heads as two men used to being in charge—and Simon suspected Jack wanted only the smallest excuse to pummel him. Well, he'd go down swinging if he had to. But he hoped that Jack remembered he had a part to play, a part that didn't include turning Simon's face into pulp—the way he'd battered those henchmen from the previous job.

"You're right," he agreed affably. "Papers can't stop you from degenerating to your basic, brutal self. But I did ask one of the clerks to summon the constabulary if you were to arrive. They'll show up just in time to see you beating a defenseless man. I can't imagine that would reflect well on your service record as a government employee."

Jack glared at him a moment longer. Absolute silence choked the room, save for the clock ticking on a bookcase. Even Simon found himself holding his breath.

Cursing, Jack spun on his heel and stormed out of the office. Cries sounded from clerks as he shoved them out of his way, and the front door banged open, then shut.

For a long while, no one within Tufton's office spoke. Simon took Alyce's hand and patted it. "All you all right, my dear?"

She pressed her hand to the center of her chest.

"My . . . goodness. What a thoroughly despicable character."

"I'm sorry I had to expose you to such unpleasantness. The world of men can be an ugly one."

"Then I'm happy to leave you to it."

Gradually, Tufton, Harrold, and Stokeham peeled themselves away from the walls. "God, Shale," Tufton said shakily, "you've got bollocks of iron. Forgive my language, Mrs. Shale."

She waved her hand. "Perfectly understandable, given the circumstances."

"Darby's well and truly gone?" Stokeham asked.

"He's my problem now, gentlemen, not yours. At the present, you've got nothing to do but take your ease for the next few days, and await the benefits of our arrangement."

Harrold came forward, his hand extended. "It was a blessed, fateful day for us you when crossed our threshold, Shale."

"Oh, but I don't believe in fate," Simon answered, shaking Harrold's hand. He glanced over at Alyce. "Fortune's in our hands. It's what we do with it that proves our character."

"I don't know how to feel."

Simon looked up from the newspaper he'd purchased at the train station to gaze at Alyce sitting across from him. They'd left Plymouth without meeting again with Eva and Jack, as had been prearranged. It would be too much of a risk for them to be seen together, but he and the other Nemesis operatives would reconnoiter as soon as his mission concluded. He didn't know when that might be . . . but it wouldn't be long, that much was certain. Finish his work at Wheal Prosperity, and then move on. As he'd always done, one job to the next.

It never troubled him, this peripatetic, rootless life of his. Until now.

Alyce watched the passing countryside, a small frown pleated between her brows.

She continued distantly, "They signed the papers. The mine belongs to us now. But I feel . . . I'm not *happy* exactly. I don't know what I am."

He folded up the paper and set it aside. Fortunately, the train car was empty, so they could speak at liberty. "The assignment's ongoing. You don't have to feel anything until it's finished."

Finally, she turned to look at him, her eyes grave. "That's another thing. I don't know how it's supposed to finish."

"We go back to Trewyn, fire the managers, and take possession of Wheal Prosperity."

"That can't be everything. The owners have had the mine for over ten years, and the managers are like pythons, strangling it slowly. There's the constabulary, too. Trewyn's been theirs to run as they please. None of them will just give up and walk away peaceably."

"They won't," he answered.

A wry smile twisted her mouth. "No pats on the hand? No 'there, there, everything's going to be fine'?"

"I'll never lie to you, Alyce. Well . . . I did, but I won't again."

Her smile turned bittersweet. "One of the things I'll miss about you." She picked at the seam of her glove as if she could pick apart her thoughts. "Henry and Sarah . . . they'd sometimes give me those little pats, tell me I had nothing to worry about. Maybe they were trying to make me feel better." She snorted. "Maybe they were just trying to shut me up." She shook her head. "Not you. After you finally revealed who you were, you always told it to me straight." Her voice thickened. "I'll . . . miss that."

Something fractured in his chest, a thread of incipient sorrow that would spread. It would be just as much of a lie if he told her that he'd stay in Trewyn, or that he'd even have the opportunity to visit her from time to time. There weren't holidays if you worked for Nemesis. At best, he could see her once or twice a year—she deserved better than that. And he couldn't do his work properly with half his heart. Better to end things cleanly.

But that didn't mean it wouldn't hurt like a bastard.

"I wish it didn't have to be like this," he murmured.

She managed a brave smile. "But it has to be."

"It does."

Her exhale was long and slightly shaky, but her control didn't break. "It's been a grand adventure."

"It's not over yet. Might get worse before it gets better."

She tilted her head, curious. "Should I be scared?"

Again, he liked and respected her too much to feed her lies. "We had a saying in the army. 'When you stop being afraid, you start being dead.'"

"Doesn't sound very soldierly. Or brave."

"We were all of those things: good, brave soldiers. But we also knew that if we thought ourselves above harm, we'd be the first to wind up with our brains splattered on the battlefield."

She winced at the graphic image. "Afraid it is, then. But not cowardly."

"Cowardly? You? Impossible. But I'm going to need your help with the rest of the workers if it comes down to a fight." He took her hands in his. "They'll need a leader."

"They'll get two." Glancing down at their interlaced hands, she smiled, though it seemed to pain her. "You and me together, we can do just about anything."

More fractures spread through his heart, even as it swelled with admiration. They just might be able to pull off this mission, but as to what came after, that was something neither of them could solve.

They switched trains in Tavistock, both to fill time until after dark, and also to give them an opportunity to change back into their usual clothing. Well, for Simon, his machinist's clothes were the disguise, but they couldn't return to Trewyn wearing the fine garments they'd had to don for the work in Plymouth.

The ladies' retiring room at the Tavistock station couldn't accommodate their needs, so Simon had taken a room at the nearest inn. It was a far shabbier room than the ones they'd had in Exeter and Plymouth, but they'd only be there for a few hours.

He avoided looking at the bed as the hotel's porter carried the trunk into the room. Once Simon got Alyce back into bed, he wouldn't want to leave. But he couldn't ignore the job's building momentum. Soon, very soon, everything would come to its climax, and he needed all his thoughts—and his body—focused.

"Why should it matter what we're wearing," Alyce asked once the porter had left, "if the ownership's been transferred?"

"Waltzing back into the village dressed like this"—he gestured at his silk waistcoat, his fine charcoal gray woolen trousers—"would tip our hand too soon. We've got to get the workers ready for what's coming before we make our next move."

She glanced down at her traveling costume and sighed. "These outfits are ruddy confining, but I'll be sorry to see them go, just the same. They're so pretty."

He stepped to her, and tugged off his glove so he could cradle her face with his bare hand. She leaned into his touch, holding him to her with her own hand. "Rough hessian or elegant moiré, nothing changes your beauty."

The pink blooming in her cheeks captivated him.

"No need for sweet talk," she murmured.

"Honesty, not flattery." He locked his gaze with hers. "I've never been able to take my eyes from you, Alyce Carr. Not for a moment."

She bit her lip. Then glanced over his shoulder at a clock sitting on a shabby deal table. "What time does our train leave?"

"Five-fifteen."

"It's three o'clock now." She looped her arms around his shoulders, gazing up at him.

He looked back, marking the way the filtered sunlight touched along the sharp edges of her jaw and chin. When he was back in London, would he see faces that reminded him of her? Would a woman's purposeful walk recall her? They'd all be pale imitations. He'd rather have nothing at all if he couldn't have the genuine article.

Which meant he'd have nothing.

"Two hours and fifteen minutes," he murmured.

"All the time we've got left to be alone." Her own voice was hardly a whisper. "Barely any time at all."

"We won't waste it." Just this once, he could be selfish, and think only of her and himself. Soon enough, they'd be forced apart.

She stepped backward, pulling him with her until they fell onto the bed. Her skirts rustled as he nestled between her legs, and he was instantly ravenous. Her own gaze was heavy-lidded, hungry. "Let's make this last a lifetime."

The sun had just set with a flash of green on the horizon as he and Alyce stepped off the train at St. Ursula. He'd given special instructions for the trunk to be delivered to London. And so, they stood on the platform wearing their coarse workers' clothes, she with her battered carpetbag, and he with his worn satchel—the leather portfolio full of documents. No one gave them a second glance. Just another poor couple back from a short-lived holiday.

Alyce watched the train pull away, chugging and steaming, until she and Simon were left in the dull quiet of a small-town train station. It was a Thursday, so people trudged home from work for their evening meal, concerned only with their comforts after a long day.

He and Alyce had eaten some meat pies on the train, so there was nothing keeping them in St. Ursula. The walk back to Trewyn would take a few hours. The sooner they started off, the sooner they'd arrive.

But they lingered on that grimy, small platform. After they returned, they wouldn't be alone together. Not the way they'd been in Plymouth—or Tavistock. God, they'd been ferocious in that threadbare hotel room, tearing at their clothes, hungry for the feel and taste of each other, knowing the sensations had to carry them for the rest of their lives. Their lovemaking had been tinged with melancholy. Rough and honest. Everything that they were and couldn't be.

That time was over.

He glanced over at her, and she gave him a small nod. Silently, they left the platform and began the long walk across the countryside, back to the village.

They hadn't gone more than thirty yards from the edge of town when she suddenly stopped and turned to him. She pulled at something on her hand, then held a small object out to him. He took it. Opening his palm, he saw it was the wedding band he'd given her a few days ago. It still held the warmth of her body, but had already begun to cool.

"Keep it," he said, his voice gruff. "A souvenir." An ache had settled in his chest, making itself at home, readying itself for a long stay.

"Memories are better. They can't get lost."

He kissed her. Once. Brief and hard. She gripped him tightly. Then they separated, and walked the dark miles back to Trewyn in silence.

It felt strange to slip back into her home, as though Alyce were waking from a dream. Or maybe this narrow cottage with its familiar table and plates and folding screen was the dream that she'd crept back into. But as she edged inside, making certain that no one in the lane had spotted her returning, she didn't feel like herself. Once, a traveling scientific fair had come through town, showing all kinds of oddities like two-headed goats and demonstrating some of the wonders electricity could do. They'd also had a whole display of specimens in jars. Malformed beasts and rare creatures.

She was one of those specimens now, floating in liquid.

Sarah sat at the table, knitting, and Henry read aloud from the Bible. Neither of them heard her enter. She watched them for a moment, in this comfortable domestic scene. Every now and then, Sarah rubbed her swollen belly, and Henry would keep reading, but reach out and give her stomach a protective, loving caress.

The thought of having what Sarah had—a baby on the way, a doting husband—something in Alyce instinctively shied away from it. She had other desires, other responsibilities. Yet a bitter thread of envy tugged on her. They had a partnership, Sarah and her brother. Someone who knew them as well as they knew themselves. Someone to trust. To . . . love.

She must've made a noise, because Henry stopped reading and Sarah's needles stilled. The moment they saw her, they leaped to their feet. In truth, Henry leaped, while Sarah levered herself up, using the table and the back of her chair for balance.

Henry's arms enfolded Alyce in a tight embrace. She froze in shock. He'd never been one for showing affection—not to her, anyway. Yet here he was, hugging her close. She let go of her bag and hugged him back, sudden hotness gathering behind her eyelids.

"We missed you," Sarah said, also embracing Alyce as best she could, given her giant stomach. "We were so worried. Henry didn't sleep for two nights."

Alyce's brows lifted.

"What kind of fool sleeps soundly when his only sister is off in the big city?" he demanded gruffly. "You could've been murdered."

"Not *this* fool." She pressed a kiss to his bristled cheek. "As you can see, I'm back, completely unmurdered."

Henry gave her a look that said her smart response wasn't appreciated, but he gave her one final squeeze before stepping back and folding his arms across his chest. "And . . . ?"

"And . . ." She allowed herself her first real smile in a long time. "It worked, Henry. The mine's ours."

She could see how he fought a whoop of triumph, but his own smile won out. Amazing how much he looked like their mother when he smiled like that. A small curl of grief circled her heart. If only their parents had lived to see this day.

"How'd it work? What did you do? What about Simon? How did he manage things? Tell me all of it."

A sharp pain at the mention of his name. But she pushed past it. She'd have to get used to that pain.

"For heaven's sake, Henry," Sarah admonished. "Look at her. She's about ready to collapse. Sit down, my dear, and Henry will make you some tea. And *when you're ready*"—she directed this at her husband—"you can tell us what happened."

Alyce barely had the energy to say thanks as she

dropped into a chair. How could she feel so light, and so heavy at the same time?

Henry clattered around the stove, muttering to himself about where was the tea caddy, and if they had any biscuits left.

As he fussed, Sarah sat down and edged her chair close to Alyce. "The mine? It belongs to us?"

"It does."

"And you're safe, unhurt? Plymouth is such a big place."

Alyce spread her hands. "I wasn't murdered once."

Sarah chuckled, then looked at Alyce with speculation. "It happened, didn't it?" she murmured. "With Simon."

Alyce answered with a shocked whisper, "Sarah!"

But her sister-in-law gently shook her head. "Henry can't see it because he's a man, and men . . . they can be good-hearted creatures, but Lord love them if they don't have the observational skills of a vole. But the moment I saw you, I knew." She glanced over at Henry, still figuring out the intricacies of how to make tea, then back to Alyce. "You made love with Simon, didn't you?"

There was no point in lying, and Alyce didn't want to, anyway. Sarah was the closest she had to a sister, the only woman she could share these kinds of secrets with. So she nodded, then waited for condemnation.

Young unmarried women didn't lie with men they didn't mean to marry—and it was clear that she and Simon had no wedding planned. More than a few sermons had warned the congregation against the dangers of lust. But there was a greater threat than being considered a sinner: having a baby out of wedlock. Girls who got pregnant and either couldn't or didn't marry the father faced bleak futures, shame following them and their babes like a trail of poison.

Simon had been careful, though. Protected her.

But Sarah was a good village girl. Alyce remembered Henry's fevered impatience to marry once Sarah had accepted him. And now she understood why. Sarah had followed the rules.

Would this drive a wedge between Alyce and her sister-in-law? Sarah had every right to throw Alyce out. It was Sarah's home, and Alyce could be a bad moral influence on the child, once the babe arrived.

"So?" Sarah pressed.

Alyce frowned. "So . . . what?"

Sarah sent another furtive glance toward Henry. "How was it? He's got the most lovely manners, but he's got a way about him, like he'd really take charge. And he's got those gorgeous hands."

"Sarah!" Alyce's mouth dropped open. *This* wasn't what she'd expected from her virtuous sister-in-law. "You're *married*. Pregnant."

"But not *dead*," Sarah answered with a little smile.

Alyce covered her face with her hands. "God. I can't discuss this with you."

"That good, eh?" Sarah let out a small sigh. "Thought it might be. And, Lord, I miss it so. But since I started getting big, Henry's too afraid to touch me."

Now Alyce clapped her hands over her ears. "For the love of all that's holy, stop."

"Everything all right?" Henry asked.

"Wonderful," Sarah trilled. "She's telling me all about the fine sights of Plymouth. So many lovely and strange hats the ladies wore. Some even covered their ears."

Apparently uninterested in hats, Henry returned his attention to fixing the tea. When his back was turned, Sarah gently pried Alyce's hands away from her ears.

"Honestly, Alyce," she said quietly, her face earnest, "he didn't force you, did he? Hurt you?"

"No. God, no. He was . . ." Now she sighed. Her heart rose then sank, a hard plunge in her chest.

Sarah's gaze softened. "Ah, I'm glad. The first time's not always so good."

"It wasn't quite, not the first time," Alyce clarified. "But . . . it got better. Much better."

Sarah pressed her hand to her mouth, holding in a giggle. "You wicked, wonderful girl. But"—her gaze grew serious—"I hope you were careful."

"We were. There won't be a baby."

Her sister-in-law's gaze grew even more sympathetic, which made Alyce feel suddenly restless and unsettled. "Did you protect yourself here?" She tapped the center of Alyce's chest.

"There weren't any promises," Alyce answered. "Temporary. That's all it is."

Sarah's eyes narrowed. "And you're cheerful as a lamb about it."

"Didn't say that. But it wasn't going to last." She forced a shrug. "It's already over." It would be better, hurt less, if she thought of it that way. He was still in Trewyn, but really, he was gone. She had to keep repeating that to herself.

"I had an uncle on my ma's side," Sarah said abruptly. "Bit of a drunkard, Uncle Fletcher. And something of a poet, too." She gave a wry smile. "Maybe those two things go together. But I remember something he once said to me—one of the few things that made any sense."

"What's that?"

"He said to me, 'Sarah, my girl, we can tell our hearts exactly what to believe, but the cheeky little bastards won't listen to anyone but themselves.'"

Alyce's smile faded.

"Oh," Sarah said, seeming to realize how true her words were, how they stripped Alyce raw. "It truly happened, then. You're—"

"Going to be fine." All that mattered was survival from one moment to the next.

Henry finally brought the cups to the table. "Put me down the bottom of a mine shaft rather than make tea. At least there, I'd know what to do."

"Lord, Henry," Alyce said, "if it wasn't for Sarah, you'd be starving, wearing filthy clothes, and talking to yourself like Barmy Sam."

"Then let's be grateful for Sarah," he answered, "for many reasons." He ran an affectionate hand down Sarah's hair, then pulled quickly away.

I miss it so. But since I started getting big, Henry's too afraid to touch me.

Alyce shook her head, trying to knock Sarah's words, and the uninvited images it brought up, from her mind. Of course Alyce knew where babies came from, and of course she knew in theory that Sarah and Henry had lain together as man and wife, but it was one thing to know it in theory. Quite different to think of it in truth. She'd always sneaked out of the cottage whenever she'd heard Henry and Sarah giggling upstairs, and the squeak of the ropes of their bed.

She took a sip of tea, then set her mug down. Somehow, her brother had completely botched it.

"I'm not so interested in hearing about hats," Henry said. "But I want to know everything that happened in Plymouth."

Shifting so she turned away from Henry, Sarah waggled her eyebrows at Alyce. Alyce glared back. Then proceeded to relate all that she and Simon had done during their trip. With a few particular things left out. She wasn't especially interested in seeing Henry march up the high street, right to the bachelors' lodging, and then threaten to murder Simon if he didn't marry her.

But not everything slipped past Henry. "You said you stayed at a hotel in Plymouth."

"In separate rooms, of course." Maybe her time working the confidence scheme had changed her, because she found it awfully easy to lie to her brother. And she seemed to do it well, because he didn't press the issue.

"And the mine," he continued. "It's ours?"

"All ours."

Grinning, he clapped his hands together. "Bloody excellent! We'll finally have the changes we wanted. A real living wage. Updated equipment. No more company store."

She hated to crush her brother's excitement, but they needed to be realistic. "Those things will come. There's still a dangerous road ahead."

"It's all taken care of," Henry objected.

"Not all of it." A few days away, and she'd changed deeply. Knew the world more. How it worked. It was far more complicated and risky than she'd ever fully understood. "There's more to be done."

"Simon has to have a plan."

"Simon and I *both* have a plan." She forced herself to drink her bitter tea, needing the warmth and the energy it would give her. Once she'd gulped the last of her drink, she stood, and wrapped herself in her cloak. "Grab your coat and hat. There's a long night ahead of us."

CHAPTER 16.

Two dozen wary faces stared at Alyce and Simon. She couldn't blame them for being chary. Again, they'd been pulled from their beds in the middle of the night—but at least this time they had a sense as to why. They'd waited in tense silence as, man by man, their collaborators had joined them. It'd taken over an hour to get everyone here, though that had been by design.

A small Cornish village didn't offer many places for people to meet in secret. They'd had no choice but to return to the caverns, with a man posted at watch in case Tippet decided to make another surprise visit. Hopefully, if the chief constable showed up, there'd be enough advance warning to get everyone out of there. Although at this point—it almost didn't matter if Tippet knew. Almost.

Simon had warned her of the risks of showing their hand too soon. It had to be handled carefully. Blunders were dangerous.

As the men had gathered in the cavern, lanterns in their hands, they'd demanded answers from Simon. He wouldn't speak until the very last of their group had arrived.

Travis Dyer finally trudged in, the final man.

"Well?" he demanded.

"The mine's ours," Simon answered.

The men started whooping, but Simon snarled at them to be quiet. "This isn't finished. Not by half."

"But you said the mine belonged to us now," Edgar said.

"The owners don't know yet that they've been gulled," Alyce answered.

"Once they do," Simon continued, "they'll put up a fight."

"Here, now," Travis grumbled, "you didn't say anything about a fight."

"You thought they'd just roll over and let us take everything away?" Simon's face and words were hard. Difficult to believe that only a few hours ago, he'd made love to her with a tender ferocity, staring into her eyes as he'd gripped the back of her neck and joined with her so intimately. That man and this one were entirely different. But somehow the same. Equally determined to have what they wanted. "Men like them don't work like that. You saw it when you tried to form a union. They'll get dirty if they have to."

The men shifted, uncomfortable. Simon hadn't seen the ugliness in the wake of the attempt to form a union, but she knew he'd seen combat before, its brutality and cruelty. He didn't speak lightly of facing battle.

"Maybe this wasn't such a good idea," said Dan Bowden.

Exhausted, edgy, the frayed threads of Alyce's patience snapped. "Simon and I have stuck our necks out for all of us. We plotted and planned and got into the heart of the spiders' nest. Everyone agreed this had to happen. No one forced your hand to sign that paper. It was *your* choice."

"Maybe we didn't know the risk," Christopher Tremaine said.

"You're a grown man, Chris," Henry said crossly. "You knew. We all did."

More grumblings rose from some of the men.

"It was never going to be as simple as a signature," Simon pressed. "But when has anything worthwhile been simple? Nothing valuable's ever been gained without a fight. That's why it means something. Because you fought and struggled and even bled for it."

The men shifted on their feet and continued to mutter, wavering.

"I never thought it wouldn't hurt," Alyce added. "The whole time, in Plymouth, and after, I knew it would. But, damn it, the pain doesn't mean anything. Not compared to what I've had . . . what *we'll* have . . . because we took that chance. Decent wages. Fresh food. Dignity. And whatever happens afterward . . . there's no regret. It was in the trying, in taking a stand."

She didn't look over at Simon, yet she felt his presence beside her, and they both heard the words spoken not just to the workers, but to each other.

"Not all of us have your bollocks, Alyce," Edgar said wryly.

"Then make a pair. Because you're going to need them."

The men turned away, gathering in a circle at the edge of the water to confer. Alyce and Simon didn't speak. She fought the impulse to reach for his hand—not because she needed his strength, but simply because she missed him. Missed his touch. The sensation of his skin against hers and the bright, lively force of him. They had been apart only a few hours, but she felt them, every one.

Could anyone tell, aside from Sarah? Alyce had been away from the village for a bare handful of days. Yet she wasn't the same woman who'd left. Not better or worse. Only different. Because she knew what she was capable of now. Because she'd pushed beyond the limits of herself. And all the while, Simon had been there, encouraging her, learning her as she learned herself.

He'd return to London, but he wouldn't be the same man who'd first arrived at Wheal Prosperity. And she tried to tell herself that maybe it was enough, to know that she'd left a mark upon him as he'd done with her. Something to carry with them through the rest of their days.

Yet they lived side by side: her concern over what was going to happen with the owners and the inevitable day when Simon left. The chambers of her heart filled with black, sticky apprehension. Somehow, some way, she'd have to endure it all. As she'd persevered her whole life.

The miners finally broke apart from their circle. It seemed that they'd elected Edgar as their spokesman, because he stepped forward, determination etched into his craggy face.

"We're with you," he said.

"You're with *you*," Simon answered.

"But you'll help us—lead us," added Christopher. "We don't have experience in this kind of business."

Simon looked at the other gathered men. "Is that what you all want?"

The men all nodded vigorously.

"Right," Simon said. "Tomorrow morning, everything changes. I want you ready for that."

"Yes, Simon."

"Good. Now go home and get some rest. These next few days are going to be rough." But he didn't sound frightened or concerned. No, he looked like a man spoiling for a fight, and wouldn't be satisfied until he got it.

Henry, Edgar, and several other miners met Simon outside the managers' office—the men restless, faces grim, with their hands stuffed into the pockets of their coats like stones ready to be thrown through windows. But it wouldn't come to that. Not today. The only weapons they'd need were the documents Simon carried.

He tried not to let his gaze linger too long on Alyce, but his eyes had a will of their own. They craved the sight of her as much as the rest of him did. She was pale, tense, her arms wrapped around herself, yet he'd never seen her look more determined. This was the beginning of the endgame. He wanted to reach for her, to reassure himself as much as her.

His arms remained at his sides. He had to get used to not touching her anymore.

"No weakness now," he said to the gathered men. "We're standing together. They've got to blink before we do."

The men all nodded their agreement. So did Alyce. One final glance around at all of them, including her, and then he pushed the office door open.

Clerks looked up from their paperwork, eyes wide with shock. It was nine o'clock in the morning. Long past the time that Simon and the others should've been at the mine.

"Get them," Simon directed one of the clerks. He glanced toward one of the manager's doors. "Get all of them."

The clerk gaped. Remained seated.

"Now," Alyce said.

The clerk leaped to his feet and scuttled out of the room. As Simon and the others waited, the chamber was utterly silent, the two other clerks staring at them as if a pack of wild dogs had stormed into the tidy office, and one slight move or sound would send them into a frenzy.

"What the hell is going on?" This, angrily, from Ware, who led Gorley, Murton, and the clerk into the room. "You're two hours late at the mine, and you've got the temerity to waltz in here like you own the place."

"We do," Alyce answered.

The managers exchanged disbelieving glances. Murton began to laugh, and soon Gorley, Ware, and the clerks joined him. Their laughter bounced off him like thrown feathers, but the other workers grew restive, uncertain. Everyone except Alyce.

"Laugh," she said coldly. "Giggle yourselves all the way up to your fancy house on the hill. Keep laughing as you pack up everything you own. Don't stop chuckling while you catch the train at St. Ursula. And then you can laugh and laugh yourselves all the way to hell."

The laughter stopped. Every eye was on Alyce. She planted her hands on her hips and returned the managers' shocked stares with her own cold glare.

Apoplectic red stained Murton's cheeks. "It's you who have to pack your bags, Miss Carr. You're sacked. And if the rest of you don't get back to work, you'll all be sacked, too."

"With no back wages," added Gorley, a child determined to get in the final word.

"None of you are in the position to make decisions about hiring and firing," Simon explained. "That's for Miss Carr and these fine gentlemen to decide."

"They'll be fired, but we'll have you sent to St. Lawrence's Hospital," Murton shot back. "Lock you up with the other madmen."

In response, Simon pulled the ownership transfer papers from his portfolio and handed them to Murton. The man put on his spectacles and read, the other two managers reading over his shoulders.

"In short, *gentlemen*," Simon said, "that document is signed by Messrs. Harrold, Tufton, and Stokeham, the owners of the Greater Cornwall Mining Endeavor, which, at one time, possessed Wheal Prosperity. By their own hands, they've transferred ownership to a collective made up of these men." He nodded to the workers standing behind him. "And Miss Carr," he added.

She tipped her head regally at him.

"They . . . they wouldn't do that!" Ware objected. He looked as chalky as the cliffs of Sussex.

"But they did," Simon noted, "and Murton holds the proof."

The managers stood like Lot's wife, pale and silent. Simon could see their minds frantically trying to come up with a way out, or considering the possibility that this could all be a hoax. Yet the more they stared at the documents, then looked up at Simon and the others, the more it seemed to dawn on them that there was no mistake.

At last, Simon plucked the papers from Murton's shaking hand, and replaced them in the portfolio. He turned to the others. "Gentlemen, and lady, the question now stands. As the owners of Wheal Prosperity, would you like these men"—he nodded to Murton, Ware, and Gorely—"to remain on as managers of the mine?"

"I believe in fairness," Alyce said. "We'll put it to a vote. New owners, all in favor of keeping them, raise your hands."

No hands went up.

"And who wants to see them sacked like so many potatoes?"

Everyone's hands rose. Not just the workers and Alyce, but the clerks, too.

"Not you?" snarled Gorley to Simon.

"I'm not one of the owners. Merely a facilitator of the process."

Alyce folded her arms across her chest. "The Yanks seem to have the right idea with this democracy idea. The owners of Wheal Prosperity have spoken. Time to grab your kits and shovel off."

Ware sputtered, "But—"

"It's not polite to argue with a lady," Henry pointed out.

"So pack it in," added Edgar.

Dazed, the three men headed toward the door. But Murton paused at the threshold. "This won't go unanswered," he spat. "Anyone can throw some papers around and say they're genuine, but the truth will be uncovered. And then you'll all be imprisoned, thrown into an asylum, or forced into a workhouse—if you're fortunate."

"You're right about one thing," Simon noted. "The truth *will* be uncovered. But it won't be the truth you want."

"Hang on," said Gorely. "You don't sound the same."

"Oh, didn't I tell you?" Simon smiled. "I'm from Nemesis."

The three men bolted, the door swinging wide open behind them like a gaping mouth.

It didn't take long for word of the managers' firing and the change of ownership to reach the mine itself. Simon watched from the doorway of the bachelors' lodging, Alyce beside him, as the high street filled with jubilant workers. An impromptu celebration broke out, full of cheers, some tears, and much shaking of hands and slapping of backs. The tavern opened casks of ale outside. Men knocked tankards together, toasting their new freedom. Someone played a fiddle and women danced. Children played in the street, reprieved from work and school.

"They don't know," Alyce murmured beside him. "It's not over."

"Some understand." A few dozen men talked quietly, soberly among themselves, their women listening attentively. Mostly they were the men who'd been involved in Simon's scheme from the beginning, and who'd heeded his warnings. Henry was among them, his arm protectively around Sarah's shoulders. Tension radiated from the group, which some of the celebrants seemed to notice. Others continued to make merry, little knowing what was coming.

"And not everyone's celebrating." She nodded toward a grim-faced Tippet, standing outside the constabulary office and watching the celebration. The constables Oliver, Freeman, and Bice stood close by. Oliver kept a tight grip on his truncheon, and Freeman had his arms crossed over his big chest. Bice's expression seemed deliberately blank. "Why don't they clear off, too?"

"The managers and owners didn't pay their salaries—that's county business. No doubt Murton and the others filled their pockets to keep things even more *orderly*. They'll stay until they know for certain that the old regime's out."

Alyce gave a small shiver. "Won't be pleasant when it sinks in."

Thus the reason why he'd declined offers of free drink. All they had were hours before the final confrontation.

Only hours left with Alyce. He'd have to go back to London as soon as the situation was resolved here—always more missions, more in need of help. Each minute now slipped by, impossible to hold.

Damn it, he just wanted to hold her sodding *hand,* touch her a little, but he couldn't. Not here, on the high street, where anyone could see and know. If he were a village lad, he could clasp her hand with his, an announcement of his intentions. He wasn't a village lad. To hold her hand in public, declaring his claim, and then to leave her—it'd be considered a humiliation. He couldn't do that to her.

He sucked in a breath when *she* took *his* hand. Pressed her palm and wove her fingers with his. A bold assertion, and when he glanced over at her, she stared back, defiant.

Let them look, her gaze said. *This is ours.*

But only for now.

A true gentleman would've pulled his hand free, protecting her from herself. But she was a grown woman and could make her own decisions. And he was selfish enough to want the feel of her skin, for a little longer. For as long as he could have it.

Edgar disengaged from the group of new owners of the mine and ambled toward Simon and Alyce. The older man's gaze snagged on their interlocked hands, and he raised a brow, but said nothing about it.

"Come and help us convince Henry to manage the mine," Edgar said.

"Couldn't think of a more perfect bloke for the job," Simon answered.

Alyce snorted. "I'd wager he's being his typical modest self."

Edgar grinned. "That's the way of it."

Without another word, Alyce marched to the group of men. She didn't relinquish Simon's hand, so they walked together, and with each step, his heart ached more. Another pleasure that was fleeting.

They reached the gathering of the mine's new owners. Everyone stopped talking, staring at Alyce and Simon's joined hands. Expressions of shock flitted across many faces, especially Henry's. Alyce returned every stare with her own cool resolve. *Judge me or don't,* her look said. *I don't give a ruddy damn.*

Listen to the lady, friends, his own countenance said. If she didn't care, neither did he. All he wanted was what he couldn't have.

"What's this nonsense about you not wanting to be the new manager, Henry?" she demanded without preface.

Her brother tore his surprised gaze from her joined hand up to her face. "I'm a miner, not a manager. You need classes or schooling or something for a big job like that."

"The only qualification the old managers had was their greed," Simon answered. "Nobody knows the working of the mine the way you do."

"You've always looked after us," Nathaniel said. "Settled differences between the workers. Tried to keep us happy even when the managers didn't give a pig's arse. There's nobody better for the job than you."

The gathered men and women added their agreement.

Uncertainty flickered across Henry's face, but beneath that was pleasure and eagerness. He'd be a good manager, if only because he couldn't dissemble.

Henry glanced down at Sarah with a worried frown. "Might not be around as much to help with the baby."

"It's too bad these are so useless." Alyce let go of Simon's hand, then held hers up. She rolled her eyes. "I'll always be there for you and the baby, and all the other babies."

The sentiment was a good one, but it only served to remind Simon that Alyce's life was here, in this village, with her family. They needed her.

So do you.

He smothered that voice. He'd given up more than he could enumerate for Nemesis. Alyce would be another loss. One he'd have to learn to endure. It might take him a lifetime to learn, but he'd force himself.

Sarah rose up on her toes and kissed her husband, pride shining in her eyes. "This is what you were meant to do."

After a moment, Henry nodded. He seemed to grow a foot taller, his chest widening, his shoulders broadening, as he accepted his new responsibility. "Edgar, Nathaniel, Travis—you'll be assisting me."

"Yes, sir," the men answered, smiling.

Uncertainty fell away from Henry. "First thing that needs to be done is a full survey of the mine itself. We've got equipment down there that's needed replacing for years. Edgar, grab Douglas and Percy to run the man-engine so we can get down into the pit."

"Now?" Edgar asked, glancing at the celebrating workers.

"Now."

Alyce grinned. "You put a Carr in charge of the mine. Did you think we'd take even a day off?"

Though he grumbled, Edgar smiled as he hurried off to find the lads to run the man-engine. Hopefully, they hadn't drunk too much of the free ale.

"Change begins today," Nathaniel said with a smile.

"Three and a half hours," Simon answered.

Questioning frowns were angled in his direction.

He pulled out his pocket watch. "By now, the managers have already made it to St. Ursula and the telegraph station. They've wired the owners in Plymouth. It'll take the owners thirty minutes to round up their attorneys, then head to the train station. Figure about two more hours by train—it won't be fast or direct. St. Ursula isn't on a main line. The owners will reach it by one-thirty, and meet up with the managers. They'll hire some carriages since they can't all fit on the managers' trap. The roads between here and St. Ursula aren't straight, and even at top speed, it'll take them an hour to get to Trewyn. That's a total of three hours and thirty minutes until we see them again."

He snapped his watch shut and slipped it back into his waistcoat pocket as the people around him gaped. Only Alyce didn't look surprised at his precise analysis. She knew him—more than anyone. Better even than Marco, Eva, and especially his family.

"Whoever isn't going with Henry to the mine," he

continued, "we'll need you here for when the managers and owners arrive."

"They won't try anything, will they?" asked Dan Bowden. "The mine's legally ours."

"Men forced into a corner do anything to survive," Simon answered. "Doesn't matter if they're street-born brutes or supposed *gentlemen*. In three and a half hours, be prepared—for anything."

"This is what we've been wanting for over ten years," Alyce added. "And if it comes down to a fight, then I'm damned ready. You'd better be, too."

The group made sounds of agreement. They dispersed, looking grim but resolute, with Henry leading several of the men in discussion.

Three hours. Thirty minutes. Less, now. Each minute crept away. He couldn't slam his boot heel down on time to keep it in place.

"You can't be nervous," Alyce said quietly.

"A little." He had to give her perfect honesty. "Wounded animals are the most dangerous, unpredictable, and the managers and owners are wounded. And it looks like Tippet and his crew are spoiling for a fight."

Standing in the doorway of the constabulary office, the chief loomed, primed as dynamite, waiting for the spark. A spark that would arrive in a little over three hours.

"Can't imagine that a bunch of fat men in bowler hats mean trouble to someone from Nemesis." She cast him a glance. "But I've learned that appearances aren't reliable. A machinist can be a gentleman's son."

"And a bal-maiden can be an Amazon warrior with a kiss like sin and redemption."

He liked that even after all they'd done together, and despite her bravado, he could still make her blush.

Hand in hand, they walked away from the high street, turning down one of the little lanes that led out of the village. In a moment, they wandered about the surrounding hills. The sky was a hazy, pale blue, not quite sunny, not quite overcast. As if it, too, held itself in suspension, waiting for what was to come.

The countryside had a spare, wild beauty, the wind brisk as it curved along the hills—so different from the racket and crowding of London. Getting used to that cacophony, beloved as it was, would be an adjustment. He imagined many restless nights when he returned.

But it wouldn't be the noise that would keep him awake, or make closing his eyes a torment.

"What's going to happen?" she asked.

It took him a moment to realize she was speaking of the managers and owners returning to the village.

"Words won't be enough," he said. "With Tippet at the ready, and the others out for any kind of blood, there'll be some kind of explosion."

Solemn, she nodded, her gaze fixed on her boots. "We'll be ready."

He stopped walking. Pulled her to him. They sank into a deep, aching kiss, and he hoped she was memorizing the taste and feel of him the way he did her sweet fire. He had a good memory. He'd never lose these sensations. Would force every part of himself to hold to her memory.

How could he miss her, when she was right here, in his arms? Yet he did.

They broke apart, their heads tipping together so their foreheads touched and their breath mingled. Though they stood in the middle of a field, with the countryside rolling all around them in green waves, the world was pared down to them, and them alone.

Her fingers laced behind his back, her arms tight and strong. A single tear coursed down her cheek. But she didn't move to wipe it away—letting him see her in her vulnerability. She, who showed her softness to no one, shared it with him. Trusting him.

I love you.

But the words wouldn't leave his mouth. He couldn't allow himself to say them. Not when they both knew he couldn't stay. The words would be more of a curse than a pleasure, offering them both something they couldn't possess. Yet they throbbed in his chest, each one a brand.

"Talk to me," she whispered.

He brushed strands of dark hair from her face, touched the damp streak on her cheek and rubbed it between his fingers. "What should we talk of?"

"Anything. Everything. What you liked to eat when you were a child. Your first memory. The sound you hate the most. The most beautiful place you've ever been."

These were intimacies greater than sex for the brief time they shared now, and he was glad to give them to her.

They resumed their walk. "Carrots," he said. "The other boys were always stealing boiled sweets from the shop in town, but I nicked carrots from the stables. The grooms pretended not to see me—maybe they were afraid they'd be sacked. But I'd eat carrots by the bushel."

"Bilberries," she answered. "I'd go out into the fields in August and stuff the berries into my mouth as soon as I found them, instead of saving them and bringing them home to make a pie. My mother always knew because I'd come back with blue lips."

They smiled softly together and continued to stroll. Leisurely. As if they were just two sweethearts courting, enjoying the day, enjoying the discovery of each other.

He continued, "I remember being very small—couldn't have been more than a year old—and my nanny slapping my hand when I tried to pull down the fire screen. Seems that was a habit of mine. Always trying to stick my hand in the fire."

"Not much has changed since then."

"Hot, dangerous things fascinate me. It's worth being burned."

She cast him a glance from beneath her lashes. "Then you get scarred."

"Something to help me remember the fire."

She shook her head, murmuring something about fool-hardy men. "I remember Henry trying to teach me how to play rugby. This was before he'd formed those foolish ideas that girls shouldn't play. I'd just learned to stand and he would try to toss me the ball. It'd knock me over."

"And you'd pull yourself back up and try to catch it again."

Her lips curved. "Not much of a mystery, am I?"

But he was serious when he answered. "It'd take life-times for me to truly know you. Time I'd gladly surrender."

She turned to him suddenly. "Simon—"

"Don't," he said roughly. "Let's . . . let's keep walking. Asking questions. Answering."

She silently acquiesced. And for hours, they roamed across the hills, talking until their voices rasped. A poem ran through his head, memorized long ago at Harrow.

But at my back I always hear
Time's wingèd chariot hurrying near;
And yonder all before us lie
Deserts of vast eternity.

Back then, he'd scoffed at Marvell, thinking the poem simply a fancy way of getting under a girl's skirts. But the aching melancholy of it now seeped into his bones. An ache he suspected would never dissipate.

They'd made a loop around the village, and were heading back toward it, when he spotted a figure running in their direction. Christopher Tremaine, one of the mine's new owners.

Both Alyce and Simon sped toward him. Christopher caught up with them, and bent over, gasping.

Simon saved him the trouble of speaking. "They've come."

Christopher, panting, nodded. He pointed down toward the village. The streets were mostly empty now, but two carriages and a trap were parked outside the managers' office.

Simon and Alyce shared a look. Time's chariot had arrived. The reckoning moment had finally come.

CHAPTER 17.

Alyce's heart thundered in her chest as she, Simon, and Christopher raced into the village. Speeding down the high street, she saw workers' faces peering out of the windows, while some braver souls lingered in the street. They all looked toward the managers' office, where two hired carriages and the managers' horse-drawn trap took up most of the space outside. She could already hear raised voices as she approached.

Simon led the way into the office. Once, Alyce had read a penny dreadful about men called cowboys in the wild American West. The end of the story had been two of those cowboys facing each other in the middle of town, waiting tensely to draw their guns. A "showdown," it'd been called.

So it looked in the managers' office as Simon entered, confronting not just the old managers, but the owners, too. At one end of the room stood the managers and owners, and at the other were some of the other miners— Nathaniel, Travis Dyer, and a few others. They looked to Simon gratefully as he stepped farther into the office.

The owners looked painfully out of place here. The managers might dress more finely than the workers, but they couldn't compare with the city elegance of the owners. Two other men stood with the owners, both of them carrying portfolios and self-importance. Solicitors.

They didn't frighten Alyce nearly as much as Tippet did, looming in one corner with the other lawmen, Oliver, Freeman, and Bice. The chief constable's face was dark with barely controlled rage, and his men clutched their truncheons, ready for a scrap.

Harrold looked almost comically shocked as Simon approached. He stared at Simon's rough worker's clothes, then up at his face.

"Good afternoon, gentlemen," Simon said, cool as November.

"I want a full accounting, Shale!" Harrold demanded. "We received a telegram a few hours ago alleging the most preposterous claims."

"Every one of those claims are true," he answered. "But I'm not Shale. The name's pure fabrication."

"I'm not his wife, either," Alyce said. "And I don't have a brother in the government. But I'm one of the owners of the collective, and that makes me the owner of Wheal Prosperity. Not you."

If Harrold and the other owners looked surprised at Simon's appearance and words, when Alyce spoke, they could've been knocked on their arses by a bit of eiderdown. From her accent to her clothes to the way she spoke to them, there wasn't anything of the simpering society lady in her now. And damn her if she didn't love seeing their shock.

"Rubbish," Stokeham declared, "the lot of it!"

Simon went to the strongbox, opened it, and took out a stack of papers. "Have your solicitors review the documentation. It's all legal, all aboveboard. Oh, but the stocks to those overseas ventures—the ones that were supposed

to shield you from taxation—those are as fraudulent as
your pretentions to gentility."

Tufton snatched the papers from Simon's hand and
thrust them at the solicitors. The men quickly donned
spectacles and spread the documents out on a table, studying them thoroughly. As they did, silence fell, tight and
thick. Tippet glared at Alyce and Simon, his knuckles
white as he clutched his truncheon. The chief constable
seemed to understand that once the old managers and
owners left, he and his brutes wouldn't be welcome in the
village anymore. They'd get no more extra pay for bullying the workers, and with the managers' protection of the
constabulary gone, anyone could file complaints with the
county government over excessive force, and likely cause
them to lose their jobs.

"Who the hell *are* you?" Harrold demanded in the
quiet.

"I don't deal in names," Simon answered. "Except
one. Nemesis, Unlimited."

While some of the owners and constables looked
blank, others seemed to know exactly what the name
meant. They turned chalky.

"But I'm really Alyce Carr," she said. "This is *my* village, these are *my* friends and family. And once your
lackeys go over those documents, I'm going to enjoy telling you to go bugger yourselves."

The men gasped, but she only stared back, ice and fire
in her veins.

Tippet and his constables weren't the only ones eager
for a fight. Murton and Gorley, two of the managers,
grew more restless by the second, flexing their fingers,
testing their fists, and muttering angrily.

Finally, one of the solicitors straightened up from the
desk. An expression of fear etched his face as he turned
to the owners and managers. "I'm afraid—" His voice

cracked, and he cleared his throat. "Everything stands up, sirs. You voluntarily signed over ownership of Wheal Prosperity to these . . . individuals."

"But they said they'd return ownership to us within three days," Harrold retorted.

"Did you sign any kind of contract binding you to that agreement?" the solicitor asked.

More silence. The owners' faces darkened as they understood that they'd been thoroughly duped.

"You traitorous son of a bitch," Murton exploded.

His hands loose at his sides, standing lightly on the balls of his feet, Simon never lost his cool expression. "Nemesis has one loyalty—to justice. At any cost."

"The fault's your own," Alyce said. She struggled to keep her voice as calm as Simon's, but long-pent-up fury boiled in her. "If you'd paid us a decent wage instead of using chit, if you'd kept the mine in good condition and stocked fresh butter in the store . . . this wouldn't have happened. We just want to work and be treated fairly. But you just want profit, and the hell with the people who make you rich." She pointed toward the door. "Now, I'm telling you as one of the new owners, the lot of you clear out. *Now.*"

It felt *so bloody good* to say those words.

"What if we don't go anywhere?" Tippet challenged.

At last, Simon smiled, but it was a brutal smile that promised a great deal of pain. "You'll go. Quick and quiet."

"Or else?" threw in Oliver, the constable. "You got no weapons, no nothing. And we got these." Grinning, he held up his truncheon.

"See here . . ." Tufton sputtered, eyes wide with fear. He backed up until he hit the far wall. "No violence, now."

Tippet sneered. "Too late for that, gov." Swinging his club, he launched himself at Simon.

Simon stepped forward, at the same time ducking Tippet's blow. The truncheon came down hard on one of the desks, crashing into the wood with a horrible, bone-splitting sound. Before Tippet could regain his balance, Simon kicked him in the side of the knee. The chief constable staggered and swore foully.

Alyce glanced around the office, but couldn't find anything heavy to use as a weapon. She threw a brass inkwell in Oliver's face as he moved to help Tippet. The constable winced and spluttered as ink and blood spattered across his face.

Edgar grabbed all the paperwork and threw it into the strongbox, then slammed the door shut, protecting the documents.

Caught up in the chaos, everyone within the office spilled out into the street, scuffling.

"If we can't have the mine," Harrold barked, "then nobody gets it. You two"—he pointed at Gorley and Murton—"take me to the mine."

The managers didn't argue. All three men leaped into the trap waiting nearby. With a flick of the reins, they sped off.

"Have to stop them," Simon ordered. "They'll try to sabotage the mine."

It made sense that they'd do something so dirty. At least the mine was empty, since everyone had taken the day as an unofficial holiday. Except . . .

"Oh, God," Alyce cried. "Henry!" He was in the pit with Edgar and several other men.

Tippet, stumbling out of the office, sneered. "I ain't going to let you catch 'em." He swung again at Simon. Simon countered with a fist into the chief constable's stomach. The man doubled over, gagging.

With Simon busy with Tippet, he didn't see Constable Freeman moving to slam his truncheon across Simon's back. Alyce rushed forward, hoping to block him some-how. But then Freeman stumbled and fell to the ground with a groan.

Constable Bice stood behind him, lowering his trun-cheon.

Simon spun around and gave Bice a respectful nod. "Glad you've finally showed your colors."

"*Constable Bice* wrote the letter to Nemesis?" Alyce asked, shocked. "But . . . he's one of them."

"Got hired on here," the young man said sheepishly. "Thought I'd be keeping things peaceful and orderly. Not roughing up workers and keeping them afraid. But I couldn't speak out. I needed the job. So . . ." He looked at Simon. "Sorry if I didn't come forward sooner."

"You sent the letter," Simon answered. "That's what matters. Right now, I've got to get to the mine and stop Harrold, Murton, and Gorley." He didn't spare a glance for any of the reeling constables, and he didn't look at any of the terrified owners, huddled together. Instead, he strode toward the door.

Alyce was immediately beside him. "*We're* stopping Murton and Gorley."

He nodded once, briskly, his face a mask of purpose and determination. "Get down," he ordered to one of the drivers of a hired carriage. The man immediately scram-bled off the seat and ran for safety. Simon climbed up onto the driver's seat.

Instead of getting inside the carriage, Alyce clambered up to sit beside him. He snapped the reins and the car-riage lurched forward.

She raised a brow. "Would've wagered you'd try to stop me."

At this, his stony façade broke slightly, a hint of a smile at the corner of his mouth. "You'd come along, any-way. This way I can keep an eye on you."

She gripped the edge of the seat for balance as the carriage quickly sped out of the village, then took the rutted track leading toward the mine. "*Keep an eye on? Like a child?*"

"Like a wild tiger that's escaped its cage." He peered ahead. "Damn it, I can't see them."

"Do you think they're at the mine already?"

He looked grim. "It's two miles from the village to Wheal Prosperity. Given their head start, they're either there already or will be soon." He urged the horses on, and the beasts raced. The carriage wasn't well sprung, and the road furrowed, so Alyce held to the seat tightly, sure she'd be thrown from the vehicle. It'd been a show of bravado, choosing to sit beside Simon, but maybe she ought to have ridden inside the carriage. She'd still be heaved around, but at least she wouldn't have to worry about being tossed to the ground.

For all the rough terrain, and the fact that the carriage wasn't built for moving this fast, Simon handled the drive capably. He never once seemed to lose control of the horses or the vehicle. But that didn't stop fear from coursing through her, thinking of her brother and friends in danger. God, what were the men planning?

A brief, terrifying eternity, and the hulking forms of the mine and its equipment rose into view. She and Simon cursed when she saw the trap was parked outside the engine house. The men were nowhere to be seen.

"Jesus," Simon snarled, leaping down from the carriage. "The pump."

Alyce jumped down, too, following Simon as he raced inside the engine house. Both the former managers stood beside the giant machine, Harrold looking on, with Gorley holding a massive wrench. Abel, a machinist who kept the pump running, lay slumped on the ground, out cold.

Gorley saw Simon and Alyce, grinned, and lifted the wrench above his head. "Wheal Prosperity won't be any use to anybody."

"No!" Alyce shouted. "Men are down there!" The man-engine was running, but even at top speed, Henry and the others wouldn't be able to get out in time to keep from drowning.

"Even better." Harrold sneered.

As Simon darted forward, the wrench came down, smashing into the pump. Gorley moved to swing again. Simon leaped to stop him, but Murton threw a punch. Simon dodged the blow, yet Murton managed to graze his chest, knocking Simon off balance. Alyce, too, hurried to stop Gorley, but by the time she reached him, he'd already slammed the wrench into the pump once more.

The machine sputtered and wheezed. Air now moved through the pipes, not water. The tunnels below were no longer being drained. They were flooding.

And Henry and the others were down there. The mine would flood completely in an hour. If Henry and the surveyors were at the bottom of the pit, it'd take them too long to climb out.

"Can you fix it?" she demanded of Simon.

He gathered his balance. "Need time."

"Then get it working!"

"Do something, goddamn it," Harrold shouted at Murton and Gorley.

As Harrold hid himself behind a large piece of equipment, the two managers attacked. Gorley used his wrench like a club, swinging it wildly. Murton didn't have a weapon, except his sizable fists. Both men came at Simon and Alyce.

She did her best to duck and dodge as Gorley swung at her. Other than scrapping with Henry when they were children, she hadn't been in a fight in almost fifteen years. All she could do was move instinctively. She wove to one side just as Gorley struck, the wrench leaving a massive dent in one of the tanks.

Simon bellowed in anger, but Murton's fists held him back. The two men traded punches, Simon narrowly avoiding Murton's clumsy but strong blows as he himself moved with precision, peppering Murton with sharp jabs to the torso.

All the while, the pumps whistled, no longer pulling water out of the mine.

Remembering Simon's move from the managers' office, she kicked Gorley in the side of the knee. Just as Tippet had, Gorley went down, groaning in agony. The wrench dropped from his hand.

She scooped up the tool. "Simon!" She tossed it to him, and he snatched it out of the air.

Simon whacked Murton across the jaw with the wrench. The man stumbled back, into Harrold's arms. The owner slapped at Murton's face, trying to rouse him. Instantly, Simon began to work on the pump, using the wrench and other tools lying nearby.

It wouldn't be long before one or both of the managers collected themselves. If only she had a damn weapon of her own!

Oh, but I do.

She ran outside, and straight to the dressing floor. Rows of hammers and bucking irons were lined up, waiting for bal-maidens to use them to smash ore into pieces. If there was one thing Alyce knew how to use, it was a bucking iron. She grabbed one and hurried back toward the engine house.

She skidded to a stop at the sound of hoofbeats. There, riding up on horseback, were Tippet, Oliver, and Freeman. Blood trickled down the side of Freeman's face from the blow Bice had given him earlier. Alyce's lungs burned as she ran full out to the engine house. She had to get there before the constables.

Just as Tippet and his men pulled up outside the building, Alyce positioned herself in front of the door, brandishing her bucking iron.

Tippet dismounted, as did his men, and he swaggered toward her. "Out of the way, lass, or you'll get a nasty little hurt."

"Back on your horses and ride the hell away," she snarled back, "or you'll get a nasty *big* hurt."

He chuckled, then nodded at Oliver to remove her.

"Don't care for women who try to fight back," Oliver growled, ink from the thrown inkwell still staining him. He moved to shove her aside. His snicker turned into a shout of pain when she brought her bucking iron down on his arm, and there was a snapping sound.

Oliver cradled his wounded limb. "Sodding bitch broke my arm!"

The three constables stared at her, disbelieving. She could hardly believe it herself. But her heart raced and her blood cried out for justice.

She clutched the bucking iron like the weapon it was, ready to swing again. "Not another step," she growled. Without taking her eyes off Tippet and his men, she shouted over her shoulder to Simon. "How's the pump?"

"Getting there," he yelled back. There came the sounds of grunting and fists hitting flesh—he must be fighting off Murton and Gorley as he kept working on the machine. Doubtful that Harrold would join in the brawl.

Damn, she needed to keep them from interrupting his task, but if she tried to help, Tippet and Freeman would attack. Oliver continued to hold his arm close, alternating between whimpers and furious curses. How could she and Simon do this on their own, with Henry and the others trapped?

The air filled with the sound of many angry voices and someone on horseback. Craning her neck, Alyce saw Constable Bice atop a horse, leading a small marching army of workers. They headed toward the engine house, looks of determination and defiance on their faces.

Alyce's heart lifted. She and Simon weren't alone.

Tippet sneered at Bice. "Think you and these weaklings can stand in our way?" He glared insolently at the workers. "We've kept you maggots beaten down for over ten years. Nothing changes." He lifted his truncheon, and despite the fact that the workers outnumbered Tippet and his men, the habit of fear must've been too deeply rooted for the workers to lose it in an instant. Many shrank back. Bice looked too uncertain of his role to rally anybody.

It fell to her. "Brody, Wendell," she shouted at two men, "get down into the pit. Carefully. We've got men trapped down there and the mine's flooding."

The two miners hesitated, eyeing Tippet.

"Go!" she yelled.

They took off at a run, heading to the entrance to the pit.

"Stop 'em," Tippet ordered Freeman.

The huge constable looked uncertain. "What about this lot?"

Baring his teeth, the chief constable said, "They're going to be good little maggots and stay put."

She stared at him. Any mask Tippet had once worn—the one that painted him as a protector of the village and the mine—had slipped. The loss of his rule showed him for what he really was: a power-hungry bully who didn't give a damn about the welfare of the people.

"He's got no hold on us anymore," she cried to the assembled workers. "No control."

"He's got a truncheon," someone pointed out.

"Then grab it!" she fired back.

There were murmurs of uncertainty, and Alyce ground down on her frustration. She couldn't be the only one to stand up for the workers. They had to do it for themselves.

But then a wave of energy moved through the crowd, and they surged toward Tippet and his men. The constables looked momentarily stunned, surprised that anyone would really dare to defy them.

Alyce began to turn toward the engine house. She needed to help Simon. But then the sound of a carriage's wheels froze her in her steps.

One woman in the crowd gave a quiet scream, and a few men cursed. She almost joined them.

Leaping out of the carriage was the owner Stokeham. And he held a shotgun.

As her blood chilled her mind whirled, trying to figure out exactly where the gun had come from. Even Tippet and his men were armed only with truncheons. But then she remembered once seeing the managers on the hills, cradling shotguns, as men beat at the shrubbery, flushing birds out into the sky. When things went mad at the managers' office, Stokeham must've sneaked out in the remaining carriage and gone to get the gun from the managers' house. Then ridden out to the mine to put an end to the rebellion.

A gun meant one thing: someone was going to get shot.

And she had a horrible feeling that someone would be Simon.

As Simon worked furiously on the pump, he had to continually beat back Gorley and Murton, with Harrold shouting them on. Didn't surprise him that the owner and two managers fought so hard to destroy the mine. Men pushed to the edge acted like unchained beasts. He finally landed a blow to Gorley's chin that had the man crumple to the floor, out cold. Murton didn't go down quite as easily. Simon kept switching between replacing a cracked fitting as it whistled, sucking air, and dodging the other manager's punches. His own back and arms were riddled with bruises. Tomorrow, he'd look like spoiled meat. If they made it to tomorrow.

Outside, he heard Alyce and Tippet arguing. Damn, but he wanted to go to her, but there was too much holding him in the engine house. Then Simon heard one of the other constables—Oliver?—scream in pain, and cry out, "Sodding bitch broke my arm!"

Simon grinned to himself. That was his woman.

Fixing the pump would take all his concentration. He needed to rally and end the fight now. Spinning around from the pump engine, he laid a combination on Murton— jab, hook, uppercut. Murton didn't have his training and couldn't keep up. Soon, he was lying beside Gorley, insensate.

He took a step toward Harrold. The man pressed himself against the wall of the building, bleached as bone, unmoving.

"Can't do anything on your own," Simon said, disgusted. Harrold only whimpered.

He got back to work. He heard more voices outside. Miners had come from the village to protect what was theirs. Another grin for himself. *This* was what Nemesis meant. Not simply coming in to play rescuer, but to help the oppressed find the means in themselves to push back, to give them the tools they'd never had to fight. Alyce's voice rose above the others as she served as general, issuing orders.

Christ, but he'd miss her. Pain in the midst of everything.

He'd lick his wounds and suffer later. Now was for fixing the pump and seeing to the next step, whatever that might be.

Only a few adjustments left, and the pump would be working again. Already, water was beginning to flow out of the mine, giving the men inside a fighting chance to get out in time. Ironic that this was how he'd begun his mission here at Wheal Prosperity, by fixing this very same piece of equipment. The stakes had been high then, but nothing compared to now.

He froze when he heard a carriage approaching, and then a woman's scream and men's alarmed cursing.

Something or someone even more frightening than Tippet was out there, which meant Alyce was in even greater danger.

He moved without thinking, stalking away from the pump and out of the engine room. Harrold had sunk down into a crouch, continuing to whimper.

Alyce stood just outside the door, holding her bucking iron like a club. Tippet and his two men—one who clutched his arm to his chest—faced her. The workers and Bice had gathered in a panicky cluster. Everyone stared at Stokeham.

The former owner held a twelve-gauge double-barreled shotgun. He swung it violently back and forth between Alyce and the workers, his own expression wild. All of Simon's muscles tightened. Few things were as dangerous as an untrained idiot with a firearm.

"Put that goddamn gun down," Simon growled. "You'll blow your own ruddy brains out."

Stokeham spun toward Simon, who crouched in defense. But the former owner didn't pull the trigger—yet.

"You've taken everything," Stokeham shrilled. "Bloody tricked us! That's not fair!"

"Fine one to speak of fair," Alyce answered.

"You!" the former owner bleated. "Pretending you're a fine lady, but you're nothing but a low-bred wh—"

Stokeham didn't get the chance to finish his sentence. Distracted by Alyce, he didn't see Simon charge him. In an instant, Simon had grabbed the barrel of the shotgun and pointed it up into the air. Stokeham spent his life behind a desk or at a dinner table. He didn't have Simon's strength. Simon slammed his fist into Stokeham's face. There was a crunch, a spray of blood from Stokeham's nose, and then the man lay sprawled in the mud, unconscious.

Tippet bellowed in fury. He and Freeman charged at the crowd, and even Oliver swung at the workers with his good arm. The wounded constable lunged for Bice, spitting words about traitors.

The air tore apart with a boom. Oliver shrank back as Simon fired over his head. The constable turned terrified eyes toward Simon, clearly understanding that Simon had missed on purpose. A warning shot.

Babbling prayers, Oliver ran. He slipped and stumbled in the mud, but didn't stop running as he crested one hill, then disappeared.

But even that wasn't enough to stop Tippet from swinging his truncheon at the rest of the crowd, holding them back.

Freeman clipped Alyce on the shoulder with his club. Rage filmed Simon's eyes as she yelped, staggered, and fell—though she didn't lose her grip on her bucking iron. She struggled to get to her feet. Freeman loomed over her, raising his truncheon for a stronger strike.

Another boom ripped through the air. Freeman screamed and collapsed. He clenched at his calf, where a large hole spewed blood into the dirt.

Simon was at Alyce's side in an instant, helping her to her feet. She stared at the ugly wound in Freeman's leg, and paled. But she didn't swoon or become ill. Only looked at the injured constable with an expression of satisfaction.

"Good shot," she said breathlessly to Simon.

"Easier than holding back a thousand Zulus." His words might be flip, but his heart shuddered. *Jesus.* Had he ever known this kind of fear?

"Tippet," she said, nodding toward the chief constable, who continued to check the crowd. They'd feint at him, but his club held them back. And when he'd try to attack, they receded.

Simon ran over to Stokeham's prone form. The man didn't make a sound as Simon patted him down, searching for more shotgun shells. Simon rolled his eyes. The sodding fool hadn't brought more ammunition, rendering the shotgun useless.

He spun back to Tippet. The chief constable saw Freeman on the ground, and knew that Oliver was long gone. Tippet's face twisted into a sneer. He stalked toward Simon, holding his truncheon out to keep Simon at a distance.

"A safe place," Tippet spat. "An orderly place. Everything under my control. Then *you.*" He and Simon circled each other, Simon holding the shotgun like a club.

"Didn't have to be their bullyboy, Tippet. That was your choice."

"And this was *my* town. You ruined it. Ruined everything."

"He *fixed* everything," Alyce retorted.

Simon wanted to point out that she'd been just as instrumental in wrangling power back into the hands of the workers as he had—but this wasn't the time.

"Shut it, bitch," Tippet snarled. "Should've run you out of town, had 'em take you away to one of those places for sluts and troublemakers."

"But you didn't," she answered. "And here I am with my bucking iron, with Simon ready to beat your head in."

"And you're all alone," added Simon.

"This place belonged to *me*. It was *mine*." Bellowing, Tippet charged. Fury glazed his eyes and forced his face into a grimace. Simon welcomed the fight. Since his first day at Wheal Prosperity, he'd been waiting for this moment. Payback for all the harm and bullying Tippet had inflicted.

As soon as the chief constable was within striking distance, he swung his truncheon. Holding the shotgun with two hands, Simon used it to block the blow. He rammed the butt of the weapon into Tippet's stomach. The chief constable doubled over, heaving, but wasn't stopped. Tippet rose up and slapped the truncheon across Simon's back.

Alyce cried out.

Blistering, choking pain and rage spread through Simon. The strike staggered him. He stumbled forward, fighting to regain his balance.

Recovering his footing, Simon turned—just as Tippet thrust the end of his truncheon toward Simon's chest. Angling his body to avoid the hit, Simon again used the shotgun to deflect the blow, forcing the truncheon down. Simon snapped the side of the shotgun up, right into the underside of Tippet's chin. Before the chief constable could even fall, Simon smashed the shotgun's wooden butt into the side of Tippet's head, the sound cracking soggily.

Tippet fell like a rotten apple. He didn't move. Not even when Simon nudged him with the toe of his boot.

The miners edged closer. Still cautious, even with the chief constable sprawled in the mud.

"Is he dead?" Bice asked.

"Alive," Simon answered, "but he and the rest of them are going to need doctoring."

"In gaol," Alyce said. There were muttered agreements from the crowd.

Simon turned to Bice. "Ride to the nearest town with a good doctor, and send him here. Then get the law."

The young constable nodded, but added, "Aren't *I* the law now?"

"You'll be a fine chief constable, but this is outside of your expertise."

"Yes, sir." He ran to his horse and climbed up into the saddle. He wheeled around to get assistance.

Simon's voice stopped him. "Constable Bice."

The young man looked at him expectantly.

"Well done," said Simon.

The new chief constable turned red, then rode off.

"The rest of you," Simon directed toward the assembled crowd, "see to our own wounded. Collect the men inside and out here and bind them with rope or whatever you can find. Bandage Freeman's wound, too."

"He should bleed to death in the mud," someone in the crowd muttered.

"Maybe that's what he deserves," Alyce said calmly, "but we'll let him face a judge. Just like the others." She called to a man emerging from the entrance to the mine. "Are they well?"

"Aye," came the answer. "Heard from Henry. They're all fine below. They'll all be up in ten minutes."

She pressed a hand to her chest, slumping with relief. Simon ached to put his arm around her, feel her strength and give her comfort, but the pump wasn't fully fixed. He gave her hand a squeeze, then, still carrying the shotgun, strode back into the engine house. Alyce was right behind him.

She herded a trembling, sniveling Harrold outside, and had other miners take the injured managers out, as well.

It didn't take much more to finalize the repairs. In a

few moments, the pump was clearing water at maximum capacity. He waited for a sense of triumph, of victory, but heaviness still clutched at him. And the reason why stood beside him, watching quietly.

"You'll have to do another survey of the mine later to see what damage was done by the flooding," he said, straightening and wiping his hands on a cloth.

"It might cost us a little," she answered, setting aside her bucking iron, "but it doesn't matter. We're all safe. A few were wounded, but we did it." She turned to him, her face streaked with dirt, hair frizzed as it came out of its bun, eyes shining. Beautiful as morning. The pain across his back and resonating through his muscles and bones was nothing compared to the other pain wrapped tightly around him, piercing his heart, his very marrow.

She wrapped her arms around him, and they pulled each other close. "It's done," she whispered against his neck. "It's over."

They both knew she spoke of more than the mine, but neither would admit it. Instead, with cheering erupting outside, Simon and Alyce remained in the engine house, wrapped tightly together, as if this one embrace could carry them through the rest of their days.

CHAPTER 18.

By the time Alyce, Simon, and the others had returned to the village, Tufton and Ware had vanished.

"What if they come back?" Alyce asked Simon.

"They won't."

He sounded so confident, she couldn't argue. Though this was her home, the business of vengeance was his—he knew the world better than she. She'd have to trust him, and she did. In everything.

Together, they organized the chaos in the village. A handful of people had been scraped and bruised when Stokeham had driven madly from the managers' house to the mine, knocking them aside. She gathered women who knew the ways of caring for injuries—including Sarah—and made the bachelors' lodging a treatment center.

Simon seemed to be everywhere at once. Making certain that Tippet and all their other enemies were secured in the village gaol. Speaking with Henry and the other new owners at length about the organization of the mine. Checking on everyone and making sure they were safe and prepared for the new transition.

Alyce kept catching glimpses of him as he strode

through the village, but they had no time alone, no moments to themselves. Every second saw him pulling further and further away. A blessing, in truth. If she'd felt time slipping away before, now it raced toward the horizon, toward the moment when Simon would leave and she'd face a life that was the same, but entirely new.

Bice came with the law—a justice and more constables, and a dark van with bars on the back window. He brought a doctor, as well. After a cursory inspection to make sure the prisoners would survive, Tippet, Gorely, Murton, Freeman, and Harrold were loaded into the van. No one cheered as the wagon rolled out of town. A curious silence fell over the gathered crowd. They'd all learned—there were no simple celebrations. Obstacles had been removed, but there were more to come. Running a mine wasn't an easy job. The challenges Alyce and everyone at Wheal Prosperity faced loomed ahead.

"Can we do it?" she asked Henry, catching him briefly on his own.

"It's what we wanted," he answered.

"The battle's not over."

He wrapped an arm around her shoulder and gave her a squeeze. "My sister can be a tremendous pain in my arse, but she's a wise one, too. She taught me that all good things are worth fighting for. For as long as it takes."

Warmth spread through her, but peace and accomplishment eluded her. She felt them more like back notes in a melancholy song, something bright and high, while the melody remained dark and low.

The sun began to set, and she found herself wandering aimlessly through the streets, strangely at a loss. There was much to do, yet she couldn't settle anywhere, couldn't get her thoughts to grab hold.

This is what you wanted. All this time.

She perched on the low wall surrounding the churchyard, wrapped in her shawl, watching the village below. As the sun dipped lower, spreading shadow, lights flickered on, one by one, as distant as stars. Behind her, everything was silent. The dead had no way of knowing the world had changed.

Movement beside her nearly made her topple backward. A pair of strong hands caught her, righted her. She knew their feel even in the darkness. And it didn't surprise her that Simon could get so close without her hearing or seeing him.

Together, they sat upon the wall and looked down at the village. He rolled a cigarette, lit it, and took a few drags, blowing smoke in long exhales. She held out her hand. Even in the darkness, she could feel his surprise, but he handed her the cigarette.

She drew on it, then spluttered and coughed. So much for being elegant and sophisticated. He patted her on the back, gently taking the cigarette from her.

"Not a habit you should cultivate," he said. "Doesn't seem healthy."

"Why do you do it?"

"I keep meaning to quit, but I've lacked proper motivation."

"Maybe if a woman asked you to stop . . ."

He flicked away some ash. "Maybe then."

But that woman wouldn't be her, and they both knew it. For a while, they sat in silence, and she felt full to bursting, almost numb with too much sensation.

"Is it always like this?" she asked quietly. "After you've finished a mission?"

He seemed to understand exactly what she meant. "No," was his simple response. "It's usually more . . . satisfying."

"I thought it'd be that way. But all I feel is . . ." She tugged her shawl closer. Words wouldn't come. None fit.

As if language itself hadn't developed to the point to capture this distant gratification mixed with strange, cold emptiness.

The world was much more complicated than she'd ever known. *She* was much more complicated than she'd known. It had always been in her, only it had lain quiet, sleeping. He'd roused that part of herself, and now it ached with longing.

He stared at the glowing tip of his cigarette before tossing it down onto the ground and crushing it beneath his heel. He stuffed his hands into his pockets. "Me, too."

Her throat was raw, as if she'd been screaming. She wouldn't look at him. Couldn't. "I don't want you to go," she rasped.

A low groan sounded in his chest. "I don't want to go."

Still, they wouldn't look at each other, staring at the village as if it were the most fascinating thing on earth, as if she hadn't seen this view a hundred times in her life and could describe it perfectly with her eyes closed. Anything rather than look at him, the shape of his face that seemed to be the shape of her own heart.

"But I have to," he finally said.

"I know." Another long silence. Then, "When?"

"Tonight. Harriet told me we've got cases piling up. Marco's tied up in something. Desmond and Riza are just coming back, but they won't be enough."

"It doesn't stop."

He shook his head. "Not for a minute."

"Ugly old world." She sighed.

"Except when it's beautiful." He did look at her then, and she could feel the heat of his gaze on her. She soaked it in, the way one might catch the last rays of the sun before the winter solstice. "Come with me."

The words she'd longed to hear punctured her now, each one a pickaxe.

"You know I can't," she answered. "Especially now."

He pushed away from the wall and stood in front of her, lean and solid, determination and purpose radiating from him. He took hold of her hands. "We can visit. There are trains, and the post, telegrams."

"Sarah, and the baby . . ."

"It's a village full of women who like nothing better than to help each other. She won't be alone."

But her gaze slid away from his. "Simon."

Again, silence. He dropped her hands. "You're afraid."

Instinctive anger coursed through her. "I'm not."

"Yet you're making excuses."

She shot to her feet, inches separating them. "Don't. Trewyn is my *home*. It's where I'm meant to be. Who I am. I'm a bal-maiden, a Cornish village girl. Take those away from me, and I'm nothing."

"You're *Alyce*. It doesn't matter where you are or what you do. Nothing changes."

The need to believe him was a fury within her. But, damn him, fear was there, too. Icy and belittling.

"Goddamn it, Alyce," he said, cupping her face. His hands were warm and coarse against her skin, and she soaked in the feel of him. "I love you."

She shriveled inside and she burst with life and wonderment. "I love you, too."

They kissed, searching and hungry, and she devoured his taste, his fire. She could stand like this all night. All week. For the rest of her life. But those were fantasies. And this was the real world, where fantasies couldn't live. They needed sunshine and limitless possibility to thrive.

He broke the kiss first. "Addison-Shawe." When she frowned in confusion, he explained, "My last name. I'm Simon Augustus Kirkwood Addison-Shawe."

His true name. The last disguise falling away. She could find him now, if she wanted. No hiding.

She forced out her words. "This doesn't change anything."

"Alyce—"

"If you have to go, do it tonight. As soon as possible. Now." The longer he stayed, the more she thought of things that couldn't be, things she craved but would never have, and there was only so much she could endure before breaking down and howling like a beast.

He took a step back. His face was frozen, unbearably beautiful and withdrawn, like a stone angel. Anger crackled around him. But he said nothing.

She held out her hand. "At least, let us say good-bye as . . . as friends."

He stared coldly down at her hand, then at her face. "No."

And then he turned and strode down the hill, leaving her as alone as she'd been a month ago. No, she was even more alone, because she'd had him, and they'd belonged to each other, but now—now she knew what she'd lost, and what she'd never have again.

He didn't have much to pack, and most of his belongings were already in his satchel from his recent travels. Simon sat on his cot and shoved the remainder of his clothes into his bag, followed by the photographs of his supposed "family" and letters from his "sister." He had his own actual family to return to in London—though he seldom crossed paths with any of them. He didn't miss them or not miss them. They felt the same about him. Handshakes, a few polite inquiries, and then they'd exhausted all points of contact. Months would go by, and then the routine would be repeated in someone's drawing room or a ballroom. Semianonymous spaces for semianonymous encounters.

He spent more time, and exchanged more true words,

at Nemesis's headquarters, a shabby set of rooms above a chemist's in Clerkenwell. He'd probably go there first from the train station, before heading home. At least at headquarters, he wouldn't be alone. There was always someone there—Lazarus, Harriet, Marco. And the air would be thick with talk of the latest operation, schemes and plans hovering like smoke. Always something to keep him in motion, and people he could surround himself with.

He wouldn't have to face this agony alone. He'd seen men in combat with their insides blown apart. They'd died, of course. What he couldn't understand was how he continued to breathe and move and think when his heart had been ripped from his chest.

But he did. He folded up his clothes and put away his fake personal belongings, all the while attuned to the creak of the floorboards, for a woman's light tread. But all he heard was Edgar walking toward him.

The older man sat down on the cot. "That's it, then?"

"Henry and I had a long talk. He knows more about mines than I do, but we laid out a good plan for setting up a new system. I gave him the direction to send any letters and which telegraph station to direct any important messages." He fastened up his satchel. "It'll be a rocky start, but Wheal Prosperity's got the tools it needs to succeed."

"You're not staying."

"That was never the plan."

"Thought that might have changed. Because, you know . . ." Edgar raised his eyebrows meaningfully, and glanced toward the window.

More sharp pain whistled through Simon. "London's my home. Nemesis is my work. And she"—he couldn't even say her name—"won't leave. Stalemate."

"You'd be asking her to give up a hell of a lot if she left."

"And so would I, if I stayed."

"Aye, the people need you, et cetera, and so forth."

Anger poured acidly through him. "This isn't a god-damn lark, Edgar. I've given up my life to Nemesis."

Edgar held up his hands. "You and me, we haven't known each other long, but I've got eyes and a brain. I know this doesn't come easy. I also know that you and Alyce Carr are two damn stubborn people."

Simon forced a wry smile. "Edgar, the matchmaker of Trewyn?"

But Edgar didn't smile back. "If I had a lass who looked at me the way Alyce looks at you . . . and if I looked back at her the same way . . ." The creases in his face deepened. "I might not be so hot to jump on a train and put all this behind me."

"I have to go, Edgar. I can't turn away from the only purpose I've ever had." He slung his satchel over his shoulder, his bones rusty, straining with each movement.

Edgar stood. "Like I said, stubborn. Ah, well. It's been a bloody honor, Sergeant." He saluted—not at all a proper salute, but it gratified Simon just the same.

Simon returned the salute—properly—then stuck out his hand. The two men shook, and Simon was glad that in the world of men, fewer words meant more. No lingering, no explanations or declamations. Just a handshake and farewell.

"May as well take one of the constabulary's horses," Edgar added. "Seeing as how we only have one lawman right now, and a long walk to the train station isn't what any man wants after fighting a battle."

As battles went, it hadn't quite compared to Rorke's Drift—not for blood or body count—yet he now felt the same raw pain of survival. With a nod, and a final look at the drafty, privacy-free room he'd called home for a short while, he left.

He exchanged good-byes with a few people as he went to the constabulary, and accepted their thanks, but he was careful to keep everything brief. Somewhere in the village was Alyce—either still by the churchyard, or perhaps she'd gone home. Either way, he needed to leave as soon as he could. Pull the spear out of the wound quick and fast. There'd be blood and pain, but he'd never survive otherwise.

After a final farewell with Bice, and his eager offer to lend Simon one of the horses, he mounted up and rode out of town at a quick trot. Full night had fallen. He left the light and warmth of the village for the open, dark countryside. On horseback, he'd be in St. Ursula shortly and on a train to London soon after that. He'd likely be back in London before midnight. There'd be a new mission waiting for him, and his Nemesis colleagues, who'd offer him a cup of tea and catch him up on all the latest news.

As if nothing had changed. As if it would go on as it always had before.

The farther Simon rode from the village, the more he realized that one thing had changed and would never be the same again: him.

He'd keep up his work for Nemesis, live his two lives as an operative and as a gentleman, but he was as empty and hollow as an exhausted mine. The best part of him had been chipped away and melted down, and was worn around Alyce's finger as an invisible band.

"What are you doing here?" asked Sarah.

Alyce looked up from the stove as her sister-in-law stepped inside the cottage. "Getting supper ready. Don't think anyone's had a mouthful all day."

"But what are you doing *here*? I saw Simon riding out of town not twenty minutes ago."

Alyce stirred the stew bubbling on the stove. They'd

have better meat at the store, and soon. Maybe they wouldn't have to stew everything to make it edible.

"Alyce?" Sarah placed a careful hand on her arm, but her gentle touch only sparked pain and anger.

"Just leave everything behind?" Alyce snapped. "Forget my friends, my family? My work?"

"As a bal-maiden, smashing rocks for the rest of your life."

"There's nothing wrong with that work."

"Aye, but, Lord, Alyce, the things you've done these few weeks! You can do more than breaking up rocks."

Scenes flashed through Alyce's mind: sneaking into the managers' house and stealing butter, changing trains and changing identities, the looks on the owners' faces when they realized how she'd duped them, and how she'd battled against the constables like one of the mythical warrior women from long ago. And in all those scenes, Simon was there. Simon, who might not have trusted her at the beginning, but who came to believe in her as no one had. Who pushed her and made love to her and . . . *God* . . . loved her. Truly loved her.

"There's so much work to be done with the mine," she said.

"With many good and clever men taking care of that. Not that your say wouldn't be helpful, but the burden isn't yours to take." Sarah eased herself into a chair that creaked beneath her weight.

"And there's you and the baby," Alyce said. "I can't leave you now."

Her sister-in-law patted her belly tenderly. "You've already given me and the baby the best gift already—the mine. Because of you, we'll have dignity, freedom. All the things we didn't have before."

Alyce had nothing to say to this.

"As for taking care of the baby," Sarah added, "I've

got cousins and neighbors. I wouldn't be the first woman to have a baby without a sister by her side. And Henry will do his part." She smiled with determination. "I'll make sure of that."

Alyce paced away from the stove, but there was nowhere to go in the tiny room, and she found herself trapped in a corner. "So I'm useless here. Nobody wants me."

Sarah sighed. "You bloody pigheaded woman—of course we want you. Most of all, we want you to be happy."

"I *am* happy," Alyce retorted, then amended, "I will be. Someday."

"I think your happiness, and your heart, just rode out of town twenty minutes ago."

Alyce turned and braced her hands on the wall. She rested her forehead against the plaster, barely resisting the impulse to knock her head against it.

There was a groan behind her, but she couldn't tell if it was Sarah or Sarah's chair that made the noise. Her sister-in-law placed a hand on her shoulder.

"Do you know what I was most afraid of on my wedding day?" Sarah asked.

"Vomiting on the vicar?"

Sarah chuckled. "No, silly. It was *you*."

At this, Alyce turned around. "Me? Why on earth would I make you afraid?"

"Because I'd never met anyone like you. Certainly no woman. I was just a meek village lass, but you were so different." She shook her head, her eyes shining. "I wasn't afraid of pleasing Henry so much as I was certain you'd find me a little milksop. All I wanted was to be like you. Confident. Independent. Unafraid."

Alyce stared. Her sweet, kind sister-in-law admired *her*. "And now you think I'm cowardly."

But Sarah only shook her head. "I think if there's

something you want badly enough, you go after it. That hasn't changed. I suppose the question now is—what do you want?"

Alyce felt the beat of her heart, the cool of the night air as it sneaked between cracks in the wall, the breath in her own lungs, and the huge emptiness inside her. She could survive without him. But it would be a barren endurance, empty of joy or passion. Or love.

She bent and pressed a kiss to Sarah's cheek. Then grabbed her shawl from its peg and hurried out into the night. All she hoped was that she could make up the distance between them.

He hadn't gotten more than three miles out of the village when he'd stopped his horse. The dark hills rolled ahead of him, and the lights of Trewyn were dim little flecks behind him. He was nowhere—in the in-between. Ahead, the life he knew. The person he'd made himself into, and the role he knew how to play. Behind, a wholly different existence. One he couldn't truly envision living. But there was one thing, one person, who kept him anchored there.

Alyce.

Merely thinking her name filled him with fathomless pain. And immeasurable pleasure. She was both. He cursed her stubbornness, but how could he curse one of the things he loved about her so much? And curse him if he wasn't just as bullheaded as she.

So, where to go? Forward, which was really backward, or backward, which was truly forward?

Away from London, away from the village, he was completely himself, no distractions, no roles to play. Just a man. A man who wanted a woman with every ounce of his being.

He wheeled his horse around. Just as he was about to kick his mount into a canter, he heard it. His name.

Alyce, calling his name. Coming for him.

He urged his horse into a gallop. She emerged out of the darkness, a slim shape of strength and windblown beauty. Before the horse even stopped, he'd swung down from the saddle and taken her in his arms.

"I was turning around—"

"I was coming after you—"

He held her close, and her arms wrapped around him. "I can't imagine life without you."

"I can't, either," she answered. She gazed up at him, a frown between her brows. "But how can we make this work? A gentleman and a bal-maiden. London and Cornwall. It's impossible."

He kissed her, heated and deep. "I don't know," he confessed a long while later when they'd both lost their breath. "But those are details. We're clever people."

"By hammer or by confidence scheme," she agreed, "we'll find a way."

"I love you."

"I love *you*." She said it almost as a challenge, which was so like her, he almost laughed, but his heart was too solemn, too exultant for that.

"As for impossible"—he kissed her again, and she returned it, gripping him tightly—"I'm from Nemesis. And you're the bal-maiden who won't hear the word 'no.' For us, there's no such thing as impossible."

EPILOGUE

The English Channel, 1887

Alyce stood in the bow of the packet as it steamed through the choppy waters. Many of the passengers had retreated inside or taken to their cabins, sickened by the bounce of the ship upon the waves. But the ship's rising and crashing down felt like her own heart wheeling and soaring. She didn't feel ill at all. Far from it. Excitement was its own wave within her.

She leaned back into Simon's warmth when he came to stand beside her. He braced his hands on the rails, surrounding her, yet she didn't feel trapped. Only secure.

She'd imagined this very scene, long ago in Plymouth. And now it was real.

"We should make landfall in half an hour," he said.

"So soon?" She couldn't keep the disappointment from her voice. Her first ride on a ship was over almost before it began.

She heard the smile in his voice. "I think you're the only one aboard this steamer who's sorry to see this voyage end."

"Not too sorry," she answered, turning around in his

arms so she faced him. They were alone in the bow, so it wasn't too scandalous for her to press herself against him as closely as she did. "Because then we're in France, and I get to be part of a Nemesis mission."

He gazed down at her with affection. "You sound more excited to work another confidence scheme than see Paris."

"Oh, I can't wait to do both. And do them with my new husband." The plain band was back on her ring finger, except now it was genuine, placed there by Simon in the church at Trewyn a month earlier. Sarah and Henry had been there with their infant daughter, as had Harriet, Eva, Jack, and a burly but kind man named Lazarus. Even by Trewyn standards, the wedding had been small—but that had been by choice. Alyce didn't want to put on an extravagant show when she knew the next day she'd be moving away.

Since then, there'd been adjustments. She received letters regularly from Henry, keeping her apprised of developments at Wheal Prosperity, and she'd write back with her suggestions. Sarah wrote her, too, with more domestic news, and those letters she'd read and reread, feeling as though part of her were still in Cornwall.

London still baffled her, sometimes overwhelming her with its size and commotion. But she'd had an excellent guide in Simon, who explored the city with her by day. And by night, they explored each other. She was learning, too, how to live in his town house that seemed so impossibly big for just two people, yet it wasn't a cold, unwelcoming place. Little by little, it became not merely his, but theirs.

She'd sometimes catch Simon with a confused look on his face, as if he didn't quite know what to do with this new life.

"Do you regret your decision?" she'd asked him one

night, fearing the response but needing to know the truth.

"Not regret. I just . . . I think I'm *happy*." He sounded so baffled by the idea, it nearly broke her heart. But she made sure to keep him happy, even if it mystified him.

He'd introduced her to his family, too. When the dinner had been announced, terror had gripped her. His father could cut him off for marrying her. She'd wanted to use the same part she had played in Plymouth—but Simon had argued that if they couldn't accept her for who she was, he didn't want their approval or money.

In the end, she'd convinced him that he did the most good for Nemesis as a gentleman in good favor with his family. His connections to the upper ranks provided valuable information for Nemesis's objectives. So, reluctantly, he agreed, and she'd been presented to his family as a mine manager's daughter. Simon's father had been one of the most intimidating men she'd ever met, and he hadn't exactly welcomed her with a warm embrace, but she'd passed muster enough to keep Simon from disinheritance. And, if his father was any sign, Simon would age very well, indeed.

Since then, she and Simon had dined with his family twice more. It wasn't ever comfortable.

The one thing that hadn't taken much getting used to was being a part of Nemesis. She'd thought that adjusting from being a bal-maiden to someone who helped others find justice would be a rough change. The most difficult part was seeing how much injustice there truly was in the world. She'd been sheltered in Trewyn, aware only of the plight of the miners. London had opened her eyes to rampant cruelty. It was one thing to know that people could hurt one another—she'd seen it at the mine—but she'd never forget the faces of the girls rescued from a brothel, or lose the smell of the dank alleyway where children forced into thieving gangs slept.

But with each case, each wrong righted, she felt herself more and more grow into the work. Simon was easing her into it, with small bits of surveillance and collecting information. Though she'd always be a bal-maiden, she matured into this new self, and it was exactly *right*. Especially because he was with her.

Yet this trip to France marked the biggest challenge so far.

"Will Marco meet us in Calais or Paris?" she asked.

"Paris. He's got roles for us to play, and he can't leave Mrs. Parrish alone—she's in too much peril."

She nodded, fighting for calm when she could barely contain her excitement. This case promised to be a little more glamorous than the usual Nemesis work, although the stakes were no less high. Mrs. Parrish, a young widow, had been cheated out of her inheritance, with Marco taking on the mission, and it seemed the deeper he got, the more corruption and danger he uncovered. And now Alyce and Simon were going to lend their help, just as Marco had helped them a few months earlier.

"I'm sorry I didn't book us a private cabin," Simon murmured, brushing his lips against hers. "We could make use of that half hour."

She smiled against his mouth. "Half an hour isn't long enough. Besides, we've got business to take care of first."

"And a hotel room all to ourselves after." His voice was husky with suggestion. "For as long as we want. I know how much you enjoy hotel rooms."

"Only when you're in them."

With that promise in mind, they both turned their gazes to the horizon, ready to meet the next challenge.

Coming soon…

Don't miss the next novel in Zoë Archer's
Nemesis, Unlimited series

"Unforgettable…will leave readers craving more."
—*Publishers Weekly* (starred review)

WICKED TEMPTATION

Available in June 2014 from St. Martin's Paperbacks